Regency BALLROOM

Anne Herries

Anne Herries, winner of the Romantic Novelists' Association ROMANCE PRIZE 2004, lives in Cambridgeshire. She is fond of watching wildlife and spoils the birds and squirrels that are frequent visitors to her garden. Anne loves to write about the beauty of nature and sometimes puts a little into her books—although they are mostly about love and romance. She writes for her own enjoyment and to give pleasure to her readers.

In The Regency Ballroom Collection

A Country Miss
in Hanover Square

This book is dedicated to
the memory of my mother, who once told me
my books would be enjoyed by hundreds of
thousands of people worldwide.
I laughed, Mum, but you were right!

Prologue

The Spanish Peninsula—1812

Three men lay slumped on the earth, which had been baked hard by the fierce Spanish sun. Harry Pendleton had his back against a rock. Of the three he was in the best shape. Max Coleridge was lying with his eyes closed, his blood-soaked shirt stuck to his chest in this damned awful heat. Gerard Ravenshead was fanning Max with a large leaf, trying to keep the flies from settling on his wound. A neckcloth was wound around a deep cut at the side of Gerard's head.

'I thought we were done for,' Harry said. He was speaking his thoughts aloud, saying what they all felt. 'What a mess!'

'You can't blame yourself for it, Harry,' Gerard said and looked at him. 'They knew we were coming. Someone must have warned them.'

'Ten killed, and the three of us only got out by the skin of our teeth.' Harry stood up and walked over to take a look at Max. 'Somehow they must have got wind that we planned a surprise raid to take prisoners...'

'One of the servants,' Gerard replied and shrugged. 'In this damned war I'm never sure whether we are fighting the French with the Spanish or the Spanish and the French.'

'I wouldn't trust their generals as far as I could throw them,' Harry growled. He looked at the blood trickling down Gerard's face. They had wrapped a kerchief round his head, but it wasn't doing much good. 'Your wound is still bleeding. Do you want me to take another look at it?'

'You saved my life once today,' Gerard said and grinned at him. 'You don't have to nursemaid me, Harry. I'll manage. We have to get Max back to the village, and by the looks of him that means carrying him between us.'

Harry pulled a wry face. 'The way you've been behaving out here, I've sometimes felt as if you meant to throw your life away...' Gerard had gained a reputation as something of a daredevil.

'There were moments when I didn't much care if I died,' Gerard admitted. He took a swipe at a fly buzzing about his face. 'But when you're facing death things come into perspective. I intend to live and return home and one day....'

Gerard left the sentence unfinished. Harry nodded. He knew something had been eating at his friend. He suspected it was to do with a young woman Gerard had been courting—and the tiny scar at his temple that he'd noticed when they first met in Spain after a year of not seeing one another. Gerard often rubbed at it when he was thoughtful, and the look in his eyes told Harry he was remembering something that made him angry.

'I know what you mean,' Harry said. 'Soldiering is blood, sweat and tears—and that is the easy part.' It was listening to the screams of dying men and knowing you couldn't save them that hurt the worst. 'Come on, then. Help me get Max on my back and I'll carry him.'

'I can walk…' Max mumbled. 'Just give me a hand up….'

'Don't be a damned fool,' Harry replied. 'You'll be carried as far as we can make it. When we get near the village, Gerard will fetch help.'

'I could walk with help.' Max's face set stubbornly as he attempted to rise. 'Damn you, Harry. I'm not a baby….'

'But I'm the superior officer here, so you will do as you're told,' Harry muttered. He grinned at Gerard. 'There's one thing, we're bound for life by this day's experience. It's something none of us will forget—and if any one of us can help the other in future, we will….'

Max grunted as they hauled him to his feet, and Harry took him over his shoulder. Gerard nodded, his eyes hard but appreciative of his friend's stubborn determination to take on the burden. He wasn't sure he could have done it himself, though he would have tried.

'Comrades in war and peace,' he said. 'Let's get back. My head is fit to burst and Max needs attention….'

Chapter One

⁂

England—1816

Harry Pendleton saw the girl run across the narrow country road seconds before he pulled on the reins, bringing his horses to an abrupt halt. Jangling harness, the sound of snorting horses and the curses of his groom took Harry's attention for a moment as he fought to control the startled beasts. They were not used to being so roughly used! Harry cursed loudly. Another second and he would have knocked the girl down! His heart had been in his mouth for an instant—and it had done his horses little good to have their mouths sawed at in that way!

'What on earth do you think you were doing?' he thundered, tossing the reins to his groom and jumping down to confront her. He hardly noticed her pale face or trembling hands. 'That was a damned stupid thing to do! I could have killed you!'

'Had you not been driving so carelessly, it would not have happened,' the girl retorted, eyes flashing. She tossed her long hair, giving him a look filled with con-tempt. 'These country roads are not made for such haste, sir. I had no idea that you would suddenly come round that corner like a bat driven out of hell....'

'You must have heard the sound of my wheels,' Harry retorted, though he knew that she had some right on her side. 'What on earth possessed you to dash across the road in that way?'

'I saw some primroses I wanted,' the girl replied. 'This is a quiet road, sir. No one ever drives the way you were driving.'

'Possibly because they are none of them able,' Harry retorted. Even as he spoke he realised that he sounded petulant and arrogant, which was far from his nature. 'You should be more careful when crossing the road near bends in the road, miss...' Harry belatedly became aware that she was rather lovely. Her hair had been tossed by the wind and looked like spun gold, and her eyes were so clear that a man might drown in them. He found himself staring like an idiot. 'Forgive me, I do not know your name.'

'Nor shall you,' the girl replied, giving him a haughty stare. 'Sir, I find you arrogant and rude and I shall say good day to you.'

Stunned, Harry watched as she ran from him, scram-bled over a stile at the side of the road and set off swiftly across the fields. He came to himself in that instant, realising that he had handled the situation badly.

'I am sorry...' he called after her. 'I was anxious because I might have killed you. I did not mean to be so harsh.'

The girl did not falter or look back. Harry contin-ued to watch her for a few moments, then he shook his head and climbed back to the driving box. His damnable temper had let him down. It was not often he lost it, but for some reason he had done so this morning. Instead of shouting at her, he should have made sure that she was none the worse for her fright. For a moment he was tempted to go after her, but he was in a hurry; he had promised to meet his friends at a mill held locally at a certain time and was already late. He frowned as he began to drive at a slightly more sedate pace. It was obvious the girl was unharmed, but he had not made the proper enquiries. He ought at least to have asked if she needed his assistance, though it was self-evident that she did not.

A little smile touched his mouth. She had answered him with spirit. Clearly she had not suffered an irritation of the nerves, as most of the young ladies in town might have, had they been subject to such a display of bad manners from a man who was generally considered to be one of the politest men in society. However, from the look of her clothes and the way she had been roaming the countryside without a hat or a companion, she was just a country girl—possibly the daughter of the local vicar. It was unlikely he would ever see her again, and, while he felt a certain regret, the incident was soon pushed to a distant corner of his mind.

Susannah stopped running when she was out of breath. What a bad-tempered man the driver of that phaeton had been! Had he been a little more considerate, a little caring in his manner, she would have apologised, for she knew herself to be partly at fault. However, he had come round the bend at such a pace that it was a wonder he had managed to stop at all. She was fortunate that she had not been trampled beneath his horses' hooves. If she had not felt so startled, she might have

admired the way he handled his horses, which were
clearly high spirited. However, the way he had shouted
at her had put all thought of apology from her mind.

Frowning, Susannah sat down on a fallen log to recover her composure before going home. As her nerves
ceased tingling, she suddenly saw the amusing side of
the affair and laughed. It had been quite an adventure,
and she had often longed for something of the sort. However, in her dreams the gentleman would smile and speak
softly, making her heart beat faster. Her heart had indeed
slammed against her chest, but from fright rather than
pleasure. Now that she had begun to feel calmer, she
remembered that he had been rather handsome—if you
liked arrogant, rude men! She tossed her head and put
the incident from her mind as she approached the cottage
they had taken after poor Papa died. She must hurry;
she had been out a long time and her mama would be
looking for her.

Susannah walked into the cottage, carrying a basket
of herbs and wildflowers she had picked in the hedge-
row. Her fine gold hair had blown all over the place
and her cheeks were pink from the fresh air. She looked
beautiful, if untidy, and not quite the proper young lady.
Her looks were misleading—she had been taught her
manners and was in truth a well-behaved girl, though
spirited and inclined to be reckless at times. She took her
precious finds into the large kitchen, setting them down
on the scrubbed pine table. The smell of baking was
everywhere, tantalising and tempting. She felt hungry,
her mouth watering at the thought of such a treat. Her
hand was reaching towards a plate of cakes that were still
cooling when Maisie walked in. Maisie had once been
her nurse, and now she kept house for Mrs Hampton,

turning her hand to anything that needed doing, because they could no longer afford the luxury of servants.

'Now then, Miss Susannah,' the woman grumbled. 'You leave them cakes alone. Your mama has the Vicar and some friends coming for tea this afternoon, and I've used the last of the butter. At least there's none to spare for more baking.'

'Can't I have just one?' Susannah pleaded, her stomach rumbling with hunger. 'I haven't eaten since first thing this morning.'

'You should have been here for your luncheon instead of wandering about the countryside like a hoyden.' Maisie looked at her with disapproval, which masked the deep affection between them. 'Go and change your gown before anyone sees you. It will be time for tea in an hour or so. You can wait until then.'

'I'm hungry now,' Susannah said and snatched a warm and chewy oat biscuit, fleeing from the kitchen with Maisie's scolding ringing in her ears.

She sighed as she went upstairs to change out of the old gown she had worn for her walk. She had managed to get grass stains on the hem again, and there was a small rent where she had caught it on some briars, so it was a good thing she had chosen this gown. It was important to conserve her best things for special occasions these days. They had just enough money to live on and pay Maisie her meagre wage, but Susannah had no idea what they would do when they needed new clothes.

Everything had changed after her father died, for he had lost his estate by making unwise investments and at the gaming tables. Mama had a little money of her own, which she had inherited from her father, but the income was scarcely enough to keep them.

'I do not know what to do, Susannah,' her mother

had told her when they moved from their comfortable house to this modest cottage. It had seemed bare and poor compared to the comfortable house they had been forced to leave, but somehow they had managed to turn it into a home. 'If I release what little capital I have, we could afford a Season in town for you, but then we should have nothing left.'

'And if I did not take, you would have given up your living for nothing,' Susannah said. She was a good-natured girl and had accepted their downfall into poverty with good grace. 'No, Mama. We shall manage as best we can. Perhaps I shall meet someone—a prince!—who will love me for myself and carry me off to his castle. I shall have jewels and beautiful clothes, and you will never have to worry again.' Her smile was unconsciously wistful.

Mrs Hampton shook her head sadly at her daughter's flight of fancy. 'You are very pretty, my darling, but things do not often happen that way. I dare say someone will offer for you, but he may not be to your liking.'

'You are thinking of Squire Horton, I suppose.' Susannah pulled a face, for the Squire was past forty, a generous kind gentleman, who had buried two wives and had a brood of boisterous children. She appreciated his qualities, but found him rather large and a little too dull for her quick mind.

She flicked her long, honey-coloured hair back out of her eyes. It was always escaping from its ribbons and curling in tendrils about her face. She presented a charming picture, for she was truly beautiful, but she seldom considered her looks, though she knew she was pretty because everyone told her so. However, it had not turned her head, and she was generally popular with both the gentlemen and the ladies she met. Unfortunately, situated as they were, she met very few gentlemen that either she or her mama considered a suitable match. 'Well, if nothing else turns up, I may be forced to such a marriage, Mama—but it is not yet too late for something exciting to happen.'

Susannah lived in the expectation of something exciting happening. She would meet a handsome man, not necessarily a prince, of course, but rich enough to keep both her and Mama in comfort. He would sweep her up on his horse and ride off with her to Gretna Green, where they would be married and live happily ever after, preferably in an ancient castle. Failing that, perhaps a relative they had never heard of would leave them a fortune. Mama said they had no rich relatives, but perhaps there was someone somewhere who might be kind to them.

Her biscuit finished, Susannah applied her mind to the little tea party her mother had planned for friends. She changed her old gown for a favourite primrose-silk afternoon dress and brushed her hair into order, tying it back with white ribbons. A white stole draped over her arms and she was instantly transformed from the hoyden, who had been traipsing the fields to find herbs her mama might use to make lotions and seasonings, into a young lady of some considerable style and beauty.

Susannah had an English rose complexion and sea-green eyes, her mouth soft and attractive. It was the kind of mouth gentlemen found irresistible and wanted to kiss, but she had not yet been brought out into society and could not guess at what might happen if she were. She sighed as she looked at her reflection in the dressing mirror. It was true that she was not ill favoured. If only they could afford a Season in town without ruining Mama! Surely then she could make a good marriage and rescue her beloved mother from the genteel poverty in which they now lived. Susannah did not care so very much for herself that they lived in a tiny cottage, but Mama had found it hard.

With an effort she banished her dreams of romantic love and handsome gentlemen who would beg for her favours. Mama was right: these things did not often happen. She might have to marry one of the gentlemen who called on Mama with gifts of fruit and vegetables from their gardens and looked at Susannah slyly whenever they got the chance, but she would not if she could help it!

She was about to go downstairs to the parlour when her bedroom door opened abruptly and her mother swept in. Wearing a gown of grey silk, Mrs Hampton was still an attractive woman, her colouring much as her daughter's, but she often had an air of sadness, which, her daughter noticed, seemed to have vanished for the moment. Susannah had not seen her mother this animated since Papa fell into a decline after losing all his money and died of a putrid infection some nine months earlier.

'Mama! What has happened?' Susannah's heart raced with anticipation, for she sensed her mother's excitement. 'You have news.'

Mrs Hampton waved a sheet of quality vellum at her. 'I have had a letter from Amelia Royston. You must remember that we met her once in Bath? She was visiting with her sister-in-law, Lady Royston. I felt so sorry for her having to live with that harpy. Her brother is a gentleman, of course, but I am not sure that I like him…' Mrs Hampton looked pensive, for her friend had not said much about her circumstances, but she had sensed her deep unhappiness at the time. 'Well, as you may recall, I asked her to a party and took her to a dance at the Assembly Rooms. She fell into a habit of visiting us every day, and we have kept in touch ever since through letters. I remember she was so grateful for my kindness…it was before Papa—' She broke off with a little choke, the sadness back in her eyes. 'Anyway, she went to live with an elderly aunt soon after that and everything has turned out most fortunately for her.'

'Yes, I remember Miss Royston,' Susannah said. 'What does she say in her letter, Mama?'

'It is like a miracle,' Mrs Hampton said and the light came back to her face. 'Amelia's aunt—Lady Agatha Sawle, I met her once, but you did not know her—well, she has died and left Amelia a fortune. She did not expect it. Indeed, she had no idea that her aunt was so wealthy. She knew she was to have something, but she says she had no expectation of being left more than an independence.'

'How wonderful for her,' Susannah said, her lovely eyes sparkling. 'You see, Mama, exciting things do happen. Perhaps someone will leave us something one day.'

'Amelia is so generous,' her mother said and dabbed at her eyes with a lace kerchief. The scent of her favourite lavender water wafted towards Susannah. 'She has offered you a Season in town, dearest. She knows of Papa's misfortune and she wants to help us. She will pay all our expenses and give you a dowry of five thousand pounds. Five thousand pounds, Susannah! Such a huge sum—and she makes it sound nothing! It means you have a chance of making a decent marriage, my love.' Mrs Hampton was quite overcome. Her hand trembled as she touched Susannah's arm. 'I can hardly believe that anyone would do such a thing, for we are not even family. However, that may be—' She broke off mid-sentence. 'Do you realise what this means, dearest?'

'A Season in town…' Susannah stared at her, disbelief, excitement and triumph warring in her head. 'Oh, Mama, how good Miss Royston is! But what made her think of us?'

Mrs Hampton shook her head. 'I really cannot imagine why she thought of us. She said it was because I was kind to her at a time when she needed friends, but I think she has other reasons.' Susannah lifted her brows in enquiry, but Mrs Hampton merely frowned, clearly preferring to keep her own counsel. 'I cannot tell, but I think she may be lonely. Her family is not kind, though she never complains. However, one knows…' She looked thoughtful. 'To give us so much is extremely generous, Susannah. I know one should not take charity, and I should not normally do so, but it is just what I have prayed for, my love. You deserve your chance and, if we are lucky, we may be able to repay Amelia for her kindness one day. Think of it, my love. You will meet everyone—Amelia is well connected and highly thought of in society. If you are fortunate…who knows what might happen!'

Susannah nodded, her face thoughtful as she looked at her mother. Some of the euphoria faded as she realised that Mama was expecting her to make a brilliant marriage and solve all their problems. She would be happy if that happened, of course, but she could not easily relinquish all her dreams of romance. She wanted to oblige Mama, but she also wanted to be swept off her feet, to fall madly in love. For some reason the picture of the outraged gentleman who had almost run her down flashed into her mind, though she could not think why—he had been abominably rude!

However, her overwhelming feeling was one of pleasure at the thought of her Season in town. It was what she had longed for, hoped for these past months since Papa died. If she were fortunate she would fall in love with a suitable gentleman, one who made her heart beat much faster, but who was also acceptable to Mama. Someone who might look a little like the rude gentleman she had met in the lane, but who was far more romantic!

'I do not understand why Miss Royston is being so very kind to us,' Mrs Hampton was saying. 'But I shall write at once and tell her we are delighted to accept her generous invitation. She has asked us to join her at her house near Huntingdon next week so that we may all get to know one another in comfort. Then we shall journey to London together. She is sending her own carriage to fetch us.'

'That is very thoughtful of her,' Susannah said. She frowned as something occurred to her. 'What shall we do for clothes, Mama?'

'That is all taken care of,' Mrs Hampton said. 'Amelia says we must not worry about anything, for we may use her seamstress in town and send the bills to her!'

'Mama! She will buy my clothes as well?' Susannah looked at her mother in awe as she inclined her head, feeling overwhelmed. 'She must be very rich. It is beyond all expectation.'

'Yes, my dearest, I imagine she is very wealthy now, but she knows what it is to live on a small income, and to be treated ill by one's relations. I think that is why she has taken it into her head to help us.'

Susannah nodded. Her mother's friend was being extraordinarily kind to them. They could not have expected anything of the sort and it was a wonderful surprise. She could not wait for her adventure to begin!

However, the next few days would fly by—she must get out all her clothes and see what could be done with them. Some of them could surely be refurbished with fresh ribbons. It would not do to impose on Miss Royston's generosity more than was absolutely necessary!

She was smiling as she joined her mother's tea party that afternoon, unconsciously practising her society manners. Soon now she would have the chance to shine in society drawing rooms—and who knew what might happen then! Dreams did come true sometimes, it seemed, for just an hour ago her hopes of a Season in town had been just that...

Susannah looked towards the house as a groom opened the carriage door and helped her down. It was a pleasant L-shaped country residence built of yellowish stone with an imposing front door and leaded windows. However, it was no larger than Papa's house had been, modest by country-house standards, but the gardens were particularly beautiful and there were some graceful old trees. She thought that she would very much like to explore the garden at the earliest opportunity.

Susannah followed her mother into the front hall, smiling at a young maid who came to assist her. Mrs Hampton was speaking to a lady Susannah suspected must be Miss Royston's housekeeper.

'Miss Royston apologises for the delay in greeting you, Mrs Hampton,' the woman said. 'If you will allow me to take you upstairs to your rooms, she will be with you shortly. An unexpected visitor arrived just a few minutes ago...'

'Yes, of course. It is no matter,' Mrs Hampton said. 'Come along, Susannah.'

Susannah hesitated. 'Mama—do you think I might take a little stroll in the gardens? I shall be only a few minutes, but they are rather lovely. Would Miss Royston mind, do you think?' She threw an appealing look at the housekeeper.

'Miss Royston is a keen gardener. She has taken great pride in them since she came to live here,' the house-keeper said and smiled at her. 'You take a little stroll, miss. Riding in a carriage is so confining. If you stay close to the house, I can call you when Miss Royston is ready to receive you.'

'Very well, you may go,' Mrs Hampton said. 'But do not go off on one of your long walks, for that would be very rude.'

'No, Mama. I shall just wander as far as the rose arbour and back.'

Susannah went back towards the front door, which was opened for her by an obliging footman. She gave him a bright smile, feeling delighted to have a few moments of freedom before meeting her hostess.

When the carriage had stopped at the front of the house, she had caught sight of the rose garden. The bushes were well tended and growing lustily, though it was too early in the year for them to be at their best, of course. In another month or so this garden would be a riot of colour and she imagined the scent of roses would reach the house. Besides the roses there were wide beds of lavender, peonies and other perennial flowers. Miss Royston must spend a deal of her time in her garden; it was clearly well planned.

Susannah hesitated as she approached the rose arbour and heard a raised voice. The fencing had hidden the fact that there was anyone there; she was about to turn away when she heard her mother's name.

'Margaret Hampton is a good friend of mine. I made the offer, Michael. Nothing was asked of me, I assure you. I will not allow you to say such terrible things. Margaret and Susannah are not hangers-on. Nor will they take advantage of my good nature.'

'You are a fool, Amelia,' a man's voice answered sharply. 'Upon my word, I do not understand you! You refuse to make your home with Louisa and myself—and you open your home to strangers....'

'I have told you that I shall never live under the same roof as Louisa again, Michael. Your wife does not like me. She never has and she never will.'

'You were pleased enough to take advantage of my generosity before you inherited a fortune,' the man snapped back irritably. 'If Agatha had left it to me, with an income for you—as any sensible woman would!—none of this would have occurred. She might have known that you would not know how to protect yourself.'

'If Aunt Agatha had wished to leave her money to you, she would have done so,' Amelia replied, her voice calm but with an underlying anger. 'She told me that she had done all she intended to do for you or your sons. We share the same father, Michael, but it was my mother of whom Aunt Agatha was so fond.'

'I dare say, but Agatha was Father's aunt and I am as entitled as you, Amelia. I did not fight the will; it would cause a scandal, and I dislike that of all things, as you know. However, you could have put things right. You could help your cousins, at least.'

'I may do so in time if I feel they deserve it,' Amelia said. 'However, that is a matter for me. You may not command me and I shall not be bullied into...'

Susannah jumped guiltily as she heard a twig snap underfoot and realised that she had been eavesdropping.

She moved away quickly, turning back the way she had come, running now because she believed that someone was leaving the shelter of the rose arbour and she did not wish to be seen.

Susannah was overcome with embarrassment and shame. She had overheard what was clearly an argument between Miss Royston and—she presumed, for she had heard the name—Sir Michael, Miss Royston's brother. What a revealing argument! She would not have listened if she had not heard Mama's name, but she had wanted to know what was being said and could not leave when what she heard was so very shocking. Poor Miss Royston! Mama was right to suspect that she had been bullied and made unhappy by her family. It was not surprising to Susannah that she did not wish to live with them ever again.

Susannah stood at the front of the house, looking back at the tree-lined avenue, composing her thoughts. It was uncomfortable to know that Miss Royston's brother had been warning her of hangers-on. Had she heard only that, Susannah might have begged her mama to take her home at once, but she had heard Miss Royston's spirited defence of her friends—and she was quite certain that Sir Michael was merely angry because he wanted his sister's fortune for himself! What a truly unpleasant man he must be to speak to his sister in that tone!

Having made up her mind that she would not let what she had overheard spoil her pleasure in the coming visit to town, she turned towards the house just as the front door opened. The housekeeper beckoned and Susannah ran towards her.

'Miss Royston has come in now, miss. Your mama is ready to join in her the small parlour and I thought you would like to be there too.'

'Oh, thank you,' Susannah said. 'I hope I have not kept her waiting?'

'Miss Royston would not trouble if you had,' the housekeeper said. 'She is too good natured, miss—but you have not, for I cannot think you went far.'

'Just a short wander towards the rose arbour,' Susannah said, a faint blush in her cheeks. 'Does Miss Royston have many visitors, ma'am?'

'She has been living quietly since Lady Agatha Sawle's death, though she entertains now and then… just friends of her aunt…'

'Does her family visit often?'

'No, miss, they do not.' The housekeeper's mouth pulled into a prim line. 'Miss Royston has talked of your visit for days. I can't say when I've seen her so pleased with life…' She smiled at Susannah. 'Here is your mama, waiting for you. Miss Royston is in the front parlour.'

Mrs Hampton looked at her daughter. 'Well, dearest—are you ready?' She looked expectant as the housekeeper knocked, opened the door and then announced them.

Susannah looked past her and saw a woman standing by the window. She had her back to them, but turned as her housekeeper spoke, a smile on her face. Had she not overheard the quarrel, Susannah might have missed the telltale signs of distress. Her mother saw nothing, moving towards Miss Royston eagerly.

Susannah hung back a little, watching.

'Amelia, my dear friend,' Mrs Hampton greeted her with an embrace and a kiss. 'I cannot express how grateful I am for all you are doing for us!'

'I explained in my letter that you will be doing me a favour,' Amelia said and smiled in welcome. 'I do not wish to stay in town with my sister-in-law, and I cannot stay alone. As yet, I have not thought of taking a companion. Besides, it is so much nicer to have friends, is it not? Once we are invited out, we shall meet all our acquaintances, but it will be more comfortable for us to attend the various affairs together, do you not think so?'

Listening, Susannah realised how true Amelia's words were. She had felt that they were very obliged to Miss Royston for her invitation, as of course they were, but what she had overheard in the garden had brought home how very uncomfortable Miss Royston must have been in her brother's home. His angry tone, the unkindness in his words, were hurtful, and she could imagine that Miss Royston had had much to bear in the past from her family. The knowledge made her angry that anyone could be so unkind to their own sister, and it made her wish to protect and help Miss Royston.

'Yes, much more comfortable to have a friend,' Mrs Hampton was assuring her as Susannah's eyes wandered round the room. It was a large room, furnished with important, dark mahogany pieces. Comfortable rather than fashionably elegant. 'You are looking very well, Amelia. I see you are wearing grey. I myself have put on my lilac for the first time today. Shall you go into colours once we are in town?'

'I think grey and lilac would be suitable, and perhaps some dark colours as the weeks pass,' Amelia said. 'I have only just put off my blacks, but I shall wear colours again soon. Aunt Agatha would not expect me to wear black for ever. Indeed, I doubt she wished it at all, but in the circumstances I thought it right to show respect. She has been so very generous to me. I knew she intended to leave me something, but I had no idea how much that would be.'

'Well, I am sure you deserved it,' Mrs Hampton said with a look of warm approval. She turned towards Susannah, beckoning her. 'Come forward, my love. You remember Miss Royston, of course.'

Susannah made an elegant curtsy, smiling a little shyly. 'Yes, I do remember Miss Royston. It is exceedingly kind of you to invite us to stay with you in town, ma'am. I do not know how to thank you—for everything. If you are certain you wish to do so much…' She had to ask, since she had heard what Sir Michael thought of her and Mama, but there was no hesitation in Miss Royston's response.

'You may thank me by being happy,' Amelia told her with a look of such warmth that Susannah's last reservation fled. 'I knew that you must be finding things difficult since your terrible loss, and I wanted to help a little if I could. Besides, as I told your mama, I wish for friends to stay with me in town. You are doing me a great favour by agreeing to accompany me to town.'

'I think you are very kind, ma'am,' Susannah said, glowing with pleasure. Miss Royston was so exact in her manners and did not make one feel one was receiving charity at all. She had been a little nervous of meeting her, especially after hearing the argument—but her charm banished all Susannah's doubts. 'It is so exciting. I can hardly wait!'

'Once it is known we are in town, I am sure we shall be invited everywhere,' Amelia went on. 'You will make many new friends and I dare say you will be one of the prettiest girls of the Season—if not the prettiest!'

Susannah blushed and shook her head. She thought Miss Royston was beautiful with her reddish toned hair and green eyes, though she would not have dreamed of saying as much to her face. For a wealthy woman, her attire was modest. Although still in mourning, Amelia was wearing a stylish gown that owed everything to good taste and nothing to ostentation. Indeed, the only jewellery she wore was a small but pretty gold-and-pearl brooch pinned to the bodice of her gown.

Susannah remembered that she had thought Miss Royston had been a little quiet when they met in Bath, though she knew that their friend had possessed a lovely smile. She had not smiled often then, which was hardly to be wondered at in her situation! She could have had nothing to smile about living in her brother's house, for he was undoubtedly a bully.

'Come and have tea,' Amelia said and indicated that they should sit. 'You must wish for some refreshment after your journey. I am sorry that I had to keep you waiting. My brother came unexpectedly to call...' A look of anger and distress passed fleetingly across her face, but was gone so quickly that it might never have been there.

Susannah glanced around the large, square room. The décor was all in varying shades of green and cream, soft muted colours that gave it a feeling of comfort and ease. She thought that the curtains had not been changed in an age, but liked the homely feeling that prevailed. The room had an atmosphere of having been lived in happily for some years: a book lay on a table, a sewing basket stood by a comfortable elbow chair, and the pianoforte had a well-loved shine that seemed to indicate it was often used. A pretty Canterbury held sheets of music that had been much handled.

Amelia rang the bell and almost immediately a butler brought in a large silver tray displaying a handsome set of plain silver. A maid followed and set up the stand so that he could deposit his burden and another maid brought in an arrangement of dainty cakes and biscuits that she set on an occasional table.

As the tea was poured and Susannah got up to hand a cup to her mama, she observed that Miss Royston seemed more in command of her situation than before, which was understandable. In the past she had been obliged to consult her sister-in-law before making plans. Now she was free to do as she pleased, and it seemed she was full of plans for the coming Season.

'I have written to one or two friends, telling them of the date I intend to be in town,' Amelia said. 'We already have several invitations to dine, and I am certain there will be many more. I shall give a dinner the first week we are in town and I thought we might have a little dance for Susannah once she has made friends.'

'Oh, Miss Royston,' Susannah exclaimed, struck by this extra kindness. 'I had not expected a dance of my own. Do you truly wish to go to so much trouble on my behalf? You have done so much—some would say far too much. We are not even family...' She glanced away, her cheeks heating as Miss Royston's eyes flew to her face. She nibbled at a delicious almond comfit as Amelia sipped her tea and looked thoughtful.

'You are my very good friends,' she said after a pause. 'At one time your mama was the only friend I felt I might trust. To me you are as much and perhaps more than family. Besides, it will be no trouble at all,' Amelia said and laughed. 'I shall employ others to make certain that everything goes well on the night. Besides, I love to dance and to see young people enjoying themselves.'

'You speak as if you were past your youth,' Margaret Hampton said and shook her head. 'You are still young enough to dance and enjoy life yourself, Amelia.'

'Yes, perhaps I am, if anyone wished to dance with

me,' Amelia agreed, and her eyes reflected amusement. She looked at Susannah. 'Please, my dear, you must call me Amelia, at least in private. I want you to think of me as your good friend—an older sister, perhaps.'

'Oh…thank you,' Susannah said, a faint colour still in her cheeks. Had Miss Royston suspected her of over-hearing her argument with her brother? 'Yes, that would be very comfortable, when we are all together.'

'Good. I want you to be comfortable and happy, Susannah.' Amelia assured her. 'Your things have been taken to your rooms, though only the small bags have been unpacked, for the day after tomorrow we set out for London.'

'This will be my first visit to London. I have been to Bath twice. Mama took me to the theatre and the shops. I think London will be very exciting.'

'You will find it strange and new, but I am sure you will enjoy yourself. There are many theatres and excellent shops in town.' Amelia smiled at her. 'Come, we shall go upstairs, for I understand that you have not yet seen your room, Susannah.'

Susannah followed her hostess up the wide staircase, glancing at the portraits hanging on the wall. She felt excited and nervous at the same time, because she understood how lucky she was that Amelia had offered her this Season in town. Amelia's claims to need friends were mere politeness, because she could have employed a companion for far less than she was giving Susannah and her mother. It was sheer good nature on Amelia's part, and Susannah was suitably grateful.

The room she was shown into upstairs was pleasant. Decorated in various shades of blue and cream, it had a cool elegance that she guessed was Miss Royston's doing. The bedchamber had clearly been refurbished recently, and she guessed that their hostess had used her time of mourning to good purpose, ordering the house to her own taste. She had left the parlour untouched, perhaps because it was so very comfortable. Susannah approved of what had been done here and thought how nice it would feel to be in a position to do as one wished. She would love to have the task of refurbishing a large house, but it was expensive. Money was certainly important for a comfortable life.

Left to herself, Susannah sighed. She so longed for romance, but she also knew her duty to Mama. Mama belonged in a house like this, not the cottage she was forced to live in these days. Her only chance of a better life was for Susannah to make a suitable match.

Susannah had finished her examination of the room and begun to change out of her travelling gown when someone knocked at the door. Thinking it must be her mama, she called out that she might enter. A young girl with brown hair and dark eyes came in. She smiled and bobbed a curtsy, seeming a little shy.

'My name is Iris, Miss Hampton,' she said. 'Miss Royston says I am to be your maid for the next few weeks and accompany you to London.'

'Oh...' Susannah was surprised; she had grown used to looking after herself at the cottage, but it would be nice to be waited on again, if only for a few weeks. 'Please come in, Iris. I knew someone had unpacked the gown I wished to wear for this evening—was that you?'

'Yes, miss. I pressed it while you were having tea.' Iris looked at her with interest. 'You have lovely hair, miss. May I dress it for you?'

'Do you know how to?' Susannah was hesitant, for

her hair was so fine and she could never get it to stay tidy for long.

'My mother used to be a lady's maid before she married,' Iris told her. 'She taught me all the skills I need and Miss Royston took me on a few weeks ago. She has her own dresser, but I was allowed to help—and now I am to serve you. It will be exciting to visit London, miss.'

'Yes, it will.' Susannah smiled at her. 'Well, you may put my hair up for me this evening,' she said. 'I have been experimenting with it myself, but it always falls down again. We shall see what you can do, Iris.'

'I think I can manage to make it stay in place, miss,' Iris said. 'You will be surprised at the difference it will make.'

Susannah felt very grand as she went down for dinner that evening. She was wearing an expensive yellow gown Mama had bought her for her birthday a few weeks before Papa died. She had not worn it since, because she had not had reason to do so, but this evening was a celebration and she wished to look her best. Her hair was dressed softly into a double loop at the back of her head, caught back with a silk flower and a few wisps allowed to curl at the sides of her face. She looked elegant and quite different from her normal self.

'Susannah!' Mrs Hampton stared at her daughter in surprise. 'You have done your hair differently, my love. It makes you look older and more grown up.'

'I think it suits her very well,' Amelia said as she came to join them. 'Are you pleased with Iris, Susannah? I thought she would be a help to you; if this is an example of her work, I am well satisfied.'

'Iris put my hair up for me,' Susannah said. 'She says

we shall try different styles and see which looks best. I think she is very clever with her fingers, for I could never have achieved something like this.'

'I think I like it now that I am getting used to it,' Mrs Hampton said, looking slightly pensive. 'I have been used to thinking of you as my little girl, but I must get used to the idea that you are a young lady now.'

'And a very beautiful one,' Amelia said in a tone of approval. 'I believe she will create something of a stir in town, Margaret. I think you must accustom yourself to the idea that Susannah will be much sought after by the gentlemen.'

'Well, I hope she may meet someone nice,' Mrs Hampton said, giving her daughter a fond look. 'She is a good girl and has been a great comfort to me these past months. I am not sure what I should have done without Susannah's support.'

'Yes, of course she has,' Amelia said and laughed. 'But we must stop talking about her, for we are making poor Susannah blush.'

Susannah shook her head. She had always known she was pretty, of course, but with her hair styled differently she was beginning to feel like someone else—a young woman instead of a girl.

'I hope that I shall meet someone I can like well enough to marry him,' she said. 'There was a gentleman at home who might have proposed marriage, but he was some years older and I did not care for him….'

'I dare say you will be able to pick and choose when we are in town,' Amelia told her. 'I was thought pretty when I was your age. I might have married several times, but I hesitated and then…' She sighed, shaking her head. 'It was too late. I wasted my chance, Susannah, but you must make the most of yours.'

'Yes, I shall,' Susannah agreed. 'If I am lucky enough to meet a gentleman I can like.'

In her mind she substituted the word *like* for *love*. She wanted to fall desperately in love with a handsome man, one who would carry her away on his white horse to a castle where she would live happily ever after. As her mother and Amelia turned to walk into the dining parlour, Susannah laughed at her foolish thoughts. It was unlikely she would meet a prince and live in a castle, of course, but she did hope that something exciting would happen.

The evening was as pleasant as any Susannah could recall for a long time. Her mama was so happy, so clearly pleased to be with her friend, and content with the arrangement that Susannah had almost made up her mind not to mention what she had overheard. However, Amelia drew her apart when Mrs Hampton stopped to enquire a recipe from the housekeeper.

'Susannah my dearest,' Amelia said softly, 'my house-keeper tells me that you took a little walk towards the rose arbour earlier.'

'Yes...' Susannah blushed. 'I will tell you that I heard Mama's name mentioned and then...an argument. I did not listen long... Forgive me. I know I should have walked away immediately, but I could not help listening for a moment or two.'

'If you heard someone say unpleasant things of you and your mother, please forgive me,' Amelia said. 'I am sorry if you were hurt and I hope you will not let it spoil your visit—or our friendship?'

'It will not, for you said only good things,' Susannah said. 'I think he must be very unkind to speak to you so! Oh, I should not have said that—but I did not like to think he could speak to you in such a manner.'

'Yes, my brother has been unkind,' Amelia replied, a hint of sadness in her eyes. 'His wife more so. Louisa can be spiteful when she chooses. However, I do not speak of it. I did not wish to be rude by appearing in town without informing my family of my intention, but Michael came down after he had my letter and we quarrelled. I shall say no more of the affair. I just wished you to know that his thoughts were not mine. I hope you know that I am truly happy your mama accepted my invitation.'

'I do know,' Susannah said and smiled. 'You are kind and generous and I think we shall be very happy together.'

'Then that is all I ask for,' Amelia said. 'Run along to bed now, my love. You have had a long journey and you must be tired.'

Susannah kissed her cheek on impulse. 'You are so good! I hate him for being unkind to you,' she said rashly and then ran away because she feared she had said too much. However, when she looked back, she saw that Amelia was smiling.

Chapter Two

Toby Sinclair looked at his uncle and frowned. He was twenty and newly in town, on the brink of his first Season since leaving Oxford. Harry Pendleton had just promised to put him up for several clubs, excluding the one he most wanted to belong to, however, which was the Four-in-Hand driving club. The elite group consisted of a select band of Corinthians who believed themselves to be masters of style and sport, allowing only a favoured few to their ranks. Having met his uncle by chance at a society affair, he seized his opportunity.

'Dash it all, Harry! You know I've got good hands. You taught me to handle a team yourself. Why can't you put my name forward?'

'Because, my young friend, they would blackball me immediately,' Harry replied with a teasing grin. He was very fond of his sister's boy and he had taken him in hand from an early age, teaching him the things his father would have had he been able. Sir James Sinclair had married late in life and was now a semi-invalid, confined to his estate and quite often to his rooms with bouts of ill health. 'For one thing, those clothes you are wearing won't pass muster, not precise enough—and you've a way to go in your handling of a team before they would consider you up to scratch. Coleridge and Ravenshead are pretty strict about who they allow to join. If you keep your nose clean and show that you're up to snuff this Season, I'll put you forward next year.'

'Next year,' Toby said and pulled a disgusted face. 'I know they are your particular friends, but I'd back myself in a race against either of them with your blacks, Harry.'

'Always supposing I would allow you to handle my blacks,' Harry replied and flicked a speck of non-existent fluff from his immaculate coat of superfine. 'Don't look now, but Northaven has just come in. Remember what I told you, Toby. The marquis is received everywhere and you cannot avoid him and his cronies, but be careful of them. The last thing you want is to be caught in their net. Your father asked me to look out for you. He would expect me to warn you of men like Northaven.'

'Didn't you say that you won a hundred guineas from him a couple of weeks ago?'

'Yes. I found it impossible not to oblige him when he invited me to play, but I suspect he may not be completely honest at the tables.'

'You mean, he cheats?' Toby's face showed his disdain as he glanced at the man they were discussing. The Marquis of Northaven was a tall, well-formed gentleman with black hair and very blue eyes. He was generally held to be handsome and the ladies liked him. His progress through the room was causing something of a stir amongst the fair sex, though most looked at him slyly when they thought he was not aware. All the matchmaking mamas were sure to have warned their daughters that he was a rake and not to be trusted, though in some cases that probably only made him more attractive to very young ladies.

'Well, I dare say he may think I am a flat, but, thanks to you, I am up to most tricks,' Toby said, his gaze drawn to some newcomers. 'I say...she's a beauty, wouldn't you agree? I believe she is new. I haven't seen her before.'

Harry followed his nephew's gaze. A vision in white had just entered the room, accompanied by two attractive older ladies wearing grey and lilac respectively. His eyes narrowed, for the girl was certainly very lovely. Her hair was a dark honey blonde, and she stood out by virtue of the simplicity of her attire. Most of the younger ladies had frills and flounces on their gowns, but she had chosen something more elegant, plain even. Her hair was dressed simply in a loop of the back of her neck, yet it suited her perfectly. He thought perhaps she had taken her cue from the younger of her companions.

Harry frowned as he recognised the lady in grey silk. He had not seen her for some years and she had changed a great deal, but she was still beautiful, extremely elegant. Miss Amelia Royston! If he remembered correctly, his friend, Gerard Ravenshead, had once been interested in the lady, but something had gone wrong. Harry did not know all the details, but Gerard had certainly been cut up about it at the time. It was about the same time that a livid scar appeared at his left temple. Gerard had never spoken of the scar or the reason for the loss of his hopes.

'Yes, she is rather lovely,' he said, bringing his gaze back to the vision in white. 'I have no idea who she is, but I know one of her companions.'

'You couldn't introduce me, could you?' Toby asked and arched his right eyebrow.

'Fancy your chances, do you?' Harry asked and chuckled as he saw the younger man colour. 'I do not think your mama would be happy to see you ensnared too soon, Toby.'

'Oh, lord, no,' Toby said and made a grimace of horror. 'I shall not marry until I am at least as old as you and ready to set up a nursery. Far too boring to be married before you've been on the town a few years.'

'You young cub!' Harry said and made a face at him. 'What makes you think I am ready to set up my nursery?'

'Mama said it was time you did,' Toby replied innocently but with a wicked air. 'She says if you leave it much longer, it may be too late.'

'Good grief. I am three and thirty,' Harry said and grimaced. 'I do not think the case desperate yet. Lady Sinclair would have had me married ten years ago if she could, but I had no mind for it. I believe she is more desperate to see me wed than Mama!'

He smiled oddly, for he knew his sister Anne had his best interests at heart. They had always been close and she understood him, perhaps even better than he did himself. Besides, of late he had begun to feel it was time he settled down. Indeed, these days he was as happy with his dogs and horses at home in the country as cutting a dash in town. However, he had not met a lady he wished to marry. Most of the young ladies brought to London by their eager mothers were too naïve and often too timid for his taste. He knew that he would be bored by their company within months and that would be unfair to his wife. If he were to marry, it would be to a lady of spirit, someone who could retain his interest. He was not sure that romantic love existed, but it was certainly possible to admire and care for another. His mother had undoubtedly loved his father, and would never consider marrying again, though she might if she had wished. Harry felt that if he were to marry he would like to be loved in that way, though he knew that most of his friends had married for reasons other than love. Had he been satisfied with a marriage of convenience he might had wed a long time ago, but he was looking for something more.

His eyes narrowed as he noticed that a steady queue of gentlemen were making their way to the side of the beautiful young lady in white. He watched her for a while. Something about her seemed familiar, but he could not think what. He was certain he had never met her before—and yet there was something. She had pretty manners and a nice smile, he observed, before turning away to join some friends in the card room. It was very unlikely that the newcomer would be any different to the other young ladies in the room.

Harry rather thought that when he married, he would probably choose an older lady, perhaps a widow. An intelligent lady, who would fill his house with good company and give him an heir. It was all very well to hope for something more, but in the end he might be forced to marry for the sake of the family.

'No, no, please, gentlemen, you must not fight over me!' Susannah begged, her eyes bright with laughter as the two young bucks argued fiercely over the last dance on her card. 'If you cannot agree which of you should have the dance, I shall promise it to neither of you.'

'But it should be mine,' Tom Roberts asserted. 'I am sure I asked first.'

'I am the elder by birth and therefore I should take precedence over this rascal,' his twin Edgar replied, glaring at his brother. 'You must dance with me, Miss Hampton.'

'I believe this dance is promised to me, gentlemen.' The newcomer held out his hand with a touch of command that prompted Susannah to obey, even though she had not yet been introduced. However, she knew who he was, for she had remarked his progress through the room and asked Amelia.

'Thank you, sir,' she said, smiling up at the Marquis of Northaven as he led her out to join the throng of dancers. 'It was good of you to rescue me.'

'The Roberts twins are known for squabbling with each other,' Northaven said. 'Harmless enough, I dare say, but I thought you needed a little help. This is your first Season in town, I believe?'

'My first dance,' Susannah confided, her smile sparkling at him, because the evening had been far more exciting than she could ever have imagined. She had not sat out once, and the twins were not the first gentlemen to argue over her, in a friendly, teasing manner, of course. It was just good fun and she had thoroughly enjoyed being fussed over. The reality had far outweighed her dreams thus far. 'I have had such a lovely time.'

'Everyone speaks of you as the latest rage,' Northaven said, amused by her honesty. She was very young and he was usually bored by innocence, but she had spirit and an artlessness that was amusing. 'It all seems fresh and new for the moment, but you will be bored within a month.'

'Oh, no, I couldn't be,' Susannah retorted. 'We have been invited everywhere, to so many different affairs. I couldn't possibly be bored in London.'

'Do you not know that it is fashionable to be bored?' Northaven lifted an eyebrow, his expression mocking.

'Oh…' Susannah laughed because she believed he was teasing her. 'I fear that I must be unfashionable then, sir. I have not yet acquired town bronze and you must forgive my country manners—but I refuse to be bored when people have gone to so much trouble on my behalf. It would be rude and ungrateful.'

'Then you will set a new fashion,' he told her. 'Since everyone approves of you, you can do no wrong.'

Susannah looked at him uncertainly as their dance ended. She was not quite sure what to think of him, because he was very different from most of the young gentlemen she had danced with that evening. He returned her to her mother and Amelia, bowed and took his leave. She was conscious of a feeling of disappointment. There was something slightly dangerous about the marquis, and she was not sure she had made an impression on him, though she found him intriguing. He was very handsome, like one of the heroes from her dreams.

'Susannah…' She became aware of her mother speaking. 'This gentleman wishes to make your acquaintance. Lord Pendleton—my daughter, Susannah. Your father was a friend of Lord Pendleton's father, my dear.' Mrs Hampton smiled and moved away a few steps to talk to a lady who had caught her attention.

Susannah turned to look at the gentleman her mother had just introduced. He was tall, though not quite as tall as Northaven, but in his way equally attractive. His hair was not as dark as the marquis's, being a chestnut brown, and with a slight curl to it, his eyes a soft, melting brown. A little shock ran through her as she recognised him. He was the rude gentleman who had almost knocked her down in the lane. He was dressed very differently this evening, but she could not mistake those eyes, even though they were not flashing with temper. She felt hot inside as she wondered whether he would recognise her.

'Sir.' She inclined her head, but kept her eyes lowered. Her heart was racing for she hardly knew how to face him. She was almost sure that he had not recognised her and she hoped he would not. Their encounter had been so brief that he would surely have forgotten her. Her hand curled into itself, her heart beating faster. 'I am pleased to meet you.'

'It is your first visit to town, Miss Hampton?'

'Yes—how did you know?' Her heart raced. Had he recognised her as the girl he had met briefly in a country lane?

Harry hesitated, frowned, then said, 'I do not wish to seem interfering, Miss Hampton, but if I were you, I should not dance with Northaven too often.' His gaze narrowed. 'You know it is strange, but I have the oddest feeling that I have seen you somewhere quite recently.'

'I doubt it, sir.' Susannah's heart caught with fright. What would he think if he realised where he had seen her? One word from a gentleman of his stature and she might be ruined! 'Why do you warn me against Lord Northaven? He seems a perfect gentleman to me, sir.'

'I do not fault his manners or his lineage,' Harry told her. 'I think perhaps he is not a suitable partner for an innocent and very pretty young lady.'

Susannah had received so many compliments that evening that his words made little impression. She had been called beautiful, stunning, a nymph, an angel and many similar endearments. To be called pretty was not remarkable and, besides, she did not like his tone. Anyone would think he was her brother or her uncle! He was arrogant and opinionated—a bore.

'I thank you for your concern, sir,' she replied primly. 'However, I believe I am quite safe here under the eyes of Mama and Miss Royston.'

'Yes, I expect you are, as long as you take care to remain where they can see you,' Harry said and hesitated. 'Forgive me if I seemed to lecture you. It is not my place to do so—but I would never allow a niece of mine to associate with that gentleman.'

'I am not your niece, sir.'

'No, you are not. Forgive me. I have earned your displeasure. I spoke with good intent, but I should not have interfered,' Harry said, then inclined his head to her and walked off.

Susannah stared after him. His back was very straight and she understood that she had offended him. She had thought at first that he was one of the most attractive gentlemen she had met that evening—in her whole life!—but he was a stuffy bore. She did not think he could be much above thirty years, but he behaved as if he were old enough to be her father! He was certainly not the kind of man she was seeking as a husband. Her eyes searched the room for the man that had made the biggest impression on her that evening and found him.

Northaven turned his head and glanced at her. For a moment his blue eyes met hers and her heart jerked, but then he looked at his companion once more and smiled at something he was saying. Almost at once they left the room together. Susannah's gaze followed him, her feelings showing a little too well on her face.

'I could not help overhearing what Harry Pendleton said to you a moment ago,' Amelia said, and Susannah glanced round at her. 'It was not his place to say it, of course, but he is quite right, Susannah. Northaven is a rake and perhaps worse. He is received everywhere, but there has been some talk of late. I should not dream of trying to dictate to you, my dear, for there is nothing so annoying as being told not to do something—but if I were you, I should be careful of Northaven, at least until you know more of him. But please do not think that I mean to interfere, for I most certainly do not. That is something I abhor.'

Susannah caught a look in her eyes that told her she was thinking of the way her own life had been when she was forced to live in her brother's house. Once again she felt indignant that anyone should have made Amelia suffer so. She had been introduced to Amelia's brother earlier that evening, but his stiff manner had not helped to change her opinion, nor the way he had looked at her, as if she were something the cat had brought in! He obviously thought that she was an adventuress, bent on taking what she could from his sister.

'Oh…then, of course, I shall be very careful,' Susannah replied. She did not wish to offend her kind hostess, though she had liked the marquis despite the warning. However, it was Lord Pendleton's advice that rankled. It was just the same as that day he had almost knocked her down. Instead of apologising he had lost his temper—and now he was seeking to lecture her. Did he imagine that she was stupid? He had spoken to her as if she were still in the schoolroom! She had no intention of becoming compromised by any of the gentlemen, several of whom had enquired if she would like to take the air. She was enjoying her success, but she had as yet no thoughts of marrying anyone and must therefore be careful not to do anything that might seem too particular.

Susannah still felt in her heart that the most exciting man she had met that evening was the Marquis of

Northaven, yet it was Lord Pendleton who lingered in her mind long after she had said goodnight to Mama and Amelia and retired to bed. When she dreamed, annoyingly it was of Lord Pendleton, who had somehow acquired a schoolmaster's hat and waved his cane at her, telling her to behave or he would punish her.

How very ridiculous! In the morning her dreams vanished with the sight of the sunshine pouring in at her window and she rose, feeling refreshed and eager for the day to begin. She laughingly dismissed her annoyance of the previous evening. Life was too amusing to be disturbed by such a small thing for long. Lord Pendleton was rich and respected, but he did not fit her idea of a knight on a white horse. Besides, they had so many engagements, so many affairs to attend that she had no time to reflect on that particular gentleman.

She was going shopping again that morning and she wanted to buy a bonnet she had seen in the milliner's window a day or so earlier. Bonnets, pretty gowns and enjoying herself were of far more importance than one gentleman's opinion of her. She did not know why she had let it weigh with her at all!

She would put the disagreeable Lord Pendleton out of her mind and not think of him again.

Harry was undressing that evening when it suddenly came to him. At first he thought that his mind was playing tricks on him. The girl in the country lane and Miss Susannah Hampton were one and the same. In the act of removing his breeches, he swore loudly, causing his valet to turn and look at him.

'Was something the matter, my lord?'

'No, Philips, nothing at all,' Harry said and laughed ruefully. 'I am a damned fool, that's all.'

'I rather doubt it, sir,' the devoted servant said and smiled. 'If there is anything I can do to be of assistance?'

'No, nothing,' Harry replied, realising that the man was brushing the coat he had worn that evening. 'Leave all that now and get off to bed.'

He sat on the edge of the bed as the man went out, then sipped the glass of brandy Philips had thoughtfully put out for him.

'It is a small world...' Harry smiled to himself. He had wondered why the Hampton girl seemed a little prickly, but now he understood perfectly.

She had looked very different in her simple country dress, her hair blown by the wind and roses in her cheeks—but those eyes did not lie. She really did have the most remarkable eyes.

Had he given her an irrevocable dislike of him? She had called him rude and arrogant at their first meeting, and tonight he had committed the unforgivable sin of lecturing her as if she were a schoolgirl. He had no idea why he had done that, for it was certainly not his business to warn young girls he did not know of Northaven's character. Some instinct had made him want to protect her from a man he knew unworthy.

Harry pulled a face, chuckling at his own stupidity. He would have to apologise the next time they met. Or perhaps not? She might find it embarrassing to be reminded of that day in the lane. It might be better to try to mend fences before he confessed that he had remembered the incident.

'What a charming bonnet,' Amelia said as Susannah tried on the white silk tied with pale blue ribbons and trimmed with matching blue bows. 'It would compliment that blue pelisse we ordered for morning wear. Why do you not buy it?'

'I have already bought three hats,' Susannah objected, mindful that it was not her money they were spending. 'Do I really need it?'

'Thankfully, we do not have to consider need, only pleasure,' Amelia said and nodded to the milliner to indicate that they would take the bonnet. 'Now, my love—what do you think of the green bonnet in the window? It is a little older in style and I was thinking of it for myself. Do you think it will become me?'

Susannah went to the window and looked at the bonnet. A gentleman was passing at that precise moment, and by chance he happened to look up and see her. He tipped his hat to her, smiling in a manner that made her heart skip a beat. She gave him a look of disapproval and moved away swiftly. Honestly! Was it impossible to go anywhere in London without seeing Lord Pendleton? He had been present at every affair they had attended this week! It almost seemed as if he were following them. She returned to Amelia, determined to put him from her mind.

'I think the green would suit you very well—' Susannah began and then broke off as the shop door opened and her mama came in, carrying parcels and closely followed by the offending gentleman in person. 'Mama...you are loaded down. I thought you meant only to borrow one book from the library. Had you said you wished for more, I should have come with you to help carry them.'

'There was no need, dearest,' Mrs Hampton said. 'I found so many volumes that I had been wanting and I was carried away. It was all going splendidly until a large dog jumped at me and I dropped them—only two doors away from here. Lord Pendleton saw my predicament and helped me. When I told him I was coming here, he insisted on accompanying me. Was that not kind of him?'

Susannah looked at the books, which had been set down for a moment. 'Very kind, Mama. I am not sure when we shall find time to read all of these, for we are invited out every day, to more affairs than we can easily accommodate.'

'Well, I may not always wish to accompany you on every occasion,' Mrs Hampton said. 'You and Amelia are so full of life...' She smiled at the gentleman standing silently at her side, his dark eyes observing them with a hint of amusement. 'It is such a thing to be young, is it not, sir?'

Lord Pendleton's eyes were centred on Susannah as he answered, 'To be so very young is sometimes as much a trial as a pleasure, ma'am. I think we sometimes forget all the problems being young and insecure may bring.'

'Very true,' Mrs Hampton agreed, giving him a look of approval. 'Especially for a young man fresh upon the town, I dare say. I met your nephew earlier. He was just leaving the lending library. A charming young man, if I may say so.'

'Toby is charming,' Harry said. 'This is his first Season in town, you know. I have been trying to warn him of the pitfalls of deep play. There are some gentlemen who do not scruple to invite young men to play deeper than they ought.'

'Scandalous!' Mrs Hampton said. 'They should know better—it can cause real misery for their families.' Her attention turned to Amelia, who had tried on the green bonnet and was asking for her opinion. 'It looks very well on you, Amelia. I am sure you should take it—it will go well with several of your gowns, and I like you in colours.'

'Yes, I think perhaps I may.'

'Miss Hampton,' Harry said as the two older ladies discussed which gowns the bonnet would compliment, 'do you attend Lady Silverson's dance this evening?'

'Yes, I believe we do,' Susannah replied. 'Shall we see you there, sir?'

'Yes, I think you will,' Harry told her. 'Indeed, yes, I believe I shall come. Tell me, do you intend to return home shortly? I have my carriage near by if you should require help with all your parcels.'

'Oh, no,' Susannah denied. She felt a little warm as she felt his gaze upon her. 'The milliner will deliver our purchases and Mama's books will be easy enough for the three of us.'

'Then I shall continue on my way, for I have an appointment with some friends, though it could easily be postponed if you required my escort,' Harry said. 'Miss Royston, you must definitely buy that bonnet. It becomes you charmingly. The colour might have been made for you. Good day to you, ladies. I shall see you this evening.'

'How odd,' Amelia remarked as Harry went out and the door closed. 'I did not expect an opinion from Lord Pendleton. It is rare that he speaks in such a frivolous fashion these days—though he was more free in his manners when he was young, of course.'

'He is not so old, Amelia, and charming in my opinion,' Mrs Hampton said, her eyes thoughtful. 'Besides, he is right. You should buy the bonnet.'

Susannah was thoughtful as Amelia completed her purchase. Lord Pendleton had enquired if they were to attend the dance that evening before telling her that he was going. Of course he was invited everywhere, but it was a little surprising that everywhere they went he was almost certain to be near by.

'We carried Toby off to play with us last evening.' Max Coleridge grinned when Harry raised his brows as they spoke at their club a little later that morning. 'Northaven was trying to bully him into a game and he was clearly unwilling.'

'I have warned him of it, but you have my thanks,' Harry said and beckoned to the waiter to bring them more wine. 'It would be wrong to try to keep him on a leading string. He would resent it and I won't do it. However, I would be obliged if you could have a word with him. He might take it better from you.'

'Already done,' Max said and grinned. 'You don't want to smother the boy, Harry. He has to learn—and we were all young once. Hard as it may be to remember in your case.'

Since there was only a couple of years between them, this brought a shout of laughter from Harry. 'Take care, Max! I might challenge you to a duel for that!'

'You would undoubtedly have done so once,' Max replied carelessly, a spark of mischief in his grey eyes. His hair was a dark brown, thick and with a tendency to curl at the nape of his neck if he allowed it to grow longer than he liked. 'Getting a bit lazy…grumpy in your old age?'

'Damn it, I'm not that old yet,' Harry said ruefully. 'Though there are times when I feel it.' He eyed his friend thoughtfully. 'Honestly—have I become too serious of late? I feel that I may be stale…set in my ways…'

'Is there a reason for your feeling that, perhaps?'

Harry shook his head. 'Just a notion that I may be coming down a bit hard on Toby. He hasn't said anything to you?'

'Not at all, admires you,' Max assured him, his gaze narrow and thoughtful. 'No other reason?'

Harry saw the laughter hidden just below the surface. 'None at all—what makes you ask?'

'Just wondered. Lady Sinclair told me she thought it was time you set up your nursery. Wondered if you meant to oblige her?'

'Damn her—and you.' Harry scowled. 'I have no intention of it yet, Max. You seem to have a bee in your bonnet—when am I to wish you happy?'

'I have been thinking of it…'

'Really? Who is the young lady?' Harry stared in astonishment.

'There is no one as yet, but I think it is time to start looking.'

'This is sudden, isn't it?'

Max nodded and sipped his wine. 'I think perhaps I ought to consider it or the alternative,' he said and shook his head as Harry arched one eyebrow. 'No, I shall not explain, Harry. It's a small problem I have to work out for myself. Anyway, we kept Toby out of trouble for you the other evening, but Northaven ensnared another young idiot. I didn't know him, but I think perhaps Toby did.'

'There's always one,' Harry agreed. He lapsed into silence, sipping his wine and thinking about what his friend had said about it being time to think of marriage. Max was, after all, two years his junior….

Susannah's heart raced as she saw the marquis turn and look at her. He immediately began to walk towards her. She had just two dances left on her card that evening and she wondered if he would ask for them both.

'Miss Hampton,' a voice spoke at her side. Susannah turned to look, feeling a spurt of annoyance as she saw that it was Lord Pendleton. He had told her he would be there that evening, but she had not seen him earlier. Why did he have to speak to her at just the moment the Marquis of Northaven was about to approach her? Glancing back, she saw that the marquis had turned away and was speaking to another young lady, Mary Hamilton, a girl whom Susannah had come to know as they were often invited to the same affairs. 'May I hope that you have a dance for me?'

Susannah blushed, because her thoughts were unworthy. 'Yes, of course, sir. Perhaps you would like the waltz, which is just about to start? I believe it is my last...' She was not lying because the supper dance was not a waltz and all the others had been taken.

'I should be delighted,' Harry said and took her hand. 'May I say that you look delightful this evening, Miss Hampton? Not every young lady wears white as well as you.'

'I thank you for the compliment, sir,' Susannah said. She put her annoyance at his untimely interruption aside, because however annoying it might be to have missed an invitation from the marquis—who was infrequently at these affairs—Lord Pendleton was wonderful at waltzing. 'But I think there are many young ladies here this evening who look just as pretty.'

'Perhaps. Yes, I agree there are many pretty girls, but only a handful are beautiful. Miss Royston is beautiful. You are beautiful—and Miss Hamilton is beautiful. The others are pretty.'

Susannah frowned at him. 'I suppose you mean to compliment me, sir...'

'No. I mean to be truthful,' Harry told her. 'You will discover that I am usually honest in my observations, Miss Hampton.' He looked at her for a moment, as if considering something he wished to say, but nothing was forthcoming.

'Oh...' Susannah was thoughtful. She hardly knew how to answer him. She had thought he was paying her an exquisite compliment, but now he had made it seem almost a reprimand. He was such an odd man! She was not even sure that he liked her, though of course he was always polite. Lord Pendleton had some of the most exquisite manners, far more so than any gentleman she had met in the country; he was one of the most respected gentlemen in the drawing rooms of London, beloved of the hostesses. However, that did not particularly recommend him in her eyes. He seemed a little severe and she had not forgiven him for scolding her the first time they met. 'Of course I do not know you well, sir.'

'No, we are not well acquainted as yet,' Harry agreed. 'I shall hope that we may become so as the Season goes on, Miss Hampton.'

Susannah smiled at him uncertainly. She was not sure whether he was just being polite or whether he meant it—and even if he did, she was not sure that she truly wished to know him well. He was a little older than most of her admirers, and serious—though he had a habit of lingering in her mind and her dreams.

Their dance ended and Lord Pendleton left her with Amelia, but it was only a matter of some minutes before her next partner claimed her. Swept up in the excitement of the evening, Susannah forgot her disappointment at missing the chance to dance with the Marquis of Northaven. He did not approach her again and left the room long before the supper dance. In the meantime, another gentleman asked for a dance and she was obliged to give her last one to him.

Lord Pendleton did not ask her for another dance that evening, though she saw him dance with several other young ladies, including Mary Hamilton and Amelia.

It was as she was leaving the ballroom to refresh herself before supper that she happened to overhear two young ladies talking. They were whispering and giggling, and she could not help but hear what Mary was saying to her friend.

'Mama says that I should encourage Pendleton if I get the chance, but I heard that he has an expensive mistress. Mama says that gentlemen often have them, but I am not sure I approve.'

Her friend giggled and whispered something. Miss Hamilton laughed harshly. 'Well, I suppose he has for-tune enough to pay for both a wife and a mistress if he cared for them, but I shall expect him to buy me more lavish presents than he gives her—if I encourage him, of course. I prefer Northaven, but Mama will not hear of it. She says he is a rogue and...'

Susannah hurried up the stairs, not wanting to hear more of their nonsense. She had been wondering why Lord Pendleton was always to be seen at these affairs, but if he were thinking of making Mary Hamilton an offer, he would naturally make certain of every chance to fix his interest with her.

Susannah could not help feeling disappointed. Not because her feelings were engaged, for they most cer-tainly were not! However, she would not have expect-ed a man like Harry Pendleton to be caught by Mary

Hamilton. He had remarked that she was a beautiful young lady—but did he have any idea how very silly Mary Hamilton was? Susannah did not dislike her, but she would certainly not count her amongst the particular friends she had made since arriving in town.

Shaking her head over what she had learned, Susannah went into the bedchamber put aside for the ladies to use. She wondered if she ought to be shocked at the suggestion that Lord Pendleton had an expensive mistress. If it were true, she must be either very tolerant or very angry, for she could not have seen very much of her protector recently.

It was highly improper of her to think of such things, but she could not help wondering what it was like to be a gentleman's mistress. How did one go on in such a situation? Susannah did not think it could be pleasant, even if there were handsome presents. She would not like to be Lord Pendleton's mistress if he were thinking of marrying Mary Hamilton. Oh, dear, what a wicked thing to have come into her mind. She would not want to be any man's mistress! And particularly not that rather annoying gentleman. She might have been even more annoyed if she had guessed at his thoughts that evening.

Harry was wondering why he had not yet made his apology. He was still hesitating because he thought it might have embarrassed her to know that he had recalled their first meeting.

'Did you enjoy your drive, my love?' Mrs Hampton asked when Susannah returned from an engagement with her new friend Miss Terry and her brother Sir James Terry two days later. 'It was a beautiful morning for a drive in the park.'

'Yes, it was,' Susannah agreed and smiled. It had been a very pleasant morning—they had met so many people, all of whom seemed as if they wanted to stop and talk, particularly to Susannah, if they happened to be gentlemen. 'We met several of our friends, Mama, and I was introduced to some new ones by Lord Northaven.'

'I am not sure that I would wish you to know that gentleman's friends,' her mama said with a frown. 'I know he is a most attractive gentleman and no one could fault his manners—but I have heard a few things that make me feel he may not be quite suitable for you to know, Susannah. You must greet him politely, of course, should he speak to you, but I think it best if you do not go out of your way to encourage him, dearest. I have heard him described as a rake. You must think of your reputation.'

'I should not dream of encouraging the marquis any more than I would encourage the attentions of any gentleman I do not know well. I believe I have more sense than that, Mama.'

'Yes, of course you do, my love,' Mrs Hampton replied fondly. 'At least, if there should be a suitable gentleman you rather liked—someone like Lord Pendleton, say—then you might be permitted to show a little encouragement, though nothing particular, of course. I do not like to see young ladies throwing themselves at the gentlemen, it is most unbecoming. Any advance must always come from the gentleman—though a smile does not go amiss.'

'Oh, Lord Pendleton,' Susannah said dismissively. Lord Pendleton seemed always there when she looked round, his serious eyes seeming to reproach her. She had not spoken to Northaven for some days—until that morning by chance in the park. After the last time, when he had changed his mind about asking her for a dance, she had believed he was indifferent to her, but that morning he had flirted with her outrageously, bringing a blush to her cheeks. Of course she could not tell Mama that! 'Lord Pendleton is all very well, Mama, but a little stern—do you not think so?'

'He seems to me an excellent gentleman in every way,' Mrs Hampton said. 'We see him quite often. Has he given you an indication that he likes you, my dear?'

'Mama! No, of course not,' Susannah replied, a little wrinkle daring to mar the perfection of her smooth brow. 'I believe he admires Miss Hamilton. She certainly believes it, for she expects an offer—and I think he imagines me to be a foolish child, far beneath his notice, I dare say.'

'I am very certain he does not!' Mrs Hampton responded on a laugh. 'What makes you think he may have an interest in Miss Hamilton?'

'He told me he considered her beautiful—and I overheard something she said to a friend. I believe she expects an offer soon. You must not imagine Lord Pendleton comes to these affairs just to see me. He has friends everywhere. I hear him spoken of all the time and I think he must be very popular. He is invited to all the best houses!'

'Why would that be, do you imagine?' Mrs Hampton asked innocently. 'I am surprised he has an interest in Miss Hamilton. I had not noticed it myself.'

'Oh, I suppose he is popular because he is rich, and of course he does have excellent manners,' Susannah said thoughtfully. 'He fetched me a glass of champagne when mine was accidentally knocked over last evening and I did not even have to ask, though he was not sitting with me.'

'Quite an observant gentleman, as well as thoughtful,' her mother said. 'He served in the army with Wellington for a few years, you know, and was commended for his bravery; then he came home to take over the estate when his father fell ill and subsequently died. They say he has improved things considerably. He is very modern in his thinking when it comes to the land and agriculture.'

'You clearly approve of the gentleman,' Susannah said. Her mama obviously thought him a good catch! 'Since you have been talking to him a great deal.'

'Oh, not so very much,' Mrs Hampton said airily. 'One hears things, you know. I have not heard his name linked with any lady in particular.'

'He has a mistress…' Susannah blurted out and then blushed as her mama stared at her. 'Forgive me. I should not have spoken of it, Mama. I know it was not proper, but I heard someone say that she was expensive.'

'Such unfortunate ladies are to be pitied,' Mrs Hampton said. 'If Lord Pendleton does have an arrangement of the kind—which is not unusual—I dare say he will end it at the proper time. I do not think he would do anything improper. I imagine if he thought of marriage, he would end any such arrangement, Susannah.'

'No, I am sure he would not do anything improper,' Susannah said and could not think why she felt disappointment. 'It would be nice if Lord Pendleton proved to be less than perfect. It is very hard to live up to someone who is so particular.'

'Oh, I dare say he has his faults,' Mrs Hampton said with a smile. 'Do not let the idea of a mistress worry you, my love. Whoever was speaking of it in your hearing was wrong to do so.'

'Yes. I thought her a very silly girl.' Susannah looked at her with interest. 'You do not condemn him for it?'

'No, I do not. Nor, if you are sensible, should you.'

'I do not,' Susannah said. In fact, she had decided that it made him seem less dull than she had first thought him. 'And now, Mama—I have seen a picture of a gown I should like to have made for the dance Amelia is to give for me, if I may...'

Susannah frowned as she saw that Lord Pendleton was already at Lady Hamilton's musical evening when they arrived. He was talking to a very pretty young lady, but he had noticed them and smiled, nodding in their direction. Susannah inclined her head. She accepted a glass of lemonade from one of the footmen circulating and wandered over to look at some particularly fine plants that her hostess had caused to be arranged by the deep bow windows. The view was over a particularly pleasant garden, and Susannah was admiring it when she became aware of someone at her shoulder. She turned, not in the least surprised to see the gentleman standing just behind her, for he usually sought her out at some time in the evening.

'Good evening, Lord Pendleton,' she said. He was looking extremely handsome that evening dressed in a fine blue coat with pearl-grey breeches that fitted him superbly. 'I did not know you were coming this evening.'

'I was not sure of it myself,' Harry told her. 'It is odd that we seem to meet almost everywhere, Miss Hampton—but delightful. Your presence enlivens many a dull affair.'

'You flatter me, sir. I am a very ordinary girl.'

'I would not call you that,' Harry replied. 'Indeed, I

would say that you are far from ordinary, Miss Hampton. Are you looking forward to this entertainment? The tenor has an exceptional voice.'

'I have heard that he is excellent,' Susannah replied. 'Do you enjoy music, sir? I like to play the pianoforte, though I am not an accomplished musician. I enjoy good singing, though I have little voice myself.'

'Music is one of life's true pleasures,' Harry agreed. 'Reading, poetry and good works of fiction are also very agreeable—do you not think so?'

'Yes. Yes, I do,' Susannah replied. They had not often spoken at such length and she warmed to him, for he was an intelligent man and seemed to think much as she did about such things. 'I love to ride when I have a horse available and to walk in the country...' A flush touched her cheeks—she had realised that she ought to be honest with him. 'I believe I should tell you something, sir. When we met in company, it was not for the first time.'

'Did you know me at once?' Harry asked. 'I did not place you until my return home later that evening. I must apologise for my behaviour that day, Miss Hampton. I was so shocked by the knowledge that I might have killed you that I lost my temper. It was abominably rude of me.'

'I think I was as much at fault,' Susannah said, a flush in her cheeks. 'I did hear something before I dashed across the road, but I thought I had time and I was not truly thinking—I had my head in the clouds, as Mama would say.'

'You are a remarkable young lady,' Harry told her. 'However, you must allow me to bear the fault, for it was my damnable temper. I try to control it, but sometimes when I am much moved it escapes me.'

Susannah laughed, her eyes alight with amusement. 'You speak of your temper as though it is a wild beast, sir.'

'Exactly so,' Harry replied, amused by her perception. She was refreshingly honest and utterly charming, and he was becoming more and more addicted to her company. 'Perhaps we should take our places? I believe they are about to begin....'

He offered her his arm and they walked to an unoccupied sofa, sitting down next to her as the musicians began to play.

'What do you think of the latest "rage"?' Toby asked when he met his uncle outside White's the following afternoon. Harry was leaving the gentleman's club, Toby just arriving, having spent the previous night at a gaming hell where he had drunk a little too much, sleeping heavily that morning as a consequence. He grinned at his cousin. 'Have you heard the rumour that you are in the petticoat line at last? At the moment they cannot decide between Miss Hamilton and Miss Hampton, though the delightful Susannah is thought to be slightly in the lead.'

Harry grimaced. 'If you waste your time listening to gossip, you will never acquire the skills you need to join the Four-in-Hand. Had you forgotten our appointment this morning? I thought you wanted to drive my team to Richmond?'

'Good grief!' Toby smote his forehead with the palm of his hand. 'It went right out of my head, Harry. I went to a gambling hell last night and drank a little too much and slept late this morning. I'm dashed sorry!'

'So you should be,' Harry told him with a severe look. 'I dare say your pockets are to let this morning?'

'It isn't quite that bad,' Toby said with a wry grimace. 'Northaven did try to involve me in a high-rolling card game again last night, but I stuck to the dice with my friends and lost about five hundred to Jackson. It was a sum I could afford to lose, particularly as I won a thousand from Ravenshead the other evening.'

'I am relieved to hear it,' Harry said. 'I do not wish to carp, Toby, but it can be very expensive in town if you play too deep. You will end up owing your tailor and everyone else bills you cannot pay if you are not careful. If the worst happens, you may apply to me, of course—but I should warn you that I shall take a dim view.'

'I dare say I should be in trouble had I let myself be cajoled into playing with Northaven,' Toby said. 'I saw young Harlow sit down with them a few nights ago. He lost a fortune. I am not sure of the amount, but I know it was a great deal, for a crowd gathered about them at the last. When Harlow rose from the table he could not pay the whole immediately and his face was as white as a sheet.'

'I imagine he will have to apply to his father for funds, and I do not know how General Harlow will pay,' Harry said, looking thoughtful. 'I know he has had some trouble himself with his investments. If the play was too deep, he may have to sell land to pay his son's debts.'

General Harlow had served with Harry at one time on the Peninsula. Toby knew that his uncle liked and respected his neighbour.

'Would you buy?' he asked. 'If he is forced to sell?'

'If he truly wishes to sell,' Harry replied. 'I think I should post down to the country and have a word. It might be possible to arrange a loan to tide him over. I would not pay the young idiot's gambling debt—that would encourage him to play deep again—but I may help his father. What passes between them regarding this is their own affair.'

Harry was a good friend in an emergency, as Toby knew well. He had told him the tale of Harlow's downfall, knowing that he might wish to offer assistance to his neighbour. Although it was not generally known, Harry was one of the wealthiest men in England. His investments were always kept private, but Toby believed he had a finger in several pies and was not above being involved in trade if it would turn a profit. Naturally, he was too much the gentleman to discuss these things, but Toby had learned to read between the lines. He had not enquired into his uncle's business, for it wasn't done, but one day, after he'd had his fun, sown a few wild oats, he intended to ask Harry for a few pointers.

However, for the moment, he had something closer to his heart on his mind. 'Have you spoken to Ravenshead about my becoming a member of the Four-in-Hand?' he asked. He had held back from doing so himself, because he was relying on his uncle to do the business for him.

'If you remember, that was the point of our drive this morning,' Harry replied. 'I am not able to make another arrangement for the time being, Toby, for I shall leave town this afternoon and may be away for a couple of days or so. However, we shall drive together when I get back. I believe Ravenshead means to stay in town for a while. He was undecided at the start and refused all invitations, but he told me that he thought he would attend a ball next week. If you prove yourself worthy, I may speak to him for you.'

Susannah paused outside the parlour door. She had returned home earlier from an expedition than expected and was about to join Amelia for tea when she heard voices and hesitated, uncertain whether or not to go in.

'I am glad to see you, John,' Amelia was saying. 'Shall I ring for wine or tea? I am alone, as you see. My friends went out...'

'Father was put out when you invited them to stay with you,' John Royston answered in a frank tone that carried easily to Susannah's ears even as she lifted her hand to knock. She hesitated as he continued, 'I must tell you that I think Miss Hampton charming. If she had fifty thousand, I should join the queue of hopefuls, but I do not think she could afford me.'

'Susannah has too much sense to marry a man who cares only for her fortune, though she has something,' Amelia told him. 'Are you in trouble again, John?'

Susannah hesitated, knowing she ought to leave, but her feet refused to move and she continued to listen.

'Lord, no,' he said. 'I won a thousand from Carstairs last night, which will tide me over until next quarter if I am careful—which I shan't be, of course. I wondered if you would speak to Father for me, Amelia?'

'I have little influence with my brother,' Amelia replied. 'If you aren't in debt, what is the matter?'

'I have asked Father to buy me a pair of colours,' John said. 'He says I should settle down and take an interest in the estate, but he would hate it if I did. If I offered advice, he would soon tell me to take my nose out of his affairs. But he says he can't afford to support me as an officer.'

'Yes, he would,' Amelia agreed. 'Are you sure the army is for you?'

'Father will live for years yet,' John told her. 'I have nothing but my allowance, which is barely enough to support the life I lead in town. I must either look for an heiress or take myself off for a few years. Of the two, I think I prefer life in the army.'

'If I bought you the colours, and gave you an income of, say, two thousand a year, could you live within your means? Even in the army it is not cheap for an officer.'

At this point, Susannah decided that she had heard too much already and must either knock or move away. Just as she was deciding what to do, her mother called to her from the top of the stairs.

'Are you waiting for me, my dear? Go in, Susannah. Amelia will send for tea and I am ready for mine.'

Susannah raised her hand, knocked and entered, feeling awkward. She was in time to see John Royston kiss his aunt's cheek. He tucked something into his breast pocket, managing to look as if nothing unusual had happened.

'Miss Hampton,' he said and came to her, bowing elegantly. He took the hand she offered and kissed it. 'I was just saying to Amelia that you are the toast of the town. I would offer my suit, but I have no fortune to recommend me.'

'I would not accept a gentleman just for his fortune,' Susannah replied, a little reserved. She was embarrassed at having heard something that ought to have remained private, feeling herself at fault for having listened. It was the second time she had done so and something she must correct! 'I shall give my hand and heart only when I find love.'

'Quite right too,' he said, eyes twinkling. He was a handsome young man and Susannah thought him charming enough. However, it seemed that he had visited to ask for money, and she could not help thinking that Amelia was not well used by her family. Her nephew had been pleasant in his manner to his aunt, but there was sadness in Amelia's eyes. Susannah felt her heart go out to her, for she sensed that she was hiding some deep hurt. She glanced at the young man as he continued, 'Well, I shall go and leave you ladies to enjoy a good gossip about me....'

'Do not flatter yourself, John,' Amelia said drily. 'I assure you that we have far more of interest than your escapades.'

He grinned and went out, leaving them together. Susannah glanced at Amelia.

'I realised that you had company and did not wish to intrude...'

'Thank you, Susannah. My nephew came to me for help, which I gave freely. John is a charmer—as unlike his father as it is possible to be. I have promised to buy him a pair of colours. I think he will do well in the army. It could be the making of him.'

'What a fine thing to do for him,' Mrs Hampton said approvingly as she came in, in time to hear Amelia's remark. 'It could well be the making of him, as you say, Amelia. I knew you were considering what would be best for him, for you have said as much to me. If he truly wishes for an army life it will suit him, and life in town is the ruin of many a young man.'

'Yes, I think it will suit John, which is why I was happy to oblige him,' Amelia agreed and smiled at Susannah. 'You are back a little earlier from your walk than I expected.'

'It came on to rain and we thought we might as well come back for tea.'

'I am happy that you did, because I am feeling a

little low.' Amelia glanced at Susannah. 'Nothing to do with my nephew's visit—another matter entirely. Something happened when I visited the library...' She paused and that odd sadness was in her eyes. 'I thought I saw someone—a ghost from the past—and it brought back memories.'

'I am sorry if it made you sad,' Susannah said. 'I do not like to think of anyone hurting you. You are such a lovely person...' She blushed, afraid she had said too much, but Amelia laughed and shook her head.

'You are a sweet girl, Susannah. I love both you and Margaret dearly, and so I shall tell you that I once thought to marry, but the marriage was not permitted and he went away. I caught a brief glimpse of someone I thought might be the gentleman I once wished to marry, but it was probably not he. Besides, it was some years ago and I have put it all behind me.' Her eyes rested on Susannah. 'I did not wish you to imagine it was John who upset me, for I was happy to see him.'

Susannah blushed, her eyes dropping as Amelia turned away to ring for tea. She thought that Amelia was gently reprimanding her for eavesdropping again, and indeed it was very bad of her. She must not do it again, but it was so very tempting when one heard one's own name.

'Well, my dear,' Mrs Hampton said, 'you are much admired, you know, Amelia. I am perfectly certain you could marry if you wished. After all, you may please yourself now.'

'Like Susannah, I would marry only if I could both love and respect the gentleman,' Amelia said, but there was such a wistful look in her eyes that Susannah suspected she was still in love with the gentleman she had been denied—even if she would not admit it to herself.

* * *

Harry was thoughtful as he left town that afternoon. He would not have expected the gossips to latch on to his interest in Miss Hampton that quickly. He thought that he had been careful to show no particular interest in her in public, though he had spent much of the previous evening at her side. It must have been remarked, which was a nuisance—he had not meant to draw the attention of the gossipmongers just yet. He had been watching Susannah as she settled into her niche as the latest rage. Her vivacity was what set her apart from the crowd. She was clearly a girl of spirit and took to any new suggestions eagerly, showing her appreciation. He thought perhaps she might be a little reckless at times, but she would surely grow out of it—and he did find her charming company.

However, as yet Harry had not truly thought of marriage, even though Anne had been urging it on him for the past couple of years. If he were to consider the idea, Susannah Hampton might be the kind of girl he would wish to make his wife; she was certainly suitable and he liked her. For the moment he had no such intention and must be scrupulous—he would not wish to cause gossip that would affect her good name. He was therefore pleased with an excuse to leave town for a day or two. It would give him a chance for some quiet reflection, and he wanted to speak to General Harlow.

His neighbour was a proud gentleman and Harry would need to think of a scheme whereby he could help him without appearing to offer charity.

Chapter Three

Susannah glanced round the ballroom. Most of the dances she had attended so far had been modest affairs. This was the first large ball she had been invited to and it was a glittering event. Magnificent chandeliers shed their light on the assembled company, picking up the sparkle of jewels around the throats of the ladies and in the gentlemen's cravats. The wealthiest members of society had gathered at the Duke and Duchess of Morland's grand affair, their laughter and chatter making such a noise that it was difficult to hear one another speak. From a room further on, Susannah could hear the faint strains of music, but the receptions rooms were so crowded that it was almost impossible to progress, especially as people kept stopping them.

It must have been at least twenty minutes later that they finally arrived at the ballroom itself, which was so magnificent that it took Susannah's breath away. The floor had been polished so hard that it looked smooth and glossy, great glittering chandeliers of glass lit by hundreds of candles overhead as the dancers moved gracefully to the music. Banks of flowers had been arranged at the foot of the dais and the scent of the blooms was so heavy that it was almost stifling.

Susannah fanned herself. The rooms were overpoweringly hot, even though long windows opened out on to terraces that led to large gardens. However, she had been in the ballroom only a moment or two when the gentlemen began asking her for dances. She offered her card and the spaces were quickly taken, all save the one before supper, which she had reserved. Susannah was not sure why she had reserved it or for whom, but she had thought it prudent to hold one dance open just in case. Swept away to the dance floor by one partner after the other, she hardly had time to breathe, let alone think, and it was not until it was almost time for supper that she realised she had not seen Lord Pendleton.

That was a little strange, for this was one of the most important affairs of the Season and Lord Pendleton would certainly have been invited. When she thought about it, she realised that she had not seen him for two days, which was most unusual. Susannah was given no time to dwell on the small puzzle, however, for as the supper dance approached and she realised she would be left standing alone, a gentleman walked towards her and her heart caught.

'Miss Hampton—' Northaven's deep tones sent little shivers down her spine '—dare I hope that you have a dance for me? Pray excuse my tardy appearance. I had hoped to come sooner, but was delayed.'

Susannah's breath caught in her throat. She suspected that she must have been hoping for this when she saved the dance, but had not allowed herself to think of it. He was, after all, the most romantic gentleman of her acquaintance; that hint of danger about him was fascinating and caused little chills up and down her spine. She remembered her mama's warning, but almost immediately dismissed it. He might have a slightly tarnished reputation, but he was still received, so he could not be so very bad, surely?

She smiled at him, a little challenge in her eyes. 'You do not deserve it, my lord, but as it happens I kept the dance before supper free.'

'I am blessed by your good sense.' Northaven gave her a look that made her pulses race. He really was a very exciting gentleman! 'I hope you will grant me the dance—and also allow me to take you into supper?'

'I am not sure...' Susannah teased and then laughed at his expression, which was half-frustration, half-disappointment. 'Yes, of course. I should be delighted, my lord.'

'I am honoured,' Northaven said and held out his hand to her.

Susannah felt a little shiver at the base of her spine as his strong fingers closed about hers. She was not sure why, but his touch made her tremble. She had dreamed of this moment, but, now it was here, something did not feel quite right.

As they began to dance Susannah relaxed, letting him guide her about the floor, giving herself up to the music. She loved to dance so much and there was no need to feel nervous. Northaven might be a little dangerous, but he was a gentleman after all. Besides, they were in a crowded ballroom so she was quite safe. After a moment or two the slight apprehension left her and she found herself laughing at his teasing.

'You are an enchantress,' Northaven told her, giving her a burning look that sent tingles down her spine. 'I did not realise how exciting a creature you were at first,

Miss Hampton. I see that I must pay more attention to you in future.'

Susannah laughed. She had lost her shyness and was behaving exactly as she did with all the friends she trusted, natural and innocent, but with a little boldness in her eyes.

After their dance, Northaven gave her his arm, escorting her through the crush to the large room that had been set aside for supper. Several tables were set about the room, some of them already occupied. At one end there was a table laden with a magnificent buffet. Northaven guided her to a table near one of the open French windows and indicated that she should sit.

'I shall fetch you a glass of champagne and something to eat,' he told her. 'What will you have?'

'Just a syllabub, if it is no trouble,' Susannah said and smiled when he replied that it was no trouble at all.

As he went off to fetch their supper, she glanced around the room. Seeing a gentleman enter, her heart did a funny little skip. It surprised her, because until this moment she had not realised that she had missed seeing him these past couple of days. Lord Pendleton had arrived late, it seemed, because the duchess went up to him and seemed to berate him, tapping him with her fan and then nodding her approval at something he said. He glanced towards Susannah, appeared to frown and turned back to his hostess. He would in the past have smiled or inclined his head to her and the neglect was oddly hurtful. Susannah looked away, but he did not seem to notice, for he was deeply engaged in conversation.

Northaven had returned with her syllabub when Lord Pendleton glanced her way again. Susannah saw the disapproval in his eyes as the marquis handed her a glass of champagne and set a little tray on the table. Remembering his warning and those of her mother and Amelia once more, she felt uneasy. It might have been wiser not to allow the marquis to escort her to supper, but there could be no real harm in it.

'You do not eat?' Susannah asked, for he had brought only her syllabub and a bottle of champagne.

'I seldom eat much at these affairs,' Northaven told her. 'Try your champagne, Miss Hampton. I managed to find a bottle—one glass is never enough, is it?' He sipped his own glass, nodding in approval as Susannah drank hers. 'I see you like champagne,' he said and refilled her glass. 'You have excellent taste, for it is the Queen of the grape.'

'I used to giggle when the bubbles went up my nose,' Susannah confessed and laughed. 'But I am used to it now, and, yes, I do like it.' She seldom drank more than one glass, but it was making her feel warm and pleasant and she did not demur when he refilled her glass once more. However, by the time she had drunk a few sips of that, she had begun to feel too warm and fanned herself. 'It is so hot in here this evening, do you not think so?'

'Indeed, you are right,' Northaven said. 'Would you care for a stroll on the terrace, Miss Hampton? You will not wish to be too warm when the dancing begins again.'

'Yes, thank you,' Susannah said. She did feel as if she needed a little air and had quite forgot the apprehension she had felt when he took her hand earlier. Her head was a little fuzzy and she could not think clearly. She stood up and went out of the French door, feeling that she needed some air, hardly noticing whether he was following her. Her head was spinning and she felt odd, though she did not know why. She walked along the terrace, and then down the three steps that led to the lawns. She had expected the air to make her feel better, but instead she had begun to experience some sickness in her stomach and her instinct drove her towards the shrubbery where she could vomit, if need be.

Feeling oddly light-headed, she did not even remember the marquis until she felt a hand on her shoulder. Turning, she stared at him in a daze, hardly knowing or understanding what was going on. She was beginning to feel decidedly unwell. Surely two glasses of champagne should not have affected her so badly?

She tried to focus as the marquis came towards her, but his face was a blur. She blinked, because she felt that she might faint at any moment.

'My beautiful darling…' Northaven's voice sounded peculiar, perhaps because her head was whirling '…how clever of you to find somewhere we can be alone. I have been wanting to do this ever since I saw you.'

Susannah made a murmur of protest as he reached for her. The last thing she wanted was to be kissed at this moment! She held up her hands as if to ward him off, but her head was swimming.

'No! No, you should not…' she cried as his face loomed large in front of her and she knew what he intended. She put up a struggle, but it was ineffectual because she hardly had the strength to stand up, let alone defend herself. 'Please, do not—'

Her protest was in vain, for Northaven's greedy mouth fastened over hers, his tongue probing at hers in an attempt to make her open to him. She became aware of his hands at her breasts, moving beneath the satin and lace of her expensive gown, touching her flesh.

Suddenly, she was aware of danger and, gathering all her strength, pushed him away and screamed.

'Be quiet, you little fool,' he muttered, holding her arms, his fingers bruising her tender flesh.

Susannah's head was whirling as she struggled to break free of Northaven, but she was feeling so ill and dizzy that she knew she could not fight him. All at once she felt him move sharply away from her, as if he had been jerked back. She stared hazily at the little scene played out before her eyes, hardly knowing what was happening because she felt so sick and dizzy.

'Take your hands from her, Northaven! She is not some country cit's daughter you can ruin. Miss Hampton is a lady and innocent, and you are taking foul advantage!'

'You mistake the matter,' Northaven drawled. 'I assure you the little innocent brought me here with no prompting. She was willing at the start, even if she did take fright.'

'Damn you! You insult an honourable lady!' Harry Pendleton said angrily. 'Take your hands from her this instant or you will answer to me.'

'I am prepared to—' Northaven began, but at that moment Susannah made a gurgling sound and then lurched towards him, the vomit bursting out of her mouth and spraying in his direction. 'Good grief!' He jerked back in disgust, a look of horror in his eyes as some of the vile-smelling liquid splashed on his shoes. 'She is ill. Take care of her, Pendleton. I swear, I had no idea...'

As Northaven beat a hasty retreat towards the house, Harry took hold of Susannah's arm. 'You are unwell,' he said gently. 'You had best come and sit down.'

'I am sorry,' Susannah wailed and jerked away from

him to be sick behind a bush once more. Harry waited until she had finished and then handed her a large white kerchief. He watched as she wiped her mouth. She was about to hand the kerchief to him, then looked at it and crumpled the fine lawn in her hand. She felt like weeping, and his shoulder looked so broad and dependable. She found herself laying her head against it, her tears soaking into his pristine coat. After a moment, her distress subsided and she drew away from his supporting arm. 'I am so sorry. I will have the kerchief washed.'

'Do not trouble yourself,' Harry said. 'Keep it until you feel better and then give it to me. I shall dispose of it. Sit here on this bench for a few moments until you recover.'

Susannah's head was beginning to clear. She looked at him uncertainly, feeling a little unwell and ashamed. 'I do not know what happened,' she said. 'I drank two glasses of champagne, but…would they have made me ill?'

'I do not think it,' he said. 'Something may have been slipped into your glass. I did try to warn you, Miss Hampton. Northaven is known for his misdeeds. You would not be the first young woman he has seduced and led astray, though the first gentlewoman to my knowledge. He normally chooses country wenches or the daughters of merchants, I believe. I cannot say for certain that he drugged your drink, for I did not see him do it, but I think it may be so. I would never be surprised at anything that rogue did!'

'Oh…' Susannah gave a cry of distress. Her cheeks stung with humiliation as she realised what might have happened to her. 'You think me so foolish. I have been foolish, but he was…exciting. I enjoyed the idea of… an adventure.' A tear slipped from the corner of her eye and slid down her cheek. 'Is that so very silly of me? I have always dreamed of a knight who would sweep me off and ride away to his castle—' She stopped in dismay as she realised what she had said. 'Now you will think me very stupid. I should have put away such childish dreams, should I not? It is all very well for children to dream, but the real world is not like that, of course. You are so very sensible—you must despise my foolishness.'

'Dreams are pleasant at times. We all have them when we are younger,' Harry said, a little smile on his mouth. 'But men like Northaven are not to be trusted. He is a ruthless rogue and would use you for his pleasure. You would be unwise to trust men of his ilk.'

'Yes, I know,' Susannah said in a small voice. She felt so ashamed! 'I must thank you for coming to my rescue, sir.'

'Do not look so ashamed,' Harry told her gently. 'Northaven was at fault, not you. You would not have behaved so recklessly had he not given you that champagne—and perhaps some kind of a drug. I shall not scold you, Miss Hampton. I think you have learned your lesson.'

'The schoolmaster...' Susannah said and laughed. She blushed as he looked at her, for she could never tell him of her dream. 'I beg your pardon. I do not quite know what I am saying.'

'I think I should fetch your mama,' Harry said. 'Unless you feel well enough to go back to the ballroom?'

'I should like to go upstairs and wash my face,' Susannah told him. She was feeling better, but not yet ready to return to the dancing. 'Would you tell Mama that I am unwell, please? I think I should like to go home.'

'Yes, of course, that may be for the best,' Harry said.

'We will allow everyone to think you were simply taken ill—there need be no scandal.'

'You are very good, sir.' He was being so kind and she felt so embarrassed, so foolish.

'Not a bit of it,' Harry said. 'Let us return now. You must go to the room provided for your comfort, and I shall speak to your mama.'

Susannah got to her feet. She was still feeling a little shaky and felt glad of his arm. When they reached the house, she entered by one of the French doors and slipped quietly away to the bedchambers. It was not until she reached the one provided for the ladies to tidy themselves that she realised she still had Lord Pendleton's kerchief. It was stained and smelly, but she slipped it inside her reticule. She would have it washed before she returned it to him.

She was feeling a little better, having washed her face and tidied her gown, by the time her mother arrived. Mrs Hampton looked at her anxiously.

'Lord Pendleton told me that you were unwell in the garden, my love?'

'Yes, I was sick—twice, in fact,' Susannah said. 'I do not know what made me feel so ill, Mama. I am beginning to feel better, but I think I should like to go home, if you will take me?'

'Yes, of course, dearest,' Mrs Hampton said. 'I do hope you are not sickening for something, Susannah. You were doing so well, enjoying yourself...'

'I am sure it will pass,' Susannah said. She could not tell Mama what had happened, for it would distress her! 'Perhaps it is something I ate.' She had actually eaten hardly anything all day. She wondered if that might be the reason the champagne had gone to her head like that—unless the Marquis of Northaven had deliberately tried to drug her so that he could seduce her. 'We need not disturb Amelia, if you will take me home, Mama.'

'Amelia has already ordered the carriage,' her mother assured her. 'She was concerned as soon as Lord Pendleton came to tell us you were not well.'

'I am sorry to have spoiled the evening for you both,' Susannah said, feeling guilty. It was her foolishness in trusting a man she had been warned against that had led her astray. She should have listened to her mama and would make certain that she did not repeat her mistake! Instinctively, she knew that her ordeal could have been much worse had Lord Pendleton not come to her rescue.

'Nonsense, my love. We shall go home and hope that you are better by the morning.'

'Thank you,' Susannah replied and followed her mother downstairs. Lord Pendleton was talking to Amelia and looked at her with concern. Susannah could not meet his gaze, for she knew he must think her so foolish. He had come to her rescue so gallantly! Indeed, he had been more like the knight of her dreams than the marquis, who had used her so shamefully.

Her mind was confused and she was in some distress as she sought her bed. Lord Pendleton would have lost all respect for her—and she had come to realise that she liked him far more than she had imagined. However, he would think her foolish beyond anything and she would do best to avoid both him and the marquis if she could....

Harry frowned as he sat in the library at his town house later that evening, brandy glass in hand, staring at nothing in particular as he thought about the incident with Northaven. The man was a menace and deserved to be taught a lesson. Had Susannah not been so ill, he would have challenged the insolent marquis to a duel or simply thrashed him in the garden. He would be well within his rights to take a horsewhip to the rogue! No gentleman would behave so badly towards a well-bred young lady.

Harry had tackled Northaven about it before he left the Morlands' home that evening, but the marquis had insisted that Susannah had drunk two and a half glasses of champagne and that he had done nothing except follow her to the shrubbery.

'Damn it all, Pendleton. If I intended her harm, I'd hardly choose the ball of the year. It would be easy enough to run off with her, I dare say.'

'Are you implying that she is of easy virtue?' Harry bristled at the suggestion.

'Dash it, no! Don't be a fool. If we fight over her, she will lose her reputation. The kiss was an impulse. I had no idea she was feeling ill. I thought she meant me to make love to her.' Something had flickered in Northaven's eyes. Harry Pendleton was acknowledged as the best shot in London and a man would have to have a death wish to enter a duel with him! 'As you said, she is a lady of quality, though unfortunately little fortune.'

'Some would consider her dowry adequate. A gentleman would offer marriage after the way you behaved, Northaven!'

'I might consider it—but I need a substantial heiress or a run of luck at the tables. I have overdone it of late and must recoup my losses.'

'Then you should not have embarrassed her. If I hear a word of this spoken in the clubs, I shall thrash you!'

'I dare say you would try—but you have my word that it remains our secret. I apologise for my behaviour. I did not realise I was treading on your toes, Pendleton. If I'd known you were interested, I would not have taken her into the garden.'

Harry had accepted his explanation, because to call him out over the incident would cause a scandal and that might damage Susannah. To bring her harm was the last thing Harry wanted. He was developing an interest in Susannah—she was just so unlike any woman he'd ever met. The few days he had spent in the country had resolved nothing, except his neighbour's problems. Harry had cleverly managed to buy a worthless piece of land for a large amount of money, because it adjoined his park and he had told General Harlow that he wanted to build a lake. The general had probably not been fooled for one instant, but the face-saving gesture had been much appreciated.

Returning to town as swiftly as he could, Harry had put in a belated appearance at the Duchess of Morland's ball in the hope of seeing Susannah. He had seen her leave the supper room with Northaven, and, feeling that she might find herself in trouble, had followed them out. When he heard her scream he went to her rescue at once, no thought of anything but her safety in his mind. Seeing her ill and wretched aroused his desire to protect her—he hated to see anyone in trouble, and, as spirited and independent as Susannah appeared, she was still innocent to the ways of London society.

She had been subdued, of course, but she had spoken of wanting excitement—an adventure. He supposed Northaven must seem a dashing fellow to young ladies.

Clearly Susannah did not find him exciting! Though

he had no plans to settle down as yet, he'd like to think a beautiful woman like Susannah might at least show a spark of interest in him. Harry nursed his brandy ruefully. He knew that his manner might seem serious, even forbidding sometimes. He had not begun well by warning her about the marquis, and she would probably resent the fact that his warning had been necessary. Susannah had felt foolish and guilty, a look of shame in her eyes as they talked afterwards. He had tried to reassure her, for he had not meant to scold, only to reassure.

Was he really as stern and forbidding as all that? There had been a time when he'd cut enough larks, behaved as wildly as any young man, and had attracted the attentions of many attractive and available young ladies, but that was before he joined the army and learned the nature of war. Watching your friends die in agony was a sobering experience, and when his elder brother died suddenly of a fever and his father was taken ill, Harry had come home to try to save the family estate. Before Harry's brother Alan had died, he had managed to gamble away a large portion of the family wealth. It had taken some years of hard work to restore the estate to its former substance and amass the fortune he now possessed. A fortune that grew steadily as the months passed.

Harry had become respected, popular, especially amongst the sporting community, because of his prowess at fencing, shooting, driving and riding. However, most of his friends were his own age, sensible men who had known the horrors of war and, like him, were intent on making their estates secure. They would find no fault in his manner, but he was afraid that he had become dull, his time given too much to building the business that had brought him his fortune. The fact that he was prepared to indulge in trade was something that he had managed to hide from all but a few, for it would be frowned on by many. However, he now owned a flourishing import business, dealing in fine wines.

He would have to ask Toby his opinion. Harry was in the habit of offering his nephew advice, but the lad had never appeared to resent it. Indeed, Toby strove to gain his good opinion and was bent on following in his footsteps. Harry had never been given cause to imagine that he had become staid or boring, and it had shocked him. How could he expect a lively young lady like Miss Hampton to feel anything for him? He was several years older, and, while that in itself was not a barrier, if his manner had given her a dislike for him...

Sighing, Harry put down his glass and went upstairs to his bedchamber, though he did not feel inclined to sleep. What had happened to him? Once upon a time he had known how to laugh and tease. If he wanted to catch Miss Hampton's attention, he would have to change his ways. Did he want her enough to change? That evening had made him aware that his feelings for her were stronger than he had previously thought, so perhaps he should make an effort to know her better.

Harry was frowning as he picked up the book he had chosen for bedtime reading. It was a solemn treatise on the works of an eminent Russian writer. He opened it, looked at the first page and then cursed, throwing it across the room in sudden disgust. He could hardly introduce that as a topic of conversation to a spirited young lady!

Harry grinned suddenly, seeing the funny side of his situation. Here he was, courted on all sides by hopeful mamas, sighed over by at least a dozen simpering young ladies, and he was floundering like a green youth in the first throes of love!

His reading matter could be changed immediately. He would subscribe to Byron's latest and a few other popular novels that were circulating, but that would get him only so far. He enjoyed music and he rather thought Susannah did too. He knew she loved to dance and he would be certain to arrive earlier at all the best affairs in future, but he needed something more to arouse her interest. However, at this moment he had no idea what that might be.

Sighing, he retired to bed, still searching his imagination for something that would delight Susannah and make her smile for him, as she did for others. He smiled as his eyelids flickered, on the brink of falling asleep…a white knight to take her up on his charger and ride off into the sunset with her.

Didn't the foolish girl know what had probably happened to most of the young wenches who were abducted by knights? They surely suffered a fate that was very far from the happy ever after that Susannah had in mind. Unless, of course, the knight was in love with the lady…

Chuckling at an outrageous thought that popped into his head, Harry at last drifted into sleep.

Susannah entered the parlour in a rush of excitement, stopping abruptly as she saw that Amelia had a visitor— and one she knew to be Amelia's brother, Sir Michael Royston. He gave her a look of dislike, which made her blush and feel uncomfortable.

'Do forgive me for bursting in, Amelia,' she apologised. 'I had some news and I did not realise that you had a visitor.…'

'You should learn to knock, young lady, especially when you are a guest in another's house.' Sir Michael glared at her and then turned to his sister. 'Well, Amelia, you know my feelings, but I shall say no more on the subject—on your own head be it.' He nodded curtly and then strode from the room, leaving a silence behind him.

'I must apologise for my brother's rudeness,' Amelia said. She was hiding her distress, but Susannah knew that she was very upset. She wondered what Sir Michael had said to her and thought that she disliked him very much. He was a horrid man to treat his sister so badly! 'He had no right to speak to you that way, dearest.'

'He was right,' Susannah replied. 'It was thoughtless of me to come rushing in here the way I did—but I was excited.'

'I am glad you had a lovely time today,' Amelia said. 'You are enjoying your visit, aren't you? You have been quiet for a few days. I wondered if you were still unwell?'

'No, I am much better and having a wonderful time,' Susannah told her. 'The Roberts twins were there this afternoon, Amelia, and the talk was all of a race. It was between Lord Coleridge and—who do you think his challenger was?' Susannah clapped her hands as Amelia shook her head. 'I am not surprised you cannot guess, for I should never have thought it. Lord Pendleton beat him, but they say it was a close-run thing.'

'Yes, I imagine it must have been,' Amelia said and laughed softly. 'They are both Corinthians and known for their driving and other sports—did you not know that?'

'Well, I had heard something. But a curricle race

in town! I had not imagined Lord Pendleton would do something like that.'

'It does not surprise me. When he was younger, I believe he indulged in the occasional prank. Max Coleridge, Pendleton, Northaven and one other—' She stopped speaking abruptly.

'The Marquis of Northaven? Lord Pendleton does not approve of him…' Susannah looked puzzled. 'I did not think they were friends.'

'They were friends when they were first on the town, I recall; I was quite young then and did not know them well—but a friend of mine did and she told me…' Amelia hesitated, then, 'But Northaven has become more ruthless and the others have…grown up. In most respects, though it seems they are still mad enough to race through town.' She arched her brows. 'It is rather amusing, though perhaps unwise.'

'Yes, a little dangerous, perhaps,' Susannah replied. 'I would not have suspected it of Lord Pendleton—but it must have been exciting. I wish I might have seen it. I should like to take part in a race, if it were possible, which it is not, of course.'

'Yes,' Amelia agreed. 'I would like to have been there. Gentlemen have all the fun, do they not? It seems a little unfair, but there are compensations in being a lady—do you not agree?'

Susannah realised that she was being teased and smiled shyly. 'Yes, of course. I know I am foolish to long for adventures. I suspect I should not like them if they truly happened.'

'Nor should I,' Amelia agreed. 'I think to be settled and happy with someone one cares for is perhaps the best of all…'

Seeing her look so wistful, Susannah spoke without

thinking. 'I believe Sir Michael must be thoughtless to cause you so much distress, Amelia. I wish he would not visit you if he only means to quarrel with you—' Realising what she had said, Susannah clapped her hand to her mouth. 'Oh, forgive me! How very forward and rude of me! I ought not to have said it, but...'

'You were thinking it,' Amelia supplied as Susannah stared at her wide-eyed and anxious. 'Come and sit down, dearest. I am going to tell you something so that perhaps you will understand and cease to be anxious about me, for I know that you have been—have you not?'

Susannah nodded and sat down in a chair near the window. 'You do not have to tell me, Amelia. I really should not have passed an opinion...'

'Why—because you are younger and a guest?' Amelia shook her head. 'The difference is not so very great and I think of you as a friend. I shall tell you, because I think you will treat my confidence with respect.'

'I promise,' Susannah vowed fervently and Amelia smiled.

'I told you that I loved someone, but the match was denied me?' Susannah nodded. 'Well, it caused a rift between Michael and myself, a rift that has never quite healed—and there was my aunt's fortune. I stayed with her for more than two years before she died. She loved me and I loved her and she left almost everything to me. My brother resented the fact that he did not receive a share. He has tried to...persuade me to give him a substantial share, but it does not stop there. He wishes to rule my life. It was for precisely this reason that my aunt made me independent. Michael cannot touch my money, nor can I give him what he asks for, because it is tied up in property and trust funds. I should not even if I could—but I cannot give away large amounts of capital. However, my income is many times larger than I require and I am able to give smaller sums now and then. I am in no danger from my brother, for I am strong enough to resist…his arguments. It is sometimes unpleasant, but there is nothing more to cause you concern.'

'I see…' Susannah looked at her. 'Thank you for telling me, Amelia. I am honoured by your trust. I have known that your brother is unkind to you and I know how generous you are…have been to me…'

'I give what I wish to give. Both my nephews have had small incomes from me, which I can easily afford, but I shall do nothing for my brother, because he does not deserve it. Unfortunately, he believes he is entitled to control my fortune and that will cause friction at times.'

'I wish you had someone to protect you,' Susannah said. 'If you were married, you would have a husband to care for you and look after your fortune.'

'Yes, I should, but I have good friends. I have not asked them for help, because as yet I do not need it—but they are there if I should need them.'

'I am so glad,' Susannah said. 'Forgive me if I am impertinent to ask—but is there no one you like enough to marry?'

'Perhaps there may be one day,' Amelia told her and smiled. 'I hope your mind is at rest now, my love?'

'Yes, it is,' Susannah said. She stood up and went to kiss Amelia's cheek. 'It was good of you to tell me, for I know it was not easy for you.'

'No, it is never easy to speak of these things, but I wanted to set your mind at rest, Susannah—and now we shall forget it. Tell me, is there a gentleman you feel you like more than the others?'

'There might be,' Susannah confessed. 'I was not sure that I liked him, but of late I have begun to change my mind.'

'I think I might guess,' Amelia said. 'But I shall not guess for you have not yet made up your mind and I do not wish to influence you—and now we really must ring for tea. Your mother should be home at any moment—she went to fetch something I needed...' She smiled as the door opened and Mrs Hampton entered, as if to order. 'We were just about to have tea. Susannah has some interesting news...' She got up to ring the bell for tea.

'You look so lovely this evening,' Harry Pendleton said, taking Susannah's hand and lifting it to his lips to kiss it when they met at a soirée that evening.

Susannah blushed faintly but did not remove her hand from his grasp immediately. She had tried to avoid him when they met for the first time after that disastrous affair at the Duchess of Morland's ball. However, he had made a point of seeking her out and was so charming that she had overcome her feeling of awkwardness. Since then they had met everywhere. He had formed a habit of seeking her out, and Susannah could not doubt that he liked her. She had believed he must have a disgust of her for her foolish behaviour, but it was not so. No one seemed any the wiser about the incident with the marquis and she suspected that she had Lord Pendleton to thank for it. The Marquis of Northaven had not been present at any of the affairs she had attended with her mother and Amelia, and someone had told her that he was out of town. Susannah could feel nothing but relief. She would be quite happy if she never saw him again!

The knowledge that she might well have lost more

than her reputation if Lord Pendleton had not come to her rescue that night was sobering. However, Susannah was an incurable romantic and she still had her dreams of a white knight on a charger. His face was indistinct, and she had begun to accept in her heart that her romantic ideas were nonsense. The Marquis of Northaven had frightened her and opened her eyes to the nature of certain types of men. She understood better now why both Amelia and her mother had warned her against being intimate with some of the gentlemen.

'I was wondering how much longer you plan to stay in town,' Lord Pendleton was saying to her. 'And what you will do when you leave?'

'Oh…' Susannah's thoughts had wandered a little, but she gave him all her attention. 'I believe we are to stay for at least another two or three weeks. I have no idea what we shall do afterwards. I suppose we shall go home.'

Susannah frowned at the idea. If she returned home in three weeks without having secured an offer, it would be the end of her dreams. She knew her mother had hoped that she would make a fortunate match, but as yet she did not think she wished to marry any of the gentlemen she knew. At least, there was only one she might feel able to accept, but she did not imagine he would ask her, for, despite his unfailing kindness, he must think her a foolish girl. A little sigh left her lips. She had hoped for so much and it might all come to nothing.

'Does something trouble you, Miss Hampton? Or are you bored?'

'Oh…' Susannah blushed as Lord Pendleton looked at her in concern. 'No, of course I am not bored, sir. Forgive me if I gave that impression. It is just that…' She shook her head because it was impossible to explain.

She did not even know herself what was making her feel restless and hastily turned the subject. 'I heard of your race, sir. It must have been exciting.'

'Yes, perhaps,' Harry said, with what she thought a boyish grin on his lips. 'It was quite mad, but we suggested it as a joke and people started to bet on the outcome and then we had to go through with the nonsense.'

'I thought it was thrilling. I wish I had been there to see it.'

'It would not have been suitable. I believe we attracted quite a rough crowd.'

'Oh, then perhaps—' She bit back her words of protest. 'I like horses and I should enjoy watching them race—at a suitable venue, of course.'

'Perhaps one day I could take you to the races, if your mama would make up one of the party.'

'Yes, that would be interesting. I attended a balloon race with Amelia and some friends, you know. I found that great fun. We followed in the carriage and it was a great spectacle.'

'Yes, I believe it is. You enjoy music and reading, I know,' Harry said. 'Tell me, what other pursuits please you?'

'I love to walk with my dogs,' Susannah told him, realising with a shock that she missed the freedom of the countryside here in town. 'One can be so free in the country, do you not think so, sir? I am often scolded for traipsing all over the place like a hoyden but the air is so fresh…'

'You enjoy the country.' Harry smiled. 'I like it myself. The pleasures of town are well enough for a few weeks, but home is best, I believe. Do you ride or drive yourself in the country, Miss Hampton?'

'I used to ride before Papa died,' Susannah said. 'I have never driven myself, but it is something I should like to learn. Perhaps I shall one day.' She was unconscious of the wistful look in her eyes.

'I dare say your husband will teach you when you marry, Miss Hampton.'

'Perhaps...' Susannah's cheeks coloured. She dared not look at him and searched for a new topic of conversation. Her eyes lit on a gentleman who had just that minute entered the room. She did not know him and it gave her the excuse she had been looking for to avoid answering. 'I do not believe I know that gentleman....'

Harry looked across the room and smiled. 'That is the Earl of Ravenshead,' he told her. 'He is newly come into the title, for his father died a few months ago; I think he has been busy sorting out the estate. He returned from France, I think, where he had been staying for the past year or so. He came to town some days ago, but has not accepted many invitations, for at first he intended to return home almost at once.'

'I did not think I had seen him before. He looks... nice.'

Harry smiled. 'Gerard is a year or so older than myself, but a great friend. I must go and greet him, because it was I who persuaded him to come this evening. Will you forgive me if I leave you, Miss Hampton? I shall see you later this evening—perhaps at supper, if not before?'

Susannah nodded, watching as he left her to greet his friend. The warmth of their greeting left no doubt in her mind that they held each other in high esteem and, intent on observing them together, she was not immediately aware that Amelia had come up to her.

'Are you enjoying yourself, Susannah?' Amelia asked.

Susannah turned to her at once. 'Yes, of course. It is a very pleasant evening.'

'I thought you looked happy.' Amelia glançed across the room. As her gaze fell on two gentlemen talking, she seemed to stiffen for a moment and her cheeks paled. 'Oh…'

'Is something the matter?' Susannah asked. Amelia seemed distracted and did not answer. Susannah looked at her and saw that she had turned pale. 'Are you unwell? Should you like to go home?'

Amelia blinked, looked at her and smiled. 'No, nothing is the matter, my dear. I have just seen someone I once knew, but it is not important.'

Susannah followed her gaze and saw that Lord Pendleton and the Earl of Ravenshead were still talking. It must be the earl who had caused Amelia to look startled and turn pale. He was the only newcomer that evening. Her gaze narrowed in thought as she remembered Amelia's confidences.

'Do you mean the Earl of Ravenshead?'

'Oh…yes, though he was simply the earl's son when I knew him,' Amelia replied. The colour had returned to her cheeks now and she had recovered from her slight shock. 'I had heard that his father had died.'

Susannah knew immediately who the earl must be. For Amelia to have received such a shock, the gentleman must have been important to her. He was the man she had wished to marry—the love that had been denied her. From the stricken look in her eyes at the moment she saw him, it was clear that she still cared!

'He and Lord Pendleton are good friends, I think?'

'Yes, I believe they always were, despite the difference in age. I believe Ravenshead is slightly older.'

Susannah wrinkled her brow. 'Do you think age difference is important in marriage?'

Amelia gave Susannah her full attention. 'I think the gentleman should be a few years older,' she said. 'Though I do not believe in marrying very young girls off to men old enough to be their grandfathers! That is a disgusting practice in my opinion! But age is not important if there is love and mutual respect. Without it, life would be intolerable, I think.'

'I do agree with you,' Susannah said. She had the feeling that Amelia was talking for the sake of it, as though she were trying to calm herself. 'I believe they are about to begin the music once more. Shall we take our places?'

'Yes, certainly,' Amelia said. She turned away at the same instant as the Earl of Ravenshead became aware of her. Susannah was watching both him and Lord Pendleton and saw the way his expression changed. He seemed stunned and then concerned, and he spoke urgently to Lord Pendleton.

Susannah was thoughtful as she followed her friend to a small couch near where her mother was already seated. The music was just beginning as they sat down, so she could not mention the earl's reaction to Amelia, and by the time they rose to go into supper she had forgotten it.

However, she recalled it later that evening when she happened to catch sight of the earl in conversation with Amelia. His manner was everything that was correct, as was Amelia's. No one could tell from their manner whether they were old friends or new acquaintances—they were being polite, but no more.

Remembering Amelia's shock, and the gentleman's violent reaction when he saw her, Susannah was certain that she was right. The earl was the gentleman Amelia had spoken of on two occasions. She had loved him once and she was not indifferent to him now, though she was trying to give that impression.

What a wonderful thing it would be if they could find each other again now that Amelia was independent of her overbearing brother! Was the earl married? She must ask Lord Pendleton, for he was sure to know. However, this evening was not the place or the time, because she must be discreet. Careless talk might lead to hurt for Amelia and she would not wish that for the world....

Chapter Four

Susannah did not need to wait long to put her questions to Lord Pendleton—they met when she was walking with some friends in the park the next morning. He tipped his hat, asked if he might join them, and after a few minutes she found that they were side by side and somehow a little behind the others.

'Would you mind if I asked you something?' she said impulsively. There was a sparkle in her eyes that had sometimes been missing for a few days, and her smile was compelling.

'You may ask me anything you wish,' Harry said, responding with a twinkle in his own eyes. 'I assure you that any confidence you place in me will be strictly kept.'

'Well...it is not actually my confidence,' Susannah said. 'Do you know—have you any idea if there has ever been anything between your friend the Earl of Ravenshead and Miss Royston?'

'What makes you ask?' Harry said, hesitating. 'Have you noticed something?'

'Yes, I did actually. Miss Royston was startled to see him last evening, and for a few moments it quite overset her. And I think he was equally perturbed when he saw her, for I was watching him at that moment.'

'Ah...' Harry considered; he would not wish to betray his friend's confidence, but there could be little harm in admitting what she had already observed. 'I believe they may once have known each other quite well. Something occurred and nothing came of the friendship. However, I can tell you no more, for I am not certain of the details.'

'Or you are not at liberty to tell me,' Susannah replied astutely. 'I should not want you to betray a friend's confidence, sir, but you have told me enough. Amelia had already mentioned that she once knew him and I too know things that I am not at liberty to tell anyone...' She paused, a look of conspiracy on her face. 'You must know that I should not have been given a Season in town if it were not for Amelia's generosity, sir. I am very grateful for it and should like to do something for her...' She hesitated, then, 'He isn't married—is he?'

Harry frowned. 'Not to my knowledge. No, I think not...why do you ask?'

Harry was wary as he looked at her. Susannah had completely recovered from her loss of spirits after the incident with Northaven, and her eyes were bright with mischief.

'I just wished to be sure,' she replied airily.

'What are you suggesting, Miss Hampton?'

'Do you have to call me Miss Hampton all the time? Could you not call me Susannah in private? I believe we know each other well enough now, sir.'

'Only if you will reciprocate by calling me Harry.'

'Oh...I am not certain I should do that, but I could

call you Pendleton,' Susannah said, looking so adorable that he gave her a broad grin. 'Anyway, I was talking about Amelia and the earl—do you think we could sort of encourage them to get together in some way? I should so like to see Amelia happy. Nothing obvious, just making sure they are at the same affairs and that kind of thing.'

'I do not think we should meddle in things that do not concern us,' Harry said, a little doubtful. He imagined his friend had been too busy getting his estate into order to think of mixing in society much, but something had made him decide to stay on in town. 'Surely—' Harry stopped as she frowned at him. He was doing it again! He must try for lightness. She wanted a white knight on a charger and he had to become what she needed or risk losing her. 'It is true that I have always believed he cared for her, but something went wrong for them.'

'Oh, I knew I was right about him!' Susannah cried. 'It was a tragic love story. Someone prevented their happiness...but now they have a second chance. How romantic it would be if they could be together again!'

'It might be the very thing,' Harry agreed, not wanting to hurt her feelings. 'But I really think we should not interfere, Susannah. If they still like each other enough, it will happen without any interference from us.'

'All I meant was to mention her name now and then—and I will mention how handsome he is to her.'

'Gerard is very handsome, I suppose,' Harry said doubtfully. 'And Miss Royston is an attractive lady. I have wondered why she has not married before this. However, I must strongly urge caution. It would not be right to push them together. It can do no good and might do great harm.'

'Do you think it wrong?' Susannah's face fell. 'You

must think me such a foolish creature. It was merely that I so wished to do something for her. She often looks… sad…' she finished on a sigh.

'Yes, I have remarked it myself,' Harry told her. 'I will make certain that Gerard attends various functions and parties, for it is time he mixed more in company, but I will do no more, and I think you should exercise caution—you would not like to make your friend angry, I think? She would perhaps feel annoyed if she thought you were meddling in her affairs.'

'No, I should not do so,' Susannah agreed. 'Very well, I shall not go out of my way to praise him, though if the occasion arises…' She gave him a look that was a mixture of defiance and appeal. 'Surely you cannot censure that?'

'I am relieved. I had thought you would beg me to arrange an elopement!'

Susannah saw that he was teasing and shook her head. 'I should not dream of suggesting it for Amelia! I know she would dislike it of all things. It might be romantic with the right man, of course—but I do not think Amelia would care for such a thing at all.'

'I am very sure Gerard would never agree. He is very much the gentleman, you know. It would not suit his notions of propriety.'

'Is an elopement so very bad?' Susannah asked, meaning to tease him now. 'It would be an adventure—if one cared for such things….'

'Perhaps, though it might be uncomfortable, unless the lady was very sure of the gentleman's affections, of course.'

'Yes, I suppose so,' Susannah agreed. 'She would have to love him to distraction, and then she would care nothing for discomfort.'

Her inhibitions concerning Lord Pendleton had quite disappeared. She had accepted Harry as her confidant and chattered away happily, as she discussed how they could bring the star-crossed lovers together, without interfering in their lives.

Listening to Susannah's laughter and watching the changing expressions on her lovely face, Harry understood that he was fairly caught. He was not sure how it had happened, for he had had his reservations at the start. However, they had somehow melted away the night he found Northaven trying to seduce her.

Susannah held his future happiness in the palm of her soft hand. Being drawn into this enchanting intimacy was such a pleasant experience for a man who had, he admitted to himself, been very much inclined to hold his feelings in check. Harry was certain his feelings were more than the natural lust any man might feel for a beautiful girl. Yes, he wanted to kiss her until she melted against him, wanted to feel the softness of her yielding body beneath him as he taught her the pleasures of desire, but even more pressing than those very strong instincts was the need to protect her.

He smiled inwardly as she offered him a smile that was both innocent and provocative at the same time. She was enchanting! Indeed, he felt himself under her spell. He was not at all certain that she felt more than liking for him, though that in itself was an advance. He was certain that two weeks previously she would not have shared her thoughts concerning Miss Royston with him.

She had spoken of an elopement and for a moment he toyed with the idea of gratifying her wish, but he was fairly certain that she would in her heart enjoy a society wedding far more. It was merely a matter of convincing her that he was the man she ought to marry.

'We must plan your dance,' Amelia said when they had tea together that afternoon. 'I had thought we would hold it a few days before we go home and we should begin to think of what to do once we leave London...' Her gaze met Susannah's. 'Your mama and I have settled it that we shall go from here to Bath, my love. I wish to purchase a house there and I have asked my agent to find me a suitable property that I may rent and then purchase if I like it. I hope to spend quite a bit of time residing in the town in future. You are both welcome to live with me until you have other plans.'

Susannah understood that Amelia was speaking of her marriage. She could offer very little on the subject; although she liked Harry Pendleton very well and thought perhaps she might feel more, she was not certain—nor had he spoken to her.

'I told Amelia that we shall certainly stay with her until she finds herself a companion,' Mrs Hampton said. 'However, we have another two weeks at least in town. Who knows what may happen?'

'Plenty of time,' Amelia said and smiled at Susannah. 'We must draw up a guest list. We shall invite everyone who has invited us to their affairs, which is all of our close friends—but is there anyone special you would like, Susannah?'

Susannah was silent for a moment. 'I should like the Earl of Ravenshead if that is acceptable to you, Amelia? He is a close friend of Lord Pendleton and I think him a pleasant gentleman.'

'Yes, they are close friends,' Amelia said, looking

pensive. 'I suppose it would seem odd if he were not invited. I shall add his name to the list. Anyone else?'

'Mr Sinclair—but I dare say he is on the list, for he is at most of the functions we attend and he is Lord Pendleton's nephew.'

'Yes. Toby Sinclair is a pleasant young man,' Amelia agreed. 'I like him very much myself.' She smiled as she said it and Susannah wondered. Could she have made a mistake in thinking that Amelia was interested in the earl? Toby was younger than Amelia, but that would not matter if they were in love.

She must not speculate! It was not her affair. Harry Pendleton had been right to reprimand her in the park. Amelia's affairs were her own. However, she was pleased that the Earl of Ravenshead was to be invited to the dance.

The next week was the height of the Season so far, and Susannah was too busy to indulge herself with flights of fancy or even to think about her own feelings very much. They never seemed to have a free evening. Often, they attended more than one event in an evening, going first to a musical soirée and then on to a card party or something of that nature. There was a ball held on four separate occasions that week, which meant that Susannah was forced to buy another pair of dancing slippers, for hers were quite worn out.

However, she could not refrain from mentioning that she had arranged for the earl to be asked to her dance when she met Harry at a particular function.

'I think she was a little affected by my request, but you do not censure me for making it, I hope?'

'How could I? There is no harm in such an invitation. I hope you have not been doing anything worse?'

She blushed. 'You are right to scold me. I should not meddle—but I still think she likes him. I should like to see her married and safe, because I care for her. She is not so very old, you know, though I dare say some may think she is past the age of marrying.'

'I do not think it at all,' Harry replied. 'I am older than Miss Royston by some seven years, I believe.'

'Well, it is different for a man, is it not?' Susannah asked innocently. 'Do you not think it would be a fine thing—if they were to decide to marry?'

Harry hesitated. He knew that Gerard had suffered a disappointment of some kind. He was fairly certain that the young lady in question had been Amelia Royston, but he did not know what had happened. Gerard had been a changed man when they next met, slightly bitter at first, though he had changed again later. Having his life saved had seemed to instigate a new reason to live in Gerard, and then something else had happened. Harry wasn't sure what it was, because he had never asked. Gerard was a man who kept his secrets. If he wished someone to know, he would tell them. They were good friends, but they did not intrude on each other's lives.

'If they decided it for themselves—I would think it a very fine idea,' he conceded. 'However, I do not think it right that we should make a push to help bring such a marriage about, though I confess I should like to see him settled in England.'

Susannah bestowed a look of glowing approval on him. 'You are such a good friend,' she told him with a confiding air. 'I think you must be my very best friend.'

Harry hesitated. He was tempted to tell her that he would like to be much more than a friend, but she was clearly enjoying his friendship and he did not wish to startle her by declaring himself too soon. She was many years his junior and he wasn't sure that it would be fair to ask her to be his wife. She would find her life much changed—as the chatelaine of his various estates, she would have many duties.

'I should always wish to please you,' he said. 'I think you must know that, Susannah?'

'Yes, I do…' she replied and glanced away, suddenly shy.

He was on the point of pressing further when they were interrupted by the arrival of some friends, who took Susannah's attention. Harry was asked to make up a four at whist and departed. His eyes strayed across the room to where Susannah was playing a game of jackstraws with some of the younger members of the company. Her laughter was music to his ears and he felt his heart jolt when their eyes happened to meet for a moment and she lowered her eyelid, giving him a saucy wink.

Harry knew that by naming him as her very best friend she had paid him the highest honour she could accord, but it was still not quite what he wanted from her. She had learned to trust and like him, but that was not the wild passion he wanted her to feel—the passion he thought necessary in a marriage. He was certain there was passion in Susannah. He just needed to awaken it.

He had been thinking for some days of things that might make him seem a hero or a little bit exciting in her eyes. His mind kept coming back to an idea that had been growing for a while now. It was completely mad, a wild flight of fancy that he would not normally consider—but it might just work. If it did he would gain so much, but he could also lose everything on the toss of the dice.

Harry had nerves of steel at the gambling table or

in the face of the enemy, but when it came to losing Susannah, he knew himself a total coward. To have her turn away from him now might be a blow from which he could never recover. No other woman had come close to having this effect on him, and he had begun to understand what might have made Gerard lose the will to live during those hellish months in Spain.

Harry's plan was risky. He was weighing the consequences, gradually gaining more confidence in the outcome. If he managed to pull it off, he would win the best prize of his life!

It was not to be thought of until Susannah's own dance was over, of course. He knew that she was looking forward to her special evening and he would do nothing that might interfere with her pleasure. However, he might just put his risky plan into place a day or so after. Her visit to town would be nearing its end, and if it did not work…but Harry dared not allow himself to think of failure, for that would be terrible.

He would wait until after the dance, but if Susannah still seemed to think of him as simply a friend, he would do it!

Susannah retired happily to bed that night. She had noticed Amelia looking pensive a few times during the evening, which surely meant that she had been missing the earl. He had not been invited to the dinner or the card evening they attended, for it was a small affair consisting of about twenty-five guests.

'I happen to know Gerard has other things on his mind at the moment,' Harry had told her. 'Some problem with his estate, I understand. I believe he has actually left town for a few days.'

'He will be here for my dance?'

'Oh, yes, I am certain of it, for we have a meeting of the Four-in-Hand club,' he told her with a smile. 'I have proposed my sister's boy as a new member and we shall be taking a vote.'

'Oh, yes, Mr Sinclair is very keen to join, I believe,' Susannah said and laughed. 'He wants to be just like you, Pendleton! He is for ever telling me how much he admires you. I had no idea of what an excellent sportsman you are until he told me that you are held to be top of the trees by the Corinthians. He never ceases to sing your praises.'

'Indeed?' Harry looked thoughtful. 'How very kind of him. I wonder what he is after now.'

'That is unkind!' Susannah cried, scolding him, but with a gleam of mischief in her eyes. 'I am quite sure his affection for you is genuine.'

'Yes, I know it is,' Harry replied and smiled oddly. 'Toby likes to kick up a few larks, but he is actually a very sensible young man. I am thinking of taking him into a new venture I am setting up—but you will please not mention that to him. I want to give him a chance to…enjoy himself before he knuckles down.'

'Oh…' Susannah stared at him. Lord Pendleton never ceased to surprise her. Every time they spoke she discovered something new about him, and she was beginning to like him more and more. She knew that he attended every function where he might expect to see her, and he had offered to take her driving in the park whenever she wished. As yet she had not accepted that particular invitation, because she had a feeling that once she did their relationship might become more serious. She was not yet sure that she wished Harry to make her an offer. He was the most generous, easiest gentleman of her acquaintance, but she still could not help feeling that she would like something exciting to happen.

Climbing into bed, Susannah dismissed her small doubts. She had another eight days or so before they were due to leave for Bath and in three days it would be her dance. She did not know why, but she felt something exciting might happen then....

Susannah emerged from the lending library the next morning. She had been to return some books for her mother and collected two others that she hoped she might have a chance to read before they left town, though she was not at all certain she would even attempt them. Her maid was carrying a small parcel they had collected for Amelia and Susannah carried the books. She had turned aside to glance in the window of a milliner's shop when she became aware that more than one person had stopped behind her to look at the bonnets displayed there.

'When is your engagement to be announced?' a feminine voice asked behind her. Susannah stiffened as she recognised the voice and the one that answered.

'Oh, I think it must be quite soon,' Mary Hamilton said and giggled. 'He has been most particular in his attentions recently. Mama is certain he will come up to scratch before the week is out.'

Susannah stiffened her resolve and then turned to look at the two young ladies, who were giggling and clutching at each other. 'Good morning, Jane—Mary...'

'Oh, I thought it was you,' Mary said. 'Are you thinking of buying a new bonnet? I shall be making several purchases soon...' She looked coy. 'I cannot name the gentleman yet, though you may guess—but it is not official, you know.'

'I see. I must wish you happy,' Susannah said. 'Excuse me, I must go home. I am expected...'

She walked away, head high, trying not to show that she was feeling agitated. She could only imagine that Mary Hamilton was speaking of Lord Pendleton, for it was he she had been thinking of when Susannah had overheard her at a dance a couple of weeks earlier.

Susannah's heart was heavy as she walked home, accompanied by her maid. It was foolish of her to feel like this, because, kind as he was, Harry Pendleton had said nothing to her. He had never suggested in any way that he found her more enchanting than any other lady of his acquaintance. It was quite ridiculous of her to feel disappointed or let down. Indeed, she was not. Truly she was not...but it did hurt just a little that the gentleman she thought of as her particular friend should have been intending to make Mary Hamilton an offer all the time.

Susannah decided that she must put a brave face on it. She knew that she would meet both Lord Pendleton and Mary at the dance that evening. She would not let them or anyone else see that she was suffering from a heavy disappointment.

She happened to be wearing white again that evening. It was not a new gown, but one she had worn several times before. Glancing at herself in the mirror as she left Amelia's house, she knew that she looked very well. However, when Mary arrived, she looked stunning in a gown that took Susannah's breath. It was obviously very expensive, the silk sewn with diamonds across the bodice and trimmed with Brussels lace at the hem, and the necklace of rubies and diamonds she was wearing was worth a small fortune; she also wore a stunning ring on the finger of her left hand. It was hardly any wonder that she had a look of triumph in her eyes! Susannah's heart sank as she heard the news circulating. Mary Hamilton had been right to anticipate a proposal and, when it was made, she had accepted.

Susannah had not seen the party come in, but she caught sight of Harry moments before she saw the triumph on Mary Hamilton's face. It was little wonder that she should look so proud—she had claimed for herself one of the best matches of the season!

Susannah would not let herself listen to the gossip. Instead, she threw herself into the evening, flirting with her partners and laughing at their jests. Her heart was aching, for only now had she realised how much Harry meant to her—but it was too late. He had made his choice and it was not her.

It was not until more than an hour had passed that Harry came to her. She thought how handsome he looked, dressed immaculately in the style made fashionable by Mr Brummell, once the Regent's favourite, his coat and breeches black, his shirt pristine white and his cravat a masterpiece set off by a diamond stick pin that sparkled in the light of the candles. His simple elegance made him stand out from many of the other gentlemen, who appeared overdressed by comparison. He smiled ruefully. 'I am late,' he apologised. 'I suppose it is too much to hope that you saved a dance for your best friend.'

'I fear that it is,' Susannah said in a reserved manner. 'I did not think you would wish it now—and so I gave them all away.'

'What do you mean?' Harry was puzzled, but before she had time to answer, her next partner was there asking her to dance. He watched as she was whisked away and stood frowning as she laughed up at the young man. Devonshire was the heir to a duke, but it was unlikely he would look at Susannah, for he needed an heiress to support his expensive tastes.

Harry took up a position next to the French windows, watching Susannah as she went from partner to partner. He could not understand what had happened to her. She was always a lively girl, but this evening she seemed almost reckless. Yet he would swear that her laughter was not her usual carefree mirth. She was upset about something and she blamed him—but for the life of him he could not think what he had done to distress her.

Could it be that he had been deceived in her? He had thought he was gaining ground, but now it seemed they had gone back to the start. Harry shrugged. He did not care to stay and watch. He would go to his club or perhaps visit the lady who had been his mistress until a few weeks previously. He had finished his affair with Elaine, for it no longer pleased either of them, but he could talk to her—and he was in need of some female advice at this moment. Advice that he would never dream of asking from his mother or his sister.

Susannah did not see him leave, but she became aware that he was missing just before supper. Glancing round the supper room, she thought he might be found there, but he had disappeared. However, she saw Mary Hamilton, Lady Hamilton and a gentleman of about fifty years she recognised as the Marquis of Stavely. He was wearing a puce coat, tight breeches that showed off his rather large stomach and a black wig that was really rather odd. As if aware of her interest, he lifted a gold lorgnette to his eye and looked her way. Susannah blushed and hastily averted her gaze.

She had turned her attention to the food and was deciding what to eat when Mrs Hampton came up to her. 'It is good news concerning Miss Hamilton, is it not, Susannah? Have you taken the opportunity to wish her happy?'

'No, Mama—I met her this morning. She told me she expected a proposal, but I did not expect it this evening...' Her voice quavered a little and her mother gave her an odd look. Her look of distress was plain and Mrs Hampton frowned. 'He said nothing of her to me even this evening...'

'Are you thinking...?' Mrs Hampton smiled all at once. 'Susannah, my dear—Miss Hamilton is engaged to the Marquis of Stavely.'

'The marquis...' Susannah stared in dismay. 'But I thought...I knew she had thoughts of...another gentleman.' How could Miss Hamilton have accepted an offer from a man nearly old enough to be her grandfather?

'I imagine that is the reason for your behaviour this evening.' Mrs Hampton looked a little disapproving. 'I knew there was something. I told you once I did not think Pendleton was interested in Miss Hamilton. I believe you should go and congratulate her, Susannah. It may look as if you are jealous of her good fortune if you do not.'

'Yes, Mama, of course,' Susannah said. She went at once and said everything that was proper, ignoring the smirk on Mary's face. It was clear that the young lady was very pleased with her bargain—indeed, the marquis was wealthy and titled—but Susannah did not envy her one little bit. She would rather remain a spinster than marry the man Mary Hamilton had accepted.

After congratulating her, Susannah went back to the ballroom. She looked for Lord Pendleton, but could not see him. She ventured to the open door of the card room and glanced in, but he was not there. Obviously he had left at some time earlier and she had not seen him go. What must he think of her?

'If you are looking for Pendleton, he is visiting his mistress,' a harsh voice said behind her. She swung round to find herself looking at the Marquis of Northaven. 'I heard him give the address to a cab driver as I got down from one myself.' Northaven sneered. 'I know the lady well. She is not particular in the company she keeps.'

Susannah bit her lip. She would not trust herself to answer such a remark, for it was said spitefully and not worthy of notice. 'Excuse me, I must find my mama.'

She walked away from him, her heart racing. It was not her affair if Lord Pendleton had gone to visit his mistress. She regretted refusing him a dance when she might have given him a choice of two had she wished, but it would not have made any difference if he wished to spend the evening in the arms of his mistress. Susannah felt close to tears, because she had been foolish. She should have made sure of her facts before sending Harry Pendleton away. He must have thought her most rude, as she had been, a fact she now bitterly regretted.

Susannah did not see Harry the following day. He called while she was out walking with some friends and left her a posy of flowers. He renewed his promise to see her at her dance, but nothing more. She knew that she could not expect more. Indeed, she had not expected as much after her behaviour the previous evening. He must think her a flighty creature who changed her mind at the slightest whim.

She had, after some thought, decided to forget what the marquis had told her. She had no way of knowing that it was true—and even if it had been, Harry was a single man and entitled to visit any lady he chose.

Susannah knew that she cared for him more than was proper. He had not declared himself and she had no reason to expect it. However, if he should propose, she would make it clear that she would not wish him to visit other ladies if they married.

But she was foolish to consider it. Harry might not even be thinking of taking a wife. It was quite improper of her even to think such things! Yet she had begun to think of him as hers, and she could not help feeling jealous of the woman who had taken him from the ball.

It was a glorious day for her special dance. Susannah was allowed to sleep a little later than normal before Iris brought in her breakfast tray and a pile of notes and small gifts.

'What are all these?' Susannah asked, staring at them in surprise. 'It isn't my birthday for ages yet. I knew I might receive some flowers, but I didn't expect anything more.'

'Why don't you open them?' Iris asked. 'See what you've got.'

Susannah picked up the first parcel and looked at the card. 'This is from Mama—what can it be?' She tore off the pretty wrapping and found a small velvet-covered box. Opening it, she discovered a pretty pearl-and-diamond clip for her hair. 'Oh, that is lovely. It must have cost Mama some guineas to buy it for me.'

'Well, it is a special day, miss,' Iris said, smiling at her. 'Go on, open the other two.'

Susannah knew her maid was excited and curious,

so to oblige her she picked up the second parcel, which was from Amelia. Inside that she found a pair of pearl-and-diamond drop earrings, which she held up for Iris to admire. Picking up the third box, she looked for a card, but found none.

'How odd,' she remarked. 'There is no card with this one. I cannot think who sent it.'

'Perhaps it fell off,' Iris suggested. 'I'll look for it when I go down, miss. Open it and see what's inside.'

Susannah removed the wrappings and discovered a beautiful posy holder. It was fashioned of basketwork gold filigree, very delicate and pretty, and it had a large diamond set into the rim.

'Oh, how charming,' she said. 'Do you see how it works, Iris? You can insert a small posy into this and wear it pinned to your gown if you wish.'

'It is lovely,' Iris said. 'It isn't just a trinket, miss; that's a real diamond and a nice one. I expect your mama bought it for your dance.'

'Yes, perhaps,' Susannah agreed.

However, when she went to her mother's room later to thank her for the clip and show her the other gifts, Mrs Hampton immediately asked who had sent the posy holder.

'I thought it might have been you,' Susannah said and looked thoughtful as she tried to imagine who else might have sent it. 'There was no card. Iris thought it might have fallen off and she means to look for it. Amelia gave me the earrings. I do not think she would also have given me the posy holder, do you?'

'I am very sure she did not, for we discussed what we should give you,' Mrs Hampton replied with a little frown. 'The trinket may have come from a secret admirer, Susannah. If there is no card, he may not have wished you to know he had sent it.'

'Oh...' Susannah felt a thrill of excitement as she looked at the posy holder. A secret admirer! 'Do you think so, Mama? What should I do? I had thought I might use it to pin flowers at the waist of my gown, but now I am not certain....'

'Well, I should do so if I were you,' Mrs Hampton said. 'It is a little difficult to be sure, for you would wish to thank whoever sent it—but if there is no card you cannot.'

'Perhaps whoever sent it will mention it,' Susannah replied. 'Besides, I cannot return it if I do not know who sent it, can I?'

'I imagine you may receive other gifts as the day goes on,' Mrs Hampton said. 'You will almost certainly have lots of flowers, though that holder is rather valuable and I would usually tell you to think carefully about accepting such a valuable thing.'

Susannah nodded—she knew that it was not usual for gentlemen to send such an item unless there was an understanding. She could not think of anyone who would send her such a thing secretly. Had a card accompanied it from—say, Lord Pendleton, she would have taken it as an indication of his intentions to speak. It really was such a pity that there was no card, though if Iris were right... A little shiver went down her spine. She had put the incident in the garden with the Marquis of Northaven from her mind, and he had not been invited to her dance. He would surely not have sent it? No, of course not!

She smiled as she pondered on the identity of her secret admirer, but after a moment or two an odd thought occurred to her. There really was no one other than

Harry Pendleton that she wished to send her something like this beautiful trinket.

Now that was very strange, wasn't it? Susannah wondered why he had become so firmly fixed in her thoughts as the only gentleman she really wanted to admire her. She wasn't at all sure of his feelings. At times, she felt sure he would make her an offer before her Season was over, but at other times she thought that they were just very good friends. The uncertainty made her a little cautious, and yet she believed that if she were to encourage Lord Pendleton he might speak. She was beginning to think it might be pleasant to be married to a man she could really trust and like.

If Susannah were in doubt of the identity of the giver of the posy holder, Mrs Hampton was not. She felt quite sure that only one gentleman would have sent the holder and therefore she had no qualms about allowing Susannah to keep it. If it was discovered that it had come from a different source, it could be returned at a later date with a polite note explaining that the card had been missing.

Flowers and tributes poured in during the day. Susannah received several small gifts of sweetmeats in beautiful boxes, flowers and cards wishing her a lovely evening, but nothing that compared to her posy holder. These gifts were the acceptable trifles commonly sent on such an occasion, and she noted with pleasure that Lord Pendleton had sent both chocolates and a wonderful little posy of roses, which would fit very well into her holder.

She deliberated over what she ought to do as she dressed, but eventually decided that she would use the delicate trinket to hold the flowers Harry Pendleton had sent her. Wearing a gentleman's flowers was often an indication of the lady's preferences, and Susannah would not wish to give any of her other admirers the wrong impression. She knew that one or two of them might have spoken had she given them reason to think she would be pleased with an offer, but none of them had touched her heart. Only Lord Pendleton had become a true friend, one she would wish to know better than as a casual acquaintance. Therefore she would wear his flowers—and if the giver of the holder hinted at his gift she would thank him and explain that the card had gone missing.

It was very odd, for Iris had searched everywhere for the card and questioned the other servants, but no one had seen it. The only explanation was that it had become detached on the way to their house, and that was a nuisance. Unless of course it *was* from a secret admirer?

While it was exciting to think that she might have a secret admirer, Susannah had begun to understand that such a thing would only be pleasant if that admirer turned out to be someone she truly liked. The idea that a gentleman of the same nature to Northaven might admire her from afar was chilling and she almost changed her mind about wearing it. However, she decided that it must have come from a friend, because it was so perfect for her.

It might just have come from Lord Pendleton.

Harry looked for Susannah as he entered the ballroom that evening. She was wearing white, as she had been the first time he had seen her. Her gown was cut so that it wrapped about her body in swathes of silk and lace—

and at her waist was pinned the posy of pink roses he had sent.

He had not been sure that she would wear white, but hoped it might be so. His first choice was for red roses, but he had thought it might be too blatant a statement of his feelings. The last thing he wanted was to make Susannah anxious. Now he saw the pink was a good choice. She was also wearing the posy holder he had sent. He smiled as he thought of the message he had written on the card.

Wear this for me if you have forgiven me for whatever I did. I hope to be your best friend again. Harry.

She was wearing it, but he could not tell from her smile whether she had forgiven him. He was not sure what he had done to displease her, but it had made him change his plans. He had thought of declaring himself and suggesting an elopement, but he no longer considered it a good idea. He had thought Susannah might see it as an adventure, but he wasn't sure that she liked him enough to consider marriage to him exciting. He would continue to offer friendship for the moment and see what happened. In the meantime, he would begin by asking her to dance—he would ask for three dances, but she might only give him one.

Susannah danced three times with Harry Pendleton that evening. She had hoped he might take her into supper so that they could talk for a while, because she would have liked to ask him to forgive her for her behaviour the last time they met, but she found herself as part of a group of young ladies and gentlemen bent on having fun. It would have seemed rude had she refused their request to join them, for it was her dance and she was part hostess of the affair.

However, the disappointment was small, for Harry asked her if he might take her driving in the park. He suggested that she might be too tired the following morning, and arranged to fetch her the day after at nine-thirty. Susannah had decided that she would accept the next time he asked, and felt a warm glow inside when she saw his smile as she assured him she would be delighted.

He really was the most generous, considerate gentleman of her acquaintance. Indeed, when he spent some time talking to another young lady, who was reputed to be an heiress, Susannah knew a moment of jealousy. It was ridiculous, of course, but she could not help herself. However, he came to her before taking his leave, and his smile reassured her once more.

'You will not forget our appointment?' he asked, his eyes intent on her face.

Susannah felt a delicious little shiver down her spine. When he looked at her that way she was almost sure she was in love with him—and that he cared for her.

'I shall not forget,' she told him, her eyes brighter than she knew. 'I shall look forward to it.'

Susannah went to bed feeling tired, but very happy. She smiled to herself as she remembered that she had begun by disliking Lord Pendleton, but now she liked him very well indeed.

As she was brushing her hair free of tangles she thought about something else she had seen that made her smile. Amelia had danced not once, but twice with the Earl of Ravenshead! She had seemed to enjoy herself very well and she had looked happier than Susannah recalled seeing her before. There was a smile of content on Susannah's face as she got into bed and blew out her candle.

* * *

Susannah slept soundly. It had been a long day and she had danced all night. She did not wake until after twelve in the morning, and felt grateful that her mother had decided on a quiet day at home following the dance.

Several notes were delivered to her during the day, and a spray of red roses arrived. They were from Harry, reminding her of their appointment to go driving. Susannah took them up to her room, placing them in a tiny vase. Lord Pendleton had made such a point of the drive in the park that she felt he must be ready to speak. She thought that she might say yes, though at the back of her mind she was still searching for that elusive excitement. Shaking her head, Susannah laughed at herself. If she wished to be comfortable and happy in the future, she could do no better than to marry Lord Pendleton. It was time to put aside her foolish dreams of being carried off by a white knight. Having thought about it more sensibly of late, she had decided that such an occurrence would perhaps be more frightening than exciting.

She was feeling relaxed and happy as she went downstairs. She was about to enter the parlour when she heard voices coming from inside. They were raised and she could not help hearing what Sir Michael was saying. She turned away at once, for she had made up her mind she would not listen to private conversations, but the voices were so loud that she could still hear them quite clearly as she started up the stairs.

'I hope you are not thinking of becoming involved with that scoundrel again? I shall tell you now, Amelia. I will not stand for it! I sent the impudent rascal on his way once and I would not hesitate to do it again if need be.'

'You may not tell me what I shall or shall not choose

to do with my life, Michael. I am not prepared to be dictated to in this or any other manner.' Amelia was angry and her voice carried through the open door.

'You will listen to nothing I say. You were always too stubborn for your own good. Do not look to me for help when all your money has gone, Amelia. I dare say Ravenshead is sniffing around again because he has learned that you have come into a fortune.'

Susannah was halfway up the stairs by the time Sir Michael stormed out of the room. She had tried not to listen, but even as she retreated she could not avoid it for he had been shouting. What a brute he was to his sister! He did not glance Susannah's way, but stormed straight out, slamming the heavy door behind him.

Immediately, Susannah ran back down the stairs and entered the parlour. Amelia was sitting in an elbow chair, her face hidden in her hands. Her shoulders were shaking and Susannah knew that she was crying.

'Do not,' she cried. 'Oh, do not, dearest. He is an awful brute and you must not let him hurt you.'

Amelia looked up and the look of grief in her eyes tore at Susannah's eyes. 'I do not cry because of what Michael said—but because it may be partly true. All those years ago, Gerard went away without trying to see me, Susannah. Had he asked me then, I would have run away with him even though my brother forbade me—but he went without seeing me. I know that Gerard has had difficulty with his estate. It may be that he is interested now because I have a fortune. I am not sure that he cares for me at all...'

'Oh, but he does,' Susannah declared impetuously. 'I have seen the longing in his face when he looks at you—' She broke off in case she had said too much. 'Forgive me for my presumption, dearest Amelia, but I have seen the way he looks at you sometimes. I am sure that he loves you.'

'He has given me no sign,' Amelia said. She took the kerchief Susannah offered and wiped her face. 'This is foolish! It was all such a long time ago. I should not care for such foolishness now.'

'It is not foolish to wish to be loved,' Susannah said. 'Especially if the other person loves you.'

'No—not if the other person loves you,' Amelia said, returning her kerchief. 'How ridiculous of me to weep like this. I seldom do so, I assure you. It was just that we danced and I thought… But no matter. He has not spoken and I dare say he will not.'

'You cannot know that,' Susannah said and pressed her hand. 'You must not give up hope—and you must not listen to Sir Michael.'

'Well, I shall not listen to my brother, because I know that he intended to hurt and humiliate me, as he has so often,' Amelia said and kissed Susannah's cheek. 'How fortunate for me that I have such friends. I shall miss you when you marry, dearest Susannah. I have felt able to tell you things I could say to no one else, dearest.'

'I am not sure when that will be,' Susannah told her ruefully. 'Harry has not spoken, either. I do not know if he ever will. What a pair we are!'

'Yes, indeed! Gentlemen are so trying! We shall forget them and visit the milliner. A new bonnet will banish the blues as nothing else.' Amelia stood up. 'I shall tidy myself and then we shall go out.'

Chapter Five

Harry had been fencing with his regular sparring partner when he saw Northaven walk into the club. He frowned—he had not been aware that the man was a member here.

'That is enough for today, Monsieur Ferdinand,' he said and accepted a towel from one of the attendants. 'I am not sure when I shall find time to train with you again, but I have enjoyed today's session.'

'We look forward to your visits. It is seldom that I have the pleasure of sparring with so complete a swordsman. Even the Earl of Ravenshead is not as accomplished, my lord.'

'Thank you. I take that as a true compliment.' Harry inclined his head and turned away. He might have stayed for another hour, but he did not care to have Northaven watch him. 'Until we meet again.'

He frowned as he walked away. He might have to change his fencing master if Northaven and his clique were permitted here. It would be a pity, for Ferdinand was a specialist, but he did not want to find himself facing the marquis in a practice bout. He might be tempted to run him through!

'Leaving so soon?' Northaven asked, a sneer on his mouth. 'I came especially to watch you, Pendleton. They tell me you are almost as fine a swordsman as you are a shot.'

'I believe I am an adequate match for most,' Harry said. 'However, fencing for sport is one thing, fighting for your life on the battlefield is quite another.'

Their eyes met and held for a moment and Northaven looked away first. 'If you imagine I had anything to do with what happened to you and Coleridge in Spain, you are mistaken. Why should I betray my own countrymen?'

'I have no idea,' Harry said. 'Believe me, had I been able to find proof I should have had you court-martialled.'

'I am no traitor,' Northaven snarled. His eyes glittered with fury. 'I may not be as much of a gentleman as you, Pendleton—but I wouldn't have told the French of your intentions. In that you have maligned me and I resent it.'

'I heard that you were drunk, shooting off your mouth about it being a risky mission,' Harry told him, his expression hard, unforgiving. 'Surely you must have been aware that we were surrounded by spies? Even if you did not betray us intentionally, it was because of your loose talk that so many died that day....'

'Anyone can have too much to drink,' Northaven told him. 'If I did what you say, then challenge me to a duel. Let's fight it out and get this quarrel over. It has festered between us long enough.'

'Is that why you decided to take fencing lessons?'

Harry asked. 'I shouldn't bother if I were you. I have no desire to fight you, and if I did I should choose pistols.'

'You think I'm too much of a coward to face you with pistols, don't you?'

'I really could not care less,' Harry said. 'You are wasting your time trying to provoke me. I shall not challenge you to a duel—and you would do well to forget the idea. If I wanted to kill you, I had my chance when you insulted Miss Hampton. I did not think you worth the effort then and I do not now.'

'Damn you! You insult me. If I wanted you dead, a bullet in the back would do it,' Northaven retorted. 'Since you think me a coward and a scoundrel, why shouldn't I just hire someone to kill you?'

'Because you might die at the end of a rope,' Harry said. 'The best thing for all of us would be if you took yourself off abroad, Northaven. Go to Paris or Rome and fight your brawls there. Your welcome grows thin in London, believe me.' He walked away, leaving Northaven to stare after him, resentment and anger in his eyes.

One of these days Harry Pendleton was going to get what he deserved. Northaven had no idea whether or not his careless words when drunk had led to the ambush on Harry and his men, but he knew that all three of them blamed him for the death of the ten men killed that day.

Before that day he had been one of them. Since then they had treated him like a pariah—and he hated them all, Harry Pendleton more than the others. He would wait his chance for revenge! If it took him a lifetime, he would bring them down one by one. There was more than one way of skinning a cat...

He would find something—a weak spot—and then he would strike!

* * *

Susannah wore a new gown of green silk with a pelisse of pale yellow; her bonnet was green with a trim of yellow daises at the brim; her reticule was fashioned of yellow silk and trimmed with beads. She had York tan gloves and half-boots of kid, her hair peeping out from beneath her bonnet in a most fetching manner.

Harry's heart caught as he saw her. She looked so young and innocent, the very essence of spring, and he was a little sorry he had changed his mind about eloping with her. However, it was not the behaviour of a gentleman and he would never have even thought of it, had Susannah not told him that she craved adventure. He was pleased that his plans now were simply to drive her to the park and back. He might even speak to her during their excursion. He thought she liked him well enough, but in his heart he wanted her to love him wildly, passionately—the until-death-do-us-part kind of love that his saner side knew belonged only in romances. Yet if he married her without believing that she loved him, he knew that he might find it unbearable.

'You look beautiful, as always,' he told her as he handed her into his high perch phaeton. 'Are you quite comfortable, Susannah?'

'Yes, thank you,' she said, settling on the seat beside him. 'I have heard of your fabulous blacks, Harry. I understand that you have an extensive stable?'

'Yes, I have,' he replied and grinned at her. 'I cannot offer to let you drive the blacks—they would be too strong for you. However, I should feel privileged if you would allow me to teach you to drive something suitable. One day in the future, perhaps?'

'Oh...' Susannah's heart fluttered as she waited, wondering if he might go on to propose. However, as he said nothing more she went on, 'I should enjoy that very much if it could be arranged, though I am not sure how.' She rather thought it would not do to begin in a public park, though she would have considered it an adventure.

'It is my habit to invite friends to my estate in the summer,' Harry told her, though his gaze did not waver from the road. She glanced at him and saw a little nerve throbbing at his temple. 'My mother stirs herself to come down and play hostess. If Mrs Hampton would consent to the visit, you might both stay for a week or two....'

Susannah's heart raced. It was not a proposal, but it might be the first step, for it would help them to know each other better. They would be able to spend more time together at his estate. He would not have asked if he did not like her.

'I know Mama has been making plans, but, if you were to ask her, sir, I am sure she would consider it an honour to visit your home. She told me that she has heard of your modern innovations with the land.'

'Did she, indeed?' Harry gave her an odd look that brought a blush to her cheeks. 'It is true that I am thought to be forward thinking, for I have made it my business to experiment with new ideas, but few know of it.'

'I believe Mr Sinclair is an eloquent advocate for your good stewardship, sir.' Susannah smiled, a dreamy look in her eyes. 'Toby is such a charming companion. He sent me flowers yesterday, because he said that everyone sends them on the day of a ball and he thought I should have some the next day.'

'You find him good company?' Harry glanced at her, but she was smiling, looking about her.

'Oh, yes!' Susannah's eyes glowed as she turned to him. 'Toby is great fun, sir. We met him out walking yesterday and took a turn in the park together. Nothing would do but for him to join some children in their play. They had a ball and a dog and it was a noisy affair.'

'Yes, I can imagine it might have been.' His eyes narrowed as he looked at her. Toby was only twenty, perhaps a more suitable age. 'I dare say the children enjoyed it?'

'Yes, indeed. It was most amusing.'

'I imagine so...'

'I believe everyone enjoyed the dance,' Susannah remarked and smiled at him. 'It was a successful evening. Everyone has sent cards and letters to thank us.'

'Yes, I am sure they did,' Harry said, a little nerve flicking at his temple. He hastily changed the subject for fear of giving himself away. 'Did you notice that the earl danced with Miss Royston?'

'Yes, I did,' Susannah replied. The sparkle died out of her face as she recalled Amelia's brief lapse into despair after her brother's visit the previous day. 'I have decided that I will not try to promote their friendship further. You were right to scold me, sir—it is not my affair.'

Harry studied her profile. She looked serious, a little sad and he wondered at it. He would have liked to speak to her further and enquire whether her sadness was for herself or her friend, but they were entering the park at that moment and there was a press of carriages and people on foot. It seemed that quite a few of London's fashionable ladies and gentlemen had decided to take the air on such a lovely day. No sooner had they managed to get through the crush at the gates than they were forced to draw up to speak to a crowd of young gentlemen who wished to pay their respects.

Harry smiled wryly as the young bucks vied to catch Susannah's attention. She was even more popular than he had imagined and the wonder of it was that she had not received at least half a dozen proposals before now. He could not know it, for Susannah would never have boasted of her conquests, but she had already received three requests for her hand, which she had turned down with a smile, and would have had more if she had encouraged her suitors.

It was obvious that a visit to the park was not the occasion to make a proposal of marriage. Harry decided that he must be patient a little longer. He would write to his mother on his return home and ask her to invite the Hamptons and Miss Royston to stay at his home. If they consented, it would at least give him a chance of some private conversation.

On her return home, Susannah did not know whether to be disappointed that Lord Pendleton had not proposed or pleased that he had spoken of an invitation from his mother.

Mrs Hampton was of the opinion that she should take it as a sign that his intentions were serious. 'I do not see why he would invite us if it were not so,' Mrs Hampton told her and smiled. 'Did you give him to understand that you would welcome the invitation?'

'He had been saying that he would teach me to drive one day if it would please me,' Susannah told her a little uncertainly. 'I said that I would enjoy it of all things if it could be arranged—and then he mentioned a house party.'

'Yes, well, it sounds promising to me,' Mrs Hampton said. 'He does know that we leave for Bath in a few days?'

'Yes, Mama,' Susannah said. 'He said that he might post down himself soon and would have an invitation from his mother. I think the visit is intended for next month.'

'Which will give us time to see Amelia settled in her new house,' Mrs Hampton said and looked pleased.

When consulted, Amelia said that she thought the situation looked promising. 'At the very least, Pendleton must be thinking that he wishes to know you better, dearest.' Amelia lifted her brow in enquiry. 'Have you made up your mind what you will say if he asks you?'

'I believe I should have said yes if he asked me today,' Susannah said. 'As you know, I was not certain at first that I liked him, but he is such a pleasant gentleman….'

'Then I shall accept the invitation when it is given,' Mrs Hampton said. 'Shall you come with us, Amelia? I am certain you will be invited for it would seem odd if you were not, and Pendleton would never give offence.'

'It will depend on my situation in Bath,' Amelia told her. 'I shall accompany you and Susannah if I am able, for I have heard that Pendleton is very fine, but I have never seen it—though I believe parts of it are opened to the public occasionally.'

'There is so much excitement going on,' Mrs Hampton said. 'I think all this must be enough for even you, Susannah?' She threw her daughter a teasing challenge. 'I do hope Pendleton will not let you drive those wicked great brutes of his.'

'He says the blacks are too strong for me, but I dare say he may have others more suitable.' Susannah was smiling to herself as she went up to change for the afternoon. She had regretted that Harry had not spoken to her that morning, but if both Mama and Amelia believed

Harry to be on the verge of making her a proposal, then perhaps he would. She could only hope so—her dreams had all become centred on becoming his wife.

At the start she had been foolish, thinking him a stuffy bore and arrogant, but now she knew it was not so. She had dreamed for so long of a knight who would sweep her up on his white charger and ride off with her into the sunset, but that was all nonsense. Now she had a clear picture of a charming house where they would live in complete contentment with roses growing up rose-pink walls and two pretty children playing on a swing....

Susannah might not have been quite as happy had she seen the face of her prospective fiancé some twenty minutes later. He was scowling over a letter he had received from a friend, his own mood changing from one of pleasant anticipation to something rather different.

I hesitate to ask for help, the letter began. *Indeed, I would not do so, but I am at my wits' end, Harry. I am in such trouble! I became involved with some gentlemen—they were born to the name, but do not deserve it!—and now I am ill. I have debts I cannot pay—but that is not the worst of it. I beg you to come to me in haste, not for my own sake—I doubt that I shall last more than the week—but for the sake of another...my poor sister, who has no one but me and will now be alone. Your one-time friend, Hazledeane*

Harry crumpled the paper in his hand, tempted to throw it away. Frederick Hazledeane had been a friend in the years he had spent at Oxford, before Harry went into the army. He had always been on the wild side and it seemed that his bad ways had led him into the kind of trouble that might have been expected.

It was a dashed nuisance! Harry would have normally been only too willing to help a friend, even one he had not been particularly close to. However, to leave London now on such an errand was not what Harry needed or wanted. He was at a delicate stage of his courtship of Susannah and he did not wish her to think he had abandoned her.

He must go, of course! Hazledeane must be in desperate straits and his sister was younger. If she truly had no one, Harry was duty bound to help her as best he could. He sighed because this was a duty he could well have done without, but there was nothing for it. He sat down at his desk and began to write a note to Mrs Hampton, telling her that he was called away on business and would hope to see her in Bath in no more than two weeks from now. That would surely give him enough time to complete his business in Cambridgeshire!

Susannah had felt some misgiving when her mother read the short letter to her. It had sounded abrupt, as if Harry had been in a hurry, and it caused a cold shiver to run down her spine. She did not know why it should have made her feel so apprehensive—after all, it would only be a matter of a few days longer before he came to Bath. Besides, they had been so taken up with saying goodbye to their friends, returning books to the library and picking up packages that had been ordered from various shops that the time had flown.

The day for their departure to Bath arrived and they set out on the journey in good spirits. Susannah could not help looking forward to Harry's visit and the letter that might spell the beginning of her happiness.

However, she had determined that she would carry on as usual, and it was a pleasant surprise when Toby Sinclair came to call the day after they arrived in Bath.

'How nice to see you, sir,' Mrs Hampton said when he was shown into the parlour where they sat together. 'We did not know that you intended to come down, Mr Sinclair.'

'Oh…I posted down to visit some friends,' Toby said airily, but his eyes were on Susannah. 'Mama asked me to call on her, which I shall, but I think I shall spend a few days in Bath first. My visit to Mama is not urgent. I wondered whether Miss Susannah would care to drive out to see some of the sights—ma'am—Miss Royston? I have another seat in my curricle if you wish?'

'I think we may trust her to your care, sir,' Mrs Hampton said. He was a pleasant young man and his attentions to Susannah had become more particular of late. Nothing was settled with Lord Pendleton yet and there was no certainty of anything. 'I trust you have your groom with you?'

'Yes, ma'am,' Toby said, his eyes never moving from Susannah. 'Would you care for a drive, Miss Hampton? It is pleasant out today.'

'If you will give me a moment to collect my parasol and pelisse,' Susannah told him, 'I shall be happy to drive with you, sir.'

She was pleased to be on such good terms with Harry's nephew. If she had not liked Harry Pendleton so very much, she might have thought Toby a very good sort of husband.

'Lord Pendleton has offered to teach me to drive when

we visit his estate,' she told Toby when he handed her into his curricle. 'I am looking forward to it so much.'

'Harry is one of the best whips I know,' Toby said. 'However, I shall be happy to give you a few lessons myself. It would be too difficult for you on the road, but I shall be visiting with Lady Pendleton and Harry next month, and it will please me to give you a few pointers.'

'Show me how to hold the reins as we drive,' Susannah said, giving him such a brilliant smile that a passer-by grinned to himself and thought he had seen a pair of young lovers. 'I should be pleased to know a little before Harry takes me driving.'

'Well, you hold them in one hand like this,' Toby said. 'That gives you a free hand for the whip. Not that you need it often with well-trained cattle. I only use it if I have to get somewhere in a hurry, but you will drive at a sedate pace. It wouldn't be fitting for a young lady to race, of course. Not done at all.'

'Oh…' Susannah looked at him wistfully. 'Would it not, sir? I am disappointed. I should have liked to race— when I am able to drive well enough, and on a private estate, of course.'

'Dashed if you ain't a girl of spirit,' Toby said and chuckled. 'We might manage it some time—once you are safe behind a pair. You would have to keep it to yourself, of course. People talk so much, you know.'

'Do you really mean it?' Susannah's eyes lit with excitement.

'Yes…' Toby knew a moment of disquiet, for he had spoken on impulse. 'It would have to be our secret, of course. I do not think Harry would approve and your mama certainly would not.'

'No, she wouldn't,' Susannah agreed. 'However,

neither of them need know. We cannot do it until the moment is right, but I should so like to do something exciting—an adventure. It could not harm anyone and if it were in private it would not be scandalous at all, would it?'

'Lord, no,' Toby assured her airily and then wondered if he had been wise to encourage her. It did not seem that way to him, but he could not vouch for his uncle's opinion. Harry could be stern at times. However, he did not want to take the glow from Susannah's lovely face and it might never happen. It was probably just a piece of nonsense and she would forget all about it.

'Lord Pendleton should return soon,' Susannah said. 'We are being spoiled! A visit to London, now Bath and then Pendleton—I do wish it might go on for ever.'

'Well, perhaps it may,' Toby told her and grinned. 'I tell you what—we're coming to a quiet spot now. Would you like to hold the reins for a bit?'

Susannah's smile was all the reward he needed. She was a beauty and a good sport too. Toby wasn't sure if his uncle meant to offer for her or not, but she was certainly a dashed pretty girl!

Harry watched as the sick man signed what amounted to his last will and testament, making Harry his sole executor and the temporary guardian of Hazledeane's sister Jenny. The innkeeper and the scribe added their names and the innkeeper departed, clutching the small purse of gold that paid his debt in full. Harry looked at the solicitor's clerk.

'Tell your master that I will call tomorrow and discuss Mr Hazledeane's estate.'

'Yes, sir,' the clerk said and accepted the guinea

Harry offered for his pains in answering the summons. 'Mr Humberston will expect you in the morning.'

Harry turned back to the dying man. Hazledeane's breathing was growing more laboured. Time was short now. 'You understand that I shall hand the care of Miss Hazledeane over to Lady Pendleton? I am not the right person to care for your sister, Hazledeane. I shall rescue what I can from this mess, though by the sound of it the sale of your estate will scarcely pay your debts. What possessed you to play so deep when you knew you had mortgages on the land? You must have known it meant ruin?'

'They draw you in, Harry. You have no idea what kind of men they are,' Hazledeane said. 'I've known for some months that my chest was weak, that I had consumption. It was desperation, I suppose—' He broke off as a fit of coughing overtook him, the cloth stained with bright crimson. Harry gave him water and after a moment he fell back, exhausted. 'Nothing matters but Jenny. He wanted her, Harry. He said he would pay my debts if I gave Jenny to him, but he would use her and desert her. She deserves better even if I have let her down.'

'Save your breath,' Harry told him. 'You speak of these men—and of one in particular—but you have not named them.'

'It was him…Northaven…' the dying man gasped. 'I swear he cheated me in the hope of getting her, but I wouldn't…' His body arched, a bubble of blood issuing from his mouth as he twisted in pain for some minutes, then he fell back.

'You must rest and then tell me all of it—all their names,' Harry said, but as he bent over the man he saw that it was too late. Hazledeane had spoken his last, and he had named Northaven as the architect of his downfall.

Harry closed his eyelids and placed copper coins over the lids, then made the sign of the cross over the dead man. 'God rest your soul. May He pity you and give you peace.'

Glancing around the room, Harry picked up the few things of value Hazledeane had possessed and pocketed them, together with the deed of Hazledeane's will. He would make arrangements with the landlord for the vicar to be fetched and return for the funeral as soon as it could be arranged. For the moment he must make a journey of some fifteen miles to Hazledeane's estate, where he hoped to find Miss Jenny Hazledeane. She might wish to be present at her brother's funeral. Hazledeane had refused to have her fetched to his sickbed, saying that he did not deserve her forgiveness. Harry had respected his wishes, but he was not sure how Miss Hazledeane would feel about the prospect of being under his guardianship.

He sighed as he realised his business would take him a little longer than he had imagined, for he could not travel with Miss Hazledeane unchaperoned. If she had a suitable maid it might be accomplished, but otherwise he must find her one. The sooner he could deliver her to his mother, the better—and he was not sure she would thank him for it! However, he knew her well enough to believe that she would not refuse him. He prayed she would accept the burden, otherwise he would have to find either a school or a companion for Hazledeane's sister.

All he wanted was to drive to Bath to renew his relationship with Susannah, but he had been unable to refuse a dying man's request to care for his sister. He must do what he could for her and hope that his mother would take responsibility for her quite soon.

* * *

'Lord Pendleton sends his apologies,' Mrs Hampton said as she finished reading her letter that morning in the elegant parlour of Amelia's house in the Crescent. 'He will not be able to come for another day or so and...' she turned the page '...Lady Elizabeth Pendleton is to accompany them.' She looked puzzled. 'I did not know that Lord Pendleton had a ward called Miss Jenny Hazledeane, did you, Susannah?'

'No. He has never mentioned her to me,' Susannah said. She had been poring over a copy of the *Ladies' Monthly Journal*, but she laid it aside. 'But I see no reason why he should...do you?'

'No, I suppose not,' Mrs Hampton frowned. 'He says they will spend a few days here in Bath and then his mother and Miss Hazledeane will go ahead to prepare for guests. He says he shall visit us as soon as he arrives.'

'Oh, that will be nice,' Susannah said and smiled. 'I am sorry that he is not to come tomorrow as he thought, but it will not be so very long...' She turned her head as she heard the rattle of wheels on cobbles outside the house. 'Ah, I think that must be Toby Sinclair. He has come to take me driving.'

'Again?' Mrs Hampton lifted her brows. 'That is the third time this week, Susannah. He is paying you a great deal of attention, dearest.'

'Oh, it is nothing—mere friendship,' Susannah replied. She did not wish her mother to know that Mr Sinclair was teaching her the first stages of driving a curricle and pair, because she might not approve. They had, after all, been driving in public places, though Toby was careful to choose very quiet spots, and he kept a strict eye on the horses. He was a patient teacher and she had formed a strong bond with him these past few days. 'Excuse me, Mama. I must not keep the horses standing for it is very warm.'

'Run along then, dearest,' her mother told her. 'Do not forget we dine with friends at six this evening.'

'No, Mama, I shall not forget,' Susannah said. 'I promise to be home on time.' She went hurriedly to meet Toby, for she was looking forward to a little longer lesson today. He had promised that they would drive out of town and she might take the reins as soon as they reached a quiet road.

It was an hour later when the accident occurred. Susannah had been driving at a steady pace in a quiet country lane for some minutes. Toby was praising her skill with the ribbons when they heard three shots in rapid succession just to the right of the road. They had come from within the woods, and were probably some-one hunting for game, but the horses took exception and bolted for their lives. Susannah was jerked forward and quite unable to hold the terrified creatures. Toby made a grab for the reins, but it was some minutes before even he began to get them under control—and it was at that point that a farm cart came out suddenly from a concealed entrance, causing him to swerve to avoid the collision. As it happened, the wheels of the cart scraped the side of the curricle, causing it to sway violently. In that moment, Susannah was thrown to the ground and everything went black.

It was a while before her senses cleared enough to discover that Toby was bending over her, his face ashen. He was patting her face and begging her not to die, which struck Susannah as rather amusing, for she was clearly not dead.

'Toby, pray do not look so worried,' she begged and sat up. Her head went round and round for a moment and then cleared. 'I am not so very much hurt. I think I can stand if you would help me.'

'Of course.' He gently pulled her to her feet, putting an arm about her waist. Susannah swayed for a moment, but he held her steady and she leaned against him until the faintness passed again. 'Forgive me, Susannah. You might have been killed and it was all my fault....'

'Nonsense,' Susannah told him. 'You could not have known the horses would bolt. Besides, we should have been all right if that cart had not come out so suddenly.'

'I should have taken more care of you,' Toby said, looking rueful. 'Please forgive me. Had you been badly hurt, I should never have forgiven myself.'

Susannah took a step forwards and winced. 'I think I may have sprained my ankle. It hurts a little.'

'I shall carry you,' Toby said solicitously. 'If you will permit me?'

'No, no I can manage to hobble to the carriage. What of your horses and curricle?' Susannah said. 'Are they much hurt?'

'The curricle has sustained some slight damage, the horses are merely blown, which they must have been after that mad flight. However, we shall go slowly to the nearest hostelry and I shall hire a pair to get you home. I think it best if we wait for your mama to call a doctor—unless you are in such pain that you cannot go on?'

'I should be a poor dab of a thing if I let such an accident upset me,' Susannah said. 'If you could help me to the curricle and take me to the nearest hostelry. I am a little shaken—a glass of wine, perhaps, while they change the horses?'

'Anything you wish,' Toby said fervently. 'I am much at fault, Miss Hampton. I cannot bear to think what might have happened…'

Susannah touched her fingers to his lips and smiled. 'No more foolishness. Please help me to the curricle and we shall forget this, for I am as much to blame as you, sir. I teased you to let me drive.'

It was perfectly true, but Toby knew himself at fault. Had anything happened to her, he could hardly have faced her mama and friends—and he did not dare to think what Harry might say to him!

Susannah's ankle was so much better by the time they stopped that she was able to get down with Toby's assistance and hobble to an outside seat while he fetched her a glass of wine and had the horses changed. It was as she was sitting sipping her wine that a large, important-looking carriage swept into the yard and two ladies got down, making their way towards the inn. A gentleman followed them on horseback. He dismounted, spoke to the groom and then turned to go into the inn, stopping in astonishment as he saw Susannah sitting on the wooden bench, sipping her wine.

'Miss Hampton,' Harry said and frowned disapprovingly. 'What are you doing here?'

Susannah smiled up at him. 'We have had a little adventure, sir. Toby is finding us some horses, for the others are blown.'

'An adventure! What nonsense is this?' he demanded, for it was most improper for Susannah to be alone drinking wine in the sunshine at the inn. 'Has Toby got you into some trouble, Susannah?'

'It wasn't his fault, truly,' Susannah told him. 'The horses were startled by a gun firing three times close by and they bolted—and then, just as he had them just under control, a farm cart came out and—' She broke off as she saw the flash of anger in his eyes. 'It was not so very terrible and Toby says—'

'The young idiot may tell me himself!' Harry said as Toby came towards them, looking awkward. 'Miss Hampton tells me you let your cattle bolt? And you wish to be a member of the Four-in-Hand? It seems you cannot control a pair, sir! What have you to say for yourself?'

'Nothing that helps,' Toby said, looking guilty. 'However, Miss Hampton was not much hurt and—'

'Hurt? Susannah was hurt?' He swung round, staring at her accusingly. 'You did not tell me that you were hurt.'

'I—I fell when the cart struck us and banged my head,' Susannah said. 'Everything went black for a moment, but I have recovered well enough now.'

'You must go home at once and you should not be drinking wine in this heat, especially after a knock on the head.' Harry glared at Toby. 'What were you thinking of to bring her here?'

'I had no choice. We had to change the horses and Miss Hampton wished for a drink.'

'Then you should have given her water or a cordial,' Harry said. 'I shall take her home instantly in your curricle. You will take my horse and escort my mother and Miss Hazledeane. You will explain why I have left them to your care. Please see if you can escort them the short distance to Bath without causing more harm!'

Toby stared at him, his face red with embarrassment. Susannah threw him a look of sympathy and touched his arm as she followed Harry to the curricle. She tried not to limp, even though her ankle hurt, because she did not wish to bring another torrent of abuse down on Toby. Harry's outburst had shocked her. Poor Toby did not deserve it and she was not pleased with Harry's behaviour at all; he was arrogant, unfair and shockingly rude. It made her wonder if she really knew him at all. She had considered him the gentlest, kindest man of her acquaintance and it really was too bad of him to treat Toby so!

Because she was upset, she ignored Harry's hand and accepted help from Toby's groom, who was observing the shocking scene in silence. Susannah took her lead from him and kept a dignified silence as Harry climbed into the curricle with her and the groom jumped up at the back. She noticed the way Harry took the reins, how strong and powerful his hands were as he gave the order for the horses to walk on. It was odd that she had not noticed it in particular before. Perhaps it was because she had been spending so much time in Toby's company that she now understood the difference between the charming young man and his uncle.

Lost in her thoughts and feeling subdued, she did not speak once during the short drive back to Bath. She risked a glance at Harry's face once, but he still seemed angry and she discovered that she did not wish to talk to him. He had scolded her for drinking wine and he had unfairly abused Toby. She hunched her shoulder towards him, deliberately keeping a distance between them. He was too bad! To stay away so long and then return just when he was not wanted, earlier than promised. If he had not come until the day after tomorrow, as his letter said, he would have known nothing of their adventure.

Outside the house in the crescent, Harry brought the horses to a standstill, tossed the reins to the groom and offered Susannah his hand, giving her no chance to ignore him. To have done so would have been the height of rudeness, and, even though she was still a little bruised by the unfairness of his attack, she would not go to such lengths to show displeasure. She allowed him to help her down, thanking him in a small, polite voice.

'Forgive me if I have offended you,' Harry told her. 'I was perhaps a little abrupt, but I was shocked and anxious. Had anyone else drawn up and seen you…someone may have seen you in passing. It is not as bad as it might have been, for it was the middle of the day—but you might have found yourself severely censured. To sit outside an inn alone with only my nephew as your escort—'

'And his groom!'

'A groom!' Harry dismissed the man. 'It could have meant a loss of reputation, Miss Hampton.'

'It was my suggestion. We needed to change the horses and…you were unfair to Toby, sir. It was not his fault, truly it wasn't.'

'You are on intimate terms with my nephew. Am I to take it there is an understanding between you?' Harry glared at her.

'No! Of course not. How could there…?' Susannah turned away abruptly as the tears threatened. How could he even ask such a thing? He must know…he must know she would never do anything improper. The groom had rapped at the door; as it opened, Susannah went inside, managing not to hobble until she had pushed the door to after her. She went slowly upstairs, hoping that her mother and Amelia had taken their walk to the Pump Room, as they had talked of doing. She did not want to have to explain why Harry had brought her back—or perhaps she ought to think of him as Lord Pendleton, for she doubted he would make her an offer now. In his eyes she had disgraced herself!

Susannah went into her room, throwing herself down to weep until the tears were finished. When her maid came, she asked if she could put a cold compress on her ankle and the girl obliged. She wanted to summon a doctor, but Susannah refused. Quite enough fuss had been made already over a sprained ankle!

She felt hurt that Harry could accuse her of behaving badly—and to ask if she had an understanding when he must know she cared for him was the limit. She was so angry with him she almost wished that she had fallen in love with Toby just to spite him. She dashed her angry tears away as temper gave way to distress.

How could Harry think that she would wish to marry anyone but him?

In the morning Susannah's ankle was still sore. She explained it to her mama by saying that she had twisted it when getting down to walk for a little at a beauty spot and made nothing of it. She claimed that she was pleased to have a day sitting quietly at home.

'I have an appointment for tea this afternoon,' Amelia told her. 'Should I cancel it, my love? I shall sit with you if you are lonely, for your mama also has an appointment and I think hers is more important than mine. She has been asked to go driving with Lady Elizabeth this afternoon.'

'I shall do very well with a book,' Susannah said. 'Please, you must both keep your engagements. I have none until this evening when we attend the theatre and I shall be glad to rest my ankle.'

'If it is no better, I shall have the doctor brought in when I return,' Mrs Hampton said. 'Unless you would like him now, dearest?'

Susannah insisted that her ankle would be better after a day of rest and that she would be able to accompany them to the theatre that evening. Amelia and Mrs Hampton were reluctant to leave her alone, but after more objections they went and Susannah settled down to her book. She had read no more than a chapter when she decided that she was far too restless to concentrate. Oh, why had Harry been so horrible to her the previous day? She had longed for him to come so much and now it was all spoiled!

Susannah frowned and put her book aside. She got up and went out into the garden at the rear. It was not a large garden, but it was pretty and she knew Amelia had plans for the borders, which would mature the following spring. She felt wistful, as if she had lost something without knowing what it was. She found a bench in the garden and sat down, watching some birds squabbling over a piece of bread they had found.

'I trust you are feeling better, Miss Hampton?'

Susannah jumped and turned, startled by Harry's voice. 'Who let you in? I did not know you had been admitted.' Her voice was harsher than she knew and he frowned.

'Would you have forbidden me if you had?' Harry

asked. 'Forgive me. I wished to speak with you alone—but if you would rather I went...'

'No, do not go...' She blushed as she saw his look. 'I dare say Amelia and Mama will be back soon.'

'Your maid told me to go through into the parlour and I saw you out here. I think we are permitted the garden, for we may be seen from every window in the house. However, I shall not stay long. I came only to enquire if you had seen a doctor. Toby told me that you were unconscious for a short time.'

'Barely a minute,' Susannah told him. 'I did not wish to alarm Mama, and I am perfectly well. She does not know that I fell—only that I twisted my ankle a little.'

'I see—do you think that wise?'

'I wish to save her anxiety. I am perfectly recovered.'

'And yet your ankle is still a little sore.' His expression was serious, even severe. 'I came here to apologise for my outburst yesterday, Susannah. I was shocked to see you sitting there, apparently alone, and I fear that I was too harsh.'

'I do not think I deserved such censure.'

'No, you did not—but you must admit that you were careless of your reputation.'

'Perhaps...' Susannah glanced away, her cheeks pink. 'Your mother sent a note, inviting Mama to drive out with her this afternoon. They know each other a little...' She hesitated, then, 'I hope you still mean to invite me to stay at Pendleton, sir?'

'I do not withdraw my invitations or my friendship lightly, though others may,' Harry said. She glanced at him, but his friendly smile was missing. 'I shall see you tomorrow. I am glad you have recovered from your fright.'

'I was not frightened at all, even when the horses bolted,' Susannah told him, lifting her head high. 'It was an adventure and I enjoyed it—even if you do not approve of my behaviour.'

'I see...' Harry inclined his head curtly. 'I see that I have made you angry. Please excuse me, Miss Hampton.'

Susannah sat on long after he had gone, the tears trickling down her cheeks. She had quarrelled with him again and she did not know why. She wanted him to like her—to love her—just as she did him! She had not meant to do anything improper, but she was very much afraid that she had lost Lord Pendleton's good opinion. He had stood by her when the Marquis of Northaven attacked her, but this time he seemed very angry indeed.

Harry *was* angry as he walked away from the house, though he could not have been certain why he felt so very aggrieved. His business had proved more complicated than he could have expected, for Miss Hazledeane was not quite the meek child he had imagined. She was twenty, beautiful with dark brown hair and greenish brown eyes that some called hazel. She had thanked him for his care of her brother, but seemed reluctant to accept him as her guardian. However, when he told her that they were to go to Bath for a few days before going on to his mother's estate she had accepted with a good grace.

'I hope I shall not need your help for long, sir,' she had told him with a flash of her remarkable eyes. 'When I am one and twenty I shall have a small bequest that was left to me by my maternal grandmother. It is enough so that I can live independently. In the meantime, I would be glad to set up my own household—if you could arrange for me to have whatever Frederick left me.'

Harry had explained that she would be lucky to have a hundred pounds, and after that she had been more amenable to his plans, but it was clear that she was a lady with a mind of her own.

He shrugged—he had not asked to be her guardian and would have preferred to hand her over to a relation. However, he had given his word to keep her safe and he would do so—at least until two months' time when she gained her independence.

Miss Hazledeane was a mere inconvenience, but the matter of Susannah was more difficult. Before they all left London he had been on the verge of making a proposal and it had been in his mind to do so as soon as he saw her again. Now he was not sure how he felt. Indeed, she seemed to have abandoned her feelings for him. She had been seeing a lot of Toby and he was beginning to wonder if the pair were not better suited.

Once again, Harry was thrown into confusion. He was certain of his own feelings, but there was a reluctance to be married simply for the sake of wealth and position. He might have married long ago if all he required in a wife was compliance. He had this foolish notion that his wife should love him, at least as much as he loved her—and he knew that he would die for Susannah if it were necessary. While he would not expect such heroics from her, he did want her to feel that she could not happily live without him.

Perhaps he expected too much. After all, she was beautiful, charming and much admired. Most men would be satisfied with that. He knew that he must be a perverse creature, but he wanted so much more.

Chapter Six

Susannah was able to visit the theatre with her mother and Amelia that evening, but she did not enjoy it as much as usual, because as the seats were filling up she saw Harry Pendleton come in with two ladies. Her mother identified them as Lady Elizabeth and her ward Miss Jenny Hazledeane, whom she had met briefly that afternoon.

'Miss Hazledeane is very beautiful,' Susannah said and sighed. There was something about the other girl that made her feel an instant antipathy, though she knew it was unfair, for they had never met. She would not allow herself to dislike the other girl just because she was holding Harry's arm as if she were on intimate terms with him! She would instead make an effort to be friendly when they were introduced. 'Do you not think so?'

'Yes, she is,' Mrs Hampton agreed, looking reflective. 'I thought her a little cold, even reserved, but perhaps I do not know her well enough to judge. We only spoke for a moment. No, I was wrong to say it. She is in mourning for her brother, who died recently. His death left her alone in the world and that is why she has come to stay with Lady Elizabeth. It is hardly to be remarked if she had nothing to say for herself.'

'Has she no one at all?'

'No one. Her brother was once a great friend of Lord Pendleton. He was ill and Lord Pendleton is in charge of his estate.'

'Oh…' Susannah was thoughtful. 'Do you imagine she is an heiress, Mama?'

'I have no idea,' her mother said and glanced at her. 'You may be certain that the gossips will find it out if it is so—but it cannot matter. Lord Pendleton is not in need of a fortune. Besides, Lady Elizabeth was most kind to me, Susannah. She said that she would be pleased to have me visit her often in the future.'

Susannah frowned as she saw the satisfied look in her mother's eyes. Undoubtedly the two mothers had settled it all between them. Susannah was torn between a pleased feeling that an announcement was expected and annoyance that Harry should have taken her for granted. Before she left London she had been on fire for a proposal, but now she was uncertain. His anger at the inn—and when he called on her the next day—had made her feel that he must have a shocking temper. It was grossly unfair to give Toby such a set-down! He had also been very sharp with her! Surely she had not done anything so very terrible?

She tried to put their quarrel out of her mind, but she dreaded the interval, for she suspected that Harry would visit their box. Her heart sank when he did just that, accompanied by his mother and the beautiful Miss Hazledeane. The introductions were made and Susannah received a warm kiss on the cheek from Lady Elizabeth.

'I am very pleased to meet you, Susannah. I may call you Susannah, I hope? My son has told me many nice things about you, my dear.'

'Oh…thank you,' Susannah said and a faint blush warmed her cheeks as she looked at Harry. His expression was unreadable, though she did not think he was angry. However, he did not give her the warm, intimate smile she was used to receiving from him and she missed it. Had she lost his good opinion completely? 'You are very kind, ma'am.'

'You must have tea with me soon, privately, so that we may have a comfortable gossip; it will be best when we are at home,' Lady Elizabeth said and turned to the other lady, bringing her forward. 'I think you have not met Miss Hazledeane? Jenny is going to make her home with me for the time being. She recently lost her brother, as you may have been told, but we have decided she shall not go into official mourning since her brother expressly forbade it. So you must not think the less of her for wearing colours.'

'Miss Hazledeane—' Susannah dipped a small curtsy '—I am truly sorry for your loss. I have no brother, but should be sad to lose him if I had. You must be very distressed.'

'Indeed.' Jenny raised her brows. 'You are kind to say so, Miss Hampton, but you know nothing of me or my brother.'

Susannah blushed hotly, feeling that she had been slapped down. She had been sincere and had not meant to offer meaningless sympathy, but it was clear that Miss Hazledeane thought she had done so. She was too embarrassed to offer anything further and listened to the general talk, while she watched the crowd begin to move back to their seats.

'Jenny did not mean to be rude,' a voice said at her ear and she swung round to look at Harry. 'Her circumstances are awkward and she is upset.'

'Of course,' Susannah agreed, though she was certain the rudeness had been intentional. 'It does not matter. In her place I should not feel like talking much to people I did not know.'

Harry gave her a look of approval. 'It is like you to say so. I hope you will find her more amenable when you are staying with us. Jenny could do with a friend nearer her own age.'

'Yes, I expect she may,' Susannah replied. 'I am sure that is not impossible, sir. I am willing if she wishes it.'

'Thank you.' Harry hesitated and then frowned as the bell rang. 'We must return to our seats. I am engaged to take Mama and Jenny to the Pump Room tomorrow morning. I wondered if I might take you driving in the afternoon?'

'Yes, please,' Susannah said and gazed at him earnestly. 'I do not wish to fall out with you, sir. If I was rude when you called on me, I apologise.'

'I believe I made you angry,' Harry said. 'I think we should agree to put the incident behind us.'

'If you are willing to forget, then so shall I.'

Harry nodded. 'It would be a pity to spoil a friendship, Susannah. I shall call on you at two in the afternoon—and now I must go, for Mama is anxious to return to her seat.'

'I shall expect you, thank you. You must go...'

Susannah took her seat as the Pendleton party left and made their way hastily to their own box just as the curtain went up. Watching the play unfold, Susannah reviewed the brief interlude in her mind. Miss Hazledeane had clearly taken her in dislike—why? Did she want Lord Pendleton for herself?

Since she had no engagements the following morning, Susannah decided to return some books to the lending library. Her mother had agreed to go driving with friends and Amelia had arranged to pay a morning visit to Lady Jamieson. Promising to return in plenty of time, Susannah set off to the library. She returned the books, resisted the temptation to borrow more and crossed the road to the small tea shop where they sold the most delicious peppermint creams.

Amelia was very partial to peppermint creams, especially those covered in chocolate. Susannah went inside, making her way to the counter that displayed them. She had her back turned to the door when some people came in, but, hearing a voice she recognised, she turned her head to look. A lady dressed in dark blue with a rather fetching hat set on the back of her head at a jaunty angle, and a tall, distinguished gentleman, had seated themselves at a table in the far corner where they were almost, but not completely, hidden from view. A little start of surprise went through Susannah as she saw Miss Hazledeane and recognised the gentleman with her.

The Marquis of Northaven! Susannah felt cold all over as she observed the way Miss Hazledeane seemed to have come to life. At the theatre she had seemed to be cold and distant, but now her lovely face was alight with excitement, her eyes glowing. She looked like a woman in love!

Susannah looked away swiftly as Miss Hazledeane glanced her way, deliberately keeping her head averted as she bought and paid for her bonbons. She left the shop at once and walked quickly home, vaguely disturbed by the scene she had just witnessed. It was not her affair who Miss Hazledeane met, and it was certainly not her place to question the look of happiness on her face—but she could not help recalling Harry's severe warnings to her concerning the marquis. What would he think if he knew that his mother's ward had been having tea with a man he thought of as untrustworthy? She was certain he would not be pleased. He might find it necessary to scold or censure Miss Hazledeane.

Susannah could not tell him! It would be a dreadful thing to do, because she must not meddle in the affairs of a woman she did not know. To go behind her back with tales would be unkind and might be thought spiteful. If Miss Hazledeane chose to meet Northaven, it was entirely her business. Yet if anything happened to her, Lord Pendleton would think himself responsible and if he knew that Susannah had witnessed a meeting between his mother's ward and the marquis, he would be angry.

Susannah was uncomfortable with having to conceal it from him. Even so, she must say nothing. It truly was not her business to tell tales. Susannah thrust the scene from her mind as she went into the house. Amelia was just coming downstairs, having changed for nuncheon.

'I bought you some peppermint creams,' Susannah told her and handed her the little box. 'Lord Pendleton will be here soon. I must not keep him waiting.'

She ran upstairs, Amelia's exclamation of pleasure following her as she hurried to get ready for her appointment. Susannah had decided that it was quite impossible to say anything to anyone about seeing Miss Hazledeane with the Marquis of Northaven. She was not a gossip and she had no wish to bring censure on Miss Hazledeane—even though she could not truly like her.

'You look lovely, as always,' Harry said as Susannah came downstairs dressed in a dark green carriage gown. 'I am sure all the gentlemen tell you how beautiful you are, Susannah.'

'Several have done so,' she admitted with a shy look. 'However, it is all foolishness—besides, I do not think beauty is everything, do you?'

'No, though many find it so,' Harry said, giving her a thoughtful look as they went outside to where his groom was holding the horses. He handed Susannah up and told his groom to stand back as the tiger jumped up on the back behind. 'I shall not need you this afternoon, Jed. The lad is sufficient for my needs.' He smiled at Susannah. 'I think character and a good heart more important myself.'

Susannah digested that in silence. She was not sure what he thought of her character. She was a spirited girl and did not hesitate to say what she felt. Would he consider that an asset or a fault in her character?

'Good humour and kindness are important too.'

'I think I agree,' Harry told her. 'Tell me, Susannah, are you still looking forward to your visit to Pendleton?'

'Yes, of course. Your nephew has told me that the grounds are very beautiful, and you know that I love to walk and collect wildflowers—' She broke off, her cheeks hot as he glanced at her. 'It was unfortunate that your carriage came so quickly round the corner that day—but we have both apologised for that.'

'And then I shouted at you again after the accident just recently. You must think me a brute and a bear.'

Susannah blushed and looked down at her gloved hands. 'I dare say it was improper of me to sit on a bench outside the inn drinking wine, but it was such a lovely day and I felt a little shaken....'

'My concern was for your safety,' Harry said and frowned. 'Toby was an idiot to leave you there alone, but had I known of the accident I should not have condemned you.'

'I thought that I must have lost your respect.'

'My damnable temper. I was anxious and at such times I am liable to say things I perhaps ought not.'

'It is all forgotten. We decided to put it behind us.'

'Yes, we did,' Harry said. They had left the town behind now and were driving through some pretty countryside. Seeing a place where the road widened, Harry drew the horses to a sedate halt, threw the reins to his tiger and then offered his hand to Susannah. 'Walk with me for a moment, if you will.'

'Yes, of course,' she said, giving him her hand. 'It is such a pleasant afternoon, is it not?'

'The sun is certainly warm,' Harry said as Susannah put up her parasol. He offered his arm and she took it. 'I wanted to speak to you alone. I have something to say to you. Indeed, I meant to speak yesterday when I called, but we got off on the wrong foot, as it were.'

Susannah's heart missed a beat. Her cheeks felt warm and she wished for a fan so that she might cool herself.

Harry had stopped walking. He turned her to face him, looking down at her so seriously that her heart slammed against her chest and she felt breathless.

'You must know that I have a high regard for you, Susannah?'

She lowered her gaze, feeling unsure. 'I did think that you liked me when we were in London...'

'My regard is much warmer than liking.' Harry reached out, tipping her chin with his hand so that she looked up at him. 'I had hoped that you might feel something similar for me?'

'Oh...I do,' Susannah said. 'Not at first, but then...I came to like you very well, sir. Very well...' She did not know why she felt so shy all of a sudden. It would be more truthful if she told him that she loved him, but she was afraid to confess her passion, for his words had been restrained, cautious rather than passionate.

'What of this friendship with my nephew?' Harry's brows arched.

'It is mere friendship,' Susannah assured him. 'You must know that...I could not like anyone else...as much...' Once again she floundered to a halt, for she was unsure of how to behave. If he had swept her into his arms and kissed her until she could scarcely breathe, she could have shown him her feelings by her response, but this polite proposal made her shy of revealing the passion within her. Perhaps for him it was a marriage of convenience with a young lady he thought suitable to give him an heir.

'Then would you do me the honour of becoming my wife?' Harry asked, gazing down at her. At that moment his eyes seemed to smoulder with something much stronger than mere liking and her heart jerked. Surely he must love her?

Susannah swallowed hard, looking up at him, her cheeks still a little pink. 'Yes, sir, I shall.'

'I am very happy,' Harry said and bent down to kiss her softly on the lips. His kiss was tender and sweet, making Susannah long to melt into his body. Her hands were against his chest, but even as she began to slide them up over his shoulders, he moved back, releasing her. 'I think we should continue this another time, in a more private place.' Harry smiled. 'In the meantime, we must tell your mama—at least I must ask her permission.'

'Yes, of course,' Susannah agreed. She was aware of a slight disappointment, for she would have liked him to kiss her again…to show in some way that he felt all those strange and wonderful feelings that his kiss had aroused in her. 'I am sure Mama will be pleased that we are to marry.'

'I told my mother that I intended to ask you this afternoon. She knew what was in my mind and this morning was pleased to tell me that she approved my choice. When we go to Pendleton you will meet others of my family. It will be a chance for us to spend more time together, Susannah. Meeting in society is all very well, but we have seldom been alone. My estate is large enough for us to escape at times.'

'I shall look forward to it,' Susannah replied, her heart racing. It was foolish of her to feel a little disappointed and uneasy. She had dreamed of this happening so many times. She had been living in a dream world of her own, Susannah realised. She must understand that this was real and not just a dream. Harry was not the white knight of her dreams but a real man, with all the faults and passions that entailed.

'Mama and I leave for Pendleton in the morning,' Harry said. 'Miss Hazledeane too, of course. Mama needs to prepare for our visitors, and it is only fair that Jenny should have a chance to settle in before everyone arrives.'

'Yes, of course…'

Susannah felt a little guilty as she wondered whether she ought to tell him of the meeting between his mother's ward and the Marquis of Northaven. Jenny had behaved like a woman in love, but Susannah could not think that it was her place to report what she had seen. Perhaps at Pendleton she might have a chance to warn Miss Hazledeane that the marquis was a rake and not to be trusted.

'Are you looking forward to this visit?' Mrs Hampton asked as her daughter came downstairs two days later. Susannah was wearing her travelling gown of dark green cloth, and carried a lighter green parasol to match the ribbons on her straw bonnet.

'Yes, Mama, of course,' Susannah told her. 'Why do you ask? I am engaged to Lord Pendleton and it will be a chance to get to know him better.'

'Yes, naturally. I just wondered if you knew what to expect. Lord Pendleton has a very large estate, you know.'

'He told me it was quite big,' Susannah replied, looking at her in a puzzled way. 'Is something wrong, Mama?'

'Oh, no, nothing. You have been very fortunate, my dear. It is just that you will find the life very different...' Mrs Hampton nodded. 'Mr Sinclair is outside in his curricle. Will you drive with him or Amelia and I?'

'Would you mind if I were to drive with him, at least for a part of the way?'

'I should not mind at all,' Mrs Hampton said and looked thoughtful. 'It was kind of him to offer his escort, was it not?'

'Lord Pendleton suggested it,' Susannah said, 'to

make sure that Amelia's coachman did not lose his way. We have a beautiful day for the journey, Mama.'

'Yes, we do indeed,' her mother agreed. 'Ah, here is Amelia. Now we are ready.'

Susannah went outside to the waiting carriages. Her mother and Amelia were to travel in Amelia's smart coach, but she was glad that she would be in the open air, for the sun was warm. Toby smiled as he saw her, coming to hand her into his curricle.

'You look lovely, Susannah,' he told her with a smile. 'Green becomes you very well. Please make yourselves comfortable.'

'Thank you,' Susannah replied and took his hand. 'I think I must ride with Mama some of the time, sir—perhaps you will take Amelia up next time?'

'I should be delighted,' Toby said. 'I am yours to command, Miss Hampton.'

Susannah giggled as he swept her an elegant bow. He looked very handsome in his superfine coat of dark blue and buff breeches, his top boots polished to a high gloss. His cravat was tied in a new way, which she believed was a style favoured by the members of the Four-in-Hand. Toby had clearly decided that he needed to improve his image if he wanted to become one of that elite set. 'I am so glad we are friends,' she said. 'I would ask you if I could drive a part of the way—but somehow I do not think Mama would approve.'

'I am very certain she would not,' Toby said and gave her a rueful look. 'You must not ask, Susannah. I should hate to refuse you anything, but you must be patient and wait until we are at the estate. I dare not think what Harry would say if it came out, especially after he has forbidden it.'

'Yes, I shall wait. I was merely teasing you,' she said.

She threw him a look of mischief as he climbed up beside her and his groom jumped on the back.

As they set off through the crescent, she saw a gentleman walking towards them. He pulled off his hat as they drew nearer, giving her a sweeping bow, his gaze intent as he brought it back to Susannah's face.

'I wish you a safe journey, Miss Hampton,' the Marquis of Northaven said, a mocking smile on his lips and what she thought was a challenge in his eyes. 'We must pray that no unfortunate accidents occur.'

Susannah felt a chill run down her spine. There was something menacing in his look, but she could not tell what he meant by it. It was clear that he had never forgiven her for that incident in the garden, when Harry Pendleton had given him a tongue-lashing.

'What the devil was that about?' Toby asked and frowned. 'The damned cheek of the rogue!'

'Do you suppose he heard about the accident we had?'

'I do not see how he could—unless someone told him. Harry wouldn't and no one else knew.'

'No...' Susannah recalled the meeting in the teashop in Bath. It was quite possible that Miss Hazledeane had overheard something about the unfortunate accident. She might have passed it on to Northaven. Susannah would not like gossip to circulate—but there was nothing very terrible about what had happened, so it did not matter. 'Let us forget him, Toby. I think the marquis is not a very nice man.'

'The devil he isn't!' Toby agreed forcefully. 'He has tried to get me to sit down to cards with him on several occasions. It did not please him that I refused.'

'No, I suppose it would not,' Susannah agreed. She pondered over the incident for a moment and then forgot it in the pleasure of driving on such a pleasant morning. Toby's curricle was well sprung and they went at a spanking pace.

They made good time and it was scarce noon when they all stopped to partake of light refreshments at an inn. After their repast, Toby was as good as his word, taking Amelia up with him for the remainder of the journey, so Susannah was in the carriage when they reached the Pendleton estate.

They drove through impressive iron gates, which had the word Pendleton worked into the arch above them and were opened by the gatehouse keeper. However, it was half an hour later before the house was first sighted through the trees. The estate of Pendleton consisted of two farms, besides several other good properties and substantial woods, also a village of some twenty cottages, a blacksmith and a sawmill. Far larger than anything Susannah could have imagined.

She craned to see out of the window as they approached the house. It was extremely large, built in the classical style of pale buff stone with a main building and a wing at either end; the windows were long, square paned and many, and a colonnade of white pillars ran the entire length of the front. Four steps led up to the imposing front door.

Grooms came running as soon as the carriages stopped, steps were let down and the ladies assisted to alight. The front door stood open, several footmen already on hand and a housekeeper dressed in black came down the steps to meet them.

'Welcome, ladies,' she said. 'I am Mrs Saunders. His lordship is out walking with a few of the gentlemen, but Lady Elizabeth awaits you in the front parlour with some of her other guests. You are not the first to arrive—we have had carriages from eleven o'clock this morning!'

'Good afternoon—or perhaps it is almost evening,' Mrs Hampton said. 'I am Mrs Hampton—this is Miss Royston and my daughter, Miss Hampton.'

'We are expecting you, ma'am,' the housekeeper said. 'Would you like to go straight up? I shall take you up myself, and send one of the footmen to let her ladyship know you are here.'

Mrs Hampton thanked her and they followed her into the house and up the stairs. They were conducted to the end of the first landing and then up some stairs to a further floor. Here they were taken through double doors into what was obviously a suite of rooms.

'This is the green suite, ma'am,' Mrs Saunders told them with a satisfied look about her. 'Royalty has stayed here in the past and the Duke of Marlborough. His lordship wanted you to be comfortable. You have two private sitting rooms and three bedrooms. When we have a party of guests it is nice to put them together—especially unmarried ladies.'

Susannah wandered round the sitting room while her mother and Amelia explored the other rooms and settled which would suit them and her. She trailed her hand over the shining surface of highly polished mahogany furniture, thinking that she had never seen anything quite so fine. The soft furnishings were a dark green-striped satin, the hangings a paler shade of the same material. There was a handsome bookcase, a desk and chair, as well as a display cabinet containing *objets d'art*. Something she found particularly pleasing was a collection of Meissen porcelain, little figures of monkeys dressed as French courtiers from the previous century and playing musical instruments. She took one of the figures out, examining it with pleasure until her mama returned.

'Come and see the bedchamber we thought you might like,' Mrs Hampton said. 'It has a beautiful view of the park and you can just see a lake in the distance. Pendleton is a large estate, Susannah.'

'Yes, Mama.' Susannah glanced at the fine paintings on the wall as she followed dutifully through the small hall into the bedroom her mother indicated. It was less formal than the sitting room, furnished in paler shades that she preferred, but still with that majestic mahogany furniture—making her very aware that she had never stayed in a house such as this one. Amelia's house was large and comfortable, but this... A little shiver ran down her spine. Could she ever be mistress of a house like Pendleton? Surely she was not worthy of the honour? There was so much she did not know. So many tasks that she feared might be beyond her. She had not realised until this moment just how wealthy and important Lord Pendleton really was. It struck her forcibly that her life would change completely once they were married. She had been living in a dream world, but this was reality! When Susannah had dreamed up her prince on a white horse, she had never thought beyond the moment when the prince took her into his arms and told her that he loved her.

As yet, Harry had merely told her that he had a warm regard for her. What did that mean exactly? Had he proposed because he could not live without her—or because she was suitable to be the mother of his children? Susannah felt a hollow sensation inside. Was she suitable to be any man's wife or a mother? And to be the chatelaine of such a house would be such a responsibility!

'Would you like this room?'

'Yes, of course, Mama,' Susannah said, becoming aware of her mother's odd look. 'I am quite content—unless you would like it?'

'I have chosen mine. Amelia and I thought you would like this one.'

'It will do very well.'

Susannah glanced out of the window. The view was magnificent and she could see the lake sparkling in the distance. Two people were walking towards the house. She could see them clearly, Lord Pendleton and Miss Hazledeane. Mrs Saunders had told them he was out with some gentlemen, but he had returned with his mother's ward. She had linked her arm through his and they seemed intent, engrossed in their conversation. Miss Hazledeane had a presence and seemed very sure of herself, as if she felt at home here.

Susannah could not help feeling a pang of what she suspected might be jealousy. It was very wrong of her, because Harry would naturally be on good terms with his mother's ward.

She drew away from the window and looked around the bedroom again. It was very grand, but she supposed she would get used to living in these surroundings after a while. She must if she were ever to live here as Harry's wife. She had thought only of love and romance, but now a few doubts had begun to creep in. Was she the right bride for Lord Pendleton? Could she do what was expected of her?

'Yes, Mama, it is a beautiful room,' she said, making an effort to smother her doubts. She took off her pelisse and laid it on the bed with her bonnet and gloves. 'It will seem more homely once I have some of my own things unpacked.'

'Yes, Susannah, it will,' Mrs Hampton agreed. She

moved to take Susannah's hand, holding it tightly. 'Are you feeling a little overcome, dearest?'

'I do not think I had imagined the house would be quite this large—or this grand, Mama. I am not sure I belong in a house like this....'

'But of course you feel strange at first,' Mrs Hampton said. 'We have never stayed in a house as grand as this one, I know. Papa's house was modest, and Amelia's— well, she makes one feel so very comfortable when one stays with her. This is a formal house, but I dare say parts of it are more like a home. These are the best guest chambers. We have been given them because we are honoured guests.'

'Yes, of course,' Susannah agreed. She took a deep breath. Her doubts were a mere irritation of nerves. No doubt she was not the first young woman to feel this way when confronted with her husband's home and family. She had yet to meet the family! She must hope that they found her suitable. 'I shall be comfortable here once I am settled, Mama. Please do not worry about me.'

Mrs Hampton pressed her hand. 'You are a sensible girl, Susannah. You know that you can always talk to me about anything that bothers you, do you not?'

'Yes, Mama, of course,' Susannah replied and smiled. 'Do you suppose we should go down?'

Even as she spoke, they heard a voice in the sitting room. Mrs Hampton smiled. 'I believe that is Lady Elizabeth come to welcome us.'

'Yes...'

Susannah followed her mother into the sitting room. Lady Elizabeth was greeting Amelia, but she turned with a smile as they entered, her eyes finding Susannah.

'Forgive me for not greeting you the moment you arrived,' she said, coming towards Susannah, hands outstretched. 'Mrs Hampton—Susannah. I hope you like your apartments?' She kissed Susannah on the cheek. 'They are a little formal, I know, but it meant you could all be together and I thought that might be more comfortable for Susannah. We shall be quite a large party once everyone gets here—quite a few single gentlemen—so it is nice for the single ladies to have their rooms together.'

'You are very thoughtful, ma'am,' Susannah said and smiled. It was impossible to feel awkward in the face of Lady Elizabeth's warmth. 'Thank you for arranging it so....'

Lady Elizabeth's eyes were knowing, filled with understanding. 'This is such a large house. When I first visited as a girl I was situated in the east wing and I was for ever losing my way. I once ended up in the gentlemen's wing, which might have been embarrassing. I did not wish it to happen to you. Now, Susannah, take my arm. We shall go down together. I was sorry that we did not see more of each other in Bath, but it was a short visit, because I needed to make sure everything was in order here. Now, my dear, take my arm, I want you to meet my friends. They are all eager to meet you.'

Susannah did as she was bid, laying her hand on Lady Elizabeth's arm and listening to her hostess talk as they went along the landing and back down the stairs to the first floor. Lady Elizabeth was still a very attractive lady with a smile much like her son's and Susannah was feeling more comfortable when they entered the large salon together. It was elegantly furnished, as was the rest of the house, but the atmosphere was softer here and the way the sofas and tables were arranged in small groups gave it a more intimate feeling. The colours were crimson, gold and cream, the furniture heavily gilded, as were the magnificent mirrors and pictures adorning the walls. There were some fifteen or more people in the room, some of them known to Susannah, others not. She saw the Earl of Ravenshead and Lady Manners, Miss Terry and her brother and several gentlemen she did not know.

'My cousin, the Earl of Elsham—Lord Marsham and Sir Henry Booker,' Lady Elizabeth said. 'Lady Elsham and Lady Booker...Lord Coleridge and the Earl of Ravenshead. You must know that Max and Gerard are particular friends of Harry's.'

'I have met them both, though Lord Coleridge only once,' Susannah said, offering her hand to the rather large and magnificent gentleman.

'It is a pleasure to meet you again,' Max Coleridge said, bold eyes twinkling. 'Harry tells me you mean to learn to drive, Miss Hampton. I should be delighted to tool you around the park whenever you wish.'

Susannah smiled and thanked him, desperately trying to remember the names as her hostess introduced her to more ladies. Several of them were older, relatives who had not been in London during the Season, but were obviously welcome guests here. Lady Ethel Booker was in her later years and slightly deaf. She used a lorgnette to good effect, training it on anyone she wished to inspect, and for the moment that appeared to be Susannah.

'Not a bad figure,' she remarked to her husband in a voice that carried a little too far. 'Better than I expected from a country nobody.'

'Be quiet, Ethel,' her husband said. 'You are speaking too loudly again.' He directed an apologetic smile towards Susannah, who could hardly meet his gaze, let alone return the smile.

It was obvious to Susannah that Harry's family were watching her, to see if she would do, and she was much afraid that she would be found lacking. How could she—an ordinary girl—be the right wife for Lord Pendleton when he lived in such splendour?

When Miss Terry and her brother addressed her she answered softly without her usual sparkle, feeling crushed by the weight of expectation all round. When she saw Miss Hazledeane enter the room looking relaxed, self-assured, her cheeks refreshed from a walk in the air, she felt as if she would have liked to run away. However, pride would not let her give in to such an unworthy urge and a moment later Toby came to her rescue.

'Ah, there you are,' he said and smiled at her. 'My mother isn't here yet, but she shouldn't be long in arriving. My sister Anne will be with her. At least there are a couple of ladies of your age, Susannah. Most of the old *crusties* are here, but you mustn't mind them. Their collective bark is worse than their bite. Here comes Harry....'

Even as he spoke Harry saw them and came towards them, a smile of welcome on his lips. 'I am glad you arrived safely, Susannah. I was not sure when to expect you—I thought later this evening—but Toby tells me you made very good time.'

'Yes, we did, sir,' Susannah said and gave him a shy smile. 'I am very glad to be here. You have a beautiful home.'

'Pendleton is a show place,' Harry told her. 'I am not sure I would call it home. I have other houses that are more comfortable I may show you one day, but the family likes to gather here for a few weeks in summer. It is large enough to hold them all should they wish to visit, and I believe most of them are coming this year.'

A smile of unholy amusement touched his lips. 'I am sure I have no idea why. Mama assures me that she did no more than issue the usual invitation.'

'I imagine an invitation to Pendleton must always be accepted.'

'Good lord, no! There are a couple here that haven't bothered for the past five years,' Harry said. 'I dare say they have their reasons for coming this time.' His eyes twinkled at her. 'They have come to inspect the new bride—which reminds me, you do not yet have your ring, my love. I shall give it to you later.'

'Yes...' Susannah glanced down at the points of her white satin shoes. 'You have extensive grounds. I should very much like to explore them one day.' She longed for him to say that they could go for a walk immediately, but he did not.

'You may walk where you wish, of course,' Harry told her. 'However, I shall take you driving tomorrow morning and you will get an idea of where everything is. I would not wish you to get lost and come to harm, Miss Pendleton.' He looked at Toby. 'I visited the stables earlier. You have done well. I heard there was a suitable pair and I am pleased with your choice. You have a good eye.'

'Thank you, Harry.' Toby looked pleased. 'I would have suggested a walk to the lake, Susannah, but Aunt Elizabeth is determined to show you off to everyone,' he said as Lady Elizabeth came towards them with an elderly lady in tow. 'I can't take too much of this! I am off. I shall see you at dinner, Susannah.'

Harry looked amused as his nephew made a beeline for the door. 'I would emulate Toby and escape with you, but I am afraid you will have to smile and bear it,

Susannah. By tomorrow they will all have satisfied their curiosity and you may escape with me to explore.'

Susannah met so many people before she was allowed to go and change for dinner that her head was whirling and she was afraid she would not recall all the names. She had not been sure what sort of a reception she would receive, but everyone seemed friendly enough. Most of them greeted her with a polite smile and she did not hear remarks about her person from anyone but Lady Booker, who had a habit of speaking loudly because she was deaf. However, from the smiles and nods she received during and after dinner, Susannah thought that she must have been generally approved—for the moment at least.

Susannah could not help wishing that they might have had a little time together before all his relatives arrived. She was trying to accustom herself to the idea that she was engaged to a man she loved—a man she was not sure felt quite the same about her. She knew that Harry felt something for her, but most marriages were arranged for reasons other than love, and she could not yet be certain that she was loved, as she would wish to be—to distraction.

Susannah would have felt her situation a little awkward even had she been sure that Harry was in love with her; only a girl of spirit could have coped with being thrust into a family gathering of this nature, and Susannah refused to be crushed by the weight of expectation. She would make every effort to enjoy this visit and she could hardly wait for the next morning so that she could escape for a while to go driving. Perhaps by the time they returned she would have more idea of how things stood.

* * *

She was relieved when she was alone in her room. Her maid helped her to undress, brushed her hair and wished her goodnight and Susannah got into bed. The mattress was harder than she was used to and, despite her efforts to settle, she tossed and turned for some minutes before getting up with a sigh of despair. She would fetch a book from the sitting room and read for a while.

The moon was shining full in the front windows of the sitting room. Susannah found herself drawn to them. She stood looking out for some minutes, and then she saw the man and the woman emerge from the shrubbery. They paused, embraced fervently, and then the man turned and walked away. Despite the moonlight, Susannah was unable to see their faces, though she suspected that the woman was Miss Hazledeane.

Who had she been meeting? Could it be the Marquis of Northaven—had he followed her here from Bath? Susannah frowned. Harry would be angry if that were the case. However, she could not be certain. It might have been Harry himself, for he had seemed quite happy in Miss Hazledeane's company when Susannah had seen them together earlier that day. No, no, that was a terrible thought! Completely disloyal and unworthy. Susannah did not know whether Harry truly loved her or not, but she was certain that he was not the kind of rogue who would kiss another woman when his fiancée slept only a short distance away.

She would not allow herself to be jealous of the other girl. If Harry had wished to marry her, he would not have spoken to Susannah. Her mind clear on that point, she wondered about the situation between Jenny Hazledeane and her lover.

Should she speak to Harry or keep Miss Hazledeane's

secret? A meeting at a teashop in Bath was one thing, but secret meetings in the moonlight were quite another. Miss Hazledeane was Lady Elizabeth's ward and she ought to behave circumspectly while living here. However, Susannah could not be certain of what she had seen. It would seem spiteful if she accused the woman of doing something she hadn't—besides, it really was not Susannah's place to spy on her.

She sighed and put the problem from her mind. She had problems enough of her own. She was still sure that she loved Harry, even though he appeared to have a temper when roused, but she was having doubts about the future. She had promised to wed Harry and it was what she truly wanted in her heart. Yet how could she ever be mistress of a house like this—the first lady of an illustrious family whose ancestors had entertained and even married with minor royalty? She was, as Lady Ethel had said, the daughter of a country nobody. In London that small fact had not seemed to matter. She had been swept off her feet by all the adulation she received, but here in this house everything seemed different. She was very conscious that the Pendleton family were watching her—waiting for her to make a mistake? Or perhaps she was judging them now?

Why had Harry asked her to be his wife? Was he marrying her because she was charming and beautiful—a suitable match and mother for his heir?

It would explain his anger in the inn yard, Susannah thought. He had spoken of being concerned for her—but had he also been concerned that scandal would ruin her good name? His own name and family clearly meant a great deal to him. He had still asked her to marry him, but how would he feel if there should be scandal over that incident? She remembered the way the Marquis of

Northaven had leered at her when she was leaving Bath in Toby's curricle. If there should be a stain on her reputation, Harry might wish that he had not spoken! Oh, she was foolish to let silly things haunt her! Harry had intended that this visit should be a pleasure and it would be if she could put her silly fears out of her head.

Susannah hunted for and chose a book of poetry she liked, taking it back to bed with her. She read for a while, then felt sleepy and blew out her candle. As she turned over to sleep, she was aware of a feeling of disappointment. She was not sure that she cared to be married because she was beautiful and would make a suitable wife. She wanted Harry to be madly in love with her. She wanted him to kiss her, not as he had when he proposed, but hungrily with a passion that overtook them both....

Chapter Seven

Susannah ate rolls and honey and drank chocolate in the private sitting room with Amelia; Mrs Hampton had hers in bed, as was her custom. Amelia seemed a little quiet and she looked tired. Susannah suspected she had not slept as well as she might, but she refrained from asking questions. She was not as impulsive as she had been, and Amelia was entitled to her secrets. If she had news, she would tell Susannah, because they were friends.

'What do you mean to do this morning?' Amelia asked, as if making an effort to rouse herself from her reverie.

'Harry is taking me for a drive around the estate,' Susannah said. 'I do not know if he will let me take the reins, though he has promised to teach me.'

'Yes, you should learn,' Amelia said and smiled. 'I learned when I was younger than you. It is a useful skill.'

'What will you do this morning?'

'Miss Hazledeane asked me if I liked to walk. We

may walk later,' Amelia said. 'However, I shall not go down just yet for I have some letters of business to write. I advertised for a companion before we left town. I had several answers, but only one appealed to me. I have decided to ask a Miss Emily Barton to come for an interview when I return to my estate.'

'Oh...' Susannah nodded. 'Yes, you will feel lonely when Mama and I leave you. If—if I should be the mistress here, you will come and stay sometimes, won't you?'

'What do you mean, "if"? You are not thinking of crying off?'

'Oh, no, of course not. I—I was not certain where we shall live. I believe Harry has other houses...'

'Yes, I am certain he does.' Amelia looked at her thoughtfully. 'Of course I shall come to stay wherever you are, dearest, and I hope that you will stay with me now and then. If you were not mistress here, but somewhere else, it would be just the same.' She smiled. 'I know it all seems strange and overpowering at first, my love. You will be surprised at how soon you will become accustomed to living here.'

'I might have known you would see how I feel,' Susannah replied and laughed. 'I still love him, Amelia, of course I do—but this house...all those relatives looking at me as if I might suddenly grow another head! I confess it has made me wonder if I am equal to the position of Lord Pendleton's wife.'

'It really was too bad of Lady Elizabeth to invite them all so soon,' Amelia said and looked amused. 'I am glad you can laugh, dearest. Last night you looked so crushed. I wanted to comfort you, but I did not wish to interfere, for your mama will say everything necessary I am sure.'

'Mama is always good to me, but I know she has her heart set on the match,' Susannah said. 'She wants to see me settled and it is a good match, Amelia. Mama would not need to worry about paying her bills—I am sure that Pendleton would see her comfortably settled.'

'An excellent match,' Amelia agreed. 'But your mama wants you to be happy. Do not feel that you are trapped, Susannah. If you really feel unable to go through with it, you may withdraw—now I have said too much!'

'You could never do that,' Susannah said and got up to kiss her cheek. 'I am feeling a little...*trapped* is not quite the word. I think *unworthy* might be a better one.'

'Susannah, dearest,' Amelia said, 'Harry is fortunate to get you. I have found you quite the kindest, most thoughtful girl. Believe me, this feeling of being inadequate will pass. You will grow into the position, my love—and you will do it well.'

'You always understand. If it were not for you, none of this would have happened for me. I might never have met Harry at all.'

'I am glad to have been of help to you, but I should feel guilty if you married and were unhappy.'

'I think I shall be happy married to Harry,' Susannah said. 'But only if he loves me. I am not so sure that I shall ever enjoy being Lady Pendleton with all that it means.'

'I am certain he does love you, and you will grow accustomed to the responsibility in time,' Amelia said. 'But you must talk to Harry about this, dearest.'

A knock at the door interrupted them, and a maid came in. She bobbed a curtsy and looked at Susannah.

'Lord Pendleton asked if you were ready to join him, Miss Hampton.'

'Yes, I have finished my breakfast. You may tell his lordship that I shall be down in five minutes.' She headed for the bedroom as the maid departed. 'I must get ready, for I do not wish to keep Lord Pendleton waiting.'

Susannah snatched up the bonnet her maid had set ready for her, and draped a light stole over her arms, then pulled on a pair of leather gloves. She would not need a pelisse, for it was a lovely day.

Harry looked at Susannah as she came downstairs to greet him. She was wearing a carriage gown of green striped with white and trimmed with a white band at the hem. Her stole, boots and gloves were white, her straw bonnet trimmed with green ribbons. She looked beautiful and his heart turned over. He wanted to sweep her into his arms and tell her of his love, but before he could speak he saw his nephew coming towards them.

'You look beautiful, Susannah,' Toby told her as she reached the bottom of the stairs. 'Harry is fortunate to have secured you as his bride. I shall be riding to the village this morning, but this afternoon you must allow me to show you the lake from the other side. It cannot be reached except on foot.'

'How kind,' Susannah said and bestowed a warm smile on him. 'I can see it from my window and I shall enjoy the walk—but this morning I am looking forward to my drive.' She looked at Harry. 'May I hope that you will allow me to drive your horses, sir?'

'I have purchased a suitable pair for that very reason,' Harry told her and smiled as her face lit up with pleasure. 'Toby was my agent and he has proved a good judge. They are not mad devils like my blacks, but well-bred creatures that are used to a lady's hand.'

'Oh, then I shall be able to manage them more easily

than his,' Susannah said innocently, forgetting that her lessons with Toby were supposed to be a secret. Harry shot a sharp look at his nephew, who was trying to look unaffected, but failing. 'Shall we go—they will not enjoy being kept waiting, will they?'

'You understand your horses better than I imagined,' Harry said and nodded meaningfully at his nephew. 'I shall see you later, Toby. Would you be good enough to call on me in the library after nuncheon?'

'Yes, of course, Harry,' Toby said, a look of discomfort in his eyes. 'Enjoy your drive, Susannah.'

Harry followed Susannah as she went outside. She had gone immediately to the horses and was patting them, stroking their noses and admiring them. She turned to him as he came up with her.

'How lovely they are! It was so kind of you to purchase them for my benefit, sir.'

'You used to call me Pendleton. I prefer it. Sir makes me feel as if I am old enough to be your father.'

'Does it? Forgive me, Pendleton,' she said, her eyes clear and free of guile. 'I did not mean to offend you, especially after such kindness.'

'It is little enough,' Harry said, feeling cross for no reason. Anyone would think she was talking to a kind uncle instead of her fiancé! He gave her his hand, helping her up and taking his seat beside her. 'Would you like to show me what you can do?' When she hesitated, he looked at her hard. 'I know Toby has been giving you lessons—the young idiot. He drives horses I gave him as a birthday gift and they are far too strong for a lady! Now I understand why they bolted like that! He was not in control of them—you were.'

'Oh…' Susannah looked at him uncertainly. 'Please do not be angry with us, and especially not with Toby. I teased him into giving me lessons, you know. I did very well until the horses bolted and then of course I could not hold them.'

'I am not cross with you,' Harry said, though he did not smile in the way she loved.

Susannah looked at him a little uncertainly. He seemed serious but perhaps he was not angry. Some of the tightness eased in her chest. He had bought these horses to please her, so he must be quite fond of her.

She took the reins he held out to her, holding them lightly in one hand and accepting the whip he presented with the other. Harry nodded his approval. Encouraged, she gave the order to walk on. Immediately, she understood the difference, for Toby's horses had been restive, always impatient to be off. This pair of fine horses behaved perfectly, responding to the slightest flick on the reins.

'Oh, how lovely,' Susannah cried after they had been driving for a few minutes. 'So perfectly matched and such polite creatures. One feels that a society hostess has taught them their manners, for they would not dream of disobeying or doing anything outrageous!'

Harry burst into laughter, causing Susannah to glance at him, a twinkle in her eyes. 'Yes, exactly,' Harry agreed. 'I thought them just right for a lady to drive. I am glad you are pleased with them. One thing I would suggest...' He hesitated. 'If I may? If you place your thumb so, it might be a little easier. I find it better like this...' He placed his hands over hers, positioning them at a slightly different angle.

'Oh, yes, that is easier,' Susannah said. 'I have noticed before that you hold your reins in a different way. It did not occur to me that it might make the control easier, but now I see that it does.'

Harry nodded. 'It is a personal preference. Most of us have our differences. Gerard is a fine whip and Max is perhaps even better. I think Toby is getting there and in a short time he may achieve his desire to join the Four-in-Hand. He has been put on probation and, if he does nothing to arouse censure, will given full membership quite soon, I think.'

'I have driven my horses at a walk and a trot,' Susannah said, glancing at him. 'When do you think I shall be ready to race them?'

'Would you wish to?' Harry studied her face. 'It is not unknown for a lady to race her team on a private estate—but it is not encouraged. Are you brave enough to face the thought of gossip? And who do you intend to race?'

'Oh, perhaps Toby,' Susannah said, then remembered that she was about to become Harry's wife and ought to behave with the proper decorum. 'But perhaps I should not think of it. I would not wish to be thought fast.'

'It would be thought fast if the race took place in public, but some ladies have the courage and the credit to carry it off. Perhaps in a few months you might have sufficient skill to try in private, though I am not sure you would find Toby eager to race you.'

'Why?'

'If he let you win, you would be angry with him, but if he beat you, he would be afraid of being thought a bad sport and it might offend his notions of gallantry. I, on the other hand, would have no such scruples. You will have to work hard to beat me.'

Susannah stared at him in wonder. 'You would race me?'

'When I consider you have the skill,' Harry told her with a wicked smile that made her heart race. 'Now, I think you should give your horses their heads and see what they can do—don't you?'

'Oh, thank you,' Susannah said, her eyes bright with excitement. 'I shall keep you to your word, I promise you!'

Susannah had never enjoyed a drive more! As they approached the front of the house at the end of some two hours, during which she had learned so much that Toby had not thought to tell her, Susannah knew that she had discovered a pleasure that would last throughout her life. Any fear she might have had of handling the horses had fled as Harry put her through her paces, encouraging her to gallop her team for short spaces, showing her how to bring them back to a trot and then a walk. They had spent a long time perfecting a turn, and she had learned how to back her horses up, something she would never have dreamed she could do.

'You are a wonderful teacher,' Susannah declared as a groom came to take the reins and Harry helped her down from the curricle. He stood for a moment with his hands about her waist, his eyes intent on her face. 'I did enjoy myself so much!'

'Then we shall drive out again tomorrow,' Harry said. He smiled in the way that made her breath catch in her throat. For a moment she thought he would kiss her as she longed to be kissed, but he moved away from her and the moment passed. 'We must go in now, for Mama will expect us to nuncheon. I know you are engaged to Toby for the afternoon, and I have promised to keep my uncle Booker company on a tour of the estate, so I shall see you this evening, Susannah. Enjoy your walk.'

'Yes, I am sure I shall.'

Harry was being scrupulously polite, just as he was

in the drawing room in London society. Susannah felt a little bewildered. Was this the way they would always live? Behaving politely to each other, considering their guests and talking as friends, but nothing more? Susannah knew it was the way many couples lived, making the best of their marriages of convenience and taking lovers or a mistress in secret. Discretion was all, the public face everything.

It was not what she wanted! Not what she had hoped for when she dreamed of her marriage—but this was reality, not a dream.

She frowned and turned, walking swiftly up to the house. She must have the smell of the horses on her clothes and needed to change before presenting herself for nuncheon. As she was going upstairs, she met Miss Hazledeane coming down.

'You should hurry or you will be late,' Miss Hazledeane said as she came down. 'You would not wish to keep everyone waiting, I dare say—even if you are going to marry Lord Pendleton.'

Something in her tone made Susannah wonder what she had done to upset Miss Hazledeane. However, she passed by without answering—she had no wish to quarrel with her.

Having changed her clothes, Susannah went down to the dining parlour as quickly as she could. Most of the guests were already there, helping themselves to an informal buffet. Miss Hazledeane was standing next to Harry at the serving table, smiling at him as he filled her plate for her. She gave Susannah an odd smirk as she took the plate to the table and sat down. People were sitting wherever they wished rather than in the places allotted in the more formal dinner arrangements.

Susannah took a plate and joined the line, choosing some cold lamb, green peas and small new potatoes with a little mint relish.

Harry had taken his place at table, sitting between one of his elderly aunts and his friend Max Coleridge. She watched as he listened attentively to his aunt until she turned to the person at her other hand, and then began speaking to Max. Sitting further down the table, Susannah could not catch more than a few words of what they were saying, but she thought it concerned horses.

'How do you like Pendleton, Miss Hampton?'

Susannah turned to her right and discovered that the Earl of Ravenshead had taken the seat beside her. He was smiling at her and she immediately felt at ease, for his look was one of approval.

'I like it very well, sir. Lord Pendleton took me driving this morning, but I do not think we saw the half of it for we kept to good roads so that I could learn to handle my team, and I dare say there are many bridle paths that will be exciting to explore. I am to walk as far as the lake this afternoon.'

'You will enjoy that, I am certain. The lake is natural, though it has been enlarged and landscaped,' Gerard told her. 'Pendleton is a large estate, though not, I believe, Harry's favourite home. He has a smaller estate he favours when he has time to go there. I believe he spends only a few weeks of the year here.'

'Yes, I think he mentioned something of the kind.'

'These large houses are very well for a family gathering such as this,' Gerard told her. 'I would not care to live here all the time, and I do not think Harry does—but no doubt he will tell you about it.'

'Yes, perhaps,' Susannah said. 'I believe you have a fine estate yourself, sir?'

'It is not as large as Harry's,' Gerard told her. 'It was mortgaged, but I have managed to pay my father's debts. However, I am not sure whether it will suit me to live there.'

'You would not sell your family home?'

'Perhaps.' He looked thoughtful and glanced across the table, at Amelia, Susannah thought. 'I have considered living abroad, but as yet my plans are unformed...'

'I am sure all your friends would miss you if you did,' Susannah said and blushed. 'I am too forward, sir. I should not have voiced an opinion.'

'I invited it by speaking my thoughts aloud,' Gerard said. He looked as if he had surprised himself by doing so and proceeded to change the subject. 'Besides, as Harry's wife you are entitled to speak to me as a friend. I hope we shall always be friends.' He smiled at her. 'Now, tell me, Miss Hampton, how are your driving lessons proceeding?'

Susannah told him enthusiastically. She wondered why he had confided as much as he had in her—was she supposed to pass the information on to Amelia? She did not think that she would do so, for he must tell Amelia himself if he wished her to know.

After nuncheon the party dispersed. Many of the older guests had wandered out to the gardens, where chairs had been set under the trees so that they could sit in the shade and enjoy the sunshine. Susannah fetched her bonnet, stole and parasol, meeting Toby in the hall, as arranged. He smiled at her and offered his arm.

'I saw you talking to the Earl of Ravenshead at nuncheon,' Toby said. 'He is one of the members of the Four-in-Hand who will either approve or disapprove my membership. I rather wanted a word with him myself. He has proved elusive so far, but I shall see if I can corner him after dinner.'

'Perhaps in the billiard room,' Susannah suggested. 'Invite him to play and you may have a chance to speak privately.'

'You are always so easy to talk to,' Toby confided. 'I couldn't talk to most young ladies the way I do to you, Susannah. You are a good sport! You understand the way a man feels.'

'I think we are good friends,' Susannah told him with a smile. They were walking at a leisurely pace, leaving the formal gardens and the sound of laughter and voices behind. 'I am beginning to enjoy myself at last. I felt terrible yesterday, but it is better today.'

'You mustn't let the old *crusties* upset you,' Toby said. 'They are curious, that's all, mainly because Harry has never shown an interest in a young lady before. Not one he could possibly marry, anyway.'

'Never?' Susannah glanced at him. 'Not even when he was first on the town?'

'To my knowledge,' Toby said. 'My mother is delighted that he is to be married at last.' He pulled a face. 'I suppose it is time, but I hope Mama does not start making plans for my marriage next.'

Susannah went into a peal of delighted laughter, and then stopped as she saw his face fall. 'My dearest friend! Forgive me, please. It is just that I do not see you tied to a lady's petticoats. I think you enjoy your freedom too much.'

'Yes, for a few years yet. Besides, I dare say I would be lucky to get someone to take me, because I am something of a madcap,' Toby said and grinned. 'I suppose that is why I like you so much. You always tell me the truth and you make no demands. I suppose a wife might—' He stopped and pointed ahead. 'There's the lake—fine, ain't it?'

'Yes, it is lovely,' Susannah agreed, watching the play of sunlight on the water. Two swans were sailing majestically towards the far side. 'Does anyone ever go on the lake?'

'Boating, you mean?' Toby grinned. 'Harry took me when I was a lad, but I don't think the boathouse has been used in years.'

'Oh...' Susannah glanced towards the other side of the lake, at what was obviously the boathouse, though it had been built in a very grand style that looked more like a Roman temple. 'I thought I saw someone leaving as we approached, though I am not certain.'

'You intrigue me,' Toby said. 'Shall we walk to the other side and take a look inside? It may be locked, of course.' He offered her his hand. 'Come, the path is narrow and sometimes a little slippery. Let me help you.'

Susannah took his hand. However, they soon discovered that the path was quite dry and it looked as if someone had walked there recently, for the long grass had been flattened.

'Someone must have been here more often than I thought,' Toby said. 'Perhaps Harry intends to have the boats out this season.'

'Yes...' Susannah's keen eyes had spotted something lying in the tall grasses to one side of the path and she bent to pick it up. She saw at once that it was a woman's kerchief. Toby was just ahead of her and had not noticed, so she slipped the scrap of lace into her pocket. 'What fun it would be to spend an afternoon here. We could have a picnic and take turns on the lake.'

Toby was striding ahead now that he knew Susannah

was in no danger of slipping. He ran the last few steps to the boathouse and tried the door, giving an exclamation of annoyance as he discovered it was locked after all. He found a large stone to stand on and put his face to the window, peering inside. Susannah stood beside him, watching as he rubbed at the glass.

'I would not say anyone has been here for years,' he said as he got down. 'However, I dare say Harry would have it opened up if we asked him.'

'Oh, yes, we must,' Susannah cried, eyes sparkling. 'I should love to go on the lake.'

'We'll ask him at tea,' Toby said and grinned at her. 'I usually find the summer visit rather a bore, but it certainly looks like being more fun this year—and that is down to you, Susannah.'

Susannah laughed and took his arm. 'You are such a good friend, Toby.'

'It is a pity all females are not as easy to please as you.'

They made their way home, arms linked, laughing and talking, in such accord that anyone who saw them together could not doubt the real affection between them.

Standing at the back of the house with one of his grooms, Harry saw the couple and felt a twinge of regret. They looked so young and eager and he felt himself to be too old for Susannah, perhaps too set in his ways. She had promised to be his wife, but he was not certain that her heart was truly engaged. He knew that he could have offered for a dozen young ladies and been accepted, but only one had made him wish for her company on a permanent basis.

Susannah had seen him. She waved and then broke

from Toby and ran to him, her face glowing with health and the fresh air.

'We have been to the boathouse,' she told him. 'Toby says that you used to have boats on the lake, Pendleton—please may we have them this year? I should so like to go on the lake.' Her eyes appealed to him, making Harry's heart lurch. She was so very lovely, so sweet and innocent.

'If you wish it, of course. I shall instruct the servants to make all ready, Susannah—but I think it will take a day or two for them to inspect the boats and make sure they are safe to use.'

'Thank you so much!' Susannah clapped her hands and turned to Toby as he came up to them. 'Harry says we can have the boats. Is that not exciting? You must promise to take me in one as soon as they are ready.'

'We shall have a picnic by the lake as we used to,' Harry told her and smiled, because her enthusiasm was infectious. 'The day after tomorrow.' He offered her his arm. 'Come, we should go in, Susannah. Mama told me that she wished for a few moments with you before tea—if you will oblige her. She is in her private sitting room. I shall take you up to her now.'

'Oh...' She gave him a tremulous smile. 'I have hardly had time to talk to her since my arrival, because there are so many people and they all wish to talk to me.'

'That is why Mama asked for a few minutes alone.' Harry smiled at her. 'There is no need to be nervous. She is already very fond of you...' He hesitated for a moment. 'Susannah...I too have been hoping for a little time alone with you. I know that we went driving this morning, but you needed to concentrate on your horses. I feel we need to talk. Do you think you might come down to the library a little earlier than usual?'

'Oh...' Susannah looked shy, her cheeks pinker than normal. 'Yes, of course—if you wish it, Pendleton.'

'I think we must talk privately,' Harry told her and stopped walking. 'Here we are—Mama's sitting room. I shall take you in and then leave you to talk together.' He carried her hand to his lips, dropping a kiss in the palm. 'Until this evening, Susannah...'

Susannah discovered that Lady Elizabeth was as kind and gentle as she appeared, making her feel at ease and assuring her of her welcome at Pendleton.

'I am sorry the relatives have been so particular with you, my dear,' she told Susannah as they sat together in her elegant sitting room, which was comfortable and pretty, just like its owner. 'You must know that Harry has never asked me to invite a young lady to this gathering before. Now that he has chosen a wife, they are all curious. Our little visit here is usually just for the family and a few of Harry's gentlemen friends. Everyone was excited to meet you, naturally, but Lady Booker does tend to be rather outspoken, and she does not realise how her voice carries. I do hope you were not uncomfortable yesterday?'

'A little at first,' Susannah admitted shyly. 'I was not expecting quite so many people—or such a magnificent house.'

'Ah, yes, the house...' Lady Elizabeth laughed softly. 'It is rather awe-inspiring. When I first came here I was terrified. I almost broke off my engagement, for I did not think that I was suitable to be chatelaine of such a house. However, my husband was madly in love with me and he persuaded me that the house was not important. He promised me that we should spend only a part of our lives here, and he kept his word.'

'You were frightened at first?' Susannah was surprised, for her hostess appeared to have been born to her role in life. 'I have never stayed in such a large house before—and there are so many treasures. I am almost afraid to touch anything.'

'Accumulated over the years and worth a king's ransom in themselves,' Lady Elizabeth agreed. 'Harry is the custodian of Pendleton, Susannah. His duty is to preserve the estate and its treasures for his sons, and he takes such things very seriously. Perhaps too seriously. He was very different as a young man, but he has had much to do to ensure that the estate is in good shape. However, I am very certain that he will not wish to live here all the time.' She gave Susannah a reassuring nod. 'His apartments are in the west wing. I have no doubt he will show you one day. If you wish it, I shall take you on a tour of the rest of the house tomorrow, after you return from driving with my son.'

Susannah looked at her thoughtfully. 'Do you think that I would be a worthy chatelaine of a house like this, ma'am?'

'Please, you must call me Elizabeth in private.' Lady Elizabeth's smile was warm. 'If you make my son happy, that is all I ask, my dear. As for the rest—I shall always be near at hand if you need me. I should not dream of interfering, but if you wish for help I am always ready to give it. I can teach you the things you need to know. Besides, the servants are so well trained that you will hardly need to do anything except keep your accounts and inspect the menus.'

'Oh…' Susannah blushed. 'I shall try, but I am sure there must be much more to marriage.'

Lady Elizabeth smiled gently. 'Harry will teach you, my dear. My son is meticulous in all things.'

'Yes, he is,' Susannah agreed. She could not tell her kind hostess that Harry's attention to detail and preference for perfection were exactly what frightened her. 'I am not certain that I can live up to his example, ma'am.'

Lady Elizabeth went into a peal of laughter. 'Oh, my dear, do not put my son on a pedestal. I assure you that he has his failings, as you will no doubt discover before too long.'

'I know that he has a temper sometimes...'

'He is also very untidy and he can be both arrogant and blind to something that is under his nose. However, he is very dear to me and the kindest of men.'

'Yes,' Susannah said and smiled. She liked Harry's mother very well indeed, and this little talk had made her feel better.

Susannah chose a simple white evening dress, which she wore with a spangled stole and a string of seed pearls. She had some pearl earrings her mama had given her and she chose those to finish her ensemble. She was trembling inside as she left the apartments she shared with her mother and Amelia and made her way to the library.

Entering, she saw that Harry was standing by the fireplace. He was dressed in a coat of blue superfine and pale cream breeches, his cravat a miracle of his valet's art and set off by a magnificent diamond pin. On the little finger of his right hand he wore a diamond ring that sparkled in the light of the candles. He smiled as she entered, his gaze intent as she walked towards him.

'You look beautiful, as always, Susannah. Thank you for coming so promptly.'

'I knew you were waiting for me,' Susannah said and

smiled at him a little uncertainly. 'You wished to talk to me?'

'Yes.' Harry reached for her hand, taking it and kissing it, as he had earlier. Susannah felt a tingle down her spine as she looked up and saw his hot gaze. She could no longer doubt that he had feelings for her. 'I wanted to give you this…' He took her left hand and slipped a beautiful diamond-and-emerald ring onto the third finger of her left hand. 'I ought to have given you a ring sooner, but I had this made specially and it arrived this afternoon.'

'Thank you. It is lovely, but…' She hesitated, gazing up at him earnestly. 'Are you certain that I am worthy to be your wife? I know you offered and I accepted, but… are you perfectly sure that you truly want me?'

'Worthy…' Harry frowned. 'I suppose you mean this wretched house and its treasures? You will discover that they are a liability we have to cope with as best we can. If I could please myself, I should sell them and live modestly, but we are merely the custodians and must preserve them for the future.'

'Your mama explained,' Susannah told him shyly. 'She said that she too felt overcome when she first came here and almost broke off her engagement.'

'Yes, she told me that too.' Harry laughed wryly. He moved closer, reaching out to touch her face. His fingers stroked her cheek lightly, sending little shivers up and down Susannah's spine and making her long for something that she did not understand. 'How can you doubt that I want you, Susannah? I have thought that perhaps it was not fair to expect so much of you. The house is a responsibility, of course, and I am older…'

'But I care for you,' Susannah said impulsively.

'Surely that is more important than any other considerations?'

'My wise little love,' Harry said in voice made deep by emotion. 'I shall speak to your mama about the date of the wedding, but we shall not rush, for we need to know each other better, I think.'

Susannah looked at her ring. The emerald was a bright, clear green and flawless, the diamonds surrounding it brilliant and white.

'It is beautiful,' she breathed. 'I have never seen anything as lovely. Thank you so much for giving it to me.'

'It pales into insignificance beside your beauty,' Harry said. He reached for her, drawing her close and kissing her softly on the lips. 'I have been wanting to kiss you all day, but it is difficult to be alone with you while everyone is here. Perhaps you will allow me to teach you the ways of love, dearest? You are very young and I prefer to take things slowly.'

'Do you, Harry?' Susannah's eyes were bright with mischief. She felt a surge of confidence as she saw the heat in his eyes. 'I rather think I should like you to kiss me again, please.'

'Minx!' Harry laughed and drew her hard against him, kissing her in a way that took her breath and was very different from the first kiss. She trembled as she felt a rush of desire, awakening feelings she had not realised existed. 'You will get more of that if you tease me, miss!'

'Shall I?' Susannah asked and giggled. 'Then I must think of ways to tease you, sir.'

'What happened to Harry?' he asked, his eyes on fire. 'You used my name just now and I like it. I think you will lead me a pretty dance, Susannah, but you have found the way to my heart and I am never happy unless you are near. I suppose we must go and face them all now, my love. My fond relatives have been eagerly awaiting the arrival of my bride. It is our duty to entertain them.'

'Did you know that Toby calls them the old *crusties*?' Susannah said innocently. She laughed as she saw his expression. 'Yes, it is too bad of him, isn't it?'

'He will lead you into trouble or you him,' Harry said and looked resigned. 'Come along then, Susannah. Dinner awaits us....'

Now that she was wearing the ring, everyone decided that their engagement was official. Before this evening the relatives had been watching her curiously, but now the barriers were down and they all tried to talk at once, wanting to be the first to wish her happiness. Susannah thought she would drown under the weight of congratulations. Everyone came to kiss her and the gentlemen shook Harry's hand. Lady Elizabeth presented her with a small gift, which turned out to be a beautiful pearl necklace.

'I thought he might give you the ring this evening and I brought this with me just in case,' she told Susannah. 'I am so pleased, my dear. Everyone is happy that Harry will be settled at last. We had begun to think he might never marry.'

Toby's mother, Lady Sinclair, added her good wishes. 'I am very fond of my brother. I have been telling Harry to find a bride for the past two years. He could not have chosen better, Susannah. I am so pleased that you accepted him, my dear. I shall look forward to having a sister.'

Since everyone seemed of the same opinion, Susannah

was carried through the evening on a wave of excitement. Harry's relatives had accepted her; they were willing to give her a chance to prove herself and she knew that she must not let them down.

'I wish you all the happiness in the world,' Toby said and kissed her cheek. 'I have a gift for you. I shall give it to you tomorrow.'

'Thank you.' Susannah smiled and glanced at Harry, surprising an odd look in his eyes. He looked serious... no, there was some other emotion in his eyes, but she was not certain of its meaning.

Toby moved on and she saw him talking with Amelia. Susannah found herself alone for the first time that evening.

'You must be very pleased with yourself. Pendleton is a wonderful catch for a girl like you.'

Susannah turned as she heard Miss Hazledeane's voice. It was clear that she was both annoyed and jealous, her eyes hard with dislike. Susannah wondered if she had hoped to catch Harry for herself.

'I am very fortunate,' she said, keeping a fixed smile in place. For some reason her eyes were drawn to a lace kerchief tucked into the sash at Miss Hazledeane's waist. She knew at once that it was exactly like the one she had found near the lake. 'Have you lost a kerchief? I found one near the boathouse this afternoon. It is in my room.'

'It cannot be mine,' Miss Hazledeane said and, if anything, her look of dislike deepened. 'I do not know why you should think it. I have never been there.'

'Oh...' Susannah frowned—she would swear that the kerchief matched the one Miss Hazledeane had and her perfume was the same as that which lingered on the kerchief. 'I must be mistaken, then.'

'Yes, you are. Besides, my kerchief is a gift from Lady Elizabeth, so if you found one it is most probably hers.'

'Perhaps…' Susannah was thoughtful as the other woman moved away from her. It had been clear to her from the beginning that Lady Elizabeth's ward did not like her. However, why stress the point that it was not her kerchief so strongly? There could be no harm in her having dropped it near the boathouse.

'Well, dearest,' Harry said, driving the thought from her head. 'We must go into dinner or my chef will hand in his notice and that would be a disaster. I have engaged to play billiards with Gerard and Max later—but if I do not see you alone again this evening I wish you sweet dreams.' He pressed her hand. 'Do not forget our arrangement for the morning, my love. I cannot wait to get you to myself again. There are far too many people here….'

Susannah laughed, forgetting the small mystery of Miss Hazledeane's kerchief. She would return it to Lady Elizabeth in the morning and then perhaps the mystery would be solved.

Chapter Eight

Susannah left the kerchief lying on the chest in her bedchamber when she went driving with Harry the next morning. It had slipped her mind in the excitement, for she had found a pile of presents by her plate when she took breakfast with Amelia in their sitting room. Everyone had sent her something—some were small gifts like lace kerchiefs, but there were several gifts of silver, and one that she liked very much was a whip of soft leather with a chased silver grip from Toby.

'Isn't that thoughtful of him?' she said, showing it to Amelia. 'Lady Elizabeth gave me those beautiful pearls last evening—and now all these. I am so fortunate.'

'They are merely tokens of affection,' Amelia told her, giving her a small box, which contained a gold stickpin to wear in her cravat when she went riding or driving. 'I am certain you will receive many more expensive gifts when you marry.'

'But everyone is so kind,' Susannah said. 'You in particular have given me so much, Amelia. I owe everything to you!'

'I have done very little,' Amelia told her. 'It was your own sweet nature that secured you Harry Pendleton's affections. However, I should like to give you a wedding at my estate—unless you plan to marry here at Pendleton?'

'I do not know,' Susannah said. 'I think I should like to be married from your house, Amelia, but I must ask Harry what he thinks. Are you sure you would wish all the trouble and expense of a wedding?'

'It would give me the greatest pleasure,' Amelia said. 'If you would prefer it, I could speak to Harry and ask him if he would be agreeable to letting me give you the wedding as my gift to you both.'

'Yes, perhaps that might be best,' Susannah agreed happily. 'And now I must go down, for I do not wish to keep Harry waiting.'

'No, you must not keep him waiting,' Amelia told her. 'I shall speak to Harry about the wedding this afternoon. Have you any idea of when it might be?'

'We have not discussed it as yet,' Susannah said. 'Perhaps I shall know more when I return.'

'Yes, I am sure you will,' Amelia said. 'I believe I shall go for a walk this morning. The weather has been so lovely of late. I am not sure how long it will last.'

'Oh, I hope it will not break before tomorrow,' Susannah said. 'Harry has promised us a picnic by the lake.' She smiled because everything was so wonderful and nothing could possibly spoil her happiness now.

That morning's expedition proved even better than her first attempt at driving Harry's horses. Harry was solicitous for her comfort and did everything possible to make the outing a happy one for her. They drove through the park and reached a secluded area, well out of sight of the house, and there he suggested they stopped, looping the reins and securing them, before helping Susannah down.

'The horses will do well enough under the trees for a few minutes,' he told her, his smile making her heart race. 'I thought we would walk for a moment, because I cannot kiss you as I would wish to in the curricle.'

'Harry...' Susannah was breathless as he took her into his arms, gazing down at her with such heat that she felt a tingle of something she realised must be desire. Her heart raced as his lips touched hers, her body melting into him, her own lips parting as she felt the touch of his tongue. His kiss made her feel very strange and filled her with longing for things she hardly understood. He caressed her cheek and pressed his lips to her throat, making her whimper his name. 'Harry...I do like that very much...'

'Do you, my dearest?' His hand caressed her breast over the softness of her habit, making her stomach spasm with desire. She wished that there was nothing between his hand and her skin, for she would have enjoyed the feel of his fingers on her flesh, but she did not dare to say it. 'I like it very much too. I want so much more of you, Susannah. I had planned to wait, but would you mind very much if we were to marry as soon as the banns are called?'

'I should like that,' she said and gave him a shy smile. 'Amelia is going to ask if you would permit her to hold the wedding at her home. I was not sure...'

'Is that your wish?' Harry asked, gazing at her. 'We must invite all my relatives and it would be easy here, but if you should like it I will agree to holding it at Amelia's home.'

'I think I should like it,' Susannah told him. 'Could

we not have a small wedding at Amelia's and then hold a large reception here for everyone?'

'Yes, we could,' Harry agreed. 'I think I should quite like a quiet wedding myself—perhaps twenty or thirty of our closest friends and relatives. Mama would enjoy giving a huge reception here a day or so later.'

'Then perhaps you would suggest that to Amelia when she speaks to you?'

'Certainly,' Harry agreed. 'We shall say one month from now—and that will give me time to make some changes to my apartments here. I had them refurbished a year or so ago, but you may wish for changes.'

'Oh, I should like to see them as they are now—will you show me?'

'Yes, of course. You might like to help choose the colours for your own bedchamber?'

'I think that would be fun,' Susannah told him. 'Amelia had made changes to her aunt's home and I thought she had done them so beautifully that I would enjoy doing something similar one day.'

'You may make as many changes to my homes as you please,' Harry said. 'I think perhaps—' He broke off as they both heard screaming and the sounds of a struggle. 'That sounds as if it is coming from over there...look! Is that not Amelia?'

'Yes...' Susannah saw her friend running towards them. She appeared to be in great distress. Without thinking, Susannah ran to meet her, Harry close behind. 'Amelia...what is it? What has happened to you?'

Amelia stopped, gasping for breath and holding her side. Her dress had been torn and it was clear that she was in some distress. Her eyes sought out Harry as she gathered her breath and panted out the words, 'I was attacked...two men...back there...' She pointed in the direction she had come. 'I think they were trying to abduct me, though I cannot be sure it was not just an attempt to rob me. I struggled and I bit one of them. He let go and I managed to escape....'

'My God! Attacked? Here at Pendleton?' Harry was astounded. 'Susannah, take the rig and get Amelia back to the house. I must investigate this and I want you both safe.'

'Harry—what of you?' Susannah cried. 'You should fetch help.'

Harry took a pistol from the pocket of his coat. 'I always carry this in case, Susannah, though I did not expect to need it on my own estate. My apologies, Amelia. A search shall be made. The culprits shall be brought to account, I promise you.'

'Pray take care, Pendleton,' Amelia said. 'I heard them say I was not to be harmed, which is perhaps why I am still alive—but they may not be so scrupulous with your person.'

'Susannah, do as I ask, please. Go now!'

'Yes, Harry.' Susannah took Amelia's hand. 'Do you feel well enough to walk to the curricle, dearest? I should get you home in case there are more of them, as Harry says. I am sure he can manage.'

'Yes, of course I can walk,' Amelia said, recovering her composure. 'I am not harmed, merely distressed. It was such a shock to be attacked like that, Susannah. Had you and Harry not been near by, I do not know what might have happened, for they pursued me—but when they heard voices I think they stopped.'

'I wish Harry had someone with him,' Susannah said. 'However, I am sure we must leave this to him and go home.' She saw Amelia safe into the curricle and then got in beside her and took the reins. 'This is the first time

I have driven without guidance, but I must be capable or Harry would not have told me to take you home.'

Amelia was silent as Susannah put her horses to a walk and then a trot. Her face was white and it was obvious that the incident had distressed her more than she would allow, even though she had tried to make light of it. When they arrived at the house, a groom came running to take the reins. Susannah explained what had happened while Amelia went up to the house.

'Please send someone to assist your master,' she begged. 'He has a pistol, but these men are dangerous and may be armed.'

'Yes, Miss Hampton,' the groom said. 'Some of the men will go immediately. Don't you worry, miss. His lordship is capable of dealing with poachers or the like—and the gamekeepers are in the woods. If they should hear a shot, they will be there in an instant.'

Susannah did not find his words reassuring. In the event of a shot it might mean that it was already too late. However, she hurried into the house and went upstairs, finding Amelia in their sitting room. She was standing by the table and about to pour herself a glass of wine from a decanter set on a silver tray, but her hand was shaking. Susannah took it from her.

'Sit down, dearest. Let me do that for you.'

Amelia obeyed. 'I am very foolish. It was the merest incident, and I am not harmed. I do not wish to make a fuss—but I am sure they meant to abduct me.'

'Why would they do such a thing? Who would wish to harm you?'

'I have no idea,' Amelia said. 'I cannot think of anyone who holds a grudge against me...' She frowned. 'I can only think that they wished to hold me for a ransom.'

'That is horrible,' Susannah said. 'Drink your wine,

Amelia. It may make you feel a little better. If Harry catches those wicked men, he may be able to discover who put them up to it.'

'Yes, perhaps.' Amelia drank her wine and then summoned a smile. 'I am better now. It was quite frightening for a moment. I should not have walked so far from the house alone, but I have always walked alone and it did not cross my mind that something of the kind could happen here.'

'No, I do not expect it would. Harry will be most distressed that something of that nature should occur on his land.'

'It was not his fault. It could have happened anywhere.' Amelia looked thoughtful. 'I suppose it is well known that I am the heiress to a considerable fortune. I shall have to take more care when walking in future.'

Susannah shivered. 'It is a sobering thought that people exist that would do such a thing,' she said. 'I am so sorry that it happened to you, Amelia. You have no idea who it might be?'

'None at all,' Amelia replied. 'We must hope that Harry and his men will catch whoever it is.' She stood up. 'I shall change my gown and then go down. You should do the same, Susannah. We do not wish to make a fuss over such a foolish incident.'

Susannah knew that Amelia was trying to make light of the affair, and decided to take her lead from her. She watched Amelia enter her bedroom and then went into her own chamber. She rang for her maid, looking at the fresh gown that had been laid out for her. It was a pretty yellow silk and she would want her seed pearls or perhaps the pearls Lady Elizabeth had given her. She had placed them in the top drawer of her chest the previous night. She opened the drawer and frowned, for the box was not where she had left it.

'You rang for me, miss?'

'Yes, Iris. I am ready to change for nuncheon. I thought I might wear my pearls. I was sure I put them in this drawer last night.'

'Yes, miss, I saw you do it,' Iris said. 'Are they not there? I put away a scarf when I tidied your room just after you left. They were there then...' Iris looked and pointed to the place Susannah had placed them, which was now empty. 'Right there, miss.' She looked horrified. 'I swear, I have not moved them. Cross my heart and hope to die!'

'Do not worry, Iris. I do not suspect you of taking them. Perhaps Mama moved them for safekeeping. I shall wear my seed pearls for now and enquire...' She frowned as she realised something else was missing. 'Did you take a kerchief to wash it, Iris? There was one on top of the chest and that has gone too.'

'No, miss. I took some undergarments that you had left lying on the chair, but nothing from the chest, Miss Susannah. You do believe me?'

'Of course I do,' Susannah said. 'Mama might have put the pearls somewhere safer, but even if they are...' she could hardly bring herself to say the word '...stolen, I should not dream of blaming you.'

'Please ask Mrs Hampton at once,' Iris said. 'The kerchief might have got in with the laundry without my knowing it, miss—but those pearls are valuable.'

'Yes, they are, and a gift, which makes them more important. However, you shall not be blamed, I promise you.'

'Thank you, miss—but others may not be so inclined to believe me.' Iris looked distressed. She began to look about the room, searching all the drawers without discovering the pearls. 'I swear to you, Miss Susannah—I would rather lay down my life than touch anything of yours!'

'Do you think I do not know that?' Susannah smiled at her. 'I had already decided to ask if you will come with me when I marry—and this does not change my opinion of you.'

'Oh, miss...' Iris held back a sob only by pressing a fist against her mouth. 'I do hope your mama has those pearls.'

'Yes, so do I,' Susannah said, for otherwise it would mean that there was a thief at Pendleton.

Coming on top of the attack on Amelia, she could imagine that Harry would find the news very distressing.

'No, Susannah, I did not touch your pearls or a lace kerchief—why ever would I do such a thing?'

'I thought perhaps...to make sure the pearls were safe.' Susannah frowned. 'I believed they would be safe in my drawer.'

'As they ought to have been,' Mrs Hampton said, looking shocked. 'I do not say that you were careless, dearest, but it is a pity that you did not ask if they could be locked away in the strong room until you needed them.'

'I have never needed to do anything of the sort,' Susannah said. 'I must tell Lady Elizabeth and apologise to her for losing her gift.'

'Yes, you must,' Mrs Hampton said. 'You questioned your maid, of course?'

'I asked Iris at once, for I thought she might have put

them somewhere she thought safer, but she says did not touch them, Mama—and I believe her.'

'Yes, I am inclined to think her honest—but someone is not, Susannah. This is most unfortunate...' She looked anxious. 'And the attack on Amelia too...I think they must be linked, do you not agree? Perhaps they are desperate rogues and they meant to rob Amelia rather than abduct her?'

'Perhaps...' Susannah was unsure. 'We must see what Harry thinks.'

'I shall tell Lady Elizabeth in private,' Mrs Hampton said. 'This is distressing for everyone.'

Susannah agreed.

She felt uncomfortable and uneasy throughout nuncheon. Afterwards, Lady Elizabeth drew her to one side.

'My son will be most distressed to hear of this,' she said. 'You are sure you did not move them somewhere else, Susannah?'

'Iris helped me to search. We looked everywhere. Besides, she saw them in the drawer after I went driving with Harry.'

'In that case, I shall speak to Harry as soon as he returns. I do not know what things are coming to. Miss Royston attacked in our woods—and your pearls stolen.'

'I should have asked for them to be locked away,' Susannah said. 'I have never had such a valuable trinket before and did not realise—'

'Do not upset yourself, my dear,' Lady Elizabeth told her. 'I would have told you they were quite safe in your keeping. I have never known such a thing to happen before. I would swear that my servants are honest.'

'Iris would never take anything of mine,' Susannah said. She considered mentioning the lace kerchief, but decided against it. If she told Lady Elizabeth the whole story, it might seem as if she were accusing the owner of the kerchief—and she did not truly know who it had belonged to.

'I shall ask Harry if he thinks we should make a search of the servants' rooms,' Lady Elizabeth said, looking bothered. 'It really is too bad of whoever did it—spiteful, in fact. I have many jewels of equal value. If they wished to steal from us, why did they not take mine? I shall find something else to give you, my dear.'

'Please do not, at least for the moment,' Susannah said. 'I should feel uncomfortable keeping them in my room—and perhaps the pearls will turn up.'

'Well…' Lady Elizabeth sighed. 'We must hear what Harry has to say on his return and decide then. If those rogues have been caught, they may have your pearls in their possession.'

Susannah agreed. She was feeling uneasy and spent most of the afternoon watching from the window for Harry's return, the idea of a tour of the house abandoned.

It was past four when Harry came at last, and the look on his face told her at once that he had not captured the rogues he sought.

'We found a place in the woods where they had left a carriage, for there were wheel marks, but there was no sign of them. The other side of the woods borders a village and they must have come that way. I have done nothing about fencing that border, for the village forms part of the estate, but I see that it makes us vulnerable. I shall instruct a master builder to construct a high wall.

Nothing like this shall happen to a lady staying under my roof again.'

'I wish that you had caught them,' Susannah said. 'But the estate is so large and you would need to be searching all day to be sure they were not hiding anywhere on your land.' She bit her lip. 'I am afraid you will be angry—but there has been more trouble since I saw you....'

Harry's gaze narrowed. 'Pray tell me at once, Susannah. Amelia is not badly hurt?'

'Oh, no. She was shocked, but not harmed, though her dress was torn. You recall that your mama gave me some pearls last evening?'

'Yes, she had shown them to me earlier.'

'They have been stolen—at least, they are not where I placed them. My maid and I searched the room, but they have gone.'

'Good grief! This is beyond anything!' Harry looked startled, a glint of anger in his eyes. 'I shall have the house searched at once in case anything else is missing. The rogues must have got in somehow during the night and taken them. I dare say they attacked Amelia because she disturbed them in the woods, or they may have had hopes of more loot. Has anyone else lost anything?'

'No one has said anything,' Susannah told him. 'Your mama did not think the servants...and I am sure it was not Iris. However, the pearls were there just after I left to go driving with you.'

'You are sure of this?'

'Iris saw them, she told me so.' Susannah frowned. Again, she was uncertain whether or not to mention the kerchief, but decided against it. 'Could someone have crept into the house unnoticed in daylight?'

'I would not have thought it,' Harry said and frowned.

'However, until earlier I would not have thought it possible for anyone to be attacked on my land. I have doubled the patrols, which will continue throughout the day and night.'

'It is all quite horrid,' Susannah said and shivered. 'It was bad enough that someone attacked Amelia—but for the pearls to be stolen right here in the house is unpleasant.'

'Yes, it is, but I am sure you are quite safe now, dearest,' Harry said. 'The rogues took what they could and fled. I am sure they are long gone by now. You must promise me this will not spoil things for you, Susannah?'

'I am not such poor stuff,' Susannah told him and smiled. 'I suppose it is an adventure in a way—but I would far rather it had not happened.'

The guests were asked if they had lost anything. Lady Ethel said that her silver evening purse was missing, but it was eventually found stuffed down the side of a sofa by one of the servants. No one else thought they had lost anything, and there was a general outcry against the rogues who had sneaked into Susannah's room and stolen her pearls. The servants were not asked to submit to a search, but after some talking between themselves they asked if it could be done as a process of elimination. Nothing was found and the general consensus was that the rogues who had attacked Amelia had somehow sneaked in and taken the pearls.

'It seems odd that just your pearls were taken,' Mrs Hampton said. 'But perhaps they were disturbed and they fled with what they had.'

'That does not explain why they tried to abduct

Amelia,' Susannah said, looking thoughtful. It did not explain the disappearance of the kerchief, either.

It was later that evening that Miss Hazledeane came up to Susannah in the drawing room. Lady Elizabeth was at the pianoforte and Susannah had been intent on the music when the other woman sat next to her on the small sofa.

'All this fuss for a string of pearls,' Miss Hazledeane said, a spiteful note in her voice. 'I dare say you will find them if you look hard enough.'

'Perhaps…' Susannah turned thoughtful eyes on her. 'It was very odd, but the kerchief I found near the boathouse was lying on my chest—and that was taken too, though I have not mentioned it for it was not important.'

'Your maid took it to be washed,' Miss Hazledeane said. 'She has probably taken the pearls too —or you mislaid them.'

'I should be very glad to think so,' Susannah said. 'I should be happy if they were found and no harm done.'

'You have caused an uproar,' Miss Hazledeane said. 'As if they mattered when you will have so much. The Pendleton heirlooms must be worth a fortune, though I dare say they are kept in the bank.'

'And may stay there, at least until we know for certain that no one can walk in and steal them,' Susannah said. 'The pearls matter to me because they were a gift from Lady Elizabeth.'

'Well, I dare say she will give you something else. She has plenty of jewels, she can well spare another trinket.' Miss Hazledeane shrugged her shoulders, got up and moved away.

Susannah stared after her. It was wrong of her to dislike Lady Elizabeth's ward. It was quite unthinkable to suspect Miss Hazledeane of taking the pearls and the kerchief, and yet Susannah had an uneasy feeling at the nape of her neck. Something was telling her that Miss Hazledeane knew more about the disappearance of the pearls than she was saying.

She could not accuse another lady of stealing! Susannah knew it would be frowned upon. Besides, it was too embarrassing. Everyone else had accepted that the mystery was solved. Harry was having all the side doors locked and the windows checked. He had increased the numbers of keepers he employed to patrol his grounds. There was nothing more to be done except put the unpleasant incident out of her mind.

As soon as Susannah went into her bedchamber, she saw that the drawer of her chest was opened a little. She felt a little shiver down her spine and went to look in the drawer. A silk scarf had been disturbed and when she pulled it aside she saw the velvet case. Taking it out, she discovered that her pearls were inside.

How had they come there? She was positive that they had not been there earlier, for both she and Iris had moved everything in their search. The pearls had gone missing, but now they were back.

Why had someone taken and then returned them? Susannah could think of only one reason—to make her look foolish. It was very embarrassing after the house had been searched and everyone made to feel uncomfortable.

However, it was clear to Susannah that she must confess to having found them, even if it did make her feel foolish.

* * *

Lady Elizabeth told her that it did not matter. She was simply relieved that the pearls had been found.

'Perhaps your maid found them and returned them to the drawer,' she suggested.

'It was not Iris, for I asked her,' Susannah said. 'I am sure they were not there earlier, for we all looked—but I suppose they must have been. I am so sorry to have caused so much fuss.'

'You must not let it upset you,' Lady Elizabeth told her. 'The pearls were lost and now they are found. It is all settled and shall be forgotten now.'

Susannah thanked her and went to bed. There was nothing more she could say, but in her own mind she was quite certain who had taken the pearls and then replaced them. The only thing she wasn't sure of was why....

The next morning dawned fine and bright. Indeed, it had the promise of being hot. Most people thought a storm would come before nightfall to break the weather, because it was too sultry.

Harry had decided that the picnic would go ahead.

'We cannot allow an unpleasant incident to put us off,' he declared. 'The boats have been brought to this side of the lake. Those who wish to go boating may join us there immediately, and those who are interested only in the picnic may wander towards the lake at noon.'

'I am so glad you have not cancelled it,' Susannah said and smiled her pleasure. 'I cannot apologise enough for causing so much trouble. I can only say that the pearls were not in the drawer when I looked.'

'No such thing,' Harry told her. 'No lasting harm done. I am more concerned with the rogues in the woods. Miss Royston has forgiven me for allowing such a terrible thing to happen in my woods, and she will leave at the end of the week to arrange our wedding.'

'Then we may forget it and be happy again,' Susannah said, her face alight. 'It was a fright for Amelia, but it is over now.'

Harry commandeered the first boat and rowed Susannah out into the middle of the lake. She smiled at him, leaning back in her seat, her parasol protecting her from the fierce heat as he pulled on the oars. She thought that he was very strong. Glancing back towards the shore, she saw that the Earl of Ravenshead was rowing Amelia and Mrs Hampton, while Toby had taken Lady Elizabeth for a turn on the water. Most of the other ladies and gentlemen were strolling about on the grass, talking and enjoying the sunshine. Susannah caught sight of Miss Hazledeane. She was wearing a white dress, wandering by herself apart from the others.

'Are you enjoying yourself?' Harry asked. 'I think we must do this more often. I had forgotten how pleasant it is to be on the water.'

'I like it very much,' Susannah said. 'Tell me, do you have a lake at your other home?'

'No, I don't—though I recently bought a piece of land for the construction of a small lake. I hadn't given it much thought, but I must set the work in hand. It will make a fine addition to the property.'

Susannah smiled and trailed her hand in the water. She closed her eyes for a moment, enjoying the tranquillity and peace of their surroundings. She was very fortunate to have the prospect of spending her life in such a lovely place.

Harry took them back to the jetty after half an hour or so, handing Susannah out. He then offered to take any other lady who wished for a trip, and Susannah was a little surprised when Lady Booker said that she would like to be rowed about the lake.

She saw that chairs had been set out, and the servants were setting up tables for their picnic.

Toby had brought his passenger to shore. He walked up to Susannah as she stood under the shade of a tree, watching everyone enjoying themselves.

'The picnic was a capital notion of Harry's, was it not?'

'Yes—' Susannah began, but broke off as she saw a woman emerge from behind the boathouse. Her attention was caught because of the way the woman was behaving—furtively, looking over her shoulder as if hoping not to be seen. She turned and ran in the opposite direction. Only moments later a man emerged from the shadows and began to walk away in yet another direction. 'Did you see that man on the far side of the lake? He came from behind the boathouse...' Susannah touched Toby's arm. 'I am not certain but I think...it was the Marquis of Northaven.'

'Where?' Toby turned in the direction of her gaze, but was only in time to see the man disappear into a clump of artistically arranged trees, too far away to be seen clearly without a spyglass. 'It couldn't have been, surely? Here at Pendleton—with all these people around? I doubt it, Susannah. He is not welcome here. Harry would want to know the reason why. It is hardly likely—the grounds are being patrolled day and night.'

'Yes, I know. It does not seem likely,' Susannah said and laughed. 'Perhaps I was mistaken, but it did look like him for a moment.'

'I cannot think he would come here. Northaven and Harry do not get along. I know for a fact that Northaven would not be invited to this estate.' Toby frowned. 'It is odd, for I do not know how anyone could be there… None of the guests are missing and the men have been warned to look out for strangers.'

'I was mistaken,' Susannah said. 'It could not have been he.'

'I should say it was one of the keepers,' Toby told her. 'I know there are a lot of them about.'

'I am sure you are right. It could not have been the marquis. It was just a trick of the light.'

Susannah dismissed the incident, because she did not want to cause a fuss. Yet she was almost certain it had been the marquis—and that the woman leaving the boathouse was Miss Hazledeane! She had seen a flash of white and Jenny Hazledeane was the only lady wearing white this morning. If it were Northaven and Miss Hazledeane, they must have met there by prior arrangement, perhaps when they had tea in Bath. She recalled the incident in the gardens the night she had arrived. She had seen a man and a woman kissing. Could it have been Jenny Hazledeane and the Marquis of Northaven?

Susannah was thoughtful throughout the rest of the morning. She managed to join in the activities and to talk about all kinds of things, but at the back of her mind was a niggling doubt that would not let her rest. If Miss Hazledeane was meeting the Marquis of Northaven here at Pendleton, Harry ought to be told about it.

Susannah knew that Miss Hazledeane had met the marquis in Bath, and she was fairly sure of what she had seen that morning. Was it her duty to tell Harry what she knew?

The question continued to tease Susannah throughout the afternoon. Several times she was on the verge of telling Harry, but Miss Hazledeane had rejoined the company, and had joined in a game of cricket. To raise doubts about her conduct might throw a cloud over the party, and after the upset of the previous day, Susannah did not feel like making a fuss. She decided that, if she got the chance, she would speak to Miss Hazledeane about it in private that evening.

However, she did not have a chance to speak to Miss Hazledeane alone until much later, because she was asked to play the pianoforte for the company when the ladies retired to the drawing room. When Amelia took her place, one of the relatives asked if she would join a hand of piquet.

Susannah found herself drawn into a lively game, which she enjoyed more than she might have expected. Harry was not a part of it, however, and when she looked for him he had disappeared.

'If you are looking for Harry, he and some of the others took themselves off to play billiards,' Lady Ethel told her in a loud voice. 'Pay attention, my dear, or you will lose points. You will have plenty of time to bill and coo tomorrow.'

Susannah laughed and put her mind to the game. She managed to win at least one hand and to share another. When she was finally released by Lady Ethel, she told her mother that she was going to bed.

'I need to be fresh for my driving in the morning,' she said. 'Please tell Harry that I said goodnight.'

After wishing the gathered company goodnight, Susannah went upstairs to her own room. However, her conscience would not let her rest and she slipped out again a few minutes later, going along the hall to the room she knew was Miss Hazledeane's She hesitated, then knocked sharply.

'Just a moment…' Miss Hazledeane opened the door in her dressing robe, staring at her for a moment. Susannah thought there was a flicker of fear in her eyes. 'What did you want?'

'I have something to say to you—in private, if I may?'

The other girl stood back, a sullen look on her face. 'I didn't steal your pearls…'

'No one stole them; they were mislaid,' Susannah said, though she suspected the other girl had taken them to punish her, not realising that it would cause so much fuss. However, they had been returned and there was no point in holding a grudge. 'I haven't come about the pearls.'

'Why have you come, then?' Jenny's eyes were suspicious, her manner uneasy.

'I thought I should warn you…' Susannah drew a deep breath. 'I saw you leaving the boathouse earlier today and I know you have been meeting someone in secret. I believe it may be the Marquis of Northaven. I think you should know that he is not to be trusted. Harry warned me against him and I think—'

'How dare you accuse me of having a lover? You have no right!'

'I did not say he was your lover…' Susannah saw the guilt and fear in the other girl's face. 'I am so sorry. I should have warned you sooner…when I first saw you with him in Bath.'

Tears hovered on Jenny's lashes. 'It would have done no good. We have been lovers for months, long before my brother died…' She brushed her hand over her cheek, pride in her eyes now. 'Edmund promised to marry me… He would have married me, but my brother wasted my inheritance and he is in debt.' Her eyes glittered. 'Edmund loves me, but he must marry a fortune.

You do not know what it is like to feel hopeless! I have nothing and I love him so much.'

'I am so sorry—'

'I do not want your pity,' Jenny flashed back at her. 'You come here interfering in what does not concern you, so smug because you are to marry into a wealthy family.' She turned away, her shoulders hunched as she fought the tears. 'Tell Lord Pendleton, then—tell Lady Elizabeth what a wanton trollop I am. I know you are dying to be rid of me.'

'No, you are quite wrong,' Susannah told her, her sympathy aroused. 'I do not hate you. I would be your friend if you would let me. If there is anything I can do to help you?'

The other girl turned, her expression desperate. 'Please, do not tell anyone what you saw. I beg you, do not betray me. I have given Edmund an ultimatum. He must wed me or I shall never see him again.'

'I am so sorry…'

'Then keep my secret…please?'

Susannah hesitated. It was her duty to tell either Harry or Lady Elizabeth, but how could she deliberately shame a girl who already had so much to bear?

'I will think about it,' she said. 'I shall not tell them tonight, but you must give me your word that you will not continue to meet the marquis here at Pendleton.'

'I promise. Please—do not betray me.'

'Very well. I shall say nothing for the moment.'

'Thank you,' Jenny said, the glitter of tears in her eyes. 'I wish that someone had warned me long ago.'

Susannah wished her goodnight and returned to her room. She was uneasy, because she was not certain she had done the right thing in promising to keep Jenny's secret.

* * *

Susannah woke suddenly. She was not sure what had woken her, but she got up and walked over to the window. It was almost morning, the dawn light just beginning to creep in through the curtains. She pulled them back and glanced out, catching sight of someone moving furtively through the gardens. Surely that was Miss Hazledeane? Susannah felt a tingling sensation at the nape of her neck. She was almost certain that Jenny was carrying a valise!

Why would Miss Hazledeane creep out in the early hours of the morning with a valise? Unless... Susannah remembered Jenny's tears of the previous night. Jenny had begged her to keep her secret and now...she had run off with her lover.

She must be wrong! Susannah shivered as the idea grew in her mind. She was almost sure that Miss Hazledeane had eloped with the Marquis of Northaven!

Susannah could not rest. She paced the floor of her bedchamber, wondering what she ought to do. She had to confide in someone! She had given her word to Jenny, but on the condition that she broke off her affair. She had made a terrible mistake. Instead of speaking to Jenny privately, she should have confided her suspicions to Harry. She should have told him the first time she saw Miss Hazledeane with the marquis. Now Jenny had run off with him and she would be ruined.

Was it too late to do anything? Susannah fretted as she went through to the sitting room. Who should she wake—her mama, Amelia or Harry?

Why hadn't she told Harry of her suspicions sooner? Susannah was overcome with guilt. She had hesitated, because she did not like to create suspicion concerning another lady, but now she was wishing that she had spoken out. She was on thorns. How long must she wait until she could tell someone?

Susannah decided that the best person to tell must be Harry. However, she could not possibly go to his bedchamber, even had she been sure of its situation. She would go downstairs and see if the servants were stirring and then ask one of them to ask him if he would come down and speak to her. If no one was about, she would take a turn in the gardens to help her summon the courage.

Looking out of his bedroom window, Toby saw Susannah pacing up and down in the garden below. She was so obviously in distress that he dressed quickly and went down. They met just as she was returning to the house.

'Susannah—are you ill?' Toby enquired in concern. 'What were you doing in the garden.'

'Oh, thank goodness!' Susannah cried, clutching at his arm anxiously. 'I wanted to talk to someone. You are just the person. I am afraid Harry will be so angry with me....'

'What have you done?'

'I kept something back that I ought to have told him,' Susannah confessed. 'And now something terrible has happened—at least, I think it may have.'

'Sit down and tell me,' Toby said, leading her to a chair. 'I am sure it cannot be anything very dreadful.'

'But it is,' Susannah said, a sob in her voice. 'You know the man we saw leaving the boathouse yesterday afternoon?' Toby nodded. 'Well, I am certain it was Northaven and that he has run away with Miss Hazledeane.'

'No! She would not...' Toby stared at her. 'She has no fortune to speak of...Northaven would not marry her without...'

'So much the worse,' Susannah said and caught back a sob. 'I saw them in Bath just before she left to come here. They were taking tea and the look on her face said it all. She is in love with him.' Susannah saw the shock in his eyes. 'She has been meeting him here and this morning she ran off. She was carrying a valise.'

'Why did you not tell someone before this?'

'Because... I was not sure and when I asked her she wept and begged me to keep her secret. I told her she must break with him and she promised she would—but very early this morning she ran away.'

Toby was stunned. 'Stay here, Susannah. I shall wake Harry, if he is not yet awake. A maid must go to check whether Miss Hazledeane is in her room.'

'Harry will be so cross...'

Toby was no longer listening. He took the stairs two at a time, clearly in a state of some anxiety. Susannah got up and began to walk about, studying the paintings in the hallway in an effort to ease her mind. However, her conscience could not be eased, for she knew that this calamity was her fault. If she had only spoken to Harry in the beginning, this could never have happened!

Some twenty minutes or more had passed before Harry came striding towards her. His expression was one of absolute fury and Susannah trembled inwardly. He did blame her and he was right to do so, for it was her fault!

'It has been confirmed that Miss Hazledeane's bed has not been slept in and that some of her things have gone.'

'I am so sorry,' Susannah said in a faint voice.

'Did she tell you of her intentions? Did you help her to run away?' Harry's gaze was stern and cold. 'Tell me now. I wish for no more lies.'

'I have not lied...' Susannah faltered. 'I did not tell you what I had seen for I thought it was not my affair... and then she wept and begged me to keep her secret. She said that Northaven would have married her, but he needs money and her brother wasted her inheritance.'

The look on Harry's face made Susannah wish to sink into the ground and disappear. 'Not your affair when you saw a young woman not much older than yourself meeting secretly with a man you know to be unworthy! Miss Hazledeane is my ward! You must have known that I should wish to be informed so that I could protect her? You deliberately went behind my back, to keep a secret you must have known was wrong! You have behaved thoughtlessly...recklessly. I had thought you had more sense!'

'I was not sure...' Susannah could not meet his eyes, because she knew herself at fault. 'She was in distress. I felt sympathy... Forgive me. I know this must pain you.'

'It pains me more that you did not see fit to tell me in the first place, Susannah. It shows a distinct lack of trust on your part, and that is serious. A marriage without trust is not worth having!'

'It was not that I could not trust you...only that I felt awkward. I had almost made up my mind to tell you what I suspected last night, but you... I did not see you to speak to alone. So I asked her for the truth and then...' It was a weak excuse and she saw the disdain in his expression. Her heart sank and she wished that the floor would open and receive her. 'I did not know what to do.'

'I am afraid our driving lesson must be cancelled for the moment,' Harry said curtly. 'I must go after Miss Hazledeane and see what can be rescued from this mess.' He glanced up as Gerard and Max Coleridge came clattering down the stairs, closely followed by Toby. 'Not you, Toby. My sister would never forgive me if anything happened to you. Northaven has done this deliberately to draw me into a fight.'

'I am prepared to shoot if I have to,' Toby declared, looking stubborn.

'Thank you, but it will be settled in the proper manner if I have anything to do with it,' Harry told him. 'Please stay here and look after Susannah. I would not put it past Northaven to arrange something for her once my back is turned.' He glanced at Susannah once more. 'I shall speak to you when I return.'

'Yes, Pendleton.' Susannah watched as Harry and his friends strode towards the front door, which was opened by a sleepy-looking footman who had just arrived at his post. Her throat was tight and the tears burned behind her eyes. She glanced at Toby, her face pale. 'He is so angry…'

'Yes, but you might have expected it,' Toby said, for once unsympathetic. 'Why on earth did you not tell one of us? Something might have been done to prevent them running off.'

'Do you think they will catch them?' Susannah asked. She was filled with apprehension. 'Is it too late? I dare say they may be halfway to Scotland by now.'

'I doubt he will have taken her to Scotland.'

'Not—but surely they are eloping?'

'Northaven will not marry her without a fortune.

Harry told me she has only a few hundred pounds from her brother's estate. Hazledeane was the guardian of her inheritance, but he misappropriated the funds—in short, he robbed his sister of ten thousand pounds. Northaven might make her his mistress, but he will not wed her.'

'But she will be ruined.' Susannah was horrified.

'That is the reason Harry is so angry. She was under his protection and he feels responsible for her. Unless he can force a deal on Northaven, Jenny Hazledeane will never be able to show her face in society again. Indeed, if her elopement becomes known, many will not receive her even if she is married.'

'Oh…that is terrible,' Susannah whispered. 'I am to blame—I should have told Harry yesterday.' The tears were so close now that Susannah could not hold them back. 'Excuse me…' she said and made a dash for the stairs before she could break down and disgrace herself further. Harry was so angry with her. No doubt he thought her careless and unfit to be his wife. He was probably wishing that he had not asked her to marry him.

'You must not blame yourself,' Amelia told her when Susannah spoke to her some half an hour later. She had conquered her tears and washed her face, but she could not ease her sense of guilt and distress. Amelia was still wearing her peignoir, a frivolous confection of white silk and lace, for she had not dressed fully. 'I can understand why you did not wish to tell tales behind Miss Hazledeane's back, Susannah. It is unfortunate that you did not mention it to me. I might have been able to help her—and I could have told her something about the marquis that would have warned her to have nothing more to do with him.'

'What do you mean?'

Amelia hesitated, then, 'I had a friend some years ago. I shall not name her for it is an old story. Suffice it to say that she was young and pretty, and very innocent. She fell in love and allowed herself to be seduced, but when she discovered she was with child her lover left her. Ashamed and distraught, she refused to tell anyone his name. Instead she chose to take her own life in the river...' Amelia paused, then, 'At the time I suspected one of three gentlemen, but I have since ruled out two of them.'

'You believe it was the marquis?'

'He was not the marquis then, but it was known that he would inherit the title from an uncle. My friend was a simple country girl. He thought her good enough for seduction, but not for marriage. Northaven is known to be in financial difficulties and may have lowered his sights since then—but he will not marry without a fortune.'

'That is what Toby and Harry say,' Susannah said, a sob in her voice. 'I am very much at fault, Amelia. I ought to have told someone. Even if I could not tell Harry, I should have asked you or Mama what to do.'

'It is easy to say so with hindsight,' Amelia agreed. 'But many of us face similar dilemmas and are as hesitant as you, Susannah. I knew that my friend was meeting a young man, but I did nothing to warn or stop her. I did not know he had seduced her, but even if I had guessed I should not have gone to her mother. You hesitated to interfere in something that was not your affair, and Harry will understand that once he is calmer.'

'I fear that I have sunk in his estimation. Do you think they will prevail upon the marquis to marry her?' Susannah asked in a subdued tone. 'I did not like her—nor she me—but I would not see her utterly ruined and banned from society.'

'She was a little strange in her manner,' Amelia agreed. 'To me she was quite friendly, but I dare say she was jealous of you. I saw her making eyes at Lord Pendleton, but he gave her no encouragement. I think if he had, she might not have run off with a man she probably knows is a rogue.'

'I am not sure. The look on her face that day was of a woman in love... I think she is in love with Northaven.'

'She may be in love with him now,' Amelia said. 'However, I doubt it will last more than a few months—if that.'

'I feel sorry for her,' Susannah said. 'If she had stayed here I am sure Harry would have given her a dowry. She might have married well.'

'He will probably give her a dowry now,' Amelia said. 'Indeed, I believe that may be her only hope.'

'I hope that he will find her,' Susannah said, her throat tight with emotion. 'But I am afraid something terrible may happen. You did not see how angry he was—and Toby told me that he did not like the marquis. Do you think they will fight?' Susannah's hand crept to her throat. 'If Harry should be killed because of this—' She broke off on a sob. 'Oh, Amelia, I feel so guilty... so responsible...'

'You must not be anxious for Pendleton,' Amelia told her. 'He is a gentleman and will not become embroiled in an unseemly fight. I dare say it will all be settled in the manner of gentlemen. Now, my love, give me a moment to put on my gown, and then I think we should go down and join the others, for everyone will be wondering where you are.'

Chapter Nine

'What makes you think he will have brought her here?' Gerard asked as the three men dismounted and looked at the house. It was a country manor of medium size, modernised some twenty years before when the estate was more prosperous, to include an imposing portico of white columns at the entrance. There were no lights at the front of the house, though there was one in an upstairs room at the back. 'If he intends to marry her, he could be on his way to Scotland even now.'

'He does not intend to wed her,' Harry said and looked grim. 'Believe me, I know his mind, Gerard. Northaven has been looking for a way to strike back at me for a long time. A bullet in the back would have been easier, but too quick. He wants to see me squirm, to make me beg him to marry the girl.'

'If that is his plan, why did he not strike closer to home?' Max asked and frowned. 'Miss Hampton means far more to you than the Hazledeane chit. If his plan was to destroy you, why not kidnap her?'

'Jenny Hazledeane means nothing to me,' Harry

agreed. 'Except that I gave her brother my word I would protect her from Northaven. I have failed in that, but I shall do what I can to put matters right. Northaven knows that if he laid one finger on Susannah I would kill him where he stood. I imagine he wants money from this….'

'You know he won't be satisfied with a few thousand,' Max said. 'Put a ball through his head and pack the girl off to a finishing school abroad.'

'Yes, the thought had occurred to me,' Harry drawled, anger mixed with amusement in his eyes. 'You do not imagine that I have come here simply to force Northaven to marry the girl?'

'He won't take her without a hefty bribe.'

Harry pulled a wry face. 'I suppose I can afford it, but that is not why I am here. I came to settle the score with Northaven, because I can no longer ignore it. If what Jenny told Susannah is true, he seduced her long before I was involved—but in meeting her at Pendleton, knowing she was my ward, he threw down the gauntlet. If I do not settle this now, he may attempt something further—something that would cause me more grief than I could bear.'

'You mean Susannah?' Gerard said and frowned. 'Good God! You think…the attempt on Amelia was a mistake. They were meant to kidnap Susannah.'

'It is my fear,' Harry said. 'I did think at first that it might simply be opportunist rogues, but now I believe they may have been after my fiancée.'

'Then you have no choice but to challenge him.'

'Exactly.' Harry's eyes glittered like cold steel. 'Shall we take a look at the back of the house, gentlemen?'

'Yes, that might be a good idea. I hardly think this is

something we can redress by calling at the front door and offering our cards.'

The three men ran swiftly across the lawns, keeping to the shadows as much as possible and turning the corner to come up at the back of the main wing. Light was blazing from a downstairs window and the French doors stood wide-open. Harry looked at his friends and made up his mind instantly.

'Wait for me here. I know it is a sultry night, but that open door is an invitation and I intend to answer it—but do not come unless I call or you hear the sound of a shot.'

'It could be too late then,' Gerard protested. 'We are coming with you. I don't trust that devil.'

Harry saw the expression on both their faces and grinned. 'Very well, if I refuse you will follow anyway. Let's see what the marquis has to say for himself.'

He set off ahead, Gerard following and Max in the rear. Harry had not drawn his pistol, but neither Max nor Gerard was taking a chance and each had his at the ready.

At the door of what was clearly a library—the walls were covered on three sides with leather-covered books—Harry paused and looked in. Northaven was sitting at a reading table, his boots crossed as they rested on the leather surface, an empty wineglass in his hand. His eyes were closed as if he were sleeping, but as Harry cleared his throat, he opened them, his lip curling back in a sneer of mockery.

'I have been expecting you, Pendleton.' His gaze went behind Harry to the other men and he smiled oddly. 'The holy trio together again, I see. Did you think it was a trap? Or have you come to be judge, jury and executioner? Should I repent my sins and ask forgiveness from my Maker?'

'Where is she, Northaven?' Harry demanded. 'What have you done to her?'

The marquis stood up, his expression one of amused malice. 'You mean the lady you were so chivalrous as to take into your home and make your mother's ward? How she disliked that, Pendleton. Your dear mama wished to turn her into a model of decorum and teach her how to behave in society,' Northaven mocked, his lip curled back in a sneer. 'Oh, yes, I knew all about that, and I admit that I was tempted to see if you would part with a small fortune to preserve her good name. I cannot say her modesty, for she lost that long ago. She was my lover before her brother died. Had she held out, I might have wed her in the end.'

'You damned seducer!' Harry's hand shot out, slapping Northaven across the mouth with his glove. 'How dare you malign the name of a lady! If you have seduced her, you will marry her!'

'It would be interesting to see if you could force me to do that,' Northaven said, eyes glittering. There was menace and hatred in his tone. 'I might oblige if the sum were large enough. However, I fear that the bird has escaped us both. She demanded that I marry her. I declined and she ran away from me.'

'She ran away?' Harry and Gerard spoke together and Northaven laughed mockingly.

'I dare say she may have gone to her aunt.' Northaven shrugged carelessly. 'Hazledeane did not tell you of her? You were duped, Pendleton. The man was a rogue. He probably hoped you would marry his sister if you thought her completely alone. Jenny has an aunt in the north of England. I dare say you will find her there if you try—though she will not thank you for it.'

'It was you he told me to watch...' Harry frowned, a little uncertain. Had he misjudged the man? 'I am not fooled by your lies. Where is she—upstairs?'

Northaven laughed mirthlessly. 'I almost wish she was,' he said. 'I should enjoy watching you play out the role of avenging angel.'

'Damn you!' Harry cried. 'You ruined an innocent girl and you should pay for it.'

'Leave it,' Gerard said. He and Max held Harry by the arms as he reached for his pistol. 'He isn't worth the bother. The girl isn't blameless, though I dare say he seduced her.'

'She was willing enough...' Northaven sneered. 'It is a pity I could not convince the innocent Miss Hampton to run off with me. I should have enjoyed seeing your face then.'

'You will meet me for this,' Harry said. 'I shall have satisfaction.'

'Delighted,' the marquis replied and his eyes gleamed with malice. 'I have been waiting for this for many years. I shall send my seconds to Pendleton to wait on you tomorrow.'

'You were not to blame for any of this,' Lady Elizabeth told Susannah as they sat in her private sitting room and drank tea. 'I cannot understand why the girl has run away. She must have known that she would be ruined.'

'It is distressing for you,' Susannah said, forgetting her own trouble for the moment. 'I did try to warn her—but she was in love with him.'

'It was very foolish of her, for she has ruined herself,' Lady Elizabeth said. 'I wish now that Harry had never brought Jenny here, for I was beginning to be fond of her—and now I feel let down.'

'She has betrayed your trust,' Susannah said. 'It is sad that she should do such a thing.'

'If only she had confided in me. I could have made it possible for her to marry. I would have given her a dowry had she told me the truth.'

'I do not think Pendleton would have permitted her to marry the marquis.'

'No, perhaps not—though Northaven is still received in many houses. It would have been better to do the thing properly than have her run off in such a sly way! I am sure marriage would have been the lesser of two evils.'

'Perhaps if I had told Harry that I saw them in Bath, he might have warned her—prevented her from throwing her life away.'

'Well, you were not to know that the foolish girl would behave so badly. No, I shall not have you blame yourself for this, and I shall give Harry a piece of my mind for upsetting you, dearest.' Lady Elizabeth frowned. 'He is inclined to be hasty at times. I hope you will forgive him. I shall tell him that he must apologise.'

'Oh, no, you must not. Truly, you must not.'

'Do not distress yourself, dearest. Well, if you do not wish it, I shall not scold him—but it was his own fault for bringing the girl here. He should have sent her to finishing school somewhere.'

Susannah did not reply. Harry had been very angry with her for not telling him what she had seen. He had accused her of not trusting him and looked at her so coldly that she had wanted to die. She did not think he could look at her like that if he truly loved her, and she felt very unhappy. Had she not consented to marry him, she would have begged her mama to take her home immediately, but that would cause such a fuss that she could not bring herself to do it. She must speak to Harry when he returned.

However, Harry had not returned by the time Susannah retired for the night. She undressed, but could not rest and sat on a stool in the window, looking out, watching for his return. It must have been the early hours of the morning when she saw the three men ride up to the courtyard at the back of the house and dismount. One of them took the reins of all three horses and headed in the direction of the stables; the other two walked towards the house. Susannah's window was slightly open and she caught a few words as they passed through the door beneath her window.

'You were a fool to challenge him! It is what he wanted, Harry, what he has been itching for these past years—his chance to kill you.'

'He may try...'

Susannah felt a chill trickle down her spine. The rest of their conversation was lost to her as they went into the house, but what she had heard was clear enough. Harry was going to fight a duel with the Marquis of Northaven!

Oh, he must not! Susannah put a hand to her mouth as she realised that Harry could be killed or badly injured. She wanted to scream and shout, but she held the agony inside, because it would not help her. She knew instinctively that if she begged Harry to withdraw he would look at her in that cold, proud way and tell her she did not understand—or he would simply lie to her and pretend that she was mistaken and there was no duel.

What ought she to do? Susannah believed that duels

had been outlawed in recent years. If she told a magistrate, he might put a stop to it…but what could she tell him? She had overheard a scrap of conversation that she believed meant Harry intended to fight a duel, but she had no proof—and she had no idea where or when the duel was to take place. Besides, he would be so angry he might never speak to her again!

Susannah paced the floor of her bedchamber. There must be something she could do… If she knew where and when the duel was due to take place, she would do something to stop them. She must do something—she could not bear it if Harry were killed.

Dared she go downstairs? She might hear a little more if she was bold enough, though it would be dangerous, for it would be thought most improper of her to be wandering about the house after everyone else had retired.

'You must know this is madness,' Gerard said as they took a glass of wine together in the library. Max had joined them after handing the horses over to a sleepy groom. 'The chit isn't worth risking your life for, Harry.'

Harry arched his right eyebrow. 'You don't imagine I am doing it for Jenny's sake? Northaven has been spoiling for a fight for a long time. If I don't settle this now, it will drag on—and who knows what he may try next? As you said, Gerard, it could have been Susannah. Oh, I do not mean that she would run off with him, for she has too much good sense. However, he might try to abduct her. He said as much—and that was why I challenged him. He hates me because of what happened in the war.'

'And you think that by fighting this duel you will put an end to the ill will between you?' Gerard asked and shook his head. 'I dare say it may if you kill him.'

'I hope that will not be necessary.' Harry looked serious. 'It will not suit me to chase after that wretched girl.' He looked at Gerard. 'I know you spoke of leaving for France soon. Could I ask you to see if you can find Miss Hazledeane before you go—make sure that she is with her aunt?'

'And if she is not?'

'Then I can do no more. She has been foolish, but Mama is fond of her—and for her sake, I would settle a small sum on Jenny.'

'Very well,' Gerard said. 'I shall leave in a day or so, and then I have business in France. I do not know if I shall manage to return for your wedding, Harry. If not, give my good wishes to your bride—and I shall leave a gift for her with Lady Elizabeth.'

'That is if there is a wedding after the way I spoke to her,' Harry remarked wryly.

'I dare say Susannah will take you—despite your show of temper,' Max said and grinned. 'I am not sure you deserve her—but she has a kind heart.'

'Thank you,' Harry said and pulled a wry face. 'I think we should seek our beds. I have no idea when Northaven's seconds will call, but I dare say the duel will take place the day after tomorrow at dawn…' He glanced at his watch. 'Good Lord, the time! Make that tomorrow, for it is past one.'

Outside the library, Susannah caught her breath. She had heard only a few words—she had wrestled with her conscience before coming downstairs and knew she had missed much that went before. Instinct had told her that the men would take a last drink together in the library. Finding the door slightly ajar, she had shamelessly listened and she had been just in time to hear Harry say that the duel would probably take place the following morning.

Hearing sounds, which told her the men were about to leave the library, Susannah fled up the stairs. Her heart was beating very fast, for she had been shocked to have her suspicions confirmed. She knew she must not let the men see her, because if Harry knew that she was aware of the duel he would be at pains to keep the location a secret from her.

Susannah knew that it would be useless to plead with Harry to withdraw from this foolish duel. He could not in all honour do so and she knew it would go ahead whatever she said. However, she was determined to discover where the gentlemen were to meet. She would follow if she could and then...

Susannah had no clear idea of what she would do. She was distressed at the thought of Harry risking his life because Jenny Hazledeane had run off with the Marquis of Northaven. Harry had clearly had some feeling for the woman or he would not have reacted as angrily. He had called Northaven out and he might be killed—and if he died Susannah would have no one to blame but herself, for if she had spoken out at the start, none of this need have happened.

Back in her room, Susannah leaned back against the door and closed her eyes, fighting the tears. She could not bear it if Harry died...but what could she do to stop him fighting this awful duel?

Susannah was walking in the formal gardens with Amelia when she saw Harry coming towards her the next morning. It was almost time for nuncheon and the two ladies had decided that a stroll in the gardens would suffice as neither of them cared to go for a long walk after Amelia's unpleasant experience in the woods.

'Good morning, Susannah—Amelia,' Harry said. His expression was serious, but not angry. Susannah felt her stomach spasm with nerves as he looked at her. 'May I ask for a few moments of your time, Susannah? You will excuse us, Amelia?'

'Yes, of course,' Amelia said. 'I am thinking of leaving the day after tomorrow...perhaps we could speak later?'

'Yes, of course.' Harry smiled briefly. 'We must talk. I hope you will allow me to send an escort with you when you leave...to be certain of a safe journey.'

Amelia inclined her head and walked away, looking thoughtful.

'That was kind of you,' Susannah said, trying to quell her nerves. 'Amelia was upset by that incident in the woods.'

'Yes, of course she must have been, for it was most unpleasant. It may have been a random attack with robbery in mind, or something more sinister, therefore I have asked Max and Gerard to accompany Amelia to her home.'

'Yes, that would be ideal,' Susannah agreed and glanced at him uncertainly. 'Your mama tells me that Miss Hazledeane was not with the marquis, but may have gone to her aunt.'

'It would appear to be the case,' Harry said. 'Gerard will journey to the north to enquire after he has escorted Amelia home. I shall do what I can for Miss Hazledeane—despite her foolishness. I would wash my hands of the business, but Mama has a fondness for her.'

'I see...' Susannah bit her lip. 'I am sorry I did not

tell you that I witnessed her meeting with Northaven. It was wrong and misjudged.'

'You did what seemed right at the time, but I dare say you have learned a hard lesson.' Harry hesitated, looking rueful. 'Once again I subjected you to a shocking show of temper. I believe in the heat of the moment I was harsh to you.'

'You accused me of not trusting you. I believe I have lost your trust—and your good opinion?' Susannah could not look at him, for she was too ashamed.

'Please look at me, Susannah,' Harry said in a gentle voice that brought her head up. 'I hope to earn your forgiveness if I can. I was angry because of what had happened, but more than that it hurt me that you did not feel you could trust me with your confidences. Even when you began to realise that Miss Hazledeane might have run off, it was to Toby you confessed your fears. I had hoped that you might feel closer to me, now that we are engaged to be married.'

'Toby saw me walking in the garden. He came down. I would have told you if I had seen you first,' Susannah said. 'Forgive me, Pendleton. It was not lack of trust that caused me to hold back. I felt that it would seem sly or ungenerous to cast doubts on a lady's character. I hardly knew her....'

'Yes, I realise that—and I do understand, Susannah. However, I should prefer it if you were to confide in me in future.' He looked grave. 'Unless anything has happened that has made you think you would prefer to be released from our engagement?'

'Oh, no!' Susannah said and then blushed. 'No, I do not wish to be released, Pendleton—but if you wish it...'

'Not at all,' he said and gave her what she felt was a

rather forced smile. He reached out to stroke her cheek with his fingertips. 'I care for you a great deal, Susannah. If...anything should happen... If anything prevented our marriage...I want you to know that you are the only lady I have ever wished to make my wife.'

'Harry...' Susannah's heart raced as he bent his head. His kiss was light, soft and brief. 'Please do not say such things! They frighten me. What could happen to prevent our marriage?'

'Nothing, of course. I should not have mentioned it,' Harry said and his smile warmed her. 'It was foolish talk. Have you forgiven me, my dearest? The force of my temper has caught you three times now. I hope it has not made you take me in dislike?'

'I could never dislike you,' Susannah told him. She was tempted to tell him that she knew about the duel, to beg him not to go through with it, but she could not find the words. 'I cannot wait for our wedding day.'

'Can you not?' Harry looked thoughtful. 'When you go to Amelia's, I shall take a trip to London, to buy your wedding gift. Tell me, Susannah, what is your favourite stone?'

'I like pearls and perhaps diamonds,' Susannah said. 'My emerald ring is lovely. I really do not mind. The pearls your mama gave me are perfect.'

'There are others of equal merit in the family jewels, but I intend to buy something new for your wedding gift—something that has not been worn by any other Pendleton lady.'

'Thank you,' Susannah framed the words, but she really wanted to say, *All I want is you, Harry. Please do not risk your life by fighting a duel*.

They heard a gong sounding from within the house. Harry turned his head and frowned—he had noticed uncertainty in Susannah and he was not sure what was causing it.

'I think we should go in, for I would not wish to keep Mama waiting, Susannah.'

'Yes, of course,' she said and smiled as they turned towards the house.

It was unlikely that she would get another chance to talk to him alone, for she had been invited to play croquet on the lawn with Lady Elizabeth and some of the others that afternoon. She felt a knot of nerves in her stomach as she wondered how she could prevent Harry fighting that duel!

Wild thoughts of sending a servant for the magistrate or locking Harry in his apartments went through her mind and were instantly dismissed. It seemed that there was nothing she could do—she was certain an appeal to Harry would fall on deaf ears.

Perhaps Toby would know what she could do? She could at least confide her fears in him this evening.

'How do you know about the duel?' Toby looked shocked when she told him she had overheard Harry talking of it with his friends. 'That sort of thing isn't for the ears of delicate ladies.'

'I am not a delicate lady,' Susannah said. 'Harry is going to risk his life to defend *her* honour and it isn't fair. She won't care if he dies, but I shall. It will break my heart, Toby. Can you not do something to stop it?'

'What would you have me do?' Toby asked and shook his head. 'Nothing I said would change his mind, Susannah. It is a matter of honour. Surely you know that?'

'Yes, I know gentlemen have foolish notions, but I do not think it is honourable for two grown men who should know better to try to kill each other!' Susannah was cross with him, for he was clearly on Harry's side. 'Couldn't you make sure Harry went to the wrong place—or persuade them to shake hands and make up their quarrel?'

'Have you tried to persuade Harry not to go ahead with it?'

'No...he wouldn't listen to me.'

'Do you imagine he would listen to me?' Toby made a rueful face. 'Harry would soon tell me to mind my own business.'

'Then you can offer me no help?' Susannah looked at him in appeal. 'Please, Toby...'

'Susannah, I would die for you,' Toby told her. 'But I cannot prevent this duel. Besides, there is no need. I dare say it will end with them both firing in the air.'

'Do you really think so?' Susannah asked. 'I could bear it if I thought it was all some silly nonsense—but I am afraid they hate each other and that the marquis will try to kill Harry.'

'Well, if he does, he will fail,' Toby said. 'I promise you that Harry is an excellent shot—the best. He was given awards for bravery when he fought with Wellington. You don't imagine he will die in a foolish affair like this?'

'There you are—you think it foolish too,' Susannah said and Toby frowned. 'At least keep this to yourself, Toby. If you tell Harry that I know, I shall never forgive you!'

She turned and left him, feeling unaccountably cross. Men were all the same with their talk of honour and their stupid duels! Well, she was going to keep watch from her window in the early hours of the next morning, and when she saw the men leave the house she would follow them. She did not know what she could do to stop the duel, but she had made up her mind that she would do something.

Susannah had lain on her bed, fully clothed, because she had had no intention of wasting time dressing later. She'd rested for a while, because the duel would not take place before dawn, then closed her eyes, but slept only fitfully, and was out of bed long before the first rays of the morning light began to creep over the silent gardens. She saw four men leave the house when it was still hardly light. A groom had horses waiting for them. Susannah waited to see which way they would ride before going quickly downstairs.

She hurried towards the stables and found a sleepy yard boy beginning to sweep the cobbles. Bestowing a brilliant smile on him, she went confidently towards him.

'Good morning, lad,' she said. 'Would you prepare my rig for me, please? I have a fancy to go driving before anyone is about.'

The lad stared at her, lifted his cap and scratched his head, clearly startled by her request, but then he laid aside his broom and went to do her bidding. Susannah waited impatiently for him to get the rig ready for her. She climbed in and took the reins from him, but on an afterthought told him to hop up beside her.

'I may need you to hold my horses for me,' she said and smiled at him. 'You won't mind that, will you, lad?''

'Me name is Tim, miss,' he told her and grinned. 'I should like to hold 'em for you. I like 'orses, but 'ead groom says I ain't fit fer nuthin'.'

'Well, if you take good care of my horses, I shall ask

his lordship to see that you are taught to be a groom. In fact, you can be my groom—if it would please you?'

'You're a good 'un, miss—a rare sport.' Tim grinned at her. 'You handle them 'orses a treat.'

'Thank you,' Susannah said. She was glad to have the lad with her, because otherwise she would have felt nervous of leaving the horses alone. 'Do you know the woods well, Tim? Is there a clearing of any kind in that direction?' She pointed out the direction that the riders had taken earlier.

'Yes, miss. I reckon I could show yer where,' Tim said and looked at her curiously. 'Yer up to somethin'—ain't yer?'

'Yes, I am,' Susannah said. 'It is our little secret, Tim. You mustn't tell anyone else about this.'

'Cross me 'eart and 'ope to die.'

Susannah smiled at him. So far her plan had worked well. She did not know what would happen when she reached the clearing, but if she was in time, perhaps she would think of something….

Harry stood with Max, Gerard and Toby as they waited for the arrival of the marquis and his seconds. A doctor had been summoned to attend and was partaking of a snifter of brandy from a small silver flask. Harry glanced at his gold watch, for it was a minute to the time agreed.

'It seems that Northaven may have changed…' he began and frowned as the sounds of horses arriving made him hesitate. 'I believe this may be he.'

Three men rode into the clearing and dismounted. Northaven walked towards them, inclining his head brusquely to the small gathering. He was immaculately dressed in black from head to toe; Harry wore a coat of blue superfine and cream breeches.

'We are not late, I hope?' Northaven asked. 'We were delayed and this clearing was not as easy to find as I imagined.'

'I believe you are on time, sir,' the physician said. 'I am Dr Barnes, my lord. I trust you are happy to accept my services if need be?'

'Certainly,' Northaven replied in a careless tone. 'My seconds, Mr William South—and Sir John Travers.'

'Pleased to meet you, gentleman,' the doctor said. 'You have agreed terms?'

'Yes, the usual rules apply,' Sir John said. 'I would like to inspect the pistols, if you please.'

'Certainly,' Doctor Barnes said. 'I have looked at the pair and they seem nicely balanced, as perfect a weapon as I have seen. Look for yourself. I can find nothing out of order.'

'Yes, a nice pair,' Sir John agreed after a brief examination.

Doctor Barnes cleared his throat. 'Gentlemen, will the seconds please confer and then we shall choose the weapons.'

Gerard and Sir John agreed. They weighed the pistols in their hands, examined them, checked the barrels and loaded each pistol with one shot and powders.

'Gentlemen, choose your weapon, please.'

Harry waved his hand to indicate that Northaven should choose first, taking his own without appearing to look at it.

'Please take your places,' Dr Barnes said. 'Are either of you inclined to reconcile your differences?'

'Damn it, no!' Northaven said, his eyes glittering.

'I believe we are agreed,' Harry said. 'Pray continue, sir.'

'I must ask you to stand back to back,' Dr Barnes said. 'Take measured paces and do not turn until I have finished the count.' He paused, then, 'Gentlemen, we shall begin. One, two, three...'

It had been darker in the woods and not easy to follow the bridle path in her rig, but the light was gathering now. Susannah could hear the voices just ahead of her. She had left Tim tending the horses after he had told her that the clearing was just through the trees. She had wondered at first if they would ever find the right place, and her nerves were tumbling low in her stomach as she crept nearer to the clearing. She could hear someone counting and she knew that she was only just in time. On the count of ten they would turn and fire at their discretion.

She reached the clearing just as she heard the count of ten. Both men turned, looking at each other. Northaven had raised his arm, Harry still had his by his side. Northaven was taking aim. Harry was not responding. The marquis was going to fire first and his pistol was pointed straight at Harry's heart. She saw him draw back the hammer on his pistol and suddenly she screamed, running from the side of the clearing towards the marquis.

'No...you must not...' she cried and her terror spurred her on, her path taking her between Harry and the marquis just as Northaven pressed the trigger. His ball struck her left arm. Her scream of pain echoed on the still air as she fell forwards on to the dry earth.

'Oh, my God!' Harry cried. He threw his pistol down and ran to where Susannah lay, unmoving. Kneeling on the ground beside her, Harry gently turned her over, looking at the blood trickling from her arm. Her eyes were closed—she had fainted from the pain—but she was still breathing. 'Thank God she is alive. The wound is to her arm…' He looked up to see Northaven standing just a few feet away. Fury erupted within him and he glared at his opponent. 'If she dies, I shall see you hang, sir.' For two pins he would have put a ball through the marquis's black heart, but that would make him a murderer and, as angry as he was, Harry could not forget that he was a gentleman. He lived by his honour, for it was his essence, what made him the man he was. 'Damn you…she is my whole life…' His voice cracked and tears glittered in his eyes. 'I love her….'

'She ran between us,' Northaven said, his face white with shock. 'I meant to wing you, Pendleton. I should not have shot to kill. I wanted to prove I am not what you think me—and I didn't see her until it was too late. I swear, I would not have wounded Miss Hampton on purpose! I may be a rogue, but I am not a murderer!' He hesitated, then, 'This settles the score between us.'

Harry was intent on his love and did not even hear.

'Let me look at her, sir.' Doctor Barnes was there beside Harry. He knelt down to examine the wound. 'She is losing a deal of blood. I must place a tourniquet on her arm until we can get her back to the house.' He reached for his bag and took out the things he required. 'Stand back, sir. Allow me to tend my patient.'

'We need a carriage.' Harry looked about him. 'Someone must go for the curricle—'

'It's just 'ere, sir,' a voice piped up to one side of the clearing. 'Lawks-a-mussy, but I never dreamed she would go and do somethin' like that, sir. She told me ter take care of the 'orses, but when I heard the shot I looped the reins over a bush and come runnin'. She's a proper sport, that 'un.'

'I shall speak to you later, lad,' Harry said and, once the physician had applied the tourniquet, gathered Susannah in his arms. His face was grim as he nodded to Tim. 'Lead on. We must get her home at once.'

He strode away from the clearing, carrying Susannah in his arms, his expression turned to stone.

'Damn you, Northaven,' Gerard said, coming up to the marquis. 'I think you should take yourself off out of the country for a while. If anything happens to Miss Hampton, I shall not answer for your life. If Harry does not kill you, one of us will—that is, if you do not hang.'

'He challenged me.' Northaven glared at him. 'He challenged me, remember? The three of you always believe you have right on your side. Damn you! I'll not run like a coward, though you think me one. If Pendleton wants to come looking for me, he knows where to find me. I am not finished with any of you.'

Gerard watched as the marquis turned on his heel, strode towards his horse, mounted and went off at a pace. His seconds lingered, looking at each other in dismay.

'This is dashed awkward, Ravenshead. Northaven did not intend harm to the lady,' Sir John said. 'I am sorry for what happened—but she ought not to have run between them like that.'

'She is a young woman and she is in love,' Gerard said and frowned. 'There is no telling what a woman in love will do. Harry thought Northaven would miss, for he is not the best shot in the world. He told me he would wait and then fire in the air, for he had no desire to kill the man, merely to put an end to this nonsense.'

He looked at Max. 'We had best get back to the house, though I doubt there is much either of us can do.'

'It is in God's hands,' Max said and looked grave. 'The devil of it is—if she takes a fever and dies, Harry will blame himself.'

'He already is blaming himself,' Gerard said. 'This is the worst thing that could have happened. It beats me how she could have discovered that the duel was to take place and where.' He frowned. 'I hope she did not learn of it from Sinclair. Harry will not forgive him if she dies.'

'I do not imagine he would forgive himself,' Max said. 'We must hope that she recovers—I do not know what Harry will do if she does not.'

'Northaven has a lot to answer for,' Gerard said. 'It is a pity that the feud was not ended today. It has dragged on too many years already. Northaven may not have intended harm to Miss Hampton, but if he wanted revenge on Harry, he has certainly had his way....'

Chapter Ten

Susannah stirred as Harry laid her gently on cool linen sheets. She gave a little cry, a whimper of pain, and a tear trickled from the corner of her eye, but she said nothing, merely staring up at him, as if she were bewildered and did not know quite what had happened to her.

'My foolish little love,' Harry said in a soft voice. 'Is the pain very bad?'

'It hurts a little,' Susannah said, trying not to cry because her arm felt so painful that she did not know how to bear it. 'You are not hurt…he did not kill you…'

'Oh, Susannah…' Harry choked. 'My dearest—'

'Stand aside, sir,' Dr Barnes ordered in a stern voice. 'You would do better to leave the room and let me attend her with the help of this good woman.' He looked at Amelia, who had seen them enter the house and led the way to Susannah's bedchamber. She hastened to pull back the covers on the bed for Harry to deposit his precious burden. She was wearing her peignoir, but made nothing of the fact that their apartments had been invaded by gentlemen before she was properly dressed.

'I am very willing to help,' Amelia said at once. 'Only command me, sir.'

'I cannot leave her,' Harry said, his expression one of near despair. 'Must you cut for the ball? How deep is it?'

'I shall tell you when I have examined the lady's arm further. At least stand aside, sir—and let me do my work.' The doctor looked at Amelia with approval. 'Pray fetch hot water, ma'am. I have everything else I need in my bag. But I may need you again in a moment.'

'I shall be as quick as I can,' Amelia promised and, with a sympathetic look at Harry, went out.

Harry watched anxiously as the doctor examined the wound carefully, prodding around the bloodied area with his fingers. He had removed the tourniquet, but a steady trickle of blood was still issuing from the tear in Susannah's flesh. She whimpered a few times, but did not cry out, and after a few minutes the doctor smiled.

'Well, you are a good, brave girl,' he told her. 'You were foolish to do what you did, Miss Hampton, but it took courage. Now you will need a little extra courage, for the ball is lodged just here and I must cut you a little to remove it and then stitch the wound. Do you think you can bear it? I shall give you a small dose of laudanum to help the pain, but I cannot pretend that you will feel nothing.'

'You must do whatever is necessary...' Her eyes moved to Harry's face, a look of appeal in their depths. 'You will not leave me? Do not let Mama come in until it is done, for she could not bear to see me in pain....'

'I promise I shall not leave you,' Harry told her. 'Shall I hold your hand, my love?'

'Ah, Miss Royston,' the doctor said as Amelia returned with a kettle of steaming hot water. 'Thank you. I shall place my instruments in this bowl. If you will pour some of the water over them, please—and then I must cleanse the wound. Perhaps you would hold the bowl for me? Lord Pendleton, if you are to stay, you may hold Miss Hampton still as I cut, for if she jerks my knife may go too deep and injure her more.'

'I am ready,' Harry replied grimly. Having endured such surgery himself on the battlefield, usually without the benefit of laudanum, he knew that Susannah would suffer terribly. He held her hand tightly as the doctor cleansed the wound. She turned her face towards him as the doctor picked up his sharp scalpel and bent over her arm. Harry was forced to hold her still as she jerked with pain despite the spoonful of laudanum she had swallowed. 'It will soon be over, dearest…and then you will sleep and the pain will ease.'

'There…' Doctor Barnes dropped the ball into a small bowl and looked pleased. 'It came out easier than I thought. You were very brave, Miss Hampton.' He frowned and laid his hand on her brow as he saw that she was lying very still. 'The laudanum is taking effect. I dared not give her too much, but she will sleep for some hours now. She will not feel the remainder of what I do.' He worked swiftly, stitching the open wound and then applying a clean linen bandage. 'The wound will heal and she should not have any lasting ill effects, though she may have a scar—but of course there may be fever. If she wakes with a fever, you must call me and I shall prescribe something.'

'Thank you,' Harry said. He bent down to kiss Susannah's brow. 'I pray that she will not take a fever, but, as you say, it may happen despite all you did to prevent it. I thank God you consented to attend this morning, sir.

Had you not, she might have bled to death before you arrived.'

'Perhaps it may help you to reflect on the evils of such events,' Dr Barnes said with a severe look. 'Had it not been Miss Hampton, it might have been you lying here, sir.'

'I wish to God it had been!' Harry said. 'I would far rather it was I who had been injured. You are right, sir. I let pride goad me into this foolishness. Well, I have learned my lesson. I hope that Northaven is satisfied. He has his revenge more surely than if he had killed me.'

'I shall leave you now, sir,' the doctor said and turned to Amelia. 'Will you walk down with me, Miss Royston? Miss Hampton will need nursing for a few days, and you seem to me a sensible young woman. Will you bear the burden of caring for her?'

'I had intended to leave in the morning,' Amelia replied. 'But I shall not leave now until I know that Susannah is recovered. I would not leave her to the care of servants, and her mama will be very distressed. I shall certainly take my share of the nursing.'

'Thank you,' Dr Barnes said. 'I shall tell you of some signs that you should look out for if she develops a fever....'

Harry bent over Susannah as the door closed behind them. Had the doctor not done so, he would have begged Amelia to stay. He had no intention of leaving Susannah alone, at least until she was safely through the worst, but there were things that only a woman could do for her.

'Sleep well, my precious, foolish love,' he murmured as he touched his lips to her cheek. 'Why did you do such a rash thing? You should not even have been there.'

Harry frowned. He could not think who had told Susannah that a duel was taking place. She must have known—she could not have stumbled upon the meeting place by accident. If Toby had told her, he would feel the sharp edge of Harry's temper—and that stable lad should never have allowed her to take the rig out without permission.

He was angry that she had put herself at risk, terrified that he might lose her—and yet at heart he admired her courage. She had seldom driven her horses without either Toby or himself to help and guide her. To have the rig made ready, drive out to the woods at such an hour and then run between opponents bent on shooting each other showed strength of purpose and courage, if a lack of good sense and decorum.

Harry smiled, his feelings of anger cooling as he admitted that the woman he loved had as much courage and determination as most men he knew. She had taken a wrong notion into her head, but he could not help feeling proud of her for what she had done. He would scold her when he was sure she was quite well, but not too severely. It puzzled him as to why she had thought it necessary. Harry had known that the likelihood of Northaven wounding him severely was small. His opponent had never been a true marksman. For himself, he had been prepared to risk it—he had decided that he would let Northaven fire first, then take his time, give the marquis a fright as he took aim and then fire in the air.

He had hoped to put an end to the feuding between them, but his plan had backfired, rebounding on him, because Susannah was suffering and there was the possibility that she would take a fever and die. Even slight wounds could become infected, and if the poison went inwards there was nothing anyone could do.

Harry prayed that it would not happen. He was not sure that he would wish to live if he lost Susannah now.

'Oh, my poor child,' Mrs Hampton said as she bent over Susannah to kiss her cheek, tears trickling down her face. 'You foolish, foolish girl! What on earth did you mean by it?'

Susannah did not answer. She could not, for the fever they all dreaded had taken hold. Once she had woken from the laudanum, the signs had all been there. She was burning up, her brow damp with sweat as she tossed restlessly and cried out in her delirium for Harry.

'Harry…' Susannah whimpered. 'Please do not die… do not leave me…'

'I am here, my love,' Harry said, coming forwards. He had stood back to allow her mother to take his place, but now he bent over her, placing a hand on her brow and brushing back the damp hair. His heart was wrung with grief, for she was so very ill and he felt so helpless. He did not think he could bear the guilt if she were to die, for the duel should never have been! 'I shall not leave you.'

'It is hardly fitting that you should be here in her bed-chamber,' Mrs Hampton said, looking at him oddly. 'I suppose since you are engaged…but it will be thought very strange if people hear that you have spent so much time alone with her, sir.'

Harry looked apologetic, his face dark with grief. 'Forgive me, ma'am. I know you must blame me for this—indeed, I blame myself. If she dies, I shall never forgive myself!'

'Well, I cannot approve of duels, though I know gentlemen think them an honourable way to solve their differences,' Mrs Hampton said, shaking her head at him. 'However, I do not blame you for Susannah's behaviour. It was foolish in the extreme—and not at all what I have taught her. She ought not to have come near that place if she knew what was happening. It was very wrong of her, Pendleton, rash and most improper.'

'Please do not be angry with her,' Harry said. 'I do not know why she took such a risk, but I am sure that she intended to save me from being killed.'

'Of course she did,' Mrs Hampton replied. 'Can it be that you do not understand how much Susannah loves you? If you imagined that she was marrying you for position or wealth, you are much mistaken. I know my daughter, sir. Once she gives her heart, she does not change, though I know she has been uncertain of your feelings for her.'

'I thought...' Harry looked rueful. 'I believed she might care for Toby. He is more her age and I fear that I am sometimes too severe for her. I have tried to please her, but I was afraid that she might find me dull.'

'Now you are being foolish,' Mrs Hampton said and smiled wisely. 'Susannah would not have accepted you if she had not fallen in love with you. My daughter is far too romantic in her notions to marry for anything but love. I thought she might have a preference for Mr Sinclair at one time, but she told me frankly that she cared for him only as a friend. She assured me that they were too much alike and would not suit. She once told me that you would be a good influence for her and help her to be a better person.'

'I think that perhaps she may teach me to be a better person,' Harry said with a rueful look at his love. She looked so flushed and ill! 'I shall admit to having a shocking temper at times, but I must—I shall learn to curb it for her sake.'

'We must pray that she comes through this fever so that you may tell her these things,' Mrs Hampton said in a practical tone. 'And now, sir—I really must insist that you take some rest. I shall not deny you my daughter's bedchamber, for I do not think you would heed me, and I have no desire to quarrel with you. However, you should rest for an hour or so. Leave her to me now. There are things I need to do for her. Amelia will be here to give Susannah her medicine shortly, and we shall call you if you are needed.'

Harry ran his hand over his face. He had not shaved in two days and was in desperate need of some sleep and a change of clothes.

'Very well, ma'am. I have your promise that you will call me at once if…'

'My daughter is stronger than you imagine, sir,' Mrs Hampton said and smiled. 'You have my promise.'

Mrs Hampton sat next to the bed after Harry had left the room. She reached for Susannah's hand as she cried out and called his name.

'He will be back soon, my love,' she said. 'You must be a good brave girl, and we shall soon have you better.' She began to pull back the covers so that she could bathe Susannah's heated flesh. 'I really do think you must get better soon, my love, or the poor man will be ill himself.'

Susannah whimpered as she felt the soreness in her arm. What was wrong with her? Her long lashes flickered against her cheek as she struggled to fight off the cotton-wool clouds that fogged her mind, and then she opened her eyes to see someone bending over her. She felt a cool cloth against her brow and sighed.

'That feels good,' she croaked. 'Thank you.'

'You are awake at last,' Amelia said and smiled in relief. 'The fever broke last night. We gave you some medicine, because you were in distress, and you slept soundly. Are you feeling better, dearest?'

'My arm is very sore,' Susannah said. 'I am so thirsty. Could I have some water, please?'

'Yes, of course,' Amelia said and sat next to her on the bed, lifting her so that she could drink from the cup. 'I had this ready, for I knew you would be thirsty when you woke. The doctor told me that you must take only a few sips at first.' She smiled as Susannah swallowed and then closed her eyes. 'You are very tired. Would you like to sleep again?'

'No, not yet,' Susannah said and forced her eyes to stay open. 'How long have I been ill? I cannot think what happened to me…'

'You were in a fever for three days and nights,' Amelia told her. 'Do you not recall what you did—the duel?'

'The…duel…' Susannah stared at her and then memory returned with a rush. 'Oh, yes, of course. Harry was not going to fire and I feared the marquis would kill him. I tried to stop him and…he must have fired. I do not remember what happened next…just that it hurt so very much. I think I must have fainted.'

'I am sure that it was very painful,' Amelia told her with a look of sympathy. 'You were fortunate that the ball did not go deeper. Had it hit your chest or your neck, you might well have been killed. The doctor says we were very lucky that you escaped so easily, dearest.'

'I did not think he would fire at me, but I suppose it was too late for him to stop,' Susannah said and winced as she pushed herself up against the pillows. Her head was aching and she felt weak. 'Indeed, if I am truthful, I did not think of anything other than my fear that Harry might be killed.'

'Toby told me that Northaven is not held to be a good marksman. It was likely that his shot would have gone wide—and then Harry would have fired in the air.'

'But he might have killed him. I could not take that risk,' Susannah said. 'I love him too much…' A little sob left her lips. 'Is he very angry with me? Do you think he will wish to break off our engagement? I know my conduct was not what it ought to have been. I ought to have pretended I knew nothing—but I could not. I love him too much.'

'I do not know how he feels about what you did,' Amelia replied. 'However, I am perfectly certain Pendleton will not wish to break off the engagement. He has hardly left your bedside since he carried you up here.'

'Harry has been here?' Susannah stared at her in surprise. 'Did Mama allow it? It was most improper for him to be in my room. I think Mama could not have been pleased?'

'Your mama knew that if she forbade it, he would ignore her,' Amelia said and laughed. 'If you had doubts concerning his feelings for you, Susannah, you may forget them. I have never seen a man more in love than Harry Pendleton. He was beside himself when he thought you might die.'

'Oh…' Susannah blushed. 'Do you think so? I have on occasion thought that my sometimes-reckless behaviour may have given him reason to regret his proposal.'

'Pendleton admits to a temper,' Amelia told her and looked thoughtful. 'However, his own behaviour has shown that he is very much in love.'

'He will still scold me,' Susannah said. 'I have caused so much anxiety and trouble.'

'Yes, you have,' Amelia agreed and laughed teasingly. 'What you did was misguided, Susannah, but I do not think you will find that you are much censured. Indeed, I have heard you spoken of as being plucky and having a deal of spunk. I imagine Harry's relatives believe him to be a lucky man to have inspired such devotion. No one has censured you in my hearing or your mama's.'

Susannah blushed again, picking at the bedcover with restless fingers. 'You had intended to leave before this,' she said. 'I am sorry, Amelia, I have kept you from your business.'

'I wrote to Miss Emily Barton and put off our interview for one week,' Amelia said. 'I could not entertain the idea of leaving while you were still so ill. Miss Barton will understand if she is the person I think her.'

'I have detained you and Harry's friends, for they were to escort you home.'

'Yes, they were. Indeed, Lord Coleridge still intends it,' Amelia said, a strange look in her eyes. 'However, the Earl of Ravenshead has had a letter, which means he must go to France.'

'A letter from France—has he business there?' Susannah looked at her curiously for she sensed that Amelia was holding her feelings in check. 'He spoke to me of that country once.'

'It appears that he has a daughter,' Amelia replied in a tone that was carefully flat and devoid of emotion. 'She has been fretting and unwell and he told me that he must go to her.'

'A daughter? But I thought...' Susannah saw the look on her friend's face. Amelia was struggling with her emotions. 'Harry did not know he had a wife.'

'He does not,' Amelia said. 'It seems that the earl was married briefly during the war in Spain—a French lady, I believe. He rescued her from some troops after her escort had been shot. She had no one and he…married her. She died after the child was born and…the earl put the child into the care of a French family. However, she pines for him when he is absent.'

'Oh…does that mean he intends to live in France?' Susannah frowned, for she recalled his having mentioned something of the kind to her. She could not quite recall what he had said, but thought he might have considered living there for a time.

'I believe he may not return to England for some months,' Amelia told her. 'But we should not be talking of this, Susannah. You need to rest and…it is not our affair after all.'

'No, it is not,' Susannah agreed. 'I am so very sorry, Amelia. Did he say nothing else?'

'What else should he say?' Amelia glanced away, but Susannah could see a pulse flicking in her throat. 'Anything that was between us is long forgotten, Susannah. I shall not allow myself to think of it again.'

'Forgive me,' Susannah said. 'I have said too much. I did not wish to hurt you.'

'You have not,' Amelia replied and turned to face her. 'Nothing has changed—I knew that there was no chance of…' She got to her feet, her expression bleak. 'Excuse me, I must tell your mama that you are awake. Everyone has been so anxious.'

Susannah lay back against the pillows, a single tear escaping to trickle down her cheek. She felt so sad for her friend, because she knew that, despite her brave words,

Amelia was hurting all over again. She was still in love with the earl, even though she would not admit it.

'Why has Harry not been to see me for two days?' Susannah asked when her mama visited her that morning. 'He popped in to say he was glad to see me recovered from the fever, but he did not stay and he has not come to visit me since then.'

'He sent you those beautiful roses,' Mrs Hampton said, indicating a vase on the dressing chest. 'You must not expect him to visit now that you are recovering, dearest. While you were in the fever he sat with you, but it would not be proper for him to do so now that you are over the worst of it.'

'Then I shall get up,' Susannah told her. 'I want to see him, Mama. I need to talk to him.'

'The doctor says that you must stay in bed for at least another week, my love. Please do not be difficult, Susannah. You were very ill, and you told me only just now that your arm is still very sore.'

'Yes, it does hurt,' Susannah agreed, 'but if Harry will not come to me, then I must go to him.'

'You know that it is extremely improper for a gentleman to visit an unmarried lady in her bedroom, do you not?'

'Yes, Mama, I know,' Susannah replied, her mouth set stubbornly. 'But if he does not come to visit me today, I shall get up.'

'Well, I believe he is out on estate business at the moment,' Mrs Hampton said and sighed. 'However, I shall tell him when he returns. It really is most improper, my love.'

'Please do tell him, Mama,' Susannah urged. 'If

he does not come, I shall dress and come down this evening.'

'You are a troublesome girl at times,' her mama said and shook her head in frustration. 'But I suppose you must have your way.'

Susannah looked through the book of poetry that Amelia had given her before she left Pendleton, tossing it aside restlessly. It was almost teatime! If Harry did not come soon, she would be forced to carry out her threat and go down, even though she did not truly feel well enough. She was about to ring the bell and summon her maid to help her dress when someone tapped at her door.

'Please come in,' she called and sat up expectantly. 'Harry…I am so glad you came!' She smiled at him as he hesitated near the door. 'Pray do come in. I am quite decent, for I have my dressing robe on.'

'You are better, Susannah,' Harry said as he walked towards the bed. 'You know I ought not to be here now—though I dare say any damage was done before this. It is just as well that we are engaged, otherwise I should have had to propose if only to save your reputation. Your mama was very cross with me, you know.'

Susannah saw the gleam in his eyes and knew he was teasing her. She laughed and shook her head at him. 'It is such a bore having to sit here, Harry. I have had lots of ladies to visit me, but I wanted to talk to you.'

'Well, I am here now—what have you to say to me?'

'I think I must apologise for all the trouble I have caused.'

Harry arched his right eyebrow. 'Must you? Perhaps you should, for everyone was very anxious for you while the fever raged. We thought we might lose you. I must tell you that several of my family have severely reprimanded me for placing you in danger—and I could not blame them. I should never have forgiven myself if you had died.'

'Would you have minded very much?' Susannah looked at him, an unconscious appeal in her eyes.

'I cannot tell you how much,' Harry said and looked stern. 'Why did you do such a foolish thing? Was it that you were afraid I should be killed?'

Susannah nodded, her cheeks on fire. 'I know it was wrong of me, Harry—but I do love you so.'

'I adore you, my brave, foolish darling,' Harry said. He advanced towards the bed, sat on the edge and took her hand. 'I was not sure if you liked Toby better, but he assures me that you are merely friends—and that he refused to tell you where the duel was. Tell me, how did you discover it, Susannah?'

'I heard you say something as you came in that night—and then I listened at the library door, which was very bad of me, I know. I watched the direction you took that morning, and I asked Tim if there was a clearing in the woods. He told me which trail to follow and—' She bit her lip. 'Why did you not fire at once? I thought you would be killed and I could not bear it.'

'So you risked your life for mine,' Harry said. He carried her hand to his lips and kissed it, his look tender. 'I am not sure that I deserve such devotion, Susannah. I must ask you to promise me that you will not take such a foolish risk again.'

'I shall promise—if you promise not to fight another duel.'

'I had to fight him, Susannah—not for Miss Hazledeane's sake, but because he was my enemy and he might have tried to harm you if I had not challenged him.'

'Oh...' Susannah's eyes widened. 'I did not know—but I still do not wish you to fight again. I should not want to live if you were killed, Harry.'

'Then I must give you my word—the word of a gentleman,' Harry said. 'For I feel much the same, my love.'

'We are agreed,' Susannah said. She tipped her head to one side, a gleam of mischief in her eyes. 'When do you think I shall be ready to drive my horses again? You promised to give me a race. I trust you have not forgotten?'

'No, I have not forgotten,' Harry replied and laughed softly. 'It will be some weeks before you are ready for such a mad adventure, my love. Your arm will be painful and stiff for some time. I think the race should wait until after the wedding—do you agree?'

'Oh, yes,' Susannah said and gave him a wicked look. 'How soon can we be married?'

'Amelia is making all the arrangements. We shall go down as soon as you are able to travel and the last banns may be called when we can attend the church.'

'I cannot wait,' Susannah said. 'I shall get up tomorrow and perhaps we can go down next week.'

'If you are well enough to get up tomorrow, I shall show you my apartments at Pendleton,' Harry said. 'I would like to set any work in hand before we leave.'

'Yes, I should like that,' Susannah replied. She looked at him thoughtfully. 'Tell me, do you think the Earl of Ravenshead will come back from France for our wedding?'

'I do not know,' Harry said and frowned. 'I know what you are thinking, Susannah—but I cannot help you. I had no idea that Gerard had a daughter until a few days ago when the letter came summoning him to France. He will need to settle his daughter—and he will try to find Miss Hazledeane and make sure that she is safe, as safe as she can be in her circumstances. I doubt that he will find time to make the trip back for our wedding. We can hardly expect it.'

'I see…' Susannah sighed and looked wistful. 'I just wondered. I do not mean to interfere, Harry. I have learned my lesson, and I know that there is nothing I can do.'

'If they are destined to be together, they will,' Harry said and leaned forwards to kiss her on the lips. 'However, I am more concerned about you—about us, Susannah. Have you forgiven me for all the things I have done to hurt you?'

'Yes, of course,' she said and laughed. 'You have done nothing but treat me kindly. It was my own fault that you were angry. I should have told you what I knew concerning Miss Hazledeane, for I should have known that you would treat her fairly. I think I must be a very troublesome girl to you at times, Harry.'

'Oh, indeed, you are,' he agreed. 'But I would not have you otherwise.'

Susannah's arm was still sore when she went downstairs the next morning. It was bound with a fresh bandage, but she wore a stole to cover it. Her appearance in the drawing room just before nuncheon caused a stir. None of the gentlemen had seen her since her unfortunate accident, and they rushed to set a chair for her, offering to bring her drinks and making such a fuss that Susannah laughed. Her fears that she might be censured for her rash behaviour were quite forgotten as she heard herself hailed as a plucky little thing and just what this family needed.

'Harry is fortunate to have found a gel of the right mettle,' Lady Ethel said in a voice that carried to everyone. 'In my day we were not so mealy mouthed and I've known ladies to fight their own duels, my dear. In fact, I once challenged a man to a duel, but the coward would not meet me!' Her eyes gleamed. 'I was a whip in my day, you know, and a good shot. I raced Harry's father round the park here once and I have sometimes shot pheasant with the gentlemen.'

'Oh, I did not know,' Susannah said, amazed at the revelations. 'I do not think I should be as brave as you, ma'am, for I should not dare to challenge anyone to a duel—but I should like to race my horses once my arm is healed.'

'You'll be as fit as a fiddle in no time,' the lady said with a nod of approval. 'I'd wager a few guineas on you against almost anyone, m'dear.'

'Really, Ethel, you are outrageous,' Lord Booker said, but winked at Susannah. 'She is quite right, m'dear. Harry kept us waiting a long time, but he certainly knows how to pick a bride!'

Since most of the relatives that still remained at Pendleton seemed to feel the same, Susannah was able to enjoy her lunch without embarrassment. However, every time she glanced across the table at Harry, she felt like laughing, so she was obliged to desist from glancing his way. However, once nuncheon was over, he claimed her for himself before anyone could ask her to play cards or sit in the gardens.

'If you feel up to it, I should like to show you where we shall stay when we visit here, though you know that

I have other houses where we may stay. I do not expect you to live here all the time, Susannah.'

'It is a very beautiful house,' Susannah said. 'I found it overwhelming at the beginning, but it has begun to grow on me. I shall not mind visiting several times a year.'

'Really?' Harry's brows went up in surprise. 'Well, perhaps we shall in that case. If our own apartments are comfortable, it will be somewhere to escape to if we choose.'

'You mean from the *crusties*?' Susannah asked and laughed. 'I think they are rather sweet, Harry.'

'You have not been on the receiving end of their displeasure,' he said and looked rueful. 'They have each and every one of them told me that it was my fault you were hurt. I have been thoroughly scolded for bringing you into danger by taking part in a duel—and risking the future to boot. I believe they know that without you there would be no heir for Pendleton.'

'Poor you,' Susannah said and giggled. 'I was praised for my courage and spirit.'

'It seems that you can do no wrong,' Harry replied and grinned. 'If I ever beat you or run mad, you will only need to tell my relatives and they will have me confined in an asylum!'

'Oh, Harry…' Susannah laughed, for this was the gentle, teasing man that she loved. 'You are wicked, truly you are.' How could she ever have thought him dull?

Harry smiled again, but said nothing until they arrived at a pair of imposing double doors. At their approach a footman sprang to throw them open. Susannah looked about her as she entered, feeling surprised at how comfortable and charming the décor was already.

'But this room is lovely, Harry,' she exclaimed,

looking round at the blend of greens, blues and cream that gave it such a restful air. 'The furniture is so pretty—and modern.'

'It is the work of Mr Adam,' Harry said and looked pleased. 'I commissioned it when I found these rooms needed refurbishment. The furniture in here is mostly satinwood, inlaid with fruit woods—and also porcelain plaques in the French style.'

'I think it beautiful,' Susannah said. 'The furniture is so light and elegant and the colours are perfect. I should not want to change anything here at all...' She ran her fingers over the top of a pretty desk, opening a cupboard to exclaim over the inlay on the tiny drawers inside. Everything was so beautifully made! A display cabinet was set with exquisite pieces of Sèvres porcelain, and some Meissen figures, which were similar to those that had amused her in the guest chambers. 'May I see the rest of your apartments, please, Harry?'

'Of course—go where you please, Susannah.' He followed behind as she ran ahead, exclaiming over the next room, which was another sitting room, furnished this time in highly polished walnut, the décor rose pinks and creams, and clearly intended for Harry's wife to be private when she chose. From there Susannah went to the bedrooms. Harry's own room was furnished in crimson, gold and touches of black, which gave it a masculine feel.

Susannah inhaled the scents of cedar and leather, lingering for a moment. Harry's valet had tidied everything away, but she imagined it with his things lying on chairs and the stool at the foot of the bed and smiled. The next room was intended for her—and Susannah stood for a moment, looking at the décor of pale yellow, gold and white, thinking how attractive it was, and how comfortable she would be in such a room. The furniture here was satinwood, again inlaid with fruit woods and porcelain, elegant and, Susannah thought, utterly charming. Letting her gaze travel round the room, she saw that Harry seemed to have thought of everything.

'This is lovely,' she told him. 'Once I have a few of my own things about me, it will be perfect. I do not think we need to change anything at all, Harry.'

'Are you sure?' he asked and came to her, gazing down at her lovely face. 'If there is anything at all, you have only to say.'

'I love it all,' she told him. 'I am quite content, though one day I may want to make changes elsewhere in the house.'

'You must tell me when you decide,' Harry said and reached out for her, pulling her close to him. He bent his head, kissing her on the lips. At first soft and tender, his kiss intensified, becoming passionate, demanding. Susannah leaned into him, her body seeming to melt into his as she gave herself up to the pleasure of the moment. 'Anything you wish for is yours….'

'Harry…' Susannah breathed, her lips parting on a sigh of content. 'You will spoil me.'

'I fully intend to,' he replied. 'Since you have nothing to complain of here, I think I shall take you for a drive about the park until it is time for tea. Otherwise one of the relatives will capture you and I shall not have you to myself again for an age.'

For the next few days Harry took Susannah driving each morning, and she spent the afternoons sitting at home in one of the parlours. Sometimes she played cards or simply conversed with the relatives. A few of them had gone home in order to prepare for the journey to Amelia's home for the wedding, but some lingered and she discovered that she enjoyed their company. Her feelings of being unequal to the task that lay ahead as Harry's wife had faded to the extent that they no longer worried her. She had much to learn before she could truly take her place as the chatelaine of a great house like this one, but she was learning and she knew that Harry and Lady Elizabeth would help her. Indeed, with such well-trained servants, she need only give her orders and keep her accounts, just as Lady Elizabeth had told her.

It was towards the end of the week that Harry let her take the reins again when they were out, and she managed to drive for half an hour before she was obliged to hand them back.

'I am afraid that my arm still aches,' she said and frowned because she did not like to give in.

'It will take time to get the full use of your arm once more,' Harry told her. 'I was out of action for at least two months when I was injured in Spain.'

Susannah looked at his profile, noticing the little pulse flicking at his temple. 'It is because of something that happened in Spain that you quarrelled with the marquis, was it not?'

'Yes.' Harry frowned. 'We were on a dangerous mission and the enemy were waiting for us. Northaven cried off sick that day and we believe that he betrayed us, though he has always sworn that he did not. He resented it when we accused him of loose talk. Since that time we have not been friends, though until recently we managed to be polite to one another in public.'

'You will not quarrel with him again, Harry?'

Harry looked at her, his expression serious. 'It shall

not come from me, Susannah. I give you my word. I cannot promise that the feud is at an end, but I shall not go out of my way to court trouble. Jenny chose her own fate. I was unwise to promise her brother so much, for I knew nothing of her. However, that is at an end. All I want now is to live happily with you, my darling.'

'And I with you,' Susannah told him, eyes bright with love. 'I cannot wait for our marriage, Harry.'

'We shall go down to Amelia's estate tomorrow,' Harry said. 'The banns have been called twice in our absence. They will be called for the third time next Sunday and we shall be in church to hear them called— and then we can be married.'

'Oh, yes,' Susannah said, her heart swelling with love. 'I can hardly wait to be your wife.'

'I can hardly wait to claim you,' he replied and the look in his eyes burned her. 'I never thought that I should ever find love like this, my darling. When you risked your life for mine, you proved yourself beyond doubt. I am humbled by such love and I shall try to make you happy for the rest of our lives.'

'Susannah, my love. I want you to meet Miss Emily Barton,' Amelia said when she took Susannah into her parlour two days later. 'Emily has been kind enough to become my companion and I think we shall suit very well.'

'Miss Barton…' Susannah studied the young woman's face as she came forward to greet her. Miss Barton was very near Amelia's own age, an attractive woman, but with an air of sadness about her. Her dark blonde hair was pulled back into a tight bun, as if she wished for no sign of softness in her appearance. Her dress was pale grey, offset by a collar of heavy cream lace and pinned with a gold cameo. She wore no other ornamentation and her manner was as gentle and self-effacing as her dress. 'I am pleased you are come to keep Amelia company.'

'I am very fortunate that Miss Royston was pleased to give me her trust,' Emily said with a gentle smile. Susannah noticed that even when she smiled the air of sadness did not leave her and she wondered what had caused it. What tragedy lay in Miss Barton's past? 'I hope to be all that she expects and needs. I know that she is fond of you and your mama and will miss you.'

'Oh, but we shall all see each other often,' Susannah said. 'Harry is to take me to his house in Devon for a week or two and then we may go to Paris to buy some clothes. After that we shall return to Pendleton, and I shall be giving a ball. It will be a grand affair. I do hope that you will both come.'

'Of course we shall,' Amelia told her. 'I would not miss it for the world. I am so relieved to see you happy and recovered from your…accident, Susannah.'

'Thank you, dear Amelia,' Susannah said and kissed her cheek. 'I do feel much better.'

'We are looking forward to your wedding—are we not, Emily?'

'Yes, we are,' Emily Barton said and smiled her gentle smile. 'Very much indeed.'

The morning of the wedding was hot. Susannah was awake early. She went down and slipped out into the gardens before anyone was stirring. It felt delicious to walk in the shade of the trees at this hour, though she could already feel the heat building. She wandered as far as the rose arbour and sat there for a while, inhaling the perfume of musk roses and feeling her happiness seep through her.

It was only as she left the shelter of the rose arbour and began to walk home that she was aware of someone behind her. A trickle of fear ran down her spine and she spun round, hardly knowing what she expected. What she saw was a man in the clothes that a gamekeeper might wear, a long gun over his shoulder. He nodded to her, but did not smile. Susannah had the oddest feeling that he had been watching her—or rather keeping watch over her—which she felt a little strange.

Was Harry concerned that the marquis might try to harm her? The thought made her a little uneasy, but she put it from her mind as she went into the house, running lightly up the stairs to her room. Harry had spent the night at the inn so as not to spoil the traditions of not seeing his bride until they met in church. Susannah had just regained her room when someone knocked at the door and then Amelia came in.

'I brought you a wedding gift,' Amelia said and handed her a small leather box. 'It is just something to bring you luck today.'

'Thank you.' Susannah took the box and opened it, gasping with pleasure as she saw the gold bangle set with pearls and diamonds. 'This is beautiful, Amelia. It will go so well with the necklace Harry has given me as a wedding present.'

'I did ask him what he would give you,' Amelia said. 'He told me it would be diamonds or pearls and I remembered the bangle left to me by my mother, which I thought would match perfectly.'

'You have been so generous to me,' Susannah said and hugged her, suddenly emotional. 'If it were not for you, I might never have met Harry. I shall never be able to thank you enough, my dearest of friends.'

'If it was meant, you probably would have met

somehow,' Amelia said and smiled a little oddly. 'I shall miss you, dearest, but I wish you all the happiness in the world. Indeed, I know you will be happy, for Harry Pendleton is a good man.'

'Yes, I know. I am very lucky.'

'He is lucky to have you, as I am sure he knows. You will both be content in your marriage, for you are well suited.'

'I wish you to be happy too,' Susannah said but did not elaborate, for she did not wish to hurt Amelia's feelings. 'Did you know someone has armed guards walking the estate? I saw one of them when I went for a walk earlier. He was dressed like a gamekeeper, but I think he was keeping watch over me rather than your pheasants.'

'Yes, I gave permission,' Amelia said. 'They have been here for the past week or so. Lord Coleridge said that he and Ravenshead discussed it—Pendleton too. Apparently, it is as much for my benefit as yours; after what happened in Pendleton Woods they feared I might be the victim of another attack, but I do not think it myself. At first I thought it was a kidnap attempt, but since then I have been inclined to think it merely a random attack, perhaps for whatever of value I happened to carry. After all, no one could have known I would walk that way.'

'Unless you had done so before?'

'Well, I have always enjoyed walking in woods, though for the moment I am content with my garden— and, of course, we shall go to Bath soon, for I intend to live there for most of the year.'

'Yes, I dare say you will be happier there,' Susannah said and frowned. 'Please be careful, Amelia. I should not wish anything untoward to happen to you.'

'Well, I am sure it will not,' Amelia said. 'I shall allow the guards for the moment, but I am certain nothing will come of it.' She shook her head, as if to dismiss the idea. 'We shall not talk of this again, dearest. This is your wedding day and I want you to be happy.'

'I am very happy,' Susannah said, and then the door opened to admit her mama. 'Isn't it a beautiful day, Mama?'

'Very warm,' Mrs Hampton replied with a look of approval. 'I do not think we could have had a better day for it, my love. I have brought you a present—just a lace kerchief of mine and a garter of blue lace. You have your wedding gown, which is new. Amelia's bracelet is old and now something borrowed and something blue. You should have lots of luck, dearest.'

'I am the luckiest girl in the world,' Susannah said and kissed her. 'I have Harry—what more could I want?'

The wedding ceremony went smoothly. The sun warmed the old church, its rays sending showers of colour through the stained-glass windows. Susannah stood beside Harry as they took their vows, her heart filled with so much joy that she thought she might burst with happiness. When they came out of church to the bells pealing and a shower of rose petals from friends and villagers, she stood for a moment on the steps looking about her, her arm through Harry's.

It was as her gaze was drawn towards some trees to her left that a shiver of ice went through her. A man was standing just at the edge of the trees, watching them with an air of menace. She shaded her eyes against the sun, sure that it was the Marquis of Northaven. What was he doing here? Had he come to try to ruin their day?

For a moment she was tense, fearing that he might

suddenly dart forward and pull a pistol. As if he sensed her tension, Northaven suddenly looked at her. For a moment she felt some intense emotion, perhaps hatred or anger—and then he inclined his head to her. For a second longer he lingered before turning and walking into the trees.

Susannah breathed again. His bowed head had reassured her—she sensed that he was showing her respect, telling her that neither she nor Harry need fear him. He might still resent his old friends, but she believed he would not try to harm her or her husband.

'Is everything all right, my love?' Harry asked, turning his head to look at her.

'Yes, perfect,' she replied and smiled at him. 'Even the weather is smiling on us.' There was no need to tell him that she had seen the marquis, no need to cast a shadow over their special day. 'I have never been happier.'

'Then we must leave for the reception,' Harry said. 'Otherwise we shall keep our guests waiting and that would never do.'

Susannah nodded, taking his hand as they ran to the waiting carriage.

'You make a beautiful bride,' Lady Elizabeth told Susannah a little later that afternoon. She kissed Susannah's cheek. 'My son was lucky to find you, my dear. Indeed, had you not acted so boldly, he might not be here today. He says that Northaven would not have killed him, but I am not so sure. That man hates him.'

'Why do you say that?' Susannah asked.

'Oh, it is just a feeling I have,' Lady Elizabeth said. 'I have heard that he is in some financial trouble. His uncle left him a fortune, but he has run through it. He must marry well or come to ruin, I dare say—but I do not know if he will find an heiress to have him.'

'Oh…' Susannah frowned. 'He was always well received in town.'

'A handsome man is always good company,' Lady Elizabeth told her. 'However, I should not have allowed a daughter of mine to marry him, had I one of a suitable age. He will probably have to elope if he finds a girl foolish enough to run off with him.'

Susannah was thoughtful as she went upstairs to change into her travelling gown. Northaven had been watching someone before he became aware of her looking at him. Could it possibly have been Amelia? She had thought he was there to see her and Harry married, but she might have been wrong. Could he have been behind that kidnap attempt in the woods at Pendleton?

Susannah felt a trickle of ice down her spine once more. She had dismissed the incident in Pendleton Woods, believing as the others did that it was by mere chance that Amelia had been attacked—but supposing someone had been trying to abduct her? Could it have been the marquis? Was he perhaps hoping that he might force her to wed him so that he could gain control of her fortune?

Susannah was unsure what to do—should she tell Harry she had seen him, or Amelia? Perhaps it was best to say nothing to Amelia. She was being protected and she did not need warning against the marquis, for she had never trusted him.

Susannah would mention it to Harry later, but not until they were alone.

'I am glad that you told me that you saw him watching us,' Harry said when they were in the carriage, having set out on their journey a few minutes earlier. 'However, I was aware that he was in the vicinity. He is being watched, Susannah, and will continue to be for a while. Max, Gerard and I considered the possibility that it might have been he who tried to have Amelia abducted. We have no proof either way. Amelia is aware that her estate is being patrolled by agents who would not hesitate to shoot anyone who refused to answer a challenge. She does not think that Northaven would attempt it, but is prepared to be careful. When she goes to Bath, she will be more in the public eye and will not need so much protection. However, I have advised her that it would be best to keep one or two of the Bow Street men on for a while.'

'How awful for her,' Susannah said and frowned. 'I do not like to think that anyone would want to hurt Amelia—or to force her into a marriage she disliked.'

'When a woman is unprotected by a husband, especially one as wealthy as Amelia, it is difficult. The property laws may seem harsh as far as women are concerned, but in a way they do protect a woman from rogues and blackmailers. Once she is married, her fortune is under the control of her husband, though in many cases she is given an income and her money secured for her children.'

'Yes, I do see that,' Susannah agreed. 'I should be happier if she were married, but I do not think she has considered it—not truly. At least, she will not marry unless she finds love.'

'Perhaps not,' Harry said and arched his brows. 'Amelia is a capable lady and protected, as much as she can be. That bonnet you are wearing is very fetching, my love—but if you were to remove it, I should be able to kiss you more easily.'

'Yes…' Susannah laughed and untied the ribbons. 'I do not think I need it for the moment—and I have been aching for you to kiss me all day.'

Susannah sat before her dressing mirror, brushing her long hair. She was in the bedroom of her new home, and she was pleased to discover that it was a comfortable house. However, the décor left much to be desired, and the prospect of being given *carte blanche* to set it right was exciting.

Her heart caught as the door opened and Harry came in. He was wearing a long dressing robe of dark blue cloth, and his hair looked damp, as if he had washed it. As he came to her, she caught the fresh scent of soap and cologne.

'You smell gorgeous,' she told him, smiling up into his eyes. 'I am so happy…so very happy.'

'I am glad,' Harry told her. 'I love you so much, my dearest wife. My wife…it seems an age since I first wondered if perhaps one day you would marry me.'

'Yes, it does seem a long time since we first met,' Susannah said. She was suddenly breathless as he put his arms about her, holding her pressed closed to his body. She could feel his heat through her fine nightgown, and she lifted her face in anticipation of his kiss. 'I love you so much.'

Harry moaned deep in his throat. He bent to catch her up in his arms, carrying her to the bed and depositing her gently amongst the silken sheets. Abandoning his robe, Harry lay down beside her, feasting his eyes on her lovely face.

'We do not need this, delicious as it is,' he said and drew her nightgown over her head, tossing it to the floor. 'I want nothing between us, my love. I have waited for this moment so long and now I want to look at you…to touch every piece of your beautiful body…'

'Love me, Harry,' she whispered, looking at him with such longing that he moaned with need. 'Teach me everything I should know to please you.'

'You please me just as you are,' he murmured hotly. 'But I shall show you how we can please each other.' His lips took possession of hers, his hand stroking the satin arch of her back. Susannah gasped as she felt the burn of desire and her body tingled with the new sensation that she knew was need for him, to feel one with him. 'I want you so much…'

Susannah gave herself up to the pleasure of his hands touching her in all the secret places where no one had touched her before, his tongue teasing and tantalising when his hands had done their work. She arched and gasped, moaning as he brought her to fever pitch, before entering her. At the moment of penetration she felt a little pain, but in another moment it had gone as she thrilled to his loving, bringing her such pleasure that she thought she might die.

Afterwards, she lay at peace in his arms, sleeping.

* * * * *

An Innocent Debutante
in Hanover Square

Chapter One

'Oh, no, you don't!' Max Coleridge said as the urchin attempted to pluck a kerchief from the pocket of his companion. His hand shot out, grasping the dirty boy around his wrist with a grip of iron. 'That is thieving, my lad, and it will land you in prison. You will end with your neck stretched at the nubbing cheat if you continue this way.'

'Let me go, guv,' the boy whined. 'I ain't done nuffin' bad, honest I ain't—but I ain't had nuffin' ter eat fer a week!'

'Indeed?' Max's right eyebrow arched. 'Should I believe you, I wonder? And what should I do with you supposing that I do?'

'Let the ruffian go and be done with it,' Sir Roger Cole advised. 'I dare say he deserves to be handed over to the beadle, but it requires far too much effort.'

'Your trouble, my friend, is that you are too lazy,' Max replied with a smile that robbed his words of any offence. 'No, I shall not let the boy go—he would simply rob someone else and eventually he will die in prison or at the rope's end.' His grasp tightened about the lad's arm. 'Tell me your name, lad. I shall take you home and tell your father to keep you off the streets.'

'Me name's Arthur,' the boy muttered sullenly. 'I ain't got no home nor no farvver or muvver neivver. Ain't got no one. Let me go like the gent said, sir. I won't trouble you no more.'

'No family at all?' Arthur shook his head and Max sighed. 'Unfortunately, if I let you go, you would trouble my conscience far more than you imagine. I shall take you with me. You are going to school, Arthur—whether you like it or not.'

'School? Wot's that?' Arthur asked and wiped his running nose on his sleeve. He eyed the large man suspiciously. 'You ain't one o' them queer nabs, are yer?'

'I am certainly not,' Max denied with a wry smile. 'If you are hungry, you will like school—you will be fed three times a day, if you behave yourself.'

'Food fer nuffin'?' Arthur stared at him suspiciously. 'Wot's the catch, guv? 'As to be a catch. No one does nuffin' fer nuffin'…'

'No, I dare say they do not where you come from,' Max said. 'In return, you will have to give up a life of crime— and grime—and learn a trade…'

'I ain't goin' up no chimneys!'

'Good grief, I should hope not,' Max said. 'You might like to be a carpenter or a groom, perhaps—or even a politician?'

'You shouldn't put ideas into the boy's head, Coleridge,' Sir Roger said. 'A politician, indeed!'

'He could not do much worse than those we have in power at the moment,' Max replied wryly. 'But I would advise an honest trade—perhaps a baker?'

'I like cake,' Arthur said, his eyes suddenly bright. 'I pinched some orf a baker's stall once on the market.'

'There you are, then,' Max said, hiding his smile. 'The future looms brighter already, Arthur—a baker you shall be.'

'You are mad, quite mad,' Sir Roger said and grinned. 'It is hardly surprising that you are not married, my dear fellow. I do not know whether any sensible woman would have you.'

'I dare say she wouldn't if she knew my habit of picking up boys from the streets,' Max replied and smiled at his friend. 'Excuse me, I have a rather dirty ruffian to scrub before I present him to someone who will teach him a few manners...' He neatly avoided a kick from the struggling urchin. 'I should give up if I were you, Arthur. I could always change my mind and hand you over to the constable, and then you might never eat cake again.'

Helene eyed the chimney-sweep wrathfully, one hand on the shoulder of the small boy at her side. Her eyes just now were the colour of wet slate, her normally generous mouth pulled tight in an expression of disgust.

'You will go and you will leave Ned with me,' she said, her voice strong and fearless despite the knots tying themselves in her stomach as she faced the great brute of a man she had caught beating his climbing boy. 'You are lucky that I do not call the magistrate and have you arrested for cruelty. This child is too ill to do his work.'

'Lazy ingrate that's what he be,' the sweep muttered. His hands were ingrained with soot, his face streaked with it. He had a fearful scar on one cheek and he squinted with his left eye. He was scowling so fiercely that Helene's courage might have deserted her had she not seen the scars on a previous climbing-boy's back. Jeb had died of his injuries. She was determined that it would not happen to Ned. 'I bought the brat from the workhouse. He belongs to me—and that's the law. You can't take him from me, miss.'

'What did you pay for him?' Helene was haughty as she faced her much larger opponent across the kitchen of her uncle's home. She knew that the sweep could fell her with a blow of his huge fist, but she refused to feel afraid. 'Tell me and you shall be paid.'

'I paid ten gold guineas for him,' the sweep growled.

Helene knew that he was lying. No one paid so much for a boy from the workhouse. However, she understood that she must pay the price if she wished to take the child from him.

'Very well, you shall be paid,' she promised. 'You may go. I will send the money to your wife tomorrow.'

The sweep scowled at her, anger flashing in his eyes. 'If you don't send the money—all of it!—I shall come and take him back,' he muttered and went off, stomping out of the kitchen in a temper.

'You've landed yourself in a pickle again, miss.' Bessie stared at her. 'Where will you find ten guineas to pay him? And what are we to do with the lad now we have him?'

Helene felt the lad tremble beneath her hand. 'Don't send me back to Mr Beazor, miss,' he said, sniffed and wiped the back of his hand across his nose and then on his disreputable breeches, smearing more soot on his face in the process. 'He'll kill me sure as hell is full of the devil.'

'You watch your language,' Bessie warned him sharply. 'Speak respectful to Miss Henderson. She just saved you from a terrible beating.'

'Please do not scold him, Bessie,' Helene said and

smiled at the maid she thought of as her best friend. Bessie was her mama's only servant and had helped Helene out of scrapes many times when she was a girl. 'I think he needs a bath and something to eat.'

'He could certainly do with a bath,' Bessie agreed. 'He doesn't smell too sweet.'

'What's a bath?' Ned eyed them suspiciously. 'Does it hurt?'

'Lord bless him!' Bessie laughed. 'We're going to put you in a tub of hot water and wash all the soot and grime off you, lad.'

'Nah…don't fancy that…' Ned backed away from them nervously.

'I promise you it won't hurt,' Helene told him. 'Afterwards, I shall put some ointment on your back and then you can eat your meal.'

'What's to eat?' Ned looked round hopefully, a sign of interest in his eyes now.

'You shall have a hot meat pie and some cake,' Bessie said, seeing the gleam and smiling inwardly. 'But you've got to be clean. I can't have dirty boys in my kitchen.'

'Are you certain it don't hurt?' Ned's nose twitched as the smell of pies baking reached his nostrils.

'I promise,' Helene said and turned as one of the other servants entered the kitchen. 'Jethro, will you fetch the tub from the scullery, please? We are going to give this lad a bath.'

Jethro nodded. 'I saw Beazor looking like thunder. He's a bad man, miss. He's already done for two workhouse lads. He's been warned that if it happens again he won't get another.'

'Is that all they can think of to threaten him with?' Helene's eyes flashed. 'In my opinion, a beating is the least he deserves. He has killed boys and no one does anything to stop him.'

'Yes, miss, a few of us were thinking the same,' Jethro said, his expression grim. 'I'll fetch the tub and give you a hand with him, Bessie. Your uncle was looking for you, Miss Henderson.'

'Yes, I know he wished to speak with me,' Helene said. 'I shall have to ask him what we should do with Ned.'

'You can leave him to me, miss,' Jethro said. 'I need a lad to help out in the yard. He'll do with me. No need to bother Mr Barnes.'

'No, I would rather not…' Helene thanked him, told Ned to be good and hurried away to keep her appointment with her uncle. Edgar Barnes was a fair-minded man. He had taken his sister and her child in when Helene's father died from a fever after a fall from his horse. However, he was not a wealthy man. He had promised to do something for her, and she knew that he had summoned her to his library to talk about her dowry that morning. She had been offered a Season in town by a good friend of her mother's. Her uncle had already given her fifty pounds towards her spending money in town, but the dowry would need to be a more substantial sum if she were to stand a chance of making a good match. Especially in view of what some might see as her unfortunate background.

Helene could ill afford to give Beazor the ten guineas she had promised him, but she must do it. Her mother had spoken of Miss Royston being very generous, but Helene was not perfectly sure what that meant, though she knew they were to be guests at Miss Amelia Royston's town house. Neither her uncle nor her mother could have afforded to give her a London Season and she felt very grateful to the lady she remembered only vaguely. It was very kind of Miss Royston to send such an invitation.

Helene hesitated outside her uncle's door, then took a deep breath, knocked and opened the door. He was writing at his desk, but looked up as she entered and smiled.

'Ah, Helene, my dear. I am pleased to see you. Come in, niece, and sit down. I want to talk to you about your visit to town.'

'Yes, Uncle. I am sorry I am a little late, sir.'

'No matter...' He waved his hand in a dismissive manner. 'I am sure you understand your great good fortune and the opportunity this visit affords you?'

'Yes, Uncle. I am very grateful to Miss Royston for inviting us.'

'You must make the most of it,' Uncle Edgar told her, his fingers touching as he placed his hands in the steeple position and looked serious. 'I have two sons to see through college and I must do something to secure the future of my younger boy. Matthew wants a set of colours and that is an expense I can scarcely bear. I had thought I might give you fifty pounds a year, but some of my investments have failed miserably and I am no longer able to make the commitment.'

'I am sorry for your loss, sir,' Helene told him, her heart sinking. Without a dowry she would stand little chance of making an advantageous match. The fact of her maternal grandfather having been in trade was a disadvantage in itself, though Helene herself was proud of being Matthew Barnes's granddaughter. He had fought his way up from lowly beginnings to become a man of some fortune, which accorded well with her notions of equality. Unfortunately, a quarrel between Helene's mama and her father had meant that Mrs Henderson had been left a mere competence.

Helene had nothing at all, for she had not been born when Matthew Barnes died. 'Then I have no dowry at all?'

'I can give you a hundred pounds extra now and that is all,' Uncle Edgar said with a sigh of regret. 'I am sorry, Helene. It is fortunate that your mother has a good friend in Miss Royston.'

'Yes, the visit will be pleasant, though I think I may not be able to oblige Mama by making a good marriage...'

'Miss Royston understands the situation and she is giving you five thousand pounds as a dowry.' Helene gasped at the news and her uncle smiled. 'Yes, it is a very large sum, Helene. It should help you to make a good match. All the more reason why you should make sure you please your benefactress. You must strive to be on your best behaviour and to make the most of your chances. You must not be too particular, Helene. Do not expect a great match, my dear. He should be a decent man, of course—and you must not go against the wishes of Miss Royston. However, I know you to be a sensible girl...most of the time. But I shall say nothing of your little lapses, which I know come from your heart. You care about others and that is not a bad thing, but sometimes you are led into the wrong paths by impulse.'

Helene wondered if he had heard anything of the scene in his kitchen earlier, but she did not ask. Her uncle would not want to be involved in the quarrel, for he always took the line of least resistance if he could, and he would probably say that Ned should be returned to his master. He certainly would not approve of paying ten guineas to the sweep!

'I do try to be sensible, Uncle,' Helene told him. 'It is just that I cannot stand cruelty in any form.'

'I do not like it myself, but sometimes one has to look the other way, Helene.'

'Yes, Uncle. I shall try to remember.'

Helene's thoughts were very different to her words. She and Bessie had done what they could to save the climbing boy who had been beaten so badly that he died. The sight of his emaciated body, the bruises and the way he had just turned his face to the wall and died had lived in her mind, because she had known that his spirit was broken, too. If she'd had a little money of her own, she would have set up a school for poor boys and alleviated the worst of their suffering. However, even then she could help only a few, and she had often thought the answer lay with men like her uncle. Edgar Barnes was not wealthy, but he had standing in the community. He and others far more powerful should put a stop to the barbaric laws that allowed children to be bought for a few shillings, half-starved and forced to work for their bread.

However, she knew better than to voice her opinion on the matter. Most gentlemen believed ladies should be seen and admired, treated with utmost gentleness, but their opinions seldom counted for anything other than in the matter of the household they ran. Such attitudes might have made Helene angry had she not understood it was simply the way of things. Because she might otherwise have said too much, Helene had fallen into the habit of saying little in the company of her uncle's friends. They were all older men, gallant, charming and entrenched in their traditions. To challenge their long-held beliefs would have been rude. As a result she was deemed to be a quiet girl, pretty enough but perhaps a little shy?

As Helene left her uncle's study, her thoughts returned to the problem of the sweep. She decided that she would consult Jethro in the matter of payment. She would give him the money and trust him to pay what was necessary.

Anything he saved could be spent on some decent clothes for Ned. She could hardly expect him to support the boy entirely from his own pocket.

As she went upstairs to her bedchamber, Helene mentally reviewed the gowns she was taking with her to London. She had four new evening dresses, one morning gown and one for the afternoon; all the others had been worn several times before she went into mourning for her father. Would they be enough to see her through the Season? If her uncle gave her the hundred pounds he had promised, perhaps she might purchase a few extra gowns, for she was certain they would be needed if they were invited to some modest affairs. It was hardly likely that she would attend the most prestigious balls taking place in the houses of the aristocracy—although her father had been a gentleman, he had never possessed a vast fortune or a title.

Helene decided that she would wait until she got to London before purchasing more gowns. It would not be long now and she might not actually need them. The money would be better saved for more important things...

Helene stood just behind her mother as their hostess received them. The house was a three-storey building in an elegant square in the heart of London, beautifully furnished and quite large.

'Marie—how lovely to see you. You are looking very well,' Miss Royston greeted them as they were shown into the comfortable parlour, which they had been told was used for private afternoons. 'And this is Helene, I believe? You have grown, my love. I knew that you would be a young lady by now, but I did not think you would be so very pretty!'

Helene's cheeks turned to a delicate rose. She felt a little uncomfortable as she bobbed a respectful curtsy. 'You are so very kind, Miss Royston,' she said. 'Indeed, Mama tells me you have been extraordinarily generous. I do not know how to thank you, ma'am.'

'Please call me Amelia when we are private together,' Amelia said. 'I need no thanks, Helene. I shall enjoy having friends to stay—and as for the other—' Helene lowered her gaze, feeling slightly embarrassed '—please do not feel under any obligation, my dear. I was very fortunate in being left a great deal of money by my aunt, far more than I could ever need, in fact. Helping my friends is a great pleasure to me. I do not wish you to feel you owe me something, for I have known what it is like to be beholden to others.'

'Mama told me that you were not happy in your brother's house,' Helene said and raised her eyes to meet Amelia's. 'Uncle Edgar has been kind to us, but I must admit it is not like living in your own home.'

'No, it cannot be,' Amelia replied. 'I have asked my dressmaker to call in the morning, Helene. We all need new gowns and it will be amusing to choose them here. We can look at patterns and materials together...but I am forgetting my manners. This lady is Emily Barton. She is my friend and my companion. I am not sure what I should do without her—she completely spoils me!'

Helene turned her gaze on the lady standing silently by the fireplace. She had dark blonde hair and the saddest eyes that Helene ever remembered seeing.

'Miss Barton,' Helene said and dipped a curtsy, 'I am pleased to meet you.'

'I am pleased to meet you,' Emily replied. 'Shall we sit together on the sofa?'

Helene went to sit by Emily. Amelia Royston turned her

attention to Mrs Henderson, drawing her to a comfortable chair near the fire and offering refreshment.

'Would you care for tea—or something a little stronger? A glass of wine, perhaps, to keep out the chill of the day. It has turned a little cold for the time of year, do you not think so?'

'How kind,' Mrs Henderson said and sat down near the fire. 'I should not mind a glass of wine, Amelia. The roads were terribly rutted in places and we were rattled so in my brother's carriage. I thought we should break a pole or lose a wheel, but we arrived safely. Edgar talks of buying a new carriage but his sons are at college and he cannot afford such luxuries for the moment.'

'When you go home, you shall be taken in my carriage,' Amelia told her. 'Had I known, I would have sent it to collect you, Marie. Forgive me for not thinking of it.'

'Oh, no—you have already done so much.'

'Really, it is very little to me,' Amelia assured her with a gentle smile. 'I am glad to entertain my friends, you know. I am not lonely now that I have Emily, but we both like to have friends to stay.'

'In the matter of Helene's clothes...I have some money,' Mrs Henderson began, a slight flush in her cheeks, but Amelia shook her head.

'We do not need to speak of it. My seamstress will send her bills to me and we shall talk about this at the end of the Season. If we are fortunate and Helene secures a good husband, neither of you will have to worry about money again.'

'Yes...' Mrs Henderson looked doubtful. 'You look... beautiful, Amelia. Scarcely older than when I last saw you.'

'Oh, I hardly think that,' Amelia said on a laugh. 'I am approaching my twenty-seventh birthday, Marie.'

'No one would know if you did not tell them.' Mrs Henderson arched her brows. 'Have you never thought of marriage yourself?'

'I thought of it some years ago, but my brother did not approve...' Amelia frowned. For a moment her expression was sad, pained, but then she raised her head in a determined fashion. 'I fear I am past the age for marrying now, Marie. You were no more than nineteen when you married, I believe?'

'Hardly that,' Mrs Henderson said and sighed. 'It was an imprudent match, for my William did not have sufficient fortune and it caused a breach with my father. In his anger he struck my name from his will. Papa did not hold with the aristocracy—he thought them proud and arrogant. I believe he would have reinstated me later, but he died suddenly, just before Helene was born, and I was left with a fraction of what might have been mine. I do not regret my marriage, for my husband was a good man and I loved him, but I have regretted the lack of fortune for my daughter's sake. I had hoped her uncle might do something for her, but he finds himself in some financial difficulty, I believe.'

'It is the way of things—and sons can be expensive,' Amelia said. 'My brother has two sons and he often complains to me of their extravagance. John has taken a pair of colours, but the younger son prefers to live in London. Your brother was widowed just before you lost your husband. Is it your intention to return and keep house for him—even if Helene should marry well?'

'Oh...I am not certain,' Mrs Henderson replied. 'Edgar has a very good housekeeper and I am not necessary to him, though he would not turn me away.' She could not prevent a sigh escaping. 'He was very good to take us in but...you understand, of course.'

'Ah, yes, I do. I was forced to reside with my brother and his wife until I went to live with my aunt,' Amelia said and gave her a look of sympathy. 'You are not alone in your predicament, Marie, for many women find themselves reduced to living on a competence when their husbands die. It cannot have been comfortable for you, my dear. Well, we must wait and see what kind of an impression Helene makes—if she is to be accepted, she needs to be well dressed.'

Helene blushed as the two ladies looked at her. It was obvious that she was expected to make a good match. She was determined to do her best, for her uncle's warning had played on her mind. She did not think he would be too pleased if she returned at the end of the Season with no prospect of a good marriage before her. However, she knew that her mama had not been well treated by her father's family, who had frowned on the marriage and cut her most cruelly because of her background. Knowing her mama's story had helped Helene to become quite radical in her thinking. She was not sure that she approved of the aristocracy and their privileged way of living. In that she probably took after her maternal grandfather. Mrs Henderson said that she had his temperament and was equally as stubborn.

It would not do for Helene to be married to one of the idle rich! She must hope that she could find a sensible man who had compassion for those less fortunate than himself. Helene knew that her mama had great hopes for her and she was afraid that she might be disappointed if her daughter's choice turned out to be less important and wealthy than she hoped.

* * *

Helene found Emily Barton easy to talk to, because she seemed genuinely interested in hearing about Helene's life. She was attractive and Helene thought she could have been lovely had she dressed her hair less severely. Her voice was soft, musical and her laugh was infectious. However, she revealed almost nothing of herself, allowing Helene to talk without interruption.

Helene did not know how it was, but she found herself confiding in her new friend about the climbing boy she had rescued from his cruel master.

'He was beating poor Ned,' she said. 'I made him stop and sent him away. He said I must pay ten guineas, but in the end Jethro made him take two. I think he would not have been pleased, but he made his mark to show that the boy was no longer his property. I think Jethro may have threatened him, though of course he said nothing of it to me.'

'How brave you were to stand up to him,' Emily said, her blue-green eyes seemingly intent on Helene's face. 'It must have been frightening, for he might have attacked you.'

'He might,' Helene admitted with a little shudder. 'To be honest, I did not consider the possibility. I just ordered him to desist and—fortunately, he did.'

'Yes, I see…' Emily smiled. 'It is a sad thing when a child can be bought and sold for a few guineas is it not?'

'Yes, it is,' Helene said and her eyes caught with an inner fire that was not often present when in polite company. 'If I were wealthy, I should open a school for orphan boys and feed them on good wholesome food so that they grow strong and healthy. It breaks my heart to see children with rickets or sores on their faces, because they do not get the proper diet. So many of them die before they reach maturity.'

Emily nodded. 'I can see that you have put a deal of thought into the matter. The situation is even worse in town than in the country, you know. There are areas where the filth runs in the gutters and the inhabitants are for ever ill with some dread fever. Some of them spend their lives drinking gin to deaden the pain of hunger and hopelessness.'

Helene's eyes brimmed with tears. 'I have heard of these places and wish with all my heart that I could do something for them…'

'Amelia does,' Emily told her and smiled. 'This winter she set up a school and a home for orphans—not just boys, girls as well. I have not been to visit yet, though I intend to quite soon.' She arched her brows at Helene. 'Perhaps you would care to accompany me? Amelia visited yesterday. She said it was heartbreaking to see the new cases, but that the ones who had been with the school for some months were a joy to behold, for they had grown strong and were gaining an education for themselves.'

'Oh, yes, I should like it above all things—may we go tomorrow?' Helene's face lit with eagerness. 'It is just the sort of thing I should do if I were rich!'

Emily smiled and shook her head. 'Amelia has many things planned for you, Miss Henderson. You must be properly dressed, you know. In a week or so, when things have quietened a little, we may choose our opportunity to slip away one morning.'

Helene wanted to protest—of what importance were fancy clothes when there was so much poverty in the world? However, she held back the words. There would be chances enough for her to discover more of what interested her. She must not forget her duty to Mama or her sense of obligation to Miss Royston. It was obvious from what Emily had told her that her hostess was a generous woman, not only to herself but to deserving cases, and therefore deserved the utmost respect and consideration.

'How long have you lived with Miss Royston?' she inquired.

'Oh, a little over nine months,' Emily replied. 'She is the kindest employer I could wish for and the best of friends.'

'I see...' Helene frowned. 'Is she the first lady you have worked for—or is it impolite of me to ask?'

'Not at all,' Emily said and her eyes clouded with sadness. 'I looked after my mother for some years after my father's death. Papa was...an intolerant man and he made Mama's life uneasy. She became an invalid some years earlier. When she died, I found myself with little money, for my father's estate went to his nephew. I...was forced to find work, but I was very fortunate—I have little to do but enjoy myself here. Amelia makes few requests of me. All she really needs is someone to keep her company.'

'Yes, I see.' Helene nodded. Emily's warm affection for her employer was further evidence of Miss Royston's goodness. Helene's sense of obligation deepened. She must take care to please Amelia in any little way she could, because it would be rude to do anything else, and she had been properly brought up. 'You must tell me if there is anything I can do to make myself useful to you or Miss Royston.'

'I am sure Amelia only wishes to see you happy. She has the kindest heart, though she can be stubborn when she chooses,' Emily said and shook her head as Helene raised her brows in enquiry. 'Now, if you are ready, perhaps I may show you to your room?'

'Thank you so much,' Helene said and stood up. She nodded to her mother and Amelia as they went out into the hall. She was a little in awe of Miss Royston, because of her goodness and generosity, and she was glad of Emily's presence. 'I should very much like it if we could be friends?' she said with a shy glance at the older woman. 'If you would like it, too?'

'Certainly I should,' Emily assured her with a smile. 'I can see that you are a lady who thinks of others and that is something I admire…' For a moment that flash of sadness was in Emily's eyes again and Helene wondered what secret sorrow she held inside. However, she would not presume to ask, for she believed that people told you things when they had learned to trust you, and Emily did not yet know her. 'Now, we must talk of other things.'

'What kind of things?' Helene asked.

'Amelia has asked me to show you the house, and to tell you how we go on here. You are to have your own maid while you stay here, Helene. I know your mama has brought her own maid, but you will have one all to yourself. Tilly is a skilled needlewoman and she can dress your hair as well as look after your clothes. She has already unpacked your trunks and will have pressed a gown for you for this evening. Amelia has no guests for this evening. She thought we should all get to know each other, and we shall do that better by ourselves.'

'Yes, that is a good idea,' Helene agreed. 'I think we shall be friends, Emily—but I must admit I feel a little in awe of Miss Royston.'

'You must not,' Emily told her. 'She would not wish it. You are not the first young lady she has helped. Last season she brought Miss Susannah Hampton to town. Susannah is now Lady Pendleton. We visited Pendleton at Christmas and she seemed very happy. I do not think you will meet her in town, for she is in a delicate situation—she is to have her husband's child this summer, I understand.'

'Oh…she must be pleased,' Helene said, her cheeks warm. 'How fortunate for her.'

'Susannah is very happy,' Emily told her. 'She fell in love with Lord Pendleton and he with her. It was a love match—and they might never have met had it not been for Amelia.'

'That is indeed fortunate. I am not sure that I shall ever truly fall in love, but I must marry if a respectable gentleman should offer for me. It is my duty to Mama.'

'Well, perhaps,' Emily said and something odd flickered in her eyes. 'I think you are very pretty, Helene. I am sure you will have a great many offers. You will not be forced to take the first man who asks for you.'

Helene looked at her curiously. She would have liked to ask Emily what she thought of marriage, but she did not yet know her well enough. Besides, she suspected that Emily had no money of her own. Helene knew that without the dowry Miss Royston had given her, she would have been unlikely to find a husband. Perhaps that was why Emily looked so sad. Helene hoped that one day Emily might like her enough to confide in her, but for the moment she would not ask.

The next morning was entirely taken up with the visit from the seamstress and her young assistant. At first Helene felt a little nervous about giving her opinions, for she was very conscious of the fact that this must be costing a great deal. However, when she discovered that Emily was also being fitted for a new wardrobe, she lost most of her inhibitions. She found it easy to confer with Emily, to discuss styles, colours and quality, and also quantity—though she found it a little shocking when she discovered just how many new gowns were considered necessary.

'Shall I really need so many?' she asked, for she could not help thinking that some of the money could be put to better use. 'I already have four evening dresses I brought with me.'

'They are very pretty and quite suitable for when we dine at home,' Emily told her and smiled as she saw Helene's doubtful look. 'I felt as you do when I first came to live with Amelia—but she has so many friends. We are invited everywhere, you know. You cannot be for ever wearing the same gown, Helene. You would not wish to appear dowdy? No, of course not. Now do look at this green silk. It would be perfect for your colouring—do you not think so, Madame Dubois?'

'*Oui*, of a certainty,' the Frenchwoman exclaimed. 'It will look well for an afternoon gown, but the young lady should wear white for evenings. White and simple will be perfect for one so young and beautiful.'

Helene held the shimmering white material to herself, glancing in the mirror. She felt that white was a little insipid for her, but hardly liked to protest. However, Emily shook her head.

'I cannot agree, *madame*,' she said. 'I believe Helene would look better in colours—that pale blue and the yellow…and perhaps that very pale pink with a deeper cerise trim.'

The seamstress pulled a face. 'Very pretty, but the petite is so young…'

'I think I agree with Emily,' Amelia said as Emily draped the yellow and blue materials against Helene. 'White is necessary if you are presented, Helene, my dear, but I am not sure that your mama wishes for a court presentation.'

'I think that might be better left for the future,' Mrs Henderson said and looked thoughtful. 'I was never presented at court even after my marriage. I doubt that Helene will be, either.'

'Oh, no, Mama, I am sure it is not necessary,' Helene assured her. Since she had no intention of marrying into the aristocracy, it would be a waste of money to invest in such elaborate gowns.

'Well, we shall see what happens,' Amelia said. 'We can always order a court gown if it seems likely that someone will offer to present you, Helene.'

'I am sure they will not,' Helene said. 'I am quite content with the gowns I already have, thank you.'

'How many have you ordered?' Amelia inquired of the seamstress and shook her head as she was told. 'That is not enough. I think you should have an evening gown made of this straw satin as well—and I think a ballgown in this beautiful peach silk, Helene. Hold it against you and look in the mirror. It is perfect for you, my dear.'

Not content with that, Amelia ordered two further morning gowns, two afternoon gowns and a riding habit in dark blue velvet. Helene felt overwhelmed—she had never owned so many gowns. She was relieved to see that Emily was also pressed to order more gowns.

'Well, I think that will do for now,' Amelia said. 'When can you deliver the first gowns, Madame Dubois? The very first should be the peach gown for Miss Henderson, please. Emily and I may wait a few days.'

The seamstress promised to have several gowns delivered by the end of the week, and the peach gown in two days.

'That is perfect,' Amelia said after she had gone. 'We

have been invited to a prestigious dance that evening. Helene will need her new gown. We shall have to shop for some spangles tomorrow. A pretty stole and some dancing shoes to complement your gown, my dear. You might like to take Helene shopping, Emily? You know all the best shops and can show her what is usually worn at these affairs.'

'Yes, of course,' Emily said. 'Would you care to accompany us, Mrs Henderson?'

'As it happens, I have agreed to accompany Amelia somewhere,' Mrs Henderson said. 'You two go and enjoy yourselves.'

'I had planned to visit the lending library this afternoon,' Emily said and looked at Helene. 'Would you like to come?'

'Yes, thank you,' Helene agreed. 'Unless Amelia needs me for anything?'

'No, I do not think so,' Amelia said. 'I am at home this afternoon. You must not stay out too long, for I am sure we shall have several callers and they will want to meet Helene.'

'It will take no more than an hour,' Emily assured her. 'A walk to the library and back will be quite uneventful. We shall be back in plenty of time for tea.'

'Then do go, my love,' Amelia said. 'It will be pleasant for Helene to see something of the town, and you may meet with some friends.'

'You may bring a book for me, Helene,' her mama told her. 'It is so nice to have the opportunity of borrowing new books. Edgar had very little of interest in his library at home.'

'Emily—look!' Helene grabbed hold of her arm as they were returning from the library. 'Do you see that man over there? He is beating that poor donkey with a stick. Oh, how wicked! It is obvious the creature is exhausted and can go no further…'

Helene had been holding Emily's arm, but she broke away from her and ran across the road to where a man dressed in filthy rags was trying to force a donkey to continue pulling the heavy wagon. The wagon was piled high with all kinds of rags, discarded furniture and metal pots. The donkey was scarcely more than skin and bone and exhausted. Its owner had lifted his arm to beat the unfortunate beast once more when a whirling fury grabbed hold of him, holding on to his arm and preventing him from carrying out his intention.

'You wicked, wicked man!' Helene cried. 'Can't you see the poor creature is exhausted? If you force it to go on, you will kill it…'

The man tried to throw her off, but Helene held on, struggling to catch hold of the stick and wrench it from his grasp. She was determined not to let go even though he was much stronger than she and obviously possessed of a nasty temper.

'Damn you, wench,' the man snarled. 'Leave me be or it will be the worse for you!' He managed to pull his arm free of her grasp and raised it again, intending, it seemed, to beat her instead of the donkey.

'No, you don't, sirrah!' a man's deep voice cried and the bully's arm was caught, this time in a grip of steel. The vagabond growled and tried to free himself, but ended with his arm up against his back, his chest pressed against the side of the wagon. 'If you do not want your arm broken, stop struggling.'

'Let me be,' the vagabond whined. 'She attacked me, sir. I were only defending meself.'

'Be quiet, rogue, or I'll break your neck,' the man commanded. His eyes moved to Helene. 'Would you like to tell me what happened here, miss?'

'He was beating that poor creature,' Helene said. 'You can see for yourself that it is half-starved—and that load is far too heavy. The poor beast is too exhausted to pull the cart another inch.'

'Did you attack him?' The man arched his brows.

'I tried to stop him beating the donkey.' Helene lifted her head proudly, refusing to be ashamed of her action.

'I see…' Max released the vagabond, turned him round and glared down at him. The vagabond opened his mouth, then shut it again. The newcomer was a gentleman and a rather large one, his expression threatening. 'What have you to say for yourself, rogue?'

'The stupid beast is useless. It is lazy and a worthless bag of bones. I have to beat it or it will not move.'

'It might work better if you fed it occasionally,' Lord Maximus Coleridge said wryly. 'Here, take this in exchange for the animal and be off with you before I call the watch!' He thrust a handful of gold coins at his victim. The vagabond stared at the money in astonishment, bit one of the coins to make sure it really was gold and then took off as fast as he could before the *mad* gentleman could change his mind.

'That was too much. One of those coins must have been sufficient,' Helene protested as the large gentleman began to undo the donkey's harness, freeing it from its burden. She patted the donkey's nose. 'The poor thing. It must have had a terrible life.'

'Yes, I dare say,' Max said and frowned. He arched his eyebrows in enquiry. 'What do you propose we should do with it now?'

'Oh…' Helene stared at him. 'I am not sure, sir. The poor creature needs a good home and something to eat. It looks quite starved.'

'I wonder if it would not be kinder to put a ball through its head and end its misery.'

'No! You must not,' Helene cried and then blushed as his dark grey eyes centred on her face. She thought him an extremely attractive man, large and powerful, and, it seemed, exactly the kind of man one could rely on in an emergency. 'I mean…could you not have it taken to a stable? At least give this unfortunate beast a chance to recover…please?'

'Helene…' Emily had waited for her chance to cross the road. 'Are you all right, my dear? I would have come sooner, but there was a press of carriages.'

'Because we are blocking the road,' Max said wryly. 'Good afternoon, Miss Barton. I did not know that you were in town. I trust you are well—and Miss Royston?'

'Lord Coleridge,' Emily said and dipped in a slight curtsy. 'We are both well. May I introduce Miss Henderson? Helene—Lord Coleridge. Helene and her mama are staying with us this Season, sir.'

'My compliments to Miss Royston. I shall call,' Max Coleridge said and turned his gaze back to Helene. 'So, Miss Henderson—what do you suggest?' He saw the pleading in her eyes. 'I hope you are not suggesting that this flea-ridden beast should rub shoulders with my cattle…'

'Could you not find a small corner for him in your stables, sir?'

'Oh, no.' Max shook his head. He turned his head and signalled to someone. A youth of perhaps fourteen years came running. 'Jemmy, this lady wants us to take care of this donkey—what do you suggest we do with him?'

'Sell 'im to the knacker's yard, sir?' the youth said and grinned.

'Much as I think you may be right, I find myself unable to agree,' Max replied, a twinkle in his eye. 'I think you should take charge of him, Jemmy. I dare say we could find a corner for him somewhere.'

'That bag of bones? You're bamming me, milord,' Jemmy said, staring at him in horror. 'We'll be the laughing stock of the *ton,* sir.'

'I dare say,' Max replied. 'However, I do not intend to drive the wretched beast. Once it has recovered—if it recovers—we may find a better home. I shall make inquiries.'

'You want me to get that thing 'ome?' Jemmy was clearly horrified. 'I dunno as it will move, sir.'

'Do your best, Jemmy. I fear we are holding up the traffic.' Max gave Helene a direct look. 'I believe we should move out of the road—do you not think so?'

'But the donkey...' Helene moved on to the path, joining Emily and Lord Coleridge. Jemmy was trying to get the donkey to move without success. 'I think you need a bribe.' She saw a barrow boy selling vegetables and darted back across the road to buy a carrot from him. It was rather wrinkled and past its best, but she thought the donkey would be hungry enough to be tempted. She paused for a moment and then dodged between a cart and a man leading a horse, narrowly avoiding being run over by a coal cart. 'Try tempting him forward with this.' She handed her prize to the lad.

'Give it 'ere, miss. I'll have a go.' Jemmy held the carrot under the donkey's nose. It snickered and then made a loud noise, trying to grab the food and succeeding. 'Blimey! He snatched it...' Jemmy's mouth fell open.

He looked so astonished that Lord Coleridge gave a shout of laughter. He tossed the lad a gold coin. 'I think you need to buy a large supply of treats,' he said. 'Be more careful next time.'

Jemmy caught the coin and started over the road. The donkey made an ear-shattering noise and trotted over the road after him. Discovering that there were many more carrots on the stall, it snatched another, and when the barrow boy yelled in anger, took off down the road at a run, Jemmy in hot pursuit.

'Not quite as exhausted as we thought,' Max said, highly amused. Helene stared at him indignantly as he laughed. He sobered as he caught the look in her eye. 'Forgive me, Miss Henderson, but you have to admit that it was funny.'

'Yes, it was,' she said and the laughter suddenly bubbled up inside her. 'Oh, dear, it seems I have cost you a great deal of money and a lot of trouble for nothing.'

'Oh, no,' Max told her. 'To see that donkey with Jemmy in pursuit was worth far more than a few guineas, Miss Henderson. I do not know how he will live it down. I can only hope that my eloquence will be enough to retain his services—he may feel that he can no longer work for such a ramshackle fellow as myself.' He glanced over his shoulder. 'My groom awaits me patiently. Ladies—may I take you up in my curricle?'

'Thank you, but we shall walk for the house is not far away,' Helene said before Emily could reply. 'It was kind of you to help us, sir—but we shall take up no more of your time.'

Max lifted his hat, his eyes bright with amusement. 'I shall see you another day, Miss Henderson. If you manage to avoid being run over by carts or attacked by rogues, of course. Good afternoon.'

Helene watched him walk away. She turned to Emily, looking thoughtful. 'He was very kind. I am not sure what would have happened if he had not come along just then. However, he seems to be one of those gentlemen who takes nothing seriously.'

'I am sure you misjudge him. Lord Coleridge is fond of a jest, but quite a gentleman. You might have been in some danger,' Emily told her. 'That rogue would have hit you if he could. It was a little reckless of you, Helene.'

'Yes, I know. My uncle has warned me of my impulsive nature—but I cannot abide cruelty, Emily.'

'No, I see that you cannot,' Emily said and gave her a look of approval. 'Well, you were impulsive, Helene—but no harm came of it.'

'No...' Helene said, but she was thoughtful. She had rather liked the large gentleman, despite his tendency to levity—but whatever must he think of her?

Chapter Two

Amelia glanced through the pile of cards on the silver salver in the hall when they all returned from an outing the following afternoon. She looked pleased as she mentioned one or two names, and then frowned as she came to the last one. Her housekeeper was hovering nearby and she beckoned to her.

'When did Lord Coleridge call, Mrs Becks?'

'Just after you all went out, Miss Royston.'

'Was he alone?'

'Yes, miss. I believe so. Is something wrong?'

'Oh…no,' Amelia said, but she still looked slightly bothered about something as she took off her hat and handed it to Mrs Becks. 'I was just a little surprised that he should call. He is Lord Pendleton's friend rather than mine.'

'Do you not approve of Lord Coleridge?' Helene asked as she followed Amelia into the small parlour, which they used when not entertaining. 'He seemed very pleasant when he…when we met yesterday.'

'You met yesterday?' Amelia glanced at her, surprised.

'You did not mention it, Helene. Are you acquainted with Lord Coleridge?'

'Oh, no,' Helene said and blushed. 'I suppose I ought to have told you about the incident, but there were visitors when Emily and I returned—' She broke off and blushed, for during the night she had lain awake, remembering her impulsive behaviour, and shuddering at the thought of what might have happened if Lord Coleridge had not come to her rescue. 'I hope you will not censure me…' She repeated what had occurred and was rendered a little anxious when Amelia frowned. 'I know it was impulsive, and perhaps I ought not to have done it, but I cannot abide cruelty.'

'No, nor can I,' Amelia said and looked serious. 'I would not recommend such behaviour, Helene, for if Lord Coleridge had not happened to be passing you might have been in some trouble. Also, your behaviour might be censured by some in society, though not by me. I can understand your feelings, my dear, though I would urge caution for your own sake.'

'I am sorry if I have displeased you.' Helene looked at her anxiously. 'You will not mention it to Mama, please?'

'No, of course not. And you have not displeased me,' Amelia told her. 'At least it explains why Lord Coleridge called this afternoon. No doubt he wanted to inquire after you, to make sure you had suffered no harm.'

'That was kind of him, was it not?'

'Yes, though I should be a little careful of becoming too friendly with that gentleman.' Amelia shook her head, an odd expression in her eyes. 'No, forget I said that, Helene. He is perfectly respectable…and it was a long time ago. I should not have said anything.'

Helene would have asked her to explain further, but her mother, who had gone straight upstairs earlier, now entered the room and looked at her. 'Have you decided which dress you will wear this evening, my dearest? It is a soirée, so you will need one of your new gowns that we brought with us. I thought the pale green satin might look well—especially with the gloves and slippers you bought this morning.'

'Yes, Mama,' Helene said. 'I think the green is perhaps the nicest of the gowns we brought with us.'

'It will be very suitable for this evening,' Amelia said. 'Lady Marsh's affair is quite small, but she is a particular friend and knows all the best people. We are fortunate to be invited to one of her musical evenings. You will meet some new acquaintances, which will make things easier for you tomorrow at the dance. You do not want to be sitting with your mama when the dancing begins, for everyone hates to be a wallflower.'

Helene smiled and thanked her. Amelia had warned her of becoming too friendly with Lord Coleridge, though she had immediately retracted her words. What had been in her mind? Despite her retraction, and her assurance that Lord Coleridge was perfectly respectable, Helene suspected that she either did not like or did not approve of Lord Coleridge. Why? What had he done that had made her feel it would be better if Helene did not form a friendship with him?

As Helene went up to change for the evening she was still pondering the question. She had liked Lord Coleridge. He had come to her rescue and dealt swiftly and firmly with what might have been an awkward situation, but, more than that, she had responded to his sense of humour and the twinkle in his eyes. However, on reflection, she recalled that he was a member of the aristocracy and perhaps it would be best to put the small incident from her mind. It would not suit her to marry a gentleman who had no idea of the value of money and wasted his blunt when it might be put to good use. Her mother had been slighted and ill used by Papa's family and Helene did not wish for something similar to happen to her. She would do much better with a gentleman of moderate fortune who thought as she did about the important things of life.

She was a thoughtful girl and was sensible of the fact that she owed her chance to enter society entirely to Miss Royston. Without Amelia's generosity, she would never have been given a Season in London. Rather than offend her hostess, she would try to avoid Lord Coleridge's company as much as possible, though of course she would speak to him when they met. He had done her a service and mere politeness demanded that she thank him at least once more. However, it was more than likely that she would not often meet him. He was a titled gentleman and she did not suppose that he would be in the least interested in a country nobody. Nor indeed was she interested in anything more than a nodding acquaintance with a man like him!

'Max!' a voice hailed him loudly from across the road as he was about to enter his sporting club. Max turned and looked round; he grinned as he saw the younger man approaching on foot. 'I am glad to have caught you. I am just this day come to town. Harry sent me to look at some decent cattle he heard of and I think they are just what I need. I wondered if you would give me the benefit of your advice in the morning?'

'Toby Sinclair...' Max clapped him on the shoulder. 'The newest member of the Four-in-Hand. So Harry put you on the right track, did he? Your uncle is one of the best judges of horseflesh I know. I doubt you need my advice.'

'I should like it none the less,' Toby said. 'I have no engagements in town as yet.'

'Ah...' Max nodded, looked thoughtful, then, 'I am promised to Lady Marsh this evening. I think you know my great-aunt Edith? I am certain she would welcome you.'

'Thank you,' Toby said, his eyes lighting up. 'I could have spent the evening at a gaming hell, but I've just accepted an offer from Harry to join him in a business venture and I am trying not too waste too much blunt at the tables.'

'Sensible,' Max said and frowned. 'I happened to see Northaven this morning. I was surprised to see him back in town after what happened at Pendleton last year. He would have done better to take himself off abroad as Harry bid him.'

'I dare say his pride would not let him.'

'I dare say you are right.'

'I have wondered if it was Northaven who attempted to kidnap Amelia Royston in Pendleton woods last summer,' Toby said. 'If, indeed, it was an attempt to snatch her and not merely a botched robbery?'

'Ravenshead has his own ideas on the subject,' Max said and looked thoughtful. 'Miss Royston is in town, you know. She has some friends staying—Mrs Henderson and her daughter Helene.'

'Really? I must call tomorrow,' Toby said. He looked round as they entered the sporting club together. 'Are you going to box or fence today?'

'I thought to see who was here,' Max said. 'Do you fancy yourself with the foils, Sinclair?'

'Well, I'm not sure I'm up to your mark, Coleridge,' Toby said and grinned. 'But I'm game if you are?'

'Delighted,' Max said and clapped him on the back.

'Tell you the truth, I've been missing Harry and Gerard. Harry invited me down to Pendleton, and I may go in a few weeks, but I have not heard a word from Ravenshead since he went to France. I am not certain he intends to return.'

'Oh, I think he may,' Toby said. 'Susannah told me that he had written to Harry. He has been delayed, but he has engaged an English nanny for his daughter and I think he will open the house at Ravenshead in another month or so.'

'Ah, that is good news. I dare say he may visit with Harry and Susannah for a while, and I shall certainly go down at the end of the Season.' Unless he found a lady to propose to in the meantime, Max thought. He said nothing of his plans to take a wife, which had been forming slowly for a while.

He did not know why he had not married sooner—he wished to have children, and not simply because he needed an heir for his estate. Max had been an only child after his younger brother died in childhood. He had joined the army more out of a desire for companionship than a wish to be a soldier and had formed some strong friendships. However, Harry Pendleton's marriage to a spirited young girl, and Gerard's absence in France, had made him aware that his life was empty.

If he could find a girl who would put up with him— one he could feel comfortable with on a daily basis—he might decide to settle down quite soon. Max was not sure whether or not he needed to love the girl. Perhaps that was not necessary for a marriage of convenience. Affection and compatibility was possibly more important? He did not think that he could put up with a simpering miss who was interested only in her new gown or some fresh trinket, though he could afford to indulge his wife with all the trinkets she required. A little smile touched his mouth as he recalled the girl and the donkey. Now Helene certainly had spirit and her indignant look had made him smile…

Helene glanced at herself in the cheval mirror. Her gown was not as stylish as some Amelia wore, but, caught high under the bust with a band of embroidery, it became her well. She had added a new spangled stole and some long white gloves and white slippers. Her dark brown hair was dressed simply in a knot at the back of her head, fastened with pearl pins, and she wore a string of pearls about her throat. They had belonged to her father's grandmother, so she had been told, and were the only jewellery she possessed, apart from a matching pair of earbobs.

A knock at the door announced a visitor. Helene had dismissed her maid once she was ready, and called out that whoever it was might enter. She smiled as the door opened and Emily entered. She was wearing a dark blue gown, very simple in design, but of quality silk and cut most elegantly.

'You look lovely,' Helene exclaimed. 'I like you in blue, Emily. I do not know why you do not wear it more often.'

'Amelia has been trying to wean me from grey for a long time,' Emily said. 'I am particularly fond of blue, but I used to think it was not a suitable colour for a companion.'

'Amelia does not think of you in that way,' Helene assured her. Her face was thoughtful as she studied the other woman. Emily looked much younger now that she had abandoned her habitual grey. 'I believe she values you as a friend.'

'Yes, she has told me so many times,' Emily agreed. For

a moment she looked sad, but it passed and she was smiling again. 'You are beautiful, Helene. That dress becomes you.'

'Thank you.' Helene glanced at her reflection once more. 'It is not as stylish as your gown, or those we have ordered, I dare say—but I do not think I shall disgrace Amelia this evening.'

'I am very certain you will not,' Emily said and laughed softly. 'You look everything you ought, Helene. I was sent to see if you were ready—shall we go down?'

'Yes, of course,' Helene said. 'I am a little nervous about this evening. It is my first outing into London society and I am not sure what to expect.'

'That is why Amelia chose carefully for you,' Emily said. 'I am sure everyone will approve of you, Helene, for your manners are good and you think before you speak—and I think you will like Lady Marsh, who is your hostess this evening, for she is very kind. She is Lord Coleridge's great-aunt on his father's side. She has been kind to me even though I am just a companion.'

'You are a lady, anyone can see that,' Helene said. 'Being a companion does not make you any the less respectable, Emily.'

Emily laughed. 'That is not always the opinion of everyone, Helene—but I am very fortunate to have Amelia as my employer. She is respected everywhere. Because of her kindness I have been accepted by most—and you will be, too, Helene.'

'Thank you, I feel a little better now. Shall we go?'

Helene's nerves returned when they alighted from the carriage and walked along the carpet that had been laid on the ground outside the large house to protect the ladies from getting their gowns soiled. Lanterns were being held for them by linkboys, and the carriage had been obliged to queue when they first arrived—and this was supposed to be a modest affair! Helene was glad of Emily's company as they walked into the house together. They were greeted first by their hostess. Lady Marsh was a small plump lady of perhaps sixty years, dressed in a purple gown and a gold turban, and she kept them talking for a moment before allowing them to pass on to the reception rooms.

The first elegant salon was half-empty, a mere half a dozen couples standing around, talking and greeting each other. Amelia smiled and greeted two ladies, who lifted their hands in welcome as they entered. She introduced Mrs Henderson and Helene.

'Lady Renton, Lady Jamieson,' she said, 'may I make you known to some good friends who have come to stay with me for a while—Mrs Henderson, and Miss Helene Henderson...and, of course, you know my dearest Emily.'

Helene felt herself being scrutinised. She dipped a respectful curtsy, wondering if she were being approved. Lady Renton seemed a little aloof in her manner, as if reserving judgement, though Lady Jamieson was friendly enough. Helene was relieved as they passed on to the next group of two ladies and a gentleman.

'Miss Royston, I am pleased to see you here,' the gentleman said and then looked at Helene, one eyebrow raised in expectation.

'Mr Bradwell,' Amelia said. 'Mrs Bradwell, Miss Bradwell...may I present my friends—Mrs Henderson and Miss Helene Henderson... Mr Nicholas Bradwell and his mama and sister.'

'Charming, quite charming,' Nicholas Bradwell said and inclined his head. 'I am happy to make your acquaintance, ma'am—Miss Henderson.' His eyes had fixed on Helene's face. 'Tell me, do you enjoy music, Miss Henderson?'

'Yes, sir, I like it very well.'

'And do you play an instrument yourself perhaps?'

'Yes, sir. I play the pianoforte, though I cannot profess to be accomplished.'

'Helene, you are too modest,' Mrs Henderson said and gave her a reproving look. 'My daughter plays very well, sir. I have heard her spoken of as talented, but she does not like to say so herself.'

'A truly modest young lady.' Nicholas Bradwell looked at her and nodded. He was a gentleman of perhaps forty years or so. Of medium height and slim build, he was dressed fashionably, his hair cut short and brushed back from his forehead, the wings sprinkled with grey. 'Perhaps you would let me take you in, Miss Henderson? I shall make you known to your fellow guests.'

Helene glanced at her mother, who nodded her consent. Feeling her stomach tighten with nerves, Helene laid her hand on his arm and allowed him to draw her into the next reception room. Here it was more crowded, and most of the chairs and sofas were occupied. Helene saw that it was here that the musical entertainment would be given a little later.

'Shall we reserve that sofa?' Nicholas Bradwell asked, gesturing towards one that was still unoccupied. 'I shall sit with you and give up my seat when your mama comes.'

'If you wish, sir,' Helene said and glanced round, feeling uncomfortable. He had promised to introduce her, but now seemed bent on reserving her company to himself. She did not mind it for he was not unattractive and she felt at home with him. He reminded her of her uncle's friends, gentlemen who had treated her kindly in the past. 'Though if older ladies are standing, I should perhaps give up my seat.'

'I dare say some of the gentlemen will repair to the card room when the music begins,' Nicholas Bradwell told her with a smile. 'I myself came for the music. We have a fine tenor to entertain us this evening. He is Italian, you know, and I think his voice one of the best I have heard. However, many of the younger gentlemen will no doubt find their way to the tables before long. Some of them have no ear.'

'Oh...' Helene was not sure what to say. Her cheeks had heated slightly because she had noticed two gentlemen enter the salon together—and one of them was Lord Coleridge. 'I thought everyone would wish to hear Signor Manzini...' She drew her breath in as she saw that Lord Coleridge was walking towards them. She looked down at her lap, her hands clasped as he bowed before them.

'Miss Henderson, I am delighted to see you this evening. Bradwell—good to see you here, sir. I heard that you had been unwell.'

Helene sensed the tension in the gentleman beside her. She had a feeling that he resented the interruption and risked a glance at him. A tiny pulse was beating at his temple.

'It was a mere chill,' Nicholas Bradwell replied. 'I may call on you in a day or so to settle the little matter between us.'

'Whenever you wish, there is no need for haste, sir,' Max said and smiled at Helene. 'I hope you suffered no ill effects of your experience the other day, Miss Henderson. I have to tell you that Jemmy is doing very well with his charge, though we have not as yet found Jezra a new home.'

'Jezra?' Helene's gaze flew to his face. She saw the laughter lurking in his eyes. 'You have given that poor creature a name? Do you expect him to recover? I know that you were uncertain of it.'

'I believe Jezra is tougher than we all imagined,' Max told her. 'He is gaining weight and I am reliably informed that with the proper treatment his appearance will improve—though whether my credit will survive his arrival I do not know.'

'Yes, I did hear that you had a donkey in your stable,' Nicholas Bradwell said, a smirk on his lips. 'Not quite in your style, Coleridge?'

'Oh, the creature grows on one, you know,' Max replied carelessly. 'I dare say it might do to pull the children of my head groom in a cart, in the country, you know—once it has recovered its strength, of course.'

'A children's pet,' Helene nodded, her expression thoughtful. 'It is the very thing, sir. You are good to consider it.'

'It was a matter of finding somewhere for Jezra to go before he quite destroys my reputation,' Max replied in a casual manner. 'Jemmy told me that he considered leaving me for Lord Carrington's employ, but he considers that I am fractionally the better whip and has decided to give me another chance. So I must count myself fortunate...'

'That tiger of yours is a deal too free in his manners,' Nicholas Bradwell said sourly. 'If a stable lad spoke to me in that way, I should instantly dismiss him.'

'Should you, Bradwell?' Max arched his brow. He was very much the aristocrat in that moment, almost arrogant, his expression unreadable. 'I must advise him not to offer his services to you should he decide that I am beneath his touch, which he may yet do. I confess that I should be devastated should he take himself off.'

'You are a wit, sir.' Bradwell glared at him. 'Forgive me

if I do not see merit in such levity.' He glanced at Helene, his mouth pulled into a grim smile. 'You must excuse me for a moment, Miss Henderson. I have seen someone I must speak to.'

'Oh, dear...' Max glanced after him, a glimmer of satisfaction in his eyes. 'I fear I have upset that gentleman. I am sorry to have lost you your admirer, Miss Henderson.'

'Do not be ridiculous, sir! I have only just met Mr Bradwell. I assure you that he is not my admirer.'

'But he will undoubtedly become so,' Max said and nodded. 'I believe you have made a conquest—the first of many, no doubt.'

'I doubt it very much, sir.' Helene shook her head at him. 'Please, make me no empty compliments, for I do not care for them. I know you were funning just now, but pray tell me why you called that creature Jezra?'

'Jemmy said he should be called Jezebel, for his temperament is uncertain to say the least—sly and devilish, my groom described him as. I explained that Jezebel was a female, and so we settled on Jezra. I hope the name meets with your approval?'

'My approval is not necessary, but I find it apt,' Helene said. His humour was infectious, though she did wish that he might be serious for a moment. 'Shall you truly send Jezra to the country? I thought you might give the beast to someone.'

'I could not be certain the poor beast would not be beaten and starved again,' Max told her. His eyes seemed to be warm and approving as they surveyed her. 'Having given Jezra a taste of what life can be like when there is a warm stable and food, I do not think it fair to abandon him. Besides, I think that would have earned me your disapproval, Miss Henderson.'

'I should have been sad had the creature gone to a cruel master, for I cannot abide cruelty,' Helene told him. 'But I have no right to approve or disapprove of what you do, sir.'

'Do you not?' Max looked thoughtful. 'Be that as it may, I would rather have your good opinion—' He broke off as her mother came up to them. 'I am remiss. I have not introduced Toby to you, Miss Henderson—Toby Sinclair, Miss Helene Henderson.' He smiled at the older lady as the two exchanged greetings. 'Ma'am, we met earlier when we arrived. Pray take your seat. Toby and I are on our way to the card room. Please excuse us.'

Mrs Henderson sat down as he walked away. She frowned at her daughter. 'I suppose Mr Bradwell introduced you. Lord Coleridge is a pleasant enough gentleman, but above our touch, Helene. I heard that he may be looking for a wife, but I dare say he will look higher. Someone said that he has been paying attention to Miss Fitzherbert. She is an heiress of some note, though not present this evening. I would not advise you to think of that gentleman as a husband, Helene. Remember my experiences. I should not wish you to be slighted by his family as I was by your papa's.'

'Mama! I was not setting my cap at him,' Helene said and blushed. 'We were merely talking. Besides, you know that I would never forget the way you were treated.'

'You seemed almost on intimate terms with him,' her mother remarked. 'I have seldom seen you look so animated in company, Helene. I dare say he would be a good catch if you could get him, but I think we must set our sights lower, my love. Mr Bradwell is of far less consequence, but I believe him to be quite warm—not an old name and fortune like Coleridge, of course. Mr Bradwell was once married, I am told, but his wife unfortunately died of a fever without giving him an heir. I feel certain that he must be looking to settle his nursery, for he is past forty. He would be a good match for you, my love.'

'Mama, please do not,' Helene begged, her cheeks hot with embarrassment. 'Supposing someone were to hear? I am very certain Mr Bradwell has no such notion, at least as far as I am concerned.'

'Well, he seemed taken,' her mother said. 'Not that there is any hurry, for this is your first evening affair…and now we should be silent for the music is about to begin.'

Helene was tempted to remind her that she had done most of the talking, but she was too well bred to argue in public. Nor would she have said much had they been at home. It was clear to Helene that her mama was anxious for her to make a good match, and she felt that she must do her very best to oblige her. She did not dislike Mr Bradwell, though she had thought that his good manners had deserted him when he was addressing Lord Coleridge. Indeed, that gentleman had made him seem almost dull and boorish in comparison.

Helene held her sigh inside. She knew which gentleman she preferred, but it was clear her mother did not wish her to encourage Lord Coleridge. Nor ought she to think of it herself. Helene did not wish for the life of a society lady. Marriage was a necessity for a girl in her circumstances, but she hoped to share her life with a gentleman who had the good of others at heart. Perhaps a member of the clergy might suit her as well as any.

She hoped that she would in the next few weeks meet someone she could like well enough to marry who also met with her mama's approval.

* * *

'You will make a fine swordsman if you continue this way,' Max said and saluted Toby with his foil. 'Harry and I both learned as young men, but fighting on a battlefield is a different affair to fencing for sport.'

'Yes, it must be,' Toby agreed as they replaced their swords in the stand and walked to the changing room together. 'I should have liked to join Wellington when Boney escaped from Elba. I was still at Oxford, of course, but that was not the reason I did not offer my services. Mama begged me not to go, because of my father's health. She said that if anything happened to me it would be the end of him. I felt obliged to do as she asked.' He looked rueful and Max smiled. 'I have always felt that I ought not to have listened to her.'

'Sometimes it takes more strength of mind to give up the chance of adventure than to take it, Toby. Do not feel that you missed out. War is something best avoided if you can. If it had not been for Harry and Gerard, I should have died in Spain. Harry carried me for more than an hour on his back. We were all of us lucky to get out...' Max frowned. 'I joined Wellington in Brussels as his aide in the last action, but saw little of the fighting. I got shot at a few times while delivering Old Hooky's messages, but I seem to have the luck of the devil.'

'That's as well,' Toby said looking at him thoughtfully. 'You have never married, Coleridge. What would have happened to the title and your estate had you been killed?'

'I have a cousin. Robert Heronsdale.' A tiny pulse flickered at Max's temple. 'My father's sister's son. I suppose Robert would inherit through his mother if I were to die without issue, but I do not think it too late to render that unnecessary.'

'Has he ever been to town?' Toby asked. 'I do not recall the name.'

'No...' A strange expression flickered in Max's eyes. 'I invited him to stay with me on my return from Brussels, but he was unwell. I have been told that he suffers bouts of periodical sickness.'

'Unfortunate for the poor fellow,' Toby said and nodded. 'Mama worried that I might have inherited Father's weakness of the chest, but thus far I am hale and hearty.'

'Nothing to fear as far as you are concerned,' Max said and the strange look disappeared as he grinned. 'If you were my heir, I should not be concerned for the future, Toby. As it is, I believe I must seriously consider marriage.'

'As to that, there was some talk of your showing Miss Fitzherbert particular attention. I heard yesterday that she had accepted the Duke of Melbourn.'

'I did consider it when we met at a house party at Christmas,' Max replied. 'However, after further consideration I decided we should not suit. Poor Jane did not find my sense of humour amusing. Indeed, she did not always realise when I was funning. I fear that I do have a rather irreverent humour and she is not alone in disapproving of levity. Nor would she approve of certain other activities of mine, I fear.'

'Mr Bradwell was not amused by your humour last night,' Toby said and arched his right eyebrow. 'However, Miss Henderson seemed to approve of your actions over the donkey. I should have liked to see her when she pounced on that rogue, Max. From what you told me, she was very brave.'

'Yes, very,' Max confirmed. 'I should not have told you had you not been so taken with that wretched donkey, Toby. You must not tell anyone else of her part in the affair.

I would not wish to damage her reputation. She seems to be taking well at the moment.'

'You need not have cautioned me,' Toby said. 'She sounds a good sort of person, Coleridge.' He threw Max a mocking look. 'Perhaps you should fix your interest with her before Bradwell does?'

'Damned young pup!' Max said and gave him a stare of mock severity. 'I shall admit to you privately that I like her. However, these things should not be rushed.'

'I'll wager that Bradwell will ask her before the week's out and be turned down,' Toby said and grinned wickedly. 'A hundred guineas she sends him away with a flea in his ear!'

'It is most improper of you to take that young lady's name in vain,' Max said, but his eyes gleamed. 'I'll take you—but if word of this wager gets out I shall skin you alive!'

'It is just between us,' Toby said. 'We must watch for the signs, Coleridge. They are both certain to be at the Marquis of Hindlesham's ball this evening.'

'Amelia was right about that colour,' Mrs Henderson said as Helene came downstairs wearing her new gown that evening. 'You look beautiful, my love.' Helene's hair had been dressed in a knot at the top of her head, and then allowed to fall to her shoulder in one elegant ringlet. Her hair was a dark, shining brown, her slightly olive-toned skin brought to life by the warmth of the deep peach silk. She was wearing a pendant of diamonds and pearls loaned to her by Amelia, and a matching pair of earrings. 'I think you need a bracelet, my love. Wear this, Helene. Your papa gave it to me as my wedding gift.' She handed Helene a small velvet pouch. Inside was a narrow bracelet of dia-monds set in gold.

'Mama, your bracelet,' Helene said and hesitated. 'Are you sure you wish to lend it to me? It is so precious to you—and I should be distressed if I lost it. Did you not say that the catch was loose?'

'I have had the catch seen to,' Mrs Henderson said. 'Had your papa been a richer man, you might have had jewels of your own, Helene. I am sorry that I could not give them to you, but you may borrow my bracelet while we are in town.'

'Oh, thank you, Mama,' Helene said. 'Will you fasten it for me, please? I shall take very good care of it, I promise.'

Helene admired the bracelet on her wrist. The stones looked well against the pristine white of her long evening gloves, but she was still a little apprehensive of wearing it, because she knew that her mama treasured the lovely thing. She had been forced to sell some of her jewellery since Papa died, but the bracelet was too precious to part with unless the necessity became too pressing. Helene tested the clasp by giving it a gentle tug. It held and she felt relieved, because it seemed that the fastening was now secure.

Amelia and Emily joined them at that moment. Emily admired the bracelet, complimenting Helene on her appearance.

'That colour looks wonderful on you,' she said. 'So much better than the white Madame Dubois would have had you wear.'

'I suppose she was thinking that white is generally favoured by young ladies,' Mrs Henderson said. 'However, I think Amelia was quite right to advise against it. I believe the carriage awaits—shall we go?'

* * *

In the carriage, Helene was careful not to sit on Amelia's gown. It was quite a squash with four of them, but, by being considerate of each other, they managed to arrive with no damage to their gowns. A red carpet had been laid for the ladies to walk on, and there were linkboys everywhere with their torches and lanterns. Footmen were waiting to conduct the guests inside, and the ladies were greeted by smiling maids who took their evening cloaks. Directed by one of the footmen, they walked up a magnificent staircase to meet the Marquis and Marquise of Hindlesham.

The marquis was a large, portly man dressed in a dark puce coat, his wife a tiny woman, exquisitely lovely in a gown of sparkling silver. She must have been at least twenty years his junior and was now recovered from the birth of her first son. The grand ball was being given in celebration of her success in producing the heir; the magnificent diamonds around her throat were evidence of her husband's delight at her cleverness.

Amelia congratulated both the marquis and his wife and received a kiss on the cheek from the young mother, who was not much above Helene's own age. Helene curtsied and thanked her hostess for the invitation.

'You are very welcome, Miss Henderson,' the marquise replied and smiled. 'Amelia Royston is a friend— any guests she cares to bring are always welcome to me. Perhaps we may talk later.'

Helene inclined her head and moved on, because there was a line of guests waiting to greet and be greeted by their hosts. She had thought there were a lot of guests at the soirée the previous evening, but this was clearly a much grander occasion. There were two large reception rooms, which were overflowing with guests. Footmen circled with trays of champagne and many people were content to linger here. However, Amelia was moving steadily through the crush, Emily, Mrs Henderson and Helene following in her wake. Beyond the two crowded reception rooms was a large, long room, which was where the ball was to be held. Helene could hear music playing and already a few couples had taken to the floor.

She looked about her, entranced by the theme. Yards and yards of some pale pink gauzy material had been draped over the stage where the musicians were grouped. Banks of pink roses and carnations were at the foot of the stage, and arranged tastefully in alcoves to either side.

'Where on earth did they find so many roses?' Helene asked of no one in particular and heard a throaty chuckle just behind her. Turning, she found herself staring up at Lord Coleridge. 'My lord...' She dipped a curtsy. 'I was just admiring the flowers. There are such a profusion and it is a little early in the year, would you not agree?'

'I believe they are all forced in a hothouse,' Max told her, a gleam in his eyes. 'Have you remarked that they have little scent? For myself I prefer a natural rose...one that is allowed to blossom in its own good time. Ours at Coleridge House begin to flower from May onwards in the most sheltered spots, and there is one white bush that always gives us a rose at Christmas. When I was a child my father always plucked it for my mother on Christmas Day.'

'How lovely,' Helene said. She felt a flutter in her stomach as she gazed up into his dark, slate-grey eyes. There was something so very attractive about him! 'Tell me, do your roses smell wonderful?'

'Yes, particularly a dark red one that was my mother's

favourite—and an old pink damask rose that no one knows anything about.'

'Someone must know something of it, surely?'

'No, it is true that no one can name it, and no one remembers it being planted. My mother was a great gardener until her health went and she died suddenly when I was young, but even she could not remember having it planted. My head gardener thinks it must have grown from a seedling—but we have no record of it. I have made inquiries, but even the experts cannot put a name to it.'

'How fascinating. If it is truly a new variety you must name it,' Helene said. 'I love gardens and gardening. I had my own at home, but my uncle's gardener does not wish for help.' She looked at him steadily. 'I am sorry that your mama died when you were young. I know what it is to lose a parent too soon.'

'Yes, your mama is a widow, I believe. We have something in common, Miss Henderson. In Mama's case, it was very sad because in his grief my father neglected her garden—and a garden gives much pleasure,' Max told her. 'I am sorry your uncle's gardener does not wish for your help, but I am sure you will have your own garden again one day.'

'Yes, perhaps I shall.'

'May I ask if you will dance this with me?' Max asked as they saw couples beginning to take the floor for a country dance. 'I hope you like to dance, Miss Henderson?'

'Yes—at least, I have not had much opportunity, though I have been given lessons.'

'I am sure you will enjoy the pastime now that you have the opportunity,' Max said and offered her his hand. 'Shall we, Miss Henderson?'

Helene gave him her hand, smiling up at him. The

answering smile in his eyes made her feel instantly at home with him, and she found the steps came easily to her. He was a large man, but she was acutely aware how well he danced, seeming to have a light step and an elegant bearing that some of the other gentlemen did not quite possess.

It was for Helene an enchanted moment—it seemed only a moment before he was returning her to her friends.

'That was most enjoyable, Miss Henderson,' Max told her as he bowed. 'May I ask you to reserve the dance before supper, please?'

'Yes, certainly,' Helene said. Her heart did an odd little flip as he wrote his name, nodded his head and walked away. Her mama was looking at her, but before she could make a remark, another gentleman approached and asked her to dance. Since she had already met Mr Peters in Amelia's company, Helene was in the happy position of being able to accept. He wrote his name in one further space at the end of their dance.

'Miss Henderson, I hope you have reserved a dance for me?'

Helene turned her head as she heard a familiar voice. 'Good evening, Mr Bradwell. I have not reserved anything, for I did not know if you were here,' Helene said. 'But there are still several spaces.' She offered him her card and he wrote in two of them.

After that, several young men she had not previously met approached Helene and it was not long before every space on her card was filled. Helene found herself swept from one dance to the next, scarcely finding the time to draw breath. When the supper dance became due, her cheeks were flushed and her eyes shone with pleasure.

She had not expected to be this popular at her first dance and felt pleasantly surprised.

'You are enjoying yourself this evening?' Max asked as he arrived to claim her for the supper dance. 'I believe this is a waltz, Miss Henderson. You do not object?'

'Not at all,' Helene said. 'Mama has given me permission to waltz and I have done so twice this evening.'

'I like it very well,' he said, placing his gloved hand at the small of her back. 'But I know some ladies find it very shocking to be held so. It was held to be fast when it was first introduced and I believe some still feel it so.'

His eyes held a gleam of humour as he gazed down at her. Helene wondered if he was trying to provoke her.

'Yes, I believe it was frowned upon at first,' she said. 'I understand that one cannot dance a waltz at Almack's unless one of the hostesses gives permission. Not that it can signify. I do not suppose that I shall be given vouchers.'

'Not be given vouchers?' Max looked at her quizzingly. 'Why should you not receive vouchers? You seem a respectable young lady to me.'

'Oh…I hope I am respectable,' Helene said and gurgled with laughter. 'But we are not important. Papa had no title and hardly any fortune. He was a gentleman, but if it were not for Miss Royston I dare say I should not have been invited here this evening. I am not certain I shall be approved by society, sir.'

'Nonsense! You have been seen, Miss Henderson. News of your beauty and good nature will spread. In the next few days you will be invited everywhere—and I am certain you will receive vouchers for Almack's. You have not lacked for partners this evening, I think?'

'No, not at all…' She wondered if she might have more

to thank him for than she knew. Had he perhaps sent his friends to ask her to dance? 'But Almack's is rather different, I believe?'

'I assure you that you will receive your invitation, Miss Henderson. It is unthinkable that you should not.'

'Perhaps…' Helene held back a sigh. 'Mama is so grateful for this chance for me.'

'It would be a pity if someone of your nature were not to grace the drawing rooms of society more often,' Max said. 'However, I am certain that I am right. By tomorrow everyone will be wanting to know you.'

'You are kind,' Helene said and smiled up at him. 'I hope you are right—for Mama's sake as much as my own.'

He nodded and looked thoughtful, but said no more. Helene was glad that there was no need to talk, because she wanted to enjoy the wonderful sensation of being in his arms. She had thought him a good dancer earlier, but waltzing with him was divine. She wished that she might stay like this for the rest of the evening, but that would be most improper. Their dance ended all too soon.

Helene hoped that he might ask her to take supper with him, but he merely bowed to her and her mother, said that he would call soon and then walked away. Watching him, Helene saw him speaking to some ladies that she did not know.

'I do not believe it would be a good thing for you to dance with Lord Coleridge too often,' Mrs Henderson said, coming up to her. 'He is a perfect gentleman, Helene, and well liked—but you must not set your heart on him. He mixes in circles that we shall scarcely enter, my dear.'

'I am very certain he would not do for me, Mama,' Helene replied primly, though a little voice at the back of her mind told her that she was not telling the whole truth.

She did like Lord Coleridge more than she was prepared to admit, but of course it would not do at all.

As they moved towards the supper room, Emily and Amelia joined them; a sumptuous buffet had been laid out on long tables and waiters were circulating with trays of champagne. Laid out for their delectation were platters of cold meats, chicken, beef, ham, tiny pies and pastries containing both sweet and savoury fillings and a huge variety of relishes, cold peas and soft sweet plums in a syrup.

Helene took a small glass of syllabub and a spoon and followed Amelia and Emily to a table by the window. She glanced back at the buffet table, discovering that an attractive lady, to whom Helene had as yet not been introduced, had detained her mother. Mrs Henderson seemed to be nodding and smiling a great deal, and when she returned to the table she had a slightly dazed expression on her face.

'Well…' she said as she put a small plate on the table. 'You could have knocked me down with a feather. I have just been talking to Lady Jersey. She asked me to bring Helene to a picnic in Richmond she is planning for next Thursday—and she has promised to send us vouchers for Almack's for the whole of the Season. I was most surprised, for I did not expect it.'

'I am so glad,' Amelia said and smiled at Helene. 'I knew all my friends would invite us to their affairs, but vouchers for Almack's are not within my gift. I thought it might happen, but that was very swift, Marie. The picnic is an honour, because Sally Jersey does not invite every young lady she meets to her more intimate affairs.'

'Are you sure she promised us vouchers for Almack's, Mama?' Helene said. She bit her lip, because the lady her mama had spoken to at the buffet was one of those she had seen Lord Coleridge conversing with before they entered the supper room. She was almost certain that he had urged the lady to invite them to her picnic and to send them vouchers.

'Yes, quite certain,' Mrs Henderson said. 'She told me that she wished to meet you, Helene—and I am to take you to her after supper. She said that she hoped we would call and take tea with her when she is at home to visitors.

'I was quite overcome—I was certainly not expecting anything of the kind,' Mrs Henderson said. 'Is Lady Jersey a particular friend of yours, Amelia? She said that a particular friend had spoken to her about Helene.'

'I know Sally Jersey quite well,' Amelia replied. 'I am not certain she would call me a particular friend. I wonder...' She shook her head as Mrs Henderson looked at her. 'It was just a thought. I shall say nothing for the moment. It is not impossible that you were asked because you are staying with me. I have many good friends in society.'

'Yes, indeed you do,' Mrs Henderson agreed. 'Well, Helene, we have been fortunate, my dear. If Lady Jersey should take a fancy to you, you will be welcomed everywhere.'

Helene did not answer. She felt uncomfortable, certain that she knew exactly who had brought about this tiny miracle. However, she did not think that it would be a good idea to mention her suspicion to her mama.

Chapter Three

Helene yawned and stretched as she woke to see the sun pouring in through the window. They had been out late again the previous evening, but she had asked her maid to wake her so that she would be dressed and ready to join the party driving to Richmond that morning. She threw back the covers and jumped out, feeling a thrill of pleasure. When they met at the Marquis of Hindlesham's ball, Lady Jersey had told her that she would send an escort for Helene and her mother, to bring them to the picnic.

Helene had not inquired further, but she had an odd, excited sensation in the pit of her stomach as she dressed. Two carriages were being sent to fetch them, because Amelia and Emily had also been invited.

Helene took her time choosing her gown for the day. In the end she decided on a striped green linen. It had a modest neckline with a white, scalloped lace collar, a wide band of white was caught up under her bust and a flounce at the bottom, the skirt slim but with sufficient play to allow her to climb into and out of carriages. She chose a pair of black leather half-boots, because there was bound to be a certain amount of walking and, since it had rained the day before, there might be wet grass and even mud in the park. Her white shoes would be ruined, but these sturdy boots would allow her to enjoy herself without worrying.

Helene was wearing a white stole and a bonnet that tied under her chin with green ribbons when she met the others downstairs. She saw that they had all chosen sensible footwear and smiled, because she was pleased to have made the right choice. When a knock sounded at the door and two gentlemen were admitted, Helene's heart leapt in her breast. She had guessed right, because Lord Coleridge and Mr Sinclair walked in, greeting the ladies with broad smiles.

'Lady Jersey has sent us to convey you to the picnic,' Max said. 'I am driving my curricle, but Mr Sinclair has his carriage and a splendid team of four.'

'Miss Royston, Mrs Henderson, would you do me the honour of driving with me?' Toby said. 'I see that Miss Henderson is wearing a bonnet that ties under the chin and will do well enough in an open vehicle. Miss Royston, that fetching hat will blow away for there is a slight breeze today. You will do better inside. Miss Barton, will you join us—and I believe you might prefer it, ma'am?' Toby smiled at Mrs Henderson.

'Yes, I believe I should.' Mrs Henderson glanced at her daughter. 'Helene, will you be all right in the curricle?'

'Yes, of course, Mama,' Helene said. She glanced at Emily. 'Your bonnet will not blow away—would you care to ride with Lord Coleridge?'

'Perhaps when we return,' Emily said. 'You go, Helene. I shall do very well in the carriage.'

'As you wish,' Helene said and looked at Lord Coleridge

as he stood aside for her to go out of the front door. 'I prefer riding in an open carriage, sir. It is such a lovely day, even if there is a breeze.'

'Oh, I think it slight,' Max said innocently and avoided her honest gaze. 'But Toby wants to show off his skill with his team. He has not long been a member of the Four-in-Hand—did you remark his waistcoat? He is wearing it in your honour today.' His mouth quirked with irreverent humour. 'I must admit I have one rather like it at home, but I do not wear it today.'

'It is a rather fine waistcoat,' Helene said, a little amused; in truth, it had looked a little odd. 'I have heard it said that you are also a member of that club—you did not choose to drive your four today?'

'I thought a curricle would be nicer. Pray tell me you are pleased with the idea, Miss Henderson—you would not prefer that I had brought Jezra?'

'Sir! You are bamming me,' Helene said and shook her head at him. 'You are a wicked tease. Are you never serious? I do not think you would drive that wretched creature in town.'

'I fear my credit would not survive it,' Max said mournfully. 'I must tell you that Jezra has to date kicked each and every member of my stable at least once. The healthier the wretched creature becomes, the more stubborn it grows. I have decided that it must be sent to the country before my grooms desert me.'

'I am sure they would not dream of it,' Helene said and laughed, for he was amusing. She glanced at Jemmy, who was with the horses, steadying them. 'You are a wicked jokester, sir. Has the donkey really been such a trial to you?'

'He be the devil in disguise, miss,' Jemmy piped up

from the back of the carriage, but subsided at a look from his master.

'I am in the fortunate position that I am the only one not to be kicked, perhaps because I take care to stand well back,' Max told her. 'I have heard of an orphanage just outside London. They are in need of a pet for the children, and the donkey would be well cared for. I can vouch for it that they are good people. Jezra may be asked to draw a small cart occasionally, but nothing too heavy. Would such a scheme win your approval?'

'An orphanage—oh, that is just the thing,' Helene said, her eyes bright as she turned to look at him. He gave her his hand, helping her into the curricle, and then swung up beside her. 'How did you come to hear of it? I know Amelia is connected with a home of some kind in London. I am hoping to visit one day. Perhaps I could visit the one you know of at some time in the future? Do you think it would be permitted?'

Jemmy made a sound, as though he intended to say something, but thought better of it. He jumped up at the back of the vehicle.

'Would you wish to?' Max asked as he gave his horses the order to walk on. 'The children are from the poorest of families. They are healthy enough these days, but boisterous. Like Jezra, the better they feel, the worse they behave. They would surround you and beg you to play with them, I fear.'

'I should like that, sir. I believe it becomes everyone who may do so to take an interest in others less fortunate than themselves. There are many ills in this world, not least the unfairness of inequality and poverty. It cannot be right that there should be such a divide between the richest and the poor,' Helene said heatedly and then blushed. 'But perhaps it would be a trouble to you to take me there? I should not have asked. I dare say you are a busy man.'

'It would be no trouble at all. I visit most weeks when I am in town,' Max told her. 'Do you think Mrs Henderson would permit it? Visiting an orphanage is not precisely the reason she brought you to town, I think.'

'No, perhaps not,' Helene said and her cheeks heated. He must think her pretentious to speak out on such a subject when she was here for the purpose of enjoying herself and in the hope of contracting a good marriage. 'I know we have engagements most days for the next week or so, but perhaps at a later date...'

'Yes, I think one day we might arrange it,' Max replied. 'When we know each other a little better, perhaps.'

Helene glanced down at her gloves. She was a little conscious that she had been too familiar and lapsed into silence. Obviously, he took some interest in the orphanage and might think it presumptuous of her to lecture him on the evils of society. It was some minutes before he spoke again, changing the subject.

'Have you visited Almack's yet, Miss Henderson?'

'Our first vouchers are for this Wednesday evening,' Helene replied, relieved that he had rescued her, for she had not known how to begin a conversation.

'Shall you go?'

'Yes, I am certain we shall,' Helene replied and looked down at her hands. 'I dare say you find the entertainment a little insipid. I have heard some gentlemen say it does not amuse them.'

'Indeed, some of my friends visit only when their sisters beg it of them,' Max said. 'I have seldom visited in the past, but Sally Jersey has been urging me to do so for an age. I believe I may oblige her this Season.'

'Oh…' Helene could not bring herself to glance at him. 'It will be pleasant if we should meet there, sir.'

She could not help but think that his words had a deeper meaning. Was he suggesting that he would visit Almack's this Season because she would be there? If so, it would be a special compliment. The thought made her feel warm inside.

No, she must not let herself be carried away! Mama had warned her that he would look much higher for his bride. To allow herself to dream of a future when he might begin to care for her would be foolish. Besides, the gap between them was too wide. Lord Coleridge was rich, titled and accustomed to spending his time amusing himself in society. She had always pictured herself as the wife of a deserving man, perhaps even a missionary who would carry her off to far lands where she would administer to the sick and dying.

The drive to Richmond was so pleasant! Helene thought that this picnic must be one of the most enjoyable events she had attended since she had come to town. The company was select, and she was made to feel very much a part of things. For a while Lady Jersey kept her at her side, talking to her and asking a great deal of questions about her life and her opinions on almost everything. However, after everyone had eaten, the company began to stroll about the park, though some of the older ladies made themselves comfortable in the shade of the trees.

'Would you like to walk, Miss Barton—Miss Henderson?' Toby asked. 'Or do you prefer to rest in the shade?'

'I should like to walk,' Emily said and Helene got to her feet at once. 'We shall join you, sir.'

'Thank you, sir. It is such a lovely day.'

Toby offered his arm to Emily. Lord Coleridge had come to join them. He offered his arm to Helene. Another lady, Miss Trevor, and her brother joined them and the six set off to walk about the park.

'This is a beautiful place,' Helene said, feeling that she needed to say something. 'I like to walk by the river—do you admire water, sir?'

'At home I have a lake, but no river, I am afraid,' Max replied. 'I am at this moment in the process of adding a little waterfall. I think there is nothing so pleasant on a warm day as the sound of water tumbling over rocks. Since we do not have a natural feature, I have decided to install one.'

'Oh, how lovely,' Helene cried. She was about to say that she would love to see it, but held the words back. They were much too forward and would sound as if she was angling for an invitation to his estate, which would be terrible. It was bad enough that she had asked him to take her to the orphanage earlier. 'I have never been to the sea—have you?'

'Yes, many times, and over it when I was with Wellington in Spain and France. My estate is not far from the sea, it is situated in Norfolk, but a few miles from the coast.'

'Oh, yes, of course. You must be fond of the sea,' Helene said. 'I think someone told me you were given a medal for your service in the last war?'

'A mere bauble,' Max said modestly. 'I rode dispatch missions, nothing more. I have also been to Brighton. You must know that the Regent has a house there and is in the process of refurbishing it. I believe it is something exotic and strange—or will be by the time he has finished it.'

'Oh, yes, someone was saying that it is a little odd,'

Helene replied. 'Does it resemble an Eastern pavilion or some such thing?'

'Some such thing would probably describe it best,' Max said and chuckled. 'Perhaps your mama will take you to Brighton for some sea air when the Season is done. Many people will go down in June or July, you know.'

'I do not think it,' Helene said and turned away, for she could not confess that they could not afford such trips. Her eyes were for some reason drawn to a stand of trees. Something had caught her notice, a splash of colour amongst the trees. She did not know why it had taken her attention, but she continued to look at the trees and then she saw the man plainly. He was wearing a dark blue coat, a black hat pulled low over his face, hiding it. Something about him caused Helene to feel a sliver of ice at the nape of her neck. She watched as he brought his arm up, a gasp of surprise on her lips as she saw that he was holding a pistol, the sunlight glinting on the long barrel. It took her a few seconds longer to realise that the pistol and the man's intense gaze was pointed in their direction—not at her, but the man by her side. 'Sir!' she cried and gave Max an almighty push, sending him staggering sidewards. So startled was he that for a moment he fell to one knee, and the crack of a pistol was an instant later, the ball passing so close that Helene felt the whistle of it as it passed between them. 'Over there...' She pointed in the direction of the trees. The man in the blue coat had turned and was running away. 'I saw him. He was going to shoot you.'

'Good grief! She is right, Max,' Toby came to him hurriedly. 'I'm not carrying a weapon or I would go after him. Damn it! I never thought I should need it today, though my groom has one.' He glanced towards the carriages, but they were too far away. No one had even heard the shot.

'It would be no good—he'll be long gone before we could fetch it and follow.'

'No, let the fellow go,' Max said in a harsh voice. 'Thankfully, he missed. We could not risk a shooting match, there are ladies present.' He gave Toby a look deep with meaning. 'It would be too much of a risk.'

'Who would want to kill you?' Helene looked at him. Her heart was beating rather quickly and for a moment she had felt sick. 'Forgive me for pushing you, but it was the only thing I could think of.'

'You may have saved my life,' Max said. 'It was quick thinking, Miss Henderson, and brave. You might have been hit yourself.' He looked angry, his eyes glinting dangerously.

'I did not think it,' Helene said. 'The pistol was clearly aimed at you—and I do not think I am important enough for anyone to wish to kill me. You were most certainly his target.'

'I am sorry that it should have happened while you were present.'

'You must set up an inquiry,' Toby said. 'If someone is trying to kill you...' He frowned as something occurred to him. 'You don't think...that business last year with Northaven?'

'I have no idea,' Max said, as puzzled as he was by the incident. 'I was not much concerned in that, you know. Besides, the ladies are anxious. We must return to the others and talk of this privately.'

'Yes, of course. My apologies, ladies,' Toby said. 'Max is right. Miss Henderson—you were very brave. Many young ladies would have screamed and fainted if such a thing had happened in their presence.'

'As I almost did,' Emily said and went to Helene. 'You

did just as you ought, but I think we should return to the others—and it may be best to say nothing.' She looked at the other lady and gentleman, who had been a little behind and had just come up to them. 'Nothing happened here—are we agreed?'

'Yes, certainly. We do not wish to cause concern,' Miss Trevor said and her brother agreed. 'But should you not call a constable, Lord Coleridge? If a dangerous man is at large, something must be done. He might have killed you.'

'Rest assured that I shall put the matter into the appropriate hands,' Max said at once. 'I apologise for the interruption to your pleasure, ladies, but I think we must return to the carriages.'

There was a murmur of agreement from the others. They turned their steps towards where the remainder of the company was beginning to stir and look for their carriages.

'I am sorry that such a thing should happen on a pleasure outing,' Max said to Helene. 'I must thank you sincerely for what you did just now. That ball came too close for comfort. Had you not acted so swiftly, I might have suffered some harm.'

'It was instinctive,' Helene said. 'I assure you that I do not regard it.'

Max looked at her, a thoughtful expression in his eyes. However, he said nothing more to her. When they reached the rest of the party, he spoke to Toby in a low voice. Toby nodded, and the context of their conversation became clear when Toby suggested that all four ladies might like to go with him.

'Lord Coleridge has noticed that one of his horses has a shoe working loose,' he said. 'There is room in my carriage for all of you. Max begs your pardon, but he must take his horses to the blacksmith in the village, and asks you to excuse him.'

'Of course,' Amelia said. 'Come along, Helene, there is plenty of room—and Toby is an excellent whip.'

Helene glanced at Lord Coleridge, who was speaking to his tiger. He turned his head as if sensing her gaze and inclined his head. She nodded and then climbed into the carriage. Clearly, he did not feel the incident was closed. She thought that perhaps he was concerned that he might be attacked again, and was making certain that she was safely inside Toby's carriage.

Helene had been quiet as they were driven home. Amelia and Mrs Henderson had seemed to have enjoyed the day and talked a great deal about Lady Jersey and how delightful she was as a companion. Emily had also been quiet for much of the time, her thoughtful gaze on Helene.

Helene went straight upstairs to her room when they reached the house. Emily followed and knocked at the door a moment later. Helene opened it and invited her to enter.

'You were very quiet on the way home, dearest,' Emily said. 'Are you all right? It was such a shocking thing to happen. You were very brave and acted promptly at the time. Has it upset you now that you have had time to think of what might have happened?'

'I am not distressed for myself,' Helene assured her. 'I am concerned only for Lord Coleridge. I saw that man and the way he concentrated his aim—I am certain that it was his intention to kill Lord Coleridge. He made light of it for our sakes, but he must know that his life was in danger—mustn't he?'

'I am sure he is perfectly sensible of it,' Emily said. 'He wanted you to ride with us, because he feared another attempt might be made on the journey home, and he was concerned for your sake. I think he will take all possible precautions in future.'

'Yes...' Helene frowned. 'But what can he do really? If someone is determined to kill him, they will try over and over.' The thought that something might happen when no one was by to warn Lord Coleridge was intolerable. She felt so upset that it forced her to sit down before her legs gave way.

'Do not distress yourself, Helene,' Emily said. 'You can do nothing more. Indeed, you did more than could have been expected. You must try to put this unfortunate incident from your mind, dearest. After all, it does not truly concern you.'

'No...' Helene turned away, because she was not sure that she could control her emotions and she did not wish to burst into tears. Emily was right to remind her that Lord Coleridge was nothing to her—but the thought of his being killed by a wicked murderer was almost more than she could bear. However, she must endeavour to put it from her mind. She must not dwell on the incident, for it was not her concern. Lord Coleridge was not a fool and he would do all he could to protect himself. 'You are very right, Emily. It is not my affair.' She must not let anyone guess how much the incident had disturbed her, least of all Lord Coleridge himself.

'Who do you imagine it was?' Toby asked when they were in Max's library later that evening drinking a glass of wine. 'Do you have enemies—anyone you know of?' He frowned. 'You don't suppose it could be Northaven, do you? He hates you and Gerard almost as much as he hates Harry.'

'I know that the Marquis of Northaven carries little love for any of us,' Max said and frowned. 'However, I believe he is in the country at the moment. A friend of mine told me that Northaven has hopes of being left something by an elderly aunt. She summoned him a day or so ago and he left town immediately. I doubt he would return and lose his chance of a small fortune for the opportunity to take a pot shot at me. He has had plenty of chances in the past—why decide to murder me now?'

'If it is not him, it must be someone who bears you a grudge. Have you won too much at the card tables recently?'

'I have lost small sums on each of the last four occasions I played,' Max replied. 'Bradwell lost five thousand to me at the tables a month ago, but he settled yesterday. I think he was annoyed over the loss, but I believe him to be warm enough to stand it. He may dislike me, but I acquit him of wanting me dead. Indeed, most of the people I play with are my friends and gentlemen of honour. If they had a quarrel with me, they would be open with it. What happened today was the act of a coward…he might have killed Miss Henderson had his aim gone astray.'

'You are right. She was very cool,' Toby said admiringly. 'I have sometimes thought her quiet. She does not always say much in company—though she talked more today.'

'I find her an interesting companion,' Max said. 'You are right in saying she is sometimes quiet in company—but she speaks intelligently when you take the time to ask her opinion on any subject.'

Toby looked thoughtful. 'Have you no idea who might want you dead?'

'No…' Max got up and wandered to the window, looking out into the courtyard at the back of his town house. Some birds had come to drink at the fountain and were squabbling amongst themselves. 'At least...I may have an idea, though I cannot truly credit that he would wish me dead. If I had been killed today, he would have inherited almost everything, for I made a will in his favour when I was in the army.'

'Are you speaking of your cousin?' Toby was incredulous. He stared as Max turned and he saw the troubled look on his face. 'Heronsdale—the fellow who is unwell at times? Surely it cannot have been he? The rogue who shot at you made off so fast that he cannot have been an invalid.'

'No, it seems unlikely,' Max said. 'It would grieve me if Robert were behind this...though it need not have been him, of course. He could have paid someone to be rid of me.'

'Surely not—your own cousin?' Toby looked shocked. 'I suppose...is he short of funds, do you suppose?'

'My aunt has been living in the dower house since her husband died. Heronsdale was deeply in debt and his estate had to be sold. I allowed them to live on my estate. I could hardly do anything else for she had little enough and Robert was...too poorly to earn a living.'

'I should have thought they would be grateful,' Toby said and frowned.

'Aunt Harriet is always grateful,' Max said. He frowned—he sometimes found her gratitude almost too much to bear. She was inclined to be too interested in his affairs. 'I have not seen Robert for two years. He has been confined to his room, too ill to allow visitors each time I am there.'

'Sounds as if he is trying to avoid you.' Toby looked

thoughtful. 'It leaves a nasty taste in the mouth, Coleridge—but the finger of suspicion would seem to point at him.'

'Yes, I suppose it looks that way,' Max replied. 'It may have been a disappointment to my cousin when I returned from the war, hale and likely to live for another forty years.'

'At least that long,' Toby said. 'It beats me why he should expect or hope for what is yours. He can only inherit through his mother. I am not even sure if he is entitled to the title...'

'It would require some documentation, I dare say, though I do not think there is anything to stop the title passing to issue from the female line. Robert would have most of what is mine if I were to die before I have a son—unless I change my will. I am loath to do it without proof of his ill intent.'

'Perhaps you should think about marriage very seriously, Max.'

'I have considered taking a wife,' Max replied. 'I do not want to rush into marriage, because that could mean a lifetime of unhappiness for us both if I chose unwisely. However, I have it in mind—but for now I am uncertain if such a step would be wise. If it was Robert or his agent in the park, and he did intend to murder me for the estate—would he stop there?'

'You mean it might put the lady you marry in danger—and your child when you have one.'

'It is possible,' Max said and frowned. 'Another thing, can we be sure that I was the intended victim this afternoon? If I was, which I believe—is it too risky for me to entertain the idea of marriage?'

'Whoever he may be, you cannot allow this rogue to order your life, Max,' Toby said. 'You would be constantly looking over your shoulder. Could you not pay your cousin a surprise visit? See if you can shock him into confessing?'

'I may have to do just that,' Max agreed. 'However, if I went down immediately, I think it might alert whoever shot at me that I have my suspicions. Besides, I have business in town. I think for the moment I shall carry on as if nothing had happened, though I shall take certain measures...'

'Yes, I see what you mean,' Toby said and nodded. 'If you need anything, you know you have only to ask. I should be happy to be of service.'

'For the moment, I would ask only that you are alert for anything that strikes you as unusual,' Max said and smiled oddly. 'I had a letter from Gerard this morning. He intends to be in London quite soon. I would not take Harry from his wife at this time, but it will be good to have both you and Gerard close by if I should need you.'

Helene looked about her eagerly as they entered the hallowed halls of Almack's, that most prestigious of clubs, the following evening. Lord Coleridge had hinted that he would be here and she was eager to see him. Thoughts of him and the rogue who had tried to shoot him had occupied her mind since the picnic. She hoped to have a chance to talk to him that evening, to ask if he had discovered anything. However, after some twenty minutes, she knew that he was not present, and she could not help feeling a deep disappointment. It was almost as if he had broken a promise to be there, for he had certainly made a point of asking if she intended to visit Almack's. Perhaps she was letting herself expect too much, as her mama had warned.

'Miss Henderson.' A gentleman's voice made Helene turn. Mr Bradwell was bowing to her. 'Lady Harris has been good enough to say that she will recommend me to you.'

'You may waltz with Mr Bradwell,' Lady Harris said, smiling on her as she gave gracious permission. 'Sally told me that you are a very well-behaved young gel.' She inclined her head and walked away, leaving Helene with no option but to accept.

'How kind of you, sir,' Helene said and offered him her hand. 'I am much obliged.'

'I am honoured, Miss Henderson,' he replied and took her hand, leading her to the dance floor.

Mr Bradwell was a good dancer. Helene could not complain of anything as he swept her into the dance, whirling her back and forth in time to the music. However, being held in his arms did not make her feel as she had when dancing with Lord Coleridge. She barely held back a sigh as she felt her keen disappointment at his absence. She had been so sure he meant to come!

When the dance was over, Mr Bradwell returned her to her mother's side. Helene saw that Amelia was talking to Toby Sinclair and walked to join them.

'Miss Henderson,' Toby said and smiled at her. 'You look beautiful as always. Will you give me the pleasure of this dance?'

'Thank you, sir,' Helene said and gave him her hand. 'I was wondering...Lord Coleridge did not accompany you?'

'No...' Toby frowned. 'I think he had a pressing engagement elsewhere, someone he needed to see. He may come later.'

'Oh...' Helene did her best to hide her disappointment. 'He is well, I trust—nothing untoward has happened?'

'No, nothing at all,' Toby assured her, but looked slightly

uncomfortable as if he would have wished to say more. 'I dare say he will be sorry to have missed you this evening, though of course he may yet turn up.'

'Yes—' Helene smiled '—perhaps an affair of this kind is not much in his line.'

'I dare say,' Toby agreed. 'I only popped in to see how you went on, Miss Henderson. I shall not stay long.'

'Oh, but you must dance with Emily,' Helene said, because she knew that Emily rather liked him. 'Surely you will?'

'Miss Barton…' Toby glanced across the room and nodded. 'Yes, certainly I shall ask her, though she does not always dance.'

'I think she might if you asked,' Helene said as the music ended. 'Come with me and ask her now.'

Toby glanced at her. 'What are you up to, Miss Henderson?'

'Nothing at all,' she said artlessly. 'It is merely that Emily has not yet danced this evening.'

Toby made no reply. However, he asked Emily for the next dance and was accepted. Helene's card was not yet full and she wandered over to the open window, standing by it to catch a little air. She had not been there more than a moment when Nicholas Bradwell came up to her.

'You are not dancing, Miss Henderson?'

'I just felt a little warm,' Helene told him. 'It is cooler here by the window.'

'It is a beautiful night. Perhaps you would care for a stroll outside?'

'I believe not,' Helene said with a smile to soften her refusal. 'I think Mama needs me.'

'Forgive me, I did not mean to be too forward. You would be quite safe with me, Miss Henderson. I admire you. Everyone speaks of your quiet manners and your dignity. I believe you must be the kind of young lady that would make any gentleman a worthy wife.'

'Please, do not say such things,' Helene said swiftly. 'It is much too soon. We hardly know each other. Excuse me, I must return to my mother.'

She left him quickly, her cheeks on fire. She was certain that he had been on the verge of proposing to her. Had she given him any encouragement, he must have done so after such a statement! Her heart was racing and she felt her stomach clench. To come so close to an embarrassing proposal on such slight acquaintance was a shock for her. She had hardly known how to cope with it and was afraid she might have offended him. It was much too soon to be thinking of marrying anyone!

Helene was relieved when her next partner claimed her. She made an effort to forget the embarrassing incident, deciding that she would stay close to her mother or Emily for the remainder of the evening.

The hour was late and Helene's mother was saying that they should leave soon when Lord Coleridge walked into the room. Helene's heart leapt in her breast, for he smiled and walked to meet her immediately.

'I believe there is one more waltz,' he said as he bowed his head to her. 'May I hope that you will forgive me for my tardy arrival and grant me the favour?'

'It should be Mr Sinclair's,' Helene said hesitantly.

'Toby will not mind,' Max said and held out his hand. Helene gave him hers, her pulses racing as they joined the last few couples on the floor. She trembled as he drew her close, his gloved hand at the small of her back. 'You look lovely, as always, Miss Henderson.'

'Thank you,' Helene said and smiled shyly up at him. Could he hear the frantic beating of her heart? Had he any idea how much pleasure it gave her to dance with him like this? Oh, it was so foolish of her to feel so happy just because he had come after all! 'I thought you were not coming this evening.'

'I had as good as given my word,' Max said. 'I was detained on a matter of importance, which I regret, for I fully intended to dance with you more than once this evening.'

'I should have enjoyed that.' Helene's cheeks were a little pink and she could not bring herself to look up at him. Her heart was beating so fast that she thought he must be able to hear it.

'I was wondering if you would like to take a drive out with me the day after tomorrow,' Max said. 'Since it is a fair distance, I thought perhaps Miss Barton might accompany us. I have business at the children's home I told you of, Miss Henderson. I thought perhaps it would please you to see Jezra settled in his new home?'

'Yes, I should enjoy such an outing on several accounts.' Helene laughed softly. 'I am sure Emily will agree. We have an evening engagement that day, but nothing for the morning.'

'Then I shall call for you both at nine-thirty in the morning—unless that is too early?'

'No, not at all. I rise early and Emily has the same habit. We are often on our way to the lending library or the shops by that time.'

'I shall look forward to it,' Max said, giving her a look of approval. 'I have engagements most of tomorrow, but I believe we may meet at Mrs Andersen's card party in the evening?'

'Yes, I am sure we had a card for that, though we may also have one for something else,' Helene said. 'I shall hope to see you, sir—if not, we shall have our drive to look forward to.'

'Yes, we shall,' Max said. He gazed down into her eyes as the music came to an end. 'I am afraid that is the end of our dance—and of the evening. I must say good night, Miss Henderson.'

'Yes…good night, Lord Coleridge,' Helene said. 'Thank you for coming this evening.'

'The pleasure was all mine,' Max told her. He lifted her hand to his lips, kissing the back briefly. 'Now I must return you to your mama, for I see that she is anxious to leave.'

Helene looked at her mother. Mrs Henderson's expression was hard to read, for she was frowning. Surely she could not be displeased because Helene had danced the last waltz with Lord Coleridge?

Max bowed his head to Helene's mama. 'Forgive me for keeping your daughter, ma'am. I was detained and was unable to come earlier, but I could not resist one dance with her.'

'Amelia has the headache,' Mrs Henderson said in a sharp tone. 'She and Emily left some minutes ago. I told her we would take a hackney and that she was not to send the coachman back for us.'

'It will be my pleasure to take you home,' Max offered at once. 'My groom is waiting downstairs. By the time you have your cloaks, my carriage will be at your disposal.'

'You should not trouble yourself, my lord,' Mrs Henderson said, but he shook his head.

'I assure you, it is no trouble at all. It will give me the pleasure of your company for a little longer.'

'You are very kind, sir,' Mrs Henderson said, but her manner was stiff and Helene sensed that she was displeased.

She looked at her mama as they went to fetch their cloaks. 'Is something the matter, Mama? You do not dislike Lord Coleridge?'

'I am sure he is quite respectable and there is nothing to dislike in his manner or his person,' Mrs Henderson replied. 'But I think you should be careful, my love. I do not wish to see you hurt.'

'Why?' Helene asked, her throat tight with suppressed emotion. 'Has he done something that makes you disapprove of him.'

'Of course not.' Mrs Henderson frowned at her. 'You cannot have forgotten what happened to me, Helene? I know that you have been well received in society, but marriage to an aristocrat is another matter. You cannot imagine that Lord Coleridge's family would accept you?'

'I am not ashamed of Grandfather,' Helene said, a militant sparkle in her eyes. 'You have told me that he was a decent man and I will not allow the fact that he owned a tannery to be a disadvantage. An honest hard-working man is the equal of any in the land.'

'You may think so, Helene. There are others in society who would not feel the same. I have not made a secret of my parentage. My mother was the daughter of a younger son and brought up as a lady, but my father had no education to speak of and was looked down on by Mama's family. You know that your papa's family shunned me. When he died I was left to struggle alone. Had my brother not taken us in, we might have ended in the workhouse.'

'Papa's family were unkind and ungenerous,' Helene told her. 'If I ever had the chance I should like to tell Papa's father what I think of him—but you should not concern yourself, Mama. I dare say Lord Coleridge will not even think of asking me to marry him. If he did, I should naturally tell him the truth.'

'Oh, Helene, be careful,' her mother warned. 'I shall not forbid you to think of him. If he should ask, you must of course tell him the truth—but be prepared for his disapproval. He comes from a proud family and may well feel that he could not marry a girl of your background.'

Helene said no more on the subject.

Later, as she lay drifting into sleep, it occurred to her that her background might be a disadvantage if she wished to marry a man of Lord Coleridge's standing. She had always thought that she did not wish for such a marriage; the image she'd carried of a worthy man who would be grateful to have her at his side as his helpmeet was still strong, but of late she had begun to think too much of a handsome gentleman with laughing eyes.

Helene did not think that she would wish to spend all her life going from one entertainment to another. She loved to dance and was enjoying her visit to London very much, but life should be about more than enjoying oneself surely?

It was all very perplexing, for she owed it to her mother to marry well. Mama was unhappy living in her brother's home. If Helene were fortunate enough to secure a man of some means, he would naturally provide for Mama. Yet the idea of marrying Mr Bradwell or some of her other acquaintance was not a pleasing one. Only one man made her heart leap when they met.

She tossed restlessly on her pillow. It was all so foolish!

She was almost sure that Lord Coleridge was not in the least interested in making her an offer, so why should she lose sleep over the idea?

Chapter Four

'I was sorry you felt unwell last evening,' Helene said the next morning. She had visited Amelia in her bedchamber, finding her sitting up in bed wearing a very pretty lace peignoir. 'Are you feeling better this morning?'

'Yes, much better,' Amelia told her. 'I do not know why I should have had a headache last evening. I do not often suffer from them.' A little sigh escaped her. 'I shall get up later. I thought we might go visiting this afternoon. We should pay a few calls—if you have nothing better to do?'

'I have promised to fetch a book from the library for Mama this morning,' Helene replied. 'I should be happy to run any errands you have, Amelia—and I should like to go visiting with you this afternoon. Emily and I have been invited to drive out with Lord Coleridge tomorrow. Did you know that he is one of the patrons of a children's home? At least, he has not actually said so, but I think he must be for he takes a great interest in the children.'

'Yes, I did know. He set it up himself, but I know he does not speak of his good works in company,' Amelia said and smiled. 'We have sat together on various committees on occasion and I know he takes an interest in the plight of unfortunate children.'

'Emily told me about the home you funded,' Helene said. 'I should like to visit that one day, if I may?'

'Of course, if you wish it—though this was supposed to be a pleasure visit, Helene. Are you sure that you wish to concern yourself with such things? Some of the children are quite well now that they have enough to eat—but some of them will never recover from their unfortunate beginnings. It can be heartrending to see them, especially those crippled by poor diet and disease.'

'That is sad and all the more reason to help if one can. I should always be willing to help in any way you think I might, Amelia.'

'Well, there is nothing for the moment, though I am planning a charity ball at the end of the Season. Perhaps you would like to help Emily write out the invitations? I have a shocking hand. Emily does it well, but there will be a great many to do, for we must invite everyone. There is no charge, of course, but many of the guests will make generous donations to the cause. I find that even those who do not concern themselves with these things are willing to give a few guineas if one asks.'

'Yes, of course I shall help,' Helene agreed at once, though she had hoped she might be given something more taxing. 'Is there anything I may do for you today?'

'Nothing, thank you,' Amelia told her. 'I shall see you at nuncheon, dearest.'

Helene nodded and went downstairs. Emily was waiting for her and they went out together, pleased to find that it was yet another warm day. They were very comfortable in each other's company and talked all the way to the library, laughing and enjoying the outing. It was when they stopped to look in the window of a fashionable milliner that Helene became aware that someone was standing a few feet away, staring at them. She turned her head to look at the gentleman. He was dressed in a style that had been fashionable some years previously, though his clothes were of the best quality. He was a man of perhaps seventy years. When he doffed his hat to her, Helene saw that his hair was snowy white.

As he turned and walked across the road to where a rather old-fashioned carriage was waiting, Helene touched Emily's arm. 'Do you know that gentleman? He was staring at us just now.'

Emily turned her head to look. She frowned and then shook her head. 'No, I do not think so. I believe I have seen that crest before... I think he must be the Duke of Annesdale, but I cannot be certain. I wonder why he was looking at us?'

'It was a little odd. He doffed his hat to me when he realised that I had noticed him. I am sure I have never seen him in company.'

'If it was Annesdale, it is unlikely you would have seen him in company. I believe he belongs to the court set, and was once an adviser to his Majesty—but he seldom comes to London these days. He is said to be a recluse, especially since his eldest son died without child. He has no heir...' Emily frowned as she looked at a bonnet in the milliner's window. 'Do you see the way that bonnet is trimmed, Helene? I think I may buy some ribbons for my straw and trim it in just that way.'

Helene looked at the bonnet. 'Yes, it is very pretty. I like the pink ribbons, but you could use almost any colour.'

'I was thinking of blue, to match my best pelisse,' Emily

said. 'If you do not mind, I should like to call at the haber-dasher on the way home.'

'Of course not,' Helene agreed immediately. 'I think I may buy some green ribbons. It is so easy to change the style of a bonnet with a new ribbon.'

They walked on in perfect harmony, the slight incident forgotten. However, when she was changing for the afternoon, Helene thought about the gentleman she had seen watching them earlier. Was he really the Duke of Annesdale—and why had he been so interested in two young ladies looking at bonnets?

The afternoon was spent calling on ladies of their acquaintance. Some were at home and they went in to take refreshment and gossip about inconsequential things. They did not spend more than twenty minutes anywhere, and at two houses they merely left their cards. It was past five when they returned home to find a small pile of visiting cards on the salver in the hall.

Amelia flicked through them. 'This note is for you, Helene. Marie, my dear—there is a letter for you. Nothing for you, Emily. The rest are simply calling cards. Mr Sinclair called and says he hopes to see us this evening.'

'I was not expecting anything,' Emily said, and for a moment her eyes were bleak, but in another moment she was smiling. 'If you will excuse me, I shall go up now for I have a bonnet I wish to trim—unless you need me, Amelia?'

'No, there is nothing I need for the moment,' Amelia told her. 'I have drunk far too much tea, so I think I shall go to my room and rest for a while before I change.'

'I shall do the same,' Mrs Henderson said.

'May I come with you?' Helene said to Emily. 'I should like to see how you intend to trim your bonnet.'

'Of course,' Emily said. 'But do you not wish to read your note?'

'It is from Miss Marshall,' Helene said. 'She said that she would be inviting me to a picnic soon. I dare say it may be that.'

'Then it will keep until later,' Emily said. 'Why do you not fetch your own bonnet and we may see what we can contrive between us?'

It was more than two hours later, as Helene was dressing for the evening that someone knocked at her bedroom door. It opened almost at once and Mrs Henderson came in. She was looking anxious, a little flustered, as she told the maid to leave them and return in ten minutes.

'Is something wrong, Mama?' Helene looked at her. 'Your letter was not bad news?'

'My letter...' Mrs Henderson frowned. 'It was of no account. Someone I have not seen for many years asked if I would be at home tomorrow. He wishes to call on me. I was wondering—did you tell me that you and Emily would be out most of tomorrow?'

'Yes, Mama. Lord Coleridge is taking us to visit his orphanage.'

'Ah, yes, I thought it was something of the sort.' An expression of relief entered her eyes. 'What was your own letter, Helene? Anything I should know about?'

'It was from Miss Marshall. She has invited me to a picnic next week.'

'Her brother is Captain Paul Marshall, is he not?' Mrs Henderson's expression was thoughtful. 'I thought him a rather pleasant young man when we met the other evening.

The family is not wealthy, but I believe he has expectations from his grandfather. It would not be a grand match, but all the better for that I think.'

'Mama! It is an invitation to a picnic. Nothing more.'

'I was making an observation,' Mrs Henderson said. 'There is time enough yet for you to meet someone you like, Helene. However, I beg you not to waste your opportunities. Once this visit is over you will have precious little—unless one of your uncle's friends should offer for you. Edgar told me that Colonel Blake rather liked you but I wanted something better than a man twice your age with a brood of children.'

'I would not marry the colonel if he asked.'

'No, I did not think you would—but you must marry someone.' Her mama sighed. 'I do not wish to seem hasty, Helene, but you know our position. I cannot afford to support a home of our own and I am not sure how long we can impose on Edgar's good nature. He made it plain to me before we left his house that he expected you to be settled before we returned.'

'I do know that I have a duty to marry respectably, Mama,' Helene said softly. 'I hope that the right person will offer for me, but as yet no one has made me an offer. We have been in town not quite two weeks, Mama.'

'I know. As I said, I do not wish to push you into anything—but think carefully if you should receive an offer. I speak only for your good, my love. I do not wish you to be in my position.'

'I promise you that if I receive an offer I feel to be acceptable, I shall not refuse it, Mama,' Helene said, her cheeks hot. 'Who is the gentleman who wishes to call on you?'

'His name is not important, for I do not wish to receive

him,' Mrs Henderson replied. 'Well, I have kept you long enough. I have decided that I shall rest this evening and read the book you fetched for me. You will be well enough with Amelia and Emily.'

'Are you unwell, Mama?'

'I am quite well, my love. I simply feel that I would prefer to stay at home this evening. You may ring for your maid. I shall leave you to finish dressing.'

Helene frowned as her mother went out, closing the door behind her. She was certain that something had upset her. She seemed on edge, uneasy—and she was clearly anxious for Helene to find a suitable husband. Was it only because she did not wish to return to her brother's house or was there something she wasn't telling Helene?

She had a feeling that her mother had lied to her about the letter she'd received that day. She did not know why she should lie, but something made her a little uneasy as she went down to join the others that evening. What was Mama hiding from her—and why?

Helene was pleased to see that Lord Coleridge was present when they arrived at the card party. They were a little late—they had also attended a soirée first and therefore arrived just as supper was being served. It was quite usual for guests to arrive later in the evening, because there were so many events in the social calendar that it was sometimes only possible to spend a part of the evening with one set of friends before moving on to another.

'I had begun to think that you were not coming,' Max said as he joined Helene at the buffet table. 'I should have been sorry to miss you, though since I was promised to Lady Sarah Annersley and Mr Hardwick for the first part of the evening, I could not have spent much time with you.

Do you intend to stay long enough for a hand of cards? If so, you may make up a four with Sinclair and Miss Trevor and myself later.'

'I believe Amelia intends to stay until eleven, so if that is time enough...'

'Ample. We are not serious gamblers. We play for pin money and amusement only.'

'Then I shall be delighted to join you, sir.'

'Do you think you could bear to call me Coleridge? At least in private.'

'Yes, if you wish it,' Helene said and blushed. 'My name is Helene, as you well know.'

'Very well, Helene.' Max grinned at her. 'When we are alone like this I shall call you by your name. You have not changed your mind about tomorrow?'

'No, indeed!' Helene said. 'I am looking forward to it very much. I think it will be most instructive, for I take a great interest in these things.'

'It will be a pleasant drive, I believe, for I think the weather is set fair for the time being.'

Helene found herself a part of a group of Lord Coleridge's friends as she ate a delicious supper. Soon afterwards, they moved back to the card room and she was soon engrossed in a light-hearted game of whisk. With Toby Sinclair as her partner, Helene pitted her wits against Max and Miss Trevor. Lord Coleridge took the first hand, but Helene trumped the second and third. The fourth was hard fought, but eventually went to Toby.

They all laughed and declared that they would call it quits for the evening. 'I have seldom enjoyed a game more,' Miss Trevor said as they rose from the table. 'It is almost a pity to leave, but I have a busy day tomorrow.'

'Yes,' Helene agreed. 'So do Emily and I, so it is time we went home.'

She said good night to Toby and then turned to Lord Coleridge, offering her hand. 'I look forward to seeing you tomorrow, sir.'

'Sweet dreams,' he replied and surprised her by lifting her hand to kiss it. 'I shall be prompt in the morning.'

Helene smiled and withdrew her hand, her pulses racing wildly. It was not the first time he had kissed her hand, but something had been different this time—or perhaps she had imagined it.

Helene slept well that night, but her maid had instructions to wake her early and she was dressed in a green carriage gown by the appointed time. Emily came downstairs a few seconds after Helene. She was wearing a dark blue pelisse over a pale grey gown, her bonnet trimmed in the new way with matching blue ribbons. Helene thought that she had seldom seen her look more attractive. They hardly had time to exchange a greeting before the doorknocker sounded and it was opened to admit both Lord Coleridge and Toby Sinclair.

'Nothing would do but that Toby should come, too,' Max told them, mischief lurking in his eyes. 'He has his curricle. I hope that you will agree to drive with him, Miss Barton?'

'Yes, of course,' Emily agreed easily, a faint colour in her cheeks. 'It is such a beautiful day that we shall do much better with an open carriage.'

'We thought so,' Max agreed. His gaze turned on Helene. 'Miss Henderson—shall we?'

'Yes, thank you,' Helene replied, her heart fluttering as she saw his intent look. She followed him outside to where the horses and carriages were waiting, held by their grooms. Max offered his hand, helping Helene into the curricle. He climbed in beside her and Jemmy scrambled up at the back as Max gave the order to move off.

Helene looked about her as they drove through the town, leaving the better houses behind as they passed through meaner streets. Here the gutters were choked with filth and the stench was often unpleasant. It was early yet and the streets were still fairly empty. A milkmaid carried her yoke, crying out her wares. Servants came out of the houses with jugs or cans to buy from her. A fish coster was pushing his barrow over cobblestones, the rattle of wheels adding to the general noise of the city as it began to wake, but as yet there were few ladies or gentlemen taking the air.

After a while they began to leave the noise and bustle of the town behind. Grimy streets and mean houses were replaced by fields and trees. Helene saw horses and cows grazing, even a few late lambs in one field. She had a sudden nostalgic feeling for home. Not the house they lived in with her uncle these days, but the small country house they had rented while her father was alive.

Max shot a glance at her when she had been silent for some minutes. 'You look pensive, Helene—anything you wish to share?'

'I was thinking of my childhood in the country,' Helene told him. 'My father would take me to see the new lambs every year. Those we passed were late, I think?'

'Yes, perhaps. We had a cold spring.' Max turned back to the road. 'Do you enjoy living in the country? I know some ladies who would never set foot there if they had their way and prefer to be in Bath or London.'

'I do not think I should care to live always in town,'

Helene replied. 'I love to dance and I enjoy the theatre. A visit to town must always be pleasant, but there is nothing so refreshing as a long walk in the country with dogs or a companion. Besides, I do not think I should care to be always at some society affair. Life should be about more than simply going from one engagement to another—do you not think so?'

'You censure society for being too thoughtless—too selfish and uncaring of others?'

'Not exactly. I see no reason why people should not enjoy themselves, but some part of life should be dedicated to more serious pursuits, do you not agree?'

'I do not see that it follows that you must be serious to lead a good life. Indeed, if one were to think only of the serious side of life, it would be very dull indeed. I fear I should find it intolerable—I must laugh at what I see or I might cry.'

'The poor have no choice. They have nothing to look forward to and nothing to sustain their spirits.'

'Yet, I think the poor are often happy with their lot.'

'No! How can they be when they do not know how to find enough money to put food in the mouths of their children?'

'To be in that situation is hard indeed, but there are degrees of poverty and most working folk find something to bring pleasure into their lives, even if it is merely a chance to dance at harvest time.'

'Yes, that is true, but I was thinking more of those who have nothing—no home or work—the unfortunates who are forced to live on the streets or wherever they can find shelter from the rain. I believe that the government should work to alleviate the plight of the destitute. In the meantime people of fortune should do much more.'

'I cannot disagree with your point of view, but we cannot expect all our friends and acquaintances to feel the same, Helene.'

She blushed. 'You think me foolish, I dare say. I am no killjoy, I assure you. I take much pleasure in my friends, though I also like the quieter pursuit of walking in the country.'

'I agree with you there,' Max said. 'I particularly like to have a house party in the country, though I have not done so for some years. I spent some time in the army. My father died just before the last campaign in Brussels, my mother some years ago, as I believe I told you. I left my estate in the care of an agent and joined Wellington for the final fling against Boney. I think the estate may have suffered for it, though it thrives now. I shall go down again in a few weeks.'

'I suppose we shall return to my uncle's house,' Helene said and smothered a sigh. 'We have lived with him since Papa died last year.'

'You must miss your own home. Was the estate entailed?'

'I do not know exactly how things stood,' Helene replied and wrinkled her brow. 'Mama has never told me—but I know we had to leave almost immediately. My uncle took us in and Mama has a little money, but we could not have come to London had it not been for Miss Royston. She is a generous friend to us.'

'Yes, I think she understands what it is to live under someone else's roof and feel unwelcome.'

'She said something of the sort,' Helene said. She noticed that he had begun to slow the pace of his horses. 'Are we nearly there?'

'Yes, this is the house,' Max said, turning in at a gateway. There were some tall iron gates, which had been opened and fastened back before their arrival. 'It had fallen into disrepair before I purchased it. I made the repairs necessary and now it is a good solid property. As you have probably realised, it is a favourite project with me.'

'Oh…it is just like a large country house,' Helene cried as she saw the faded rose bricks of an attractive house. It was not huge by country-house standards, and of a similar size to her uncle's, but she thought nicer. 'Are the children expecting us?'

'They knew I would come one day this week,' Max told her. He shot a wicked glance at her. 'I hope that very fetching gown will wash, Helene. You are likely to be touched and admired, and young lads almost always have dirty hands.'

'Oh, I did not think to warn Emily,' Helene said. 'My gown will not show every mark, but hers will.'

'Perhaps she will have the good sense to stay out of reach,' Max said. His eyes twinkled as he threw the reins to Jemmy and handed her down. 'Walk them, Jemmy—and give them a drink, please.'

'Yes, milord.' Jemmy saluted smartly and then winked at Helene. She wondered if he had once been one of Lord Coleridge's orphans.

She smiled at the lad, taking Lord Coleridge's arm as they walked up to the front door. It was flung open before they reached it and eight or nine children came streaming out, screaming and yelling with what was clearly delight. They threw themselves at Max, clinging to his legs and hanging on to his arms, their hands reaching for his pockets.

'These rascals have forgotten their manners,' he said but he was smiling. 'They think they may find something sweet in my pockets—but they have not bid my guests welcome.' He pulled one boy off him, took a handful of comfits wrapped in paper from his pocket and tossed them into the air. The children screamed and jumped to catch them. 'Enough, lads! Have you nothing to say to the guest I have brought to see you?'

'Good morning, miss,' the children chimed in unison. 'Welcome to our school.'

A woman in her middle years came to the door and clapped her hands. She was wearing a dark grey gown, her hair drawn back into a knot at the back of her head, but her smile was open and friendly.

'Now, children, that is enough,' she said and ushered them inside. 'Back to your places and allow our visitors to come in, please. My lord, forgive their excitement. You know how they love to see you.'

'There is nothing to forgive, Ann,' he told her. 'Miss Henderson, this is my angel. I call her that because she cares for these little monsters with a devotion that is nothing short of angelic. Her name is Ann Saunders—and she is schoolmistress, mother and nurse to these brats.'

'Now, sir, none of that,' Ann said and smiled. 'You will be pleased to know that Arthur is settling well after a few tantrums, my lord. Miss Henderson, I am glad to see you. The children enjoy having visitors and I am always pleased that anyone should show an interest in what we are doing here.'

Helene smiled, for she could see that the children were well cared for and happy. 'I think that Lord Coleridge is right, ma'am. You clearly take great care of these children.'

'I do my best,' Ann replied. 'Would you like to see where they have lessons and where they sleep?'

'Yes, very much,' Helene said. Toby's curricle had come to a stop and he was handing Emily down. Helene followed the schoolmistress into the house while Max greeted the others.

'This is the schoolroom. We are very proud of it,' Ann said, taking Helene into a long room with several desks and a blackboard. The ceilings were high and the cream-painted walls were covered with maps, drawings and lists of words that were clearly used to teach pupils how to spell. At one end of the large room there was a rocking horse and a box of toys, which included lead soldiers and models of animals, also wooden swords and shields. 'We have school pageants to entertain our visitors sometimes. The children dress up as knights and ladies—we play mock battles and learn about the history behind them. I find they learn things they would reject if made to recite lists, as is often the case.'

'How wonderful,' Helene said. 'I wish you had been my governess, Miss Saunders. I was made to recite the kings and queens of England until I knew them by heart, but my governess never bothered to concern herself with their history. I read that for myself from books I borrowed from the lending library.'

'I am sorry that your governess did not see fit to make your lessons a pleasure. When Lord Coleridge offered me the post here I explained that I should want to make learning fun for my children and he agreed. If he had insisted on this place being run as so many others are, I could not have taken up his offer. I never use the cane and I do not force my pupils to do lessons they hate. Instead, I try to make them curious. Usually, the new ones hang back for a start, but after a while they come and ask about what we are doing.'

'How clever of you to let them come to you,' Helene said. 'I cannot believe how well the children look. If you had seen the climbing boy I recently rescued from his master...' Helene shook her head at the memory. 'Do you not think it should be the right of all children to go to school?'

'Oh, do not start me on politics,' Miss Saunders said and laughed. 'Lord Coleridge says I am a radical. My views are outrageous and I really should not harangue the guests. If ever women are allowed to stand for Parliament, you will find me on the hustings!'

'I think I might like to join you.'

Helene was amused. She liked Miss Saunders very much, and she gave Lord Coleridge credit for having found her and giving her the freedom to run her school as she chose.

After an hour spent looking round the house, Helene wandered out into the gardens where some of the boys had badgered Lord Coleridge and Toby into playing a game of cricket with them. She was laughing as she saw Toby catch Lord Coleridge out, and did not immediately notice the young lad at her elbow.

'Please, miss,' he said and tugged at her skirt, 'will you come?'

'Come where?' Helene asked, looking down. He had sandy hair, bright green eyes and a gap in his teeth. His face was streaked with dirt and she thought he might have been crying. 'Is something the matter?'

'It's Tiddler, miss,' the lad said and wiped his nose on his sleeve. 'He's in trouble, miss—will you come?'

'Yes, of course,' Helene said. 'Where is Tiddler?'

'Over here, miss.' The boy pulled at her gown. 'He's stuck, miss...he can't get down and it's too high fer me ter climb.'

Helene was intrigued. She allowed the lad to hurry her down the path to the far end of the garden where a small apple orchard bordered the garden. She looked round for the child in trouble, but could see nothing.

'Where is Tiddler?'

'Up there, miss.' The lad pointed into the branches of an apple tree. Helene looked and saw the small tortoiseshell kitten, its back hunched as it mewed in obvious distress. 'He can't get down and I can't reach the first branch.'

'No, I see it is too high for you.' Helene glanced back towards the game of cricket. Ought she to summon Toby or Lord Coleridge? She hesitated and then saw the ladder lying on the ground near by. No need to summon help. She could quite easily go up the ladder and rescue the kitten herself. 'Help me carry the ladder…then I will fetch Tiddler down to you.'

It was not a very long ladder and Helene was able to lift it easily, the boy balancing the end for her as she carried it to the tree in which the kitten was stuck. She leaned it up against the trunk, then, glancing over her shoulder to make sure she was unobserved, tucked her skirts up so that she could climb the ladder. She scrambled onto the most substantial branch, feeling sure it would hold her weight, and then looked for a foothold to climb to the next. From there she was able to see the kitten clearly.

'Come, kitty,' she coaxed softly. 'Here, Tiddler…there's a good kitty…'

The kitten arched its back, big round eyes looking at her suspiciously. She reached up and grabbed it, holding it to her breast as she tried to step backwards down to the substantial branch just below her. Her foot seemed not to be able to find it, so she turned her head, and let go of the kitten with one hand, still holding it close with the other as she tried to negotiate her way down to the ladder. The kitten suddenly hissed, dug its nails into her neck, causing Helene to cry out and wobble. The kitten made a bid for freedom and sprang down to the ground, shooting away into the bushes as if in fear of its life.

'Tiddler...' the boy yelled and set off after it. 'Come back 'ere...'

Helene grasped at a branch, which cracked and broke, leaving her floundering as she half-fell, and half-scrambled back to the sturdy branch that she knew would hold her weight. Now if she could just reach the ladder... Her foot touched it and sent it crashing to the ground.

'Oh, no!' she cried, annoyed because she had not thought to tell the lad to hold it. It was too far to jump, which meant she was stuck here until someone came. 'Lad...help me... someone...I'm stuck... I can't get down...'

The young boy had disappeared in pursuit of the kitten. Helene could hear the sounds of laughter and cheering as the cricket match continued. She peered down at the ground. Should she try to jump—or could she find foot-holds on the trunk? She leaned forward slightly and felt something holding her back. Her dress had caught on the broken branch. She gave it a tug, but it would not budge.

Now she really was stuck until someone came!

Max looked round and smiled as Miss Saunders approached him. He had been bowling for some minutes, but now it was Toby's turn and he was merely the outside fielder.

'I came to tell you that nuncheon is prepared, sir.'

'Very well. If you would like to summon the children, we shall join you.' He glanced round, looking for Helene.

'Is Miss Henderson in the house? I thought she was watching the cricket a few minutes ago?'

'I haven't seen her since she came out, sir,' Ann said.

Emily walked up to them. 'I noticed that Helene went off with one of the boys some minutes ago. I think she went in that direction—towards the orchard.'

'I shall go and find her,' Max said. 'Please go in, all of you. We shall join you shortly.'

He strolled in the direction of the orchard. It was a little odd that Helene should go off alone. He had thought she might like to join in the game as Emily had, but before he could ask she had disappeared.

'Please...someone help me...'

Max began to run as he heard Helene call. She was in the orchard somewhere. What could be the matter?

At first he could not see her, and then he heard her voice again and looked up. Seeing the ladder lying under the apple tree, he realised what had happened.

'What are you doing up there? Or shouldn't I ask?'

'There was a kitten in distress...'

'Of course, I understand perfectly,' Max said, his eyes dancing with amusement. 'Where is the poor creature now?'

'Tiddler scratched me and made off into the bushes— the boy ran after it. When I tried to reach the ladder, it fell and my dress is caught on a broken branch so I could not jump even if I wished.'

'Naturally,' Max said. 'It is all exactly as I should have imagined. You are impulsive, Miss Henderson. Did you not think that it would be safer to ask me or Toby for assistance?'

'The boy asked me to help. You were playing cricket.

I did not wish to disturb you. I tried to climb down, but I am caught fast so I could not even jump.'

'No, of course not.' Max shook his head at her. 'Do not try anything so dangerous, Miss Henderson. You would break your ankle. Please stay exactly where you are. I shall come up and help you down.'

'Thank you. I thought I might be stuck here for some time, because no one knew where I was...'

Max did not reply immediately. He fetched the ladder and placed it against the tree, then looked for and found two large stones, which he wedged against the bottom, testing it to make sure it was safe. He then climbed up, reaching the branch Helene was now sitting on. He edged his way out to a position where he could pull her gown free. It tore slightly and he muttered his dissatisfaction, then came back to her.

'I am sorry, but there was no time to fiddle about. This branch will not bear both of us for long. I shall return to the top of the ladder. Turn so that your back is towards me and reach out with your right foot. I shall place it on the ladder and hold you as you descend—do you understand?'

'Yes, thank you. I shall be all right now the ladder is secure.'

Max stood on the ladder just below the top rung. When Helene's foot searched tentatively for the first step, he took hold of her ankle and placed it firmly in position.

'Now put your other foot on,' he encouraged. 'You cannot fall because I am right behind you. That's right... now hold the ladder and down we go.'

Helene obeyed. She came down steadily, Max's body steadying her until they reached the bottom. She turned to look at him, a smile of triumph on her lips and then saw what was clearly a scowl of displeasure.

'What on earth did you think you were doing?' he demanded. 'You might have fallen and injured yourself badly. You had only to call me and I would have fetched the wretched creature down. You are thoughtless and reckless. What would your mother have said if you had come to harm while in my care?'

'I am sorry,' Helene said, feeling as if he had slapped her. 'But there is no need to make such a fuss. I am not hurt and I should have come down myself had my gown not caught.'

'Do you make it a habit to risk your life for nothing?' Max demanded. 'Rescuing a donkey and then a stupid animal! The kitten would have come down itself in time, they usually do.'

'The boy was upset. I did not think,' Helene said defensively. Surely he had no need to scold her? 'I could not leave the poor creature up there. It was frightened.'

'So frightened that it scratched your neck,' Max said. 'You have blood on your gown. Come into the house and let Miss Saunders bathe it for you.'

Helene put her hand to her neck. 'It is only a small scratch. I can perfectly well tend it myself,' she said and set off towards the house. She was walking fast, her head bent as if in distress.

Max watched for a moment and then ran after her. He caught at her arm, swinging her round to face him. For a moment he stared at her, torn between anger, regret and amusement.

'Damn it, I'm sorry,' he said and then caught her to him. Helene's eyes widened as he bent his head and kissed her hard on the mouth. It was such an angry kiss that it aroused conflicting emotions in her. Almost immediately he drew back, an odd expression in his own eyes. 'Forgive me—that was most improper of me. I am sorry…sorry that I was harsh to you and sorry that I behaved so badly. I was shaken because you might have been seriously hurt, but I should not have spoken to you so sharply—and I should not have kissed you like that, either.'

'No, you should not,' Helene said, her expression one of pride. 'Excuse me, sir. I must tidy myself before nuncheon.'

'Yes, of course,' Max said. He stood watching as she walked towards the house. Damn it! He had been a complete fool! He could only hope that Helene had not completely lost her trust in him.

Helene rushed up the stairs to the room Miss Saunders said was kept for visitors to tidy themselves. She was relieved that it was empty when she entered. There was cold water in the jug on the washstand. Helene splashed a little on her face and neck. The scratch stung a little, but when she looked in the mirror she could see that it was only a very little one. Hopefully, no one would notice it after a few hours when the redness had gone.

She smoothed her hair into place and looked at the tear in her gown. Unfortunately, that was noticeable and Emily was sure to ask what had happened. Helene put her hands to her cheeks, feeling a hot rush of colour. Lord Coleridge must think her so foolish. She had acted like a hoyden—climbing into a tree after a kitten was something no properly behaved young lady would do. Helene hadn't hesitated. The child and the kitten had been in distress. How could she have done otherwise?

After a moment her feeling of embarrassment became anger. There had been no need for him to be so harsh—and to kiss her in that way, almost as if he wished to punish her. Just because she had climbed into a tree, it did not mean she was lost to all propriety, but he obviously thought so—a gentleman would not kiss a lady he respected in that rough manner. He had clearly lost all respect for her!

She felt close to tears, but she knew she must not give way to her feelings. The others were waiting for nuncheon. She must go down and join them. She lifted her head, pride coming to her rescue. She had been reckless and must simply take the consequences of her actions.

Helene went downstairs, making her way to the big dining hall that Miss Saunders had shown her earlier. The children were all standing behind their benches, waiting for her. She felt their eyes on her as she walked towards the high table, where the guests were already seated. Her cheeks heated, making her uncomfortable. She took a seat between Toby and Miss Saunders.

'Forgive me for keeping everyone waiting,' she said.

'She got Tiddler down,' a voice piped up as the children took their places. 'He were stuck up a tree and she got 'im down fer us.'

Helene was startled when the children stamped their feet and sent up a cheer. She blushed again, shooting a glance at Max at the other end of the table.

'Be quiet, children,' Miss Saunders said and a hush fell over the tables. 'We shall say grace and then you may eat.'

Helene looked down as the schoolmistress said the prayer. She felt embarrassed and uncomfortable. Whatever must everyone think of her?

'It was kind of you to rescue that wretched kitten,' Miss Saunders said as the children settled to their meal. 'I had to get it out of the lily pool the other day. The children thought it would drown. They do so love their pets—and they adore the donkey. Lord Coleridge sent it for them recently. He told them that a kind lady had rescued it from a cruel master and that they were to take good care of it. I think the beast will be totally useless after all the fuss they make of it.'

'Oh...' Helene glanced at Max again. He lifted his brows, as if to ask if he were forgiven. She gave a slight nod of the head and smiled. 'I should like to see Jezra. I understand that he is much recovered now.'

'Was it you that rescued the poor creature?' Ann Saunders asked. 'That explains it—I wondered why Lord Coleridge had taken a donkey under his care, but I see that you have a kind heart, Miss Henderson. I hope that you may take an interest in our little school in the future?'

'Yes, of course, though we are in town only for a short time,' Helene said. 'However, you already have the best patron you could have in Lord Coleridge.'

'Yes, indeed, we do,' Miss Saunders said. 'Would you care for some of this mutton, Miss Henderson? It comes from the Coleridge estate—or one of them, for I believe his lordship has more than one. Our patron makes sure that we never go short of anything here.'

Helene accepted a little of the pie, which was swimming in delicious gravy, the meat cooked slowly and very tender. She noticed that the children were being served the same foods as they had. In the workhouse they would have been lucky to be served bread and thin soup. The difference was so marked that she could not help feeling approval for the man who had provided them with this home.

Her anger had quite gone now. How could she be angry with Lord Coleridge when he was so generous to these children? He must think her very foolish for climbing that tree, but she would not hold the kiss against him. Indeed, it had made her tremble inwardly. Had she not been certain that he had meant to punish her, she might have found it enjoyable.

Chapter Five

After nuncheon, they were taken to see Jezra. The children took gifts of bread and carrots to feed their pet. Seeing how happy they were to have the donkey to fuss over and care for, Helene was completely satisfied that Jezra would do well in his new home.

Max told them it was time to leave after some minutes spent admiring the children's pet. They said their goodbyes and walked out to the carriages. Max glanced at Helene as they paused for a moment in the sunshine.

'Am I forgiven?' he asked. 'Or would you prefer Toby to drive you home?'

'I have forgiven you,' Helene said. 'I dare say I was foolish.'

'I would not say so. Reckless and brave, but not foolish,' Max replied. 'I was fearful for your safety but I should not have…behaved as I did. I hope it will not spoil our friendship?' His eyes quizzed her, making her look down quickly, her heart racing.

'It is forgotten,' Helene said and gave him her hand. Max

inclined his head, helping her to climb into the curricle. 'I think, after what I have seen today, I should forgive you almost anything, sir.'

'You are pleased with our school?' Max glanced at her before giving his horses the order to walk on.

'How could I fail to be?' Helene said, but did not look at him. 'These children would be forced to live in the workhouse if it were not for you and I dread to think of their fate in that terrible place.'

'There are other decent homes. Miss Royston is the patroness of one in London, as I am sure you know.'

'Yes, Emily told me of it, but I doubt that it is quite like yours. You were fortunate to find Miss Saunders, sir. Her ideas and beliefs are very different, as I am sure you agree.'

'Yes, I was fortunate. I am glad you approve,' Max said, looking thoughtful. 'I trust you are satisfied with Jezra's new home?'

'How could I not be?' Helene said and smiled. 'I think those children will spoil the wretched creature.'

'I dare say Jezra will find it preferable to pulling an impossibly heavy cart and almost starving to death.'

'I am certain that he will,' Helene replied. She glanced at him, seeing that he was smiling. She had a warm feeling inside, because it seemed that their argument was forgotten. 'I think you are very kind, sir.'

'Do you, Helene?' he asked and turned to look at her for a moment. Something in his eyes at that moment sent a tingle down her spine. 'Jezra owes his good fortune entirely to you—and the children need help. Someone has to do something until the laws are changed to protect them. I am certain you agree?'

'Yes, of course.'

'I knew you would think as I do.' His dark eyes sent

little tingles through her entire body. She remembered the way she had lectured him on the evils of poverty and felt embarrassed. He needed no such instruction from her! She was sure he knew far more about these things than she did.

Helene blushed and looked away. She had a strange feeling that something in their relationship had changed, though she was not sure what or why. Her heart raced for a moment, but she clasped her hands in her lap. She must not read too much into that kiss. She had thought he was angry, his kiss meant to punish...but that look in his eyes had seemed to say something very different.

Max stopped the curricle outside Miss Royston's house. He got down to help Helene alight, holding her hand for a moment, gazing down at her as they stood in the street.

'I have enjoyed your company,' he told her. 'I have taken a box at Vauxhall next week. If I were to send Mrs Henderson an invitation for all of you, would it be acceptable, do you think?'

'I am sure Mama would be pleased to accept. Amelia has spoken of taking a box, but we have had so many engagements that there has been no time.'

'You must visit Vauxhall,' Max told her. 'You will enjoy the fireworks, and the gardens are pleasant. I shall write to your mama—and perhaps we shall meet soon?'

'I expect we shall,' Helene said. She gave him her hand, her manner outwardly calm, though her heart was beating very fast. 'Thank you so much for today. I have enjoyed myself.'

'Despite my show of temper?' Max lifted his brows.

'I think it was more my fault than yours, sir.'

'Well, we shall agree to forget a disagreeable incident,'

Max said and lifted her hand to kiss it. 'Goodbye for the moment...'

Helene walked into the house, leaving Emily to offer her thanks for the outing. She paused by the silver salver on the hall table. To her surprise there was a letter addressed to Miss Helene Henderson. She picked it up and slipped it into her glove as she went upstairs.

Her mother came along the landing towards her as she reached her bedchamber. 'Helene, my love. Did you have an interesting day?'

'Yes, Mama. Miss Saunders is the schoolmistress at the orphanage and she is wonderful with the children. I think it must be so satisfying to do such worthwhile work.'

'Yes, I dare say it may be more rewarding than life as a governess,' Mrs Henderson said. 'However, you are in the fortunate position of not having to work, my love. I am confident that you will receive an offer very soon, Helene. Mr Bradwell called today. He seemed most disappointed that you were not at home. Had you been, he might have had something to say to you.'

Helene nodded, but made no answer as she went into her bedroom. She thought that she would prefer to work, as Miss Saunders did, than marry a man she could not truly love. She was almost certain now that there could be no true happiness in marriage without love. She had not thought that she would ever wish to marry a member of the class that had treated her mama so badly, but Lord Coleridge seemed to think just as he ought about so many things.

Yet it was foolish to allow herself to dream, for she had no real reason to suppose that he had any intention of asking her to marry him.

* * *

Max took his leave of Toby with the promise to meet later that evening at a card party to which both were invited. Leaving his tiger to see to the horses, he went into the house. He stopped to glance through the calling cards and pocket a sealed letter before going upstairs to change for the evening.

Max's valet had laid out the clothes he would need, and a bath had been set for his use in the dressing room. His valet gave the order and servants began to fill the hipbath with hot water. Sinking into the fragrant water some minutes later, Max closed his eyes, allowing his thoughts to drift back to the moment he had seen Helene in the apple tree. Her skirt had been caught up, revealing shapely ankles and more. The glimpse of white silk stockings going right up to her thighs had been tantalising; she looked beautiful, the picture of lovely womanhood, making him very aware of his feelings for her.

Max thought that perhaps it was this awareness that had made him suddenly angry. The desire to crush Helene in his arms and kiss her had come swiftly, making him act in a way he would not normally have dreamed of doing. He had made her angry in her turn. Max knew that he was lucky she had forgiven him so easily. He did not doubt that it was Jezra who had worked that particular magic, and promised himself he would take the donkey an apple when they came in season.

Max admitted to himself that he was intrigued with Miss Henderson. She was a very spirited lady and courageous, though her compassion tended to make her reckless at times. She had rushed to the defence of the donkey without thought for her own safety, and she had not hesitated to attempt the rescue of the kitten, making nothing of either the scratch or her plight when the ladder fell. He could not help but admire her, and she was certainly both intelligent and beautiful.

If he wished to marry, he surely could not do better than to make Miss Henderson an offer. She would make a companionable wife and a good mother for his children. Seeing her in the apple tree had made him aware that he found her desirable. He was not certain that his feelings went deeper and because of that he was still hesitating about making her an offer.

Harry Pendleton had fallen deeply in love with Susannah, and she with him. Max had witnessed the moment when she risked her life for Harry's, running between Harry and Northaven at the very moment the marquis pressed the trigger. His ball had struck her in the shoulder and she had made a complete recovery, but she might have died—and she had done it out of love for Harry. They were the happiest couple of his acquaintance. Most of Max's friends had married for reasons other than love: fortune, property and consequence. He knew that two of his friends who married in the last eighteen months already had mistresses; bored with their wives, they looked elsewhere for their pleasure. That would not do for him!

Max stood up, water dripping off the body of a superbly fit Corinthian, his well-toned muscles rippling beneath the skin as he dried himself. It was too soon to think of making Miss Henderson an offer, even though he had experienced a flood of intense desire when he kissed her. Even now he could feel himself hardening at the memory of those shapely ankles. Yet desire was not reason enough for marriage. He would wait for a time, he decided, get to know her better.

Wrapping a robe about himself, he walked into the bed-chamber. He remembered the letter he had thrust into his pocket on his arrival home and discovered that his thought-

ful valet had placed it on the dressing chest before taking
the coat away to brush and clean it.

Max broke the seal and read the contents. He frowned
as he digested the letter, which had come from a neighbour.
General Tyler had written to tell him of some unfortunate
events that had taken place in the district of late. A young
woman had been attacked when walking home from her
place of work late at night, and another had barely escaped
the same fate. Some other girls had reported that a man
had followed them—and all the incidents had taken place
in the last six months.

It was six months since his cousin, Mrs Heronsdale and
the doctor she insisted was the only physician to care for
her son properly had moved into the dower house. Max had
an uncomfortable feeling about what his neighbour had not
written. Could he be implying that one of the newcomers
was responsible for these despicable attacks?

Max frowned as he dressed for the evening. It would
be inconvenient to leave town at the moment. He felt that
he was just beginning to get to know Miss Henderson.
He thrust the disturbing letter into a drawer. Robert could
surely have had nothing to do with these attacks, for he was
never well. Max was not sure about the physician. He did
not care for the man much, but he would not have thought
him capable of such wickedness.

He would give the matter some thought. No doubt it
would keep for a few weeks. The problem of his marriage
was more important for the moment. He needed to make
a decision.

Helene opened her letter. She read the contents quickly,
frowned and then puzzled over the spidery script. What
did the rather cryptic message mean?

Lady Annersley requests the pleasure of a private interview at her house in Berkeley Square tomorrow at three in the afternoon.

Helene recalled that Lord Coleridge had once mentioned the lady as being an acquaintance, and she had been introduced to her at an evening party. However, she had not been invited to the small dance given by that lady only a few days previously. Since they were not intimately acquainted, why would Lady Annersley ask her to call for a private interview? It was puzzling, for Helene could not think that she had done anything to arouse that lady's interest—or to upset her. However, she was already engaged for the following afternoon to some friends, and would be unable to oblige.

She sat down at the little desk in the window and took out some notepaper, penning a short note of regret. She would be happy to call on her ladyship at another date, but did not have a free afternoon for some ten days. Having sanded and sealed her note, she went downstairs with it and placed it on a salver with others waiting to be delivered by hand. One of the footmen delivered letters to houses in the near vicinity each morning, which saved the cost of some sixpences unless they could be franked. They also collected post from the receiving house, which was left in the hall together with hand-delivered post.

The letter had taken up more time than she had anticipated, and Helene had to hurry to dress. That evening they were attending the theatre with some friends of Amelia's and would call at their house for a glass of wine first. She must not keep the others waiting!

In her haste to be ready on time, Helene did not give much thought to the day she had spent with Lord Coleridge. It had seemed for a moment as he looked at her that something had changed between them. However, he had not pressed his advantage. Apart from the invitation to Vauxhall, which she was looking forward to, he had merely said that he would see her when they met in company.

Helene could not in honesty tell herself that he had done anything to give her reason to think he intended to offer for her. His kiss had been an impulse, she was certain, meant to punish, perhaps, or in frustration at her reckless behaviour. Her pulses had raced while he held her so fiercely, but she had decided that she should not dwell on the small incident. Had it meant anything, he would have spoken on the way home—if only to request an interview with Mama. One kiss meant nothing, even though it had left her shaken and breathless.

She must not expect anything. Helene knew that, despite his harsh tone, she had felt pleasure as he kissed her. She was not sure how it felt when you fell in love, for she had no experience of such things. However, she did know that she enjoyed being with Lord Coleridge more than any other gentleman of her acquaintance. Since she must marry for Mama's sake, she would accept an offer from Lord Coleridge should he make it, providing he could accept her humble background—but of course he would not. She would be foolish to let herself hope for such a thing.

Helene finished dressing, thanked her maid for making her look elegant and then ran downstairs to join the others. She must put all her foolish notions from her mind! Perhaps there was someone else she could happily marry…

Helene was engrossed in the play; it was *The Taming of the Shrew* by William Shakespeare and vastly amusing. She laughed in delight, enjoying the performance so much that she did not become aware of being watched until the interval. As the curtain came down and people began to move about, Helene saw that some people in the box opposite Amelia's were staring at her hard. She felt an odd uneasiness as she saw that Lady Annersley was looking at her through a pair of opera glasses, which she then handed to a gentleman sitting beside her with a comment.

Helene shivered, a sliver of ice sliding down her spine. She was sure that she had seen the gentleman once before in his coach. He had seemed to stare at her then, though she had not been certain the first time, for he might have been looking at Emily. This evening she was sure that he was watching her—and had been for some time.

Helene picked up Amelia's opera glasses and lifted them, studying the gentleman. He was a man of advanced years, aristocratic with a proud face, his nose long and his lips thin. He was not unattractive even now and she thought he must have been very handsome when younger. He became aware of her scrutiny and bowed his head towards her, a slight smile on his mouth.

Helene put down the opera glasses at once. She did not know who he was or why he—and Lady Annersley— were taking such an interest in her, but she did not wish to encourage him. It was not unheard of for a gentleman of advanced years to take a much younger bride. Helene would not wish him to imagine that she was giving him encouragement.

She turned her gaze back to the stage, feeling glad that she had refused Lady Annersley's invitation. When she thought about it, the letter had been couched in terms that made it more of a command than a summons. A shiver went through Helene, because she was very sure that she would not wish to become that gentleman's bride!

'Is something the matter?' Emily whispered in her ear. 'Did you notice that gentleman staring at you, Helene?'

'Yes. I did not like it.'

'I am sure it is the Duke of Annesdale,' Emily told her. 'Lady Annersley is the wife of the late Marquis, Annesdale's daughter-in-law. She was married to his eldest son, but they had no children—at least none that survived infancy. Her husband died some years ago, but she has never married again.'

'I am sorry for her,' Helene replied. She might have told Emily about the lady's letter, but the curtain was going up and the play was about to begin.

Helene took the letter from her drawer and read it again that evening. The more she puzzled over it, the less she understood. Clearly both Lady Annersley and the Duke of Annesdale had taken an interest in her—but why?

Helene was uneasy as she blew out her candle and tried to sleep. She had never met the duke, so she could only imagine that he found her attractive. He was a widower and had been for some years. His sons had failed to provide him with an heir before they died. It was quite possible that he was looking for a young wife to give him the heirs he needed.

She could appreciate his feelings. His title was an old one and unless he married again and had a son it would pass on to some distant cousin—perhaps there was no one. The title would then die with him, his estate pass to whomever he chose or perhaps the Crown if he made no will. It was sad, Helene thought, and felt sympathy for his plight. However, she had no wish to be the Duchess of Annesdale.

No, she must be wrong! Helene laughed at herself as she snuggled down into the comfort of her feather mattress.

She had imagined it all. He was merely curious about a new face or there was some other perfectly simple explanation.

Helene went driving with Miss Marshall and her brother Captain Paul Marshall the next day. He was a handsome man only a few years her senior, and of a teasing disposition. The afternoon passed so swiftly that Helene was reluctant to take leave of her friends, but felt happy in the knowledge that she was sure to meet them again that evening, for they were all to attend a small dance given by Mr Henry Marshall.

'My uncle does not often stir himself to visit town,' Miss Marshall told Helene, 'but when he does he gives wonderful parties. Everyone has been sent a mask to wear this evening, and we shall unmask at midnight—is that not amusing?'

'Yes, it is,' Helene said. 'I have not been to a masked ball before, but I have heard of them. Amelia says that she shall give a costume ball for her charity at the end of the Season.'

'Oh, yes, I have received my invitation and I am looking forward to it,' Miss Marshall told her. 'Paul has a wonderful idea for us, but I must not tell you because it is a secret.'

'I am not sure I should have told you, Lily,' Captain Marshall replied with mock severity. 'Ten to one you will tell everyone and I shall have to think of something else.'

Miss Marshall denied it and they all joined in the laughter.

It was just gone four when Helene was taken home. She parted from her friends happily and went into the house, pausing to glance at the cards and letters on the salver in the hall. A little shiver went down her spine as she recognised the hand of the sender of a letter addressed to her. Snatching it up, she ran upstairs to her own room. She broke the seal and scanned the contents.

I urge you not to ignore my request. Please visit me in the morning tomorrow. It is of the utmost importance...

Helene felt cold all over. What could be of such importance? She stared at the letter for some minutes, wondering what best to do about it. Ought she to show it to Mama?

Helene was reluctant to do so, though she was not certain why. Mama would certainly not even consider any offer the duke might make her. He was far too old to make a suitable husband.

Helene shook her head. She must be mistaken. The duke did not know her. They had not even met. He could not be thinking of making her an offer—and yet he had been staring at her in such an intent way.

Suddenly, Helene went cold all over. There was one very plausible explanation of why the duke and his daughter-in-law could be taking an interest in her! It had not occurred to her at first, but now she was wondering if the duke could be Papa's father. Mama had told her that his family had been unkind to her, refusing to accept her and cutting her father off without a penny when he married. She had never told Helene the name of her paternal grandfather and Helene had not thought to ask, but now things began to fall into place.

Mama had been upset by a letter she had received a few days earlier. Had the duke written to Mama? Had he threatened her? She had been so upset that she had gone to bed with a headache.

Why had she not told Helene the truth?

* * *

Helene knew Lord Coleridge as soon as he approached her, even though he was wearing a handsome black-and-gold mask over the top half of his face.

'My lady,' he said, bowing to her. 'I do not know your name, but it would give me pleasure if you would dance with me.'

Helene laughed and shook her head. 'I am afraid your mask does not hide your identity from me, sir. You would need to wear something to cover your whole face—and then your size would betray you. You are rather larger than most other gentlemen, Lord Coleridge, and your height gives you away.'

'Woe is me. I hoped to surprise you later,' Max replied and chuckled. 'You were too clever for me, Miss Henderson.'

'Not clever, sir, just observant,' she told him and smiled, glancing round at the assembled company. 'I believe Mr Sinclair is very fond of that blue coat, for I have seen him wear it before this evening…and I know Captain Marshall is wearing a black mask—his sister told me. Hers is gold, I think—but there are certainly some others here that I would not recognise.'

'Perhaps one has to know the other person quite well to recognise them wearing a mask. I certainly knew you immediately, and I do not think I have seen this delightful gown before?'

'No, you would not—it is new,' Helene told him and laughed. 'I will not ask you to explain how you knew me, for it might embarrass us both.'

'Perhaps,' he agreed and his mouth curved. 'I should have known you as soon as you spoke. You have a most unusual way of cutting to the heart of things, Miss Henderson.'

'Am I too direct?' Helene asked. 'I am not always so in company, but somehow I have found myself able to talk to you without reserve. You must tell me if I am too free. I know that some gentlemen prefer a lady to have no opinions or at least to keep them to herself. It is the reason that I am often quiet, for I do not wish to offend.'

'Do they? More fool them,' Max said drily. 'I am not one of them. You may be as direct as you please, and your opinion will always weigh with me. You will certainly not offend me, whatever you say.'

'Oh…' Helene blushed beneath the mask. She was thrown into confusion by his manner, which she thought more intimate than before, and her heart raced. 'Mama says that she will be quite happy for me to be a part of your party at Vauxhall, sir. She says that she shall not come, but Amelia and Emily are both looking forward to the evening.'

'I am glad to hear it,' Max said. 'Does your mama not care for fireworks? I know that some people find them frightening.'

'I do not believe Mama is frightened of them,' Helene said. 'It is a little odd—she has cried off one or two engagements recently. I wondered if she found London tiring, but she says she is perfectly well. It is just that she prefers to stay at home sometimes—and I am well chaperoned with both Amelia and Emily for company.'

'Indeed you are,' Max said. He stopped dancing as the music ended, gazing down at her ruefully. 'Why is it that whenever I dance with you the duration is always too short? I must ask you to grant me at least one more dance this evening, Miss Henderson.'

'I have reserved the dance before supper, if that will suit you?'

'It will do very well,' he said and held her hand for a moment longer than necessary. 'I shall see you later, sweet Helene. Now I must see if I can guess the identity of some others. I think I see Sally Jersey. I shall discover if I am correct. Please excuse me...'

Helene smiled as he released her. She was about to rejoin her mother and Amelia, who were sitting at the side of the room, when a lady dressed in a dark blue gown and a mask of silver came up to her. Helene turned in enquiry as she laid a hand on her arm.

'Yes, ma'am—may I help you?'

'I have written to you twice, but you refuse to see me,' the lady said in a harsh tone. 'Has someone forbidden you to visit me?'

'Lady Annersley...' Helene gasped. 'Forgive me, I truly have been engaged every day. I am sorry if you feel that I have slighted you, but I could not break my engagements. Besides, I do not know why you would wish to see me, ma'am. I hope I have done nothing to offend you?'

'The only offence is in your stubborn refusal to meet him. He has the right to make himself known to you.'

'I beg your pardon—of whom do you speak?' Helene felt a shiver down her spine. Could she mean the Duke of Annesdale? 'I am not aware that I have refused to meet anyone.'

'You did not answer his letter.'

'I must ask your pardon once more, but I have not received a letter from a gentleman. If I were to receive one—which would be most improper—I should give it to my mother.'

'And she would of course destroy it,' Lady Annersley

said. Her mouth drew into a thin line. 'This is not the place to discuss anything of a private nature. I must have your promise that you will call on me as soon as you have time. I have something of importance to tell you, Miss Henderson—something that could change your life.'

'Indeed? I do not know what that might be, ma'am.' Helene's manner was stiff. If this woman were a member of the family who had treated Mama so badly, she had no wish to know her!

'It is not for me to say, at least not here. Come to my house next Tuesday morning and all shall be revealed.'

'If that is your wish,' Helene said. 'If you will excuse me, ma'am, I see a friend approaching and I believe he means to ask me to dance.'

Helene walked to meet Toby Sinclair. He grinned at her and lifted his mask slightly. 'I dare say you knew me anyway, but I wanted to be sure you would dance with me, Miss Henderson.'

'I should be delighted,' Helene replied and went to him with relief. She felt safe with Toby Sinclair—her brief interlude with Lady Annersley had left her feeling uneasy.

Helene danced all evening, going from one friend to another. It was amusing to guess the identity of her partners, though she had little trouble with most of them—they all had some little mannerism or habit that made it easy. However, the company was enjoyable; she had begun to make many friends, both gentlemen and ladies, and she particularly enjoyed her time with Miss Marshall and her brother.

Dancing twice with Lord Coleridge made the evening perfect. The supper dance was a waltz and Helene felt that she was floating on air as he whirled her around the floor. Afterwards, he took her into supper and was so attentive that she felt people must notice. Her happiness was complete when he asked if he might join her when she walked with Toby and some others in the park the following afternoon.

'I should be delighted if you would join us,' Helene said. 'I am to drive there with Miss Marshall and her brother. Mr Sinclair will bring Emily and Mr Osbourne is driving his sister. We shall listen to the band playing in the park. It has been arranged for some days, but one more will only make the afternoon more enjoyable.'

'I am grateful that you feel my company will add to your enjoyment of the afternoon, Miss Henderson.' His look was so intimate at that moment that butterflies set up a crazy dance in her abdomen.

Helene felt her cheeks becoming warm. She glanced down, for she could not quite meet his eyes. She felt that his attentions were becoming more particular, but she was not sure that anything would come of their growing friendship. It was rumoured that he had paid court to an heiress the previous year for a while, but that had fallen through. Perhaps he was fickle in his relationships, though she could not truly think it of him.

After supper, Lord Coleridge took his leave of her, promising to keep his appointment the following afternoon. Helene was sorry to see him go, though she knew she could not dance with him again that evening unless she wished for it to be thought that he was the admirer she favoured. She was not yet ready to make that commitment in public and she did not think Lord Coleridge had any intention of making her an offer just yet. They liked each other very well, and they enjoyed being together. Helene thought that perhaps there was more, because when he kissed her she had felt something stir inside her. Had his kiss been tender rather than punishing, she might have felt that he cared for her. As it was, she was still uncertain.

She danced the last of the evening with Mr Nicholas Bradwell. It was he who was standing with her when the unmasking happened at midnight. Helene smiled and laughed as she removed her own mask.

'I think we had guessed long since, sir,' she said. 'I must admit it has been vastly amusing this evening.'

'Dancing with you must always be a pleasure,' he replied with a little bow. 'Will you be at home if I should call one day this week, Miss Henderson? I thought we might drive out one day.'

'I am sorry to disappoint you, sir,' Helene said. 'I have engagements all this week and some of next. Indeed, I do not have a free morning until Thursday next.'

'Then perhaps you will engage with me for that morning?'

Helene hesitated, feeling reluctant to commit herself to such an engagement. 'I am not certain of Miss Royston's plans,' she said. 'Pray let me consult with her and I shall give you my answer when we next meet.'

He looked displeased with her answer, but inclined his head, leaving her as her mother came up to her.

'Are you ready to leave, Helene?' Mrs Henderson asked. 'I think the others have already gone up to retrieve their cloaks.'

'Then I shall go at once—I should not want to keep Amelia waiting,' Helene said. She saw that her mother was looking tired, a little anxious perhaps. 'Is something troubling you, Mama?'

'I have a little headache,' her mother said and frowned.

'This is not the time or the place but I must talk to you alone soon, Helene.'

'Yes, of course, Mama. Whenever you wish.'

Helene leaned forward and kissed her cheek impulsively. She was startled to see what looked like tears in her mother's eyes, but in another moment they had gone.

'We must not keep the others waiting,' Mrs Henderson said and appeared to make an effort to be brisk. 'Come along, my dearest. I think you have had a good evening, for you have many friends now. You are enjoying yourself, Helene?'

'Yes, of course, Mama.'

'Then I must be content with that for the moment,' Mrs Henderson said. 'I just hope that I have not harmed you, my love. I thought only to secure your future...'

'Mama! What do you mean?'

'Not now, Helene. I must think about something and then I shall tell you what I have decided.'

Helene stood patiently that morning as the dressmaker pinned and pulled, moulding the new evening gown about her so that it fit her like a second skin. It was made of a flame-coloured silk and was quite the most sophisticated gown that Helene possessed.

'You have lost a little weight about the waist,' the seamstress remarked. 'The gown will require a little alteration, Mademoiselle Henderson.'

'I am sorry to put you to extra trouble,' Helene said. 'Will it be ready for the Duchess of Marlborough's ball next week? I believe it is meant to be the highlight of the season and I was hoping to wear this.'

'*Oui,* of a certainty,' the seamstress said. 'I assure you

that the alterations will be made and the gown delivered before the ball.'

'Thank you,' Helene said. 'I dare say you have many calls on your time, *madame?*'

'*Oui,* I am busy all the time, but this is good—no?' She looked pleased. 'I believe the gown will be a triumph. I hope you will ask me to make your wedding gown?'

'I have not yet been asked to marry anyone,' Helene said, her cheeks pink. 'However, I shall certainly ask if I am…if you have time.'

'I should make time for you, *mademoiselle*. It is not always that the figure is so good. Of a certainty it will not be long before milord speaks. I have heard your name mentioned by one of my clients.'

'Someone spoke of my marriage?' Helene frowned. 'Surely not, *madame!* I do not think that I have done anything to occasion gossip.'

'Forgive me, I should not have spoken…' The French-woman looked uncomfortable. 'It was a conversation I overheard. Perhaps I did not hear correctly.'

'What exactly did you hear?' Helene was both curious and annoyed that people should be discussing her.

'It was something about the marriage being suitable… and a name was linked with yours. I heard nothing more, Miss Henderson. I should not have assumed, but I imagined the engagement to be imminent.'

'Who mentioned my name?'

'I do not think I should say…'

'Please tell me. It will go no further.'

'I believe it was Lady Annersley. I called on her to fit her new gown. She was behind the screen and talking to the gentleman.'

Helene felt a sliver of ice slide down her spine. 'Do you recall the gentleman's name?'

'I think he was the Duke of Annesdale. He is her father-in-law, I believe. They seem close.'

'I see, thank you,' Helene said. She did not press the seamstress further, for she could see that she was embarrassed. She felt angry that Lady Annersley and the duke should discuss her in such an intimate way.

Why did they feel that her marriage was important enough to be discussed? If the duke was her grandfather, he had abandoned the right to influence her life. She decided that she would keep her appointment with Lady Annersley the following week. Before that, she would find a moment to speak privately with her mama.

After the dressmaker had gone, Helene went up to her mother's bedchamber. She knocked and went in, finding her mother still in bed, a tray with the remains of her breakfast on a table beside the bed. She did not appear to have eaten very much.

'Mama, are you unwell?' Helene asked, looking at her in concern. 'You have not been quite yourself of late. Last evening you spoke of wanting to speak with me alone. Is something on your mind?'

'Yes, dearest,' Mrs Henderson said and patted the bed beside her. 'Please sit down, Helene. I have searched my conscience and I think I must tell you. I had hoped that you would receive a suitable offer and none of this need have come out, but now I believe I must confess the truth.'

'Tell me what, Mama?' Helene frowned. 'What can be so dreadful that you have tortured yourself, for I know that you have been anxious for some days now?'

'Firstly, I must ask you if you have received any offers that you have not mentioned to me, Helene?'

'No, Mama...' Helene blushed. 'There are three gentlemen I think may make me an offer in time, but none of them have spoken.'

Mrs Henderson sighed. 'I was afraid of that. It is unfortunate, for if you had chosen wisely it might all have been settled to your advantage. I am afraid he will make things awkward for us.'

'Of whom do you speak, Mama?'

Mrs Henderson shook her head. 'Papa's father. He is come to town and wishes to see you, Helene.'

'I have thought...' Helene hesitated. 'You have not told me Papa's family name, Mama—was it Annesdale? Was Papa the duke's younger son?'

'Yes, though he never used his title.' Mrs Henderson frowned. 'Who told you? Have you see him?'

'He was staring at me at the theatre—and Lady Annersley has written to me.'

'Why did you not tell me?'

'I did not think it was important at first—and you did not tell me that my grandfather was in town.'

'I did not wish to have anything to do with the family. You know that I was not treated well as a bride, Helene. I was given the cold shoulder. One lady told me that she did not wish to mix with people of my class.' She fiddled with her lace kerchief, as if she found the words difficult. 'I have never forgotten or forgiven them.'

'Oh, Mama, I am so sorry,' Helene said. 'I know it still hurts you—and of course I shall have nothing to do with them if you do not wish it. I told Lady Annersley I would call, but I can cancel the appointment.'

'I wish it were that simple.' Mrs Henderson sighed. 'As

you know, your father would have nothing more to do with his family. When they refused to receive me, he cut them out of our lives. Even when his father wrote and offered him a small allowance, he refused it. He was too proud to accept charity and we managed on what he earned from his copying. He had a beautiful copperplate hand, but the work did not pay much money.'

'That was hard for you, Mama.'

'I did not mind, though there were times when I wished we had a little more money. My father gave me five thousand when we married, even though we quarrelled. He did not approve of my marrying into the aristocracy and he cut me out of his will—but he still gave me something. Annesdale gave us nothing, not one penny. What little I had is almost gone, and if you do not marry well I do not know what we shall do.'

'Oh, Mama…' Helene did not know how to answer her. 'I am so sorry.'

'Well, it is not your fault. I had hopes that Mr Bradwell might speak. He seems to like you, and he is the kind of man that would make me an allowance—even provide me with a home of my own, perhaps. He is a gentleman, but not an aristocrat, and would make nothing of the fact that my father was in trade. I know that you like Lord Coleridge, but I fear his family might shun you, Helene. I do not want you to suffer as I did, my love.'

'I am sure something good will happen soon, Mama.'

'The duke is demanding to see you, Helene,' Mrs Henderson said. 'I have never told you, but he made me an infamous offer once…just after your father died. He said that he would take you into his family and give you everything that I could not—but that I must give you up entirely.'

'Mama!' Helene was shocked. 'How could he say such a wicked thing to you? I hope you told him that I should not go?'

'To be honest I was nervous of telling you, Helene. Our lives have been hard since Papa died, and I was afraid you might be tempted by what Annesdale had to offer.'

'Mama! You should have known I would never leave you in such circumstances.'

'I have felt guilty over it. I refused without asking if you would like to live under his roof. You would have so many advantages...'

'None that would compensate for having to give you up,' Helene said. 'I shall certainly not visit Lady Annersley. How dare they write to me, knowing how they behaved to you in the past?'

'I think perhaps you should keep your appointment, Helene. Hear what they have to say. I thought if you married well you would be safe, but I do not think Annesdale will rest until he hears your denial from your own lips.'

'You are sure, Mama? I do not wish to have anything to do with these people—they do not deserve it.'

'Hear him first and then we may put an end to this business.' Mrs Henderson smiled. 'Go and change for your outing this afternoon, Helene. It is not your fault that you have not received an offer of marriage. I dare say I can live in Edgar's house a little longer if I am forced to it.'

'Is it so very bad, Mama?' Helene asked. 'If a gentleman asked for my hand, I should naturally tell him that my grandfather was in trade. I know it is not considered the done thing, but if there was genuine affection between us, it could not matter.'

'It might matter to others,' her mother warned. 'If a

gentleman loved you for yourself, he might not care—but his family might think otherwise.'

'What are you trying to tell me, Mama?'

'Lord Coleridge...his father was second cousin to Annesdale...' Mrs Henderson put a hand to her face. 'It is the reason I tried to warn you from the start, my love. Max Coleridge is said to be fond of the duke—I fear that he would give you up rather than risk a breach with him. I dare say Coleridge may even be his heir...though I am not certain of it.'

'Oh, Mama!' Helene stared at her in dismay. The discovery that Max Coleridge was distantly related to Papa's father was shocking. How could she ever marry him in the circumstances? The duke had ruined her mother's life, thereby forcing Papa to work as a secretary for barely enough money to keep his family alive.

If she married Max, he would expect her to welcome his friends and family. How could she be civil to a man she must hate?

Helene dashed away the angry tears. She was being ridiculous, for Max had not asked her to marry him, and it was unlikely that he would—especially if she told him exactly who she was.

Chapter Six

'I do not know how much longer this weather can last,' Max said as they strolled together in the park that afternoon, waiting for the band to start. 'We have been lucky this year and it must rain before long.'

'I do not mind the rain,' Helene said. She directed an uncertain look at him, for her secret was playing on her mind. She felt that she was deceiving him, because he could not know that she was the daughter of a woman the duke had hated so much that he had cut his son off without a penny for marrying her. 'At home I sometimes walk when it is wet. Everything in the country smells so clean and fresh after the rain—do you not think so?'

'Yes, particularly new-mown grass,' Max said and gave her an approving look. 'I can see that you are truly a country girl at heart, Helene. Would you consider being a guest at my home when the Season ends? I am thinking of having a house party for friends. I have not done so for some years. Indeed, no one but Harry Pendleton and the Earl of Ravenshead have been there since my father died—apart from my widowed aunt and her son. They live in the dower house, but it is time that the main house was opened up to guests again.'

'I dare say you were away for long periods in the army, sir?'

'Yes, I was. My father was ill for a while, but he would not send for me and I did not know until I came home. I was with him when he died, but he was a very proud man. Had he asked, I would have resigned my commission and come home to be with him sooner. He was one of the old school. His name and family were everything to him. He was proud because I was doing my duty for my country. Pride and honour were all. He would not summon me simply because he had only a few months to live.'

'You must have been sad when you knew,' Helene said, the expression in her eyes thoughtful. 'My father died some years ago. We live with Mama's brother. I know very little of my family.' It was on the tip of her tongue to confess what she knew, but she held back.

'I was fortunate enough to know my grandparents well,' Max said. 'I recall that Grandfather was a stiff, cold man— but his wife was a sweet lady. She more or less brought me up after my mother died when I was a child. My mother's father died only last year. He left me everything. I was very fortunate to have such relations.'

'How sad for you that your mama should die, but fortunate that your grandparents were kind to you,' Helene said. She turned her head as they heard the music begin. 'I think we should rejoin the others, sir.'

'Yes, I am sure we should. I must not monopolise your time or your friends will not be pleased with me.'

Helene laughed and shook her head. 'Tell me, Lord

Coleridge, have you ever discovered who shot at you when we were at Richmond?'

'I fear nothing has been discovered as yet,' Max said and frowned. 'It may be that I shall have to go down to the country for a few days—but that will not be until after we have visited Vauxhall.'

'I dare say your estate takes a great deal of your time?' Helene glanced at him, noticing the tiny nerve flicking in his cheek.

'Yes, sometimes,' Max agreed. 'There may be some changes necessary before I can hold my house party. Nothing of any great moment, I assure you.'

'I see.' Helene nodded. 'I shall look forward to our visit to Vauxhall. I have been thinking that I might buy a few comfits and trinkets for the children. Shall you be visiting them again soon?'

'Perhaps on my return,' Max said. 'I see that Miss Marshall is looking for us. We'd best rejoin our party now.'

'So Lord Coleridge told you he may be going out of town for a few days? And he asked if we would join him at his estate at the end of the Season?' Mrs Henderson frowned when they spoke in Helene's room later that evening. 'He has certainly paid you some attention. I do not think he can be aware that you are Annesdale's granddaughter.'

'Oh, Mama—' Helene felt her throat tighten '—do you think it would distress him if he knew the truth?'

'I told you that they are close,' her mother said and sniffed. She waved her kerchief, sending waves of lavender water in Helene's direction. 'I am not sure what he would say, but I fear he might take Annesdale's part. If you married him, I might not be able to visit you often.'

'Do you want to go home, Mama?' Helene felt a strange ache in her breast. It was as if she had been stabbed to the heart, because all her dreams must end now.

'Not yet. There are other gentlemen, Helene. Could you not bring yourself to marry Mr Bradwell if he asked you?'

'I am not sure, Mama,' Helene said, her face very white. 'I do not truly like him, but if you say I must...'

'No, I shall not force you to take him,' Mrs Henderson said. 'But there must be someone else you've met that you like enough to marry—someone who will not be influenced by Annesdale?'

'I do not know...' Helene felt overwhelmed by her disappointment. 'I think I am in love with Lord Coleridge, but I am not sure that he loves me—or that he would accept me if he knew the truth.'

Helene went driving in the park with Miss Marshall and her brother Paul the next morning. She had decided that she must carry on as usual until they could leave town, but she had kept a distance between herself and Captain Marshall. Helene sensed that he was considering making her an offer, but she could not allow it—she knew she did not love him. Her heart belonged to another. When Captain Marshall suggested that she might like to attend a balloon race with a party of his friends the following week, she smiled and told him that she had a prior engagement. His expression showed that he was disappointed, and perhaps a little offended, but her pride would not let her continue as an intimate friend when she knew that she could never accept an offer from him.

She returned home just before noon, a little surprised to see a large travelling coach moving away from the house. A gentleman was staring out of the window, and he seemed to sit forward as the coach drew near to her. Helene frowned, for she knew that he was the Duke of Annesdale. How dare he call here? He must know he was not welcome after the way he had behaved to Mama.

She went straight upstairs to take off her bonnet, but she had not yet changed for nuncheon when someone tapped at the door. A moment later it opened and her mama entered.

'Helene dearest,' Mrs Henderson said. 'Did you enjoy your drive?'

'Yes, Mama,' Helene replied. 'Have you had visitors this morning? I saw a coach leaving just as I returned from the park. I believe it may have belonged to the Duke of Annesdale...'

'Yes, he was here. He asked to speak to you or, failing that, to me. I was lying down with a headache and refused him.'

'Was that wise, Mama? I think perhaps he might be a dangerous enemy.'

'What more can he do to me—except take my daughter from me?'

'He shall not do that, Mama.'

'Then I have nothing to fear.' Mrs Henderson smiled at her. 'I cannot blame him for wanting you—but I do not think I could bear to give you up, my love. I know I am selfish and—'

'You are not selfish!'

'Supposing it comes to a choice between Lord Coleridge and me?'

'If he could not see how unfair such a choice was, he would not be the man I care for.'

'You do care for him,' her mama said and sniffed. 'If I have caused you unhappiness, I shall never forgive myself.'

'Please do not cry, Mama,' Helene begged. 'Lord Coleridge has not asked me to marry him—and I dare say he will not.'

'You say it does not matter, but I know you will break your heart,' Mrs Henderson said. 'But I am being foolish. You must get ready. Amelia is taking you to visit her orphanage this afternoon...'

'Well, what do you think of my children?' Amelia said as they finished their tour of the house. 'I like to think that they are being taught to become responsible citizens of the future.'

'They all look happy and well fed,' Helene said. 'I enjoyed sitting in on their lessons, Amelia. Do you know, I think I could be content as a teacher. I know I could be a governess if I wished, but I think it must be more rewarding to teach in a school like yours. They have come from misery and poverty and yet they show such courage and resilience.'

'Some of the boys were very unruly when they first came,' Amelia said and looked thoughtful. 'I suppose the girls would do well with a woman to teach them how to sew—but surely you will not think of it, Helene? Would you rather not be married?'

'I suppose I might,' Helene said and wrinkled her brow. It was impossible to explain, for she could not tell Amelia about the duke or that infamous letter. 'But I cannot marry unless someone asks me—and I would only wish to marry if I could like the gentleman. I have not yet given up hope of meeting someone I can like well enough to wed.'

'I thought...' Amelia hesitated and shook her head. 'No, I should not say. You know your own feelings best, Helene.' She glanced at Emily, who had lingered to talk to the housekeeper. 'I believe we ought to be leaving, for we have an engagement this evening. I have thought of setting up another home in the country—somewhere I can send those who need a little extra care. Do you think that would be a good idea? I have been fortunate here for Mrs Rowley was looking for a position, and her husband is very good about the place. Mr Makepeace is an excellent tutor and he does not mind helping with other things. I am not sure that I should be as lucky again. I would not wish to employ someone who would treat the children badly, though I know they need a firm hand.'

'I dare say that is the difficult thing, finding the right staff,' Helene said and looked thoughtful. 'As you say, you have been lucky here, Amelia. Perhaps it is enough.'

'I do not think it will ever be enough,' Amelia replied. 'My brother thinks me foolish, of course. He says it is a waste of money and that the children are slum rats and will remain so whatever I do.'

'Oh, no,' Helene said. 'I think you are doing a wonderful thing, Amelia. More people of consequence should set up homes of a similar kind, there must always be a need for them, I believe.'

'There certainly is,' Amelia replied. 'There are few other places these children can go. Most of them would be sent to the workhouse if they were not here. Have you any idea of what happens to them there? They are given poor food, made to do physical, hard work, and when they are old enough they are sold to masters who will work them even harder. They have no choice, no control over their lives at all.'

Helene nodded agreement. She told Amelia about the climbing boy she had rescued at her uncle's house. 'His master demanded to be paid ten guineas for him. In the end I paid much less, but it was not right that he should be able to buy and sell the boy.'

'It certainly was not,' Amelia said and smiled at her. 'When you are married, you must set up your own charity, Helene. You may invite gentlemen of influence to your salon and try to influence them to use their power in government to change the laws. Until that happens, we can only do so much.'

Helene had enjoyed her visit to the orphanage, because the children had looked healthy, well fed and content. It was proof of what could be done when one had money. Lord Coleridge's orphanage was in the country, and Amelia's was in the poorest part of London, but they were both doing excellent work.

It would be pleasant to be the wife of a wealthy man, Helene thought, a little wistfully. She would have had many interests in common with Lord Coleridge, but there was no point in thinking of it. She could not marry him even if he asked. He was related to the Duke of Annesdale and fond of him. Helene could never accept that man in her life.

It was obviously best if she put all thought of Max Coleridge from her mind.

Mrs Henderson had decided to keep to her bed. On the Sunday morning, Amelia was worried and called the doctor to her. He came, prescribed a tonic and said that it was either a chill or an irritation of the nerves.

'I am well enough,' Mrs Henderson said when Helene took a tray of tea and comfits up to her. 'I think I have a summer cold and should stay in bed for a few days. You must not think of giving up your pleasures for my sake, Helene. If I feel no better in a few days, I may go home—but you will stay here with Amelia for the time being. At least until…' She sniffed and held a small bottle of smelling salts to her nose. 'Do not worry, my love. In a day or so I shall be better. If you would be so kind as to fetch me some books from the lending library, I shall do well enough here.'

'Of course, Mama,' Helene agreed. 'I have engaged to go to an art collection with Miss Marshall and Emily this morning. I can quite easily call in at the lending library on my way home.' She looked at her mother anxiously. 'Are you sure you do not wish for company? Emily may go in my stead and I could read to you.'

'You are a sweet girl to think of it, but I shall not hear of it. Run along now and make the most of your visit. I do not know when we shall come to town again.'

'Do not worry, Mama. I shall think of something,' Helene promised. 'If you are so unhappy living under my uncle's roof, we shall not live there for ever.'

'I wish things might be different.' Mrs Henderson shook her head, tears brimming in her eyes. 'Go away now, Helene. I want to rest.'

Helene was obedient to her wish. She collected her pelisse for there was a little chill in the air that morning—the first sign, perhaps, that the weather might turn. Joining Emily downstairs, the two of them went out to the carriage.

Miss Marshall was waiting when they arrived at the gallery. Her mother accompanied her, but there was no sign of her brother.

'Paul had another engagement,' she said. 'He says he has danced attendance on me long enough and has only a few days before he must leave for his regiment. They are based near Lyme Regis at the moment, but he expects a posting to India quite soon.'

'Oh, I did not know that.' Helene looked at the other girl as Emily fell into step with Lady Marshall. 'Does Captain Marshall mean to make a career in the army? I thought perhaps he might give up the life in time to help your father manage the estate.'

'Paul is my younger brother,' Miss Marshall told her. 'I have two older brothers, Helene. He has a small estate of his own, but employs an agent. He says that he shall stay in the army for some years to come...though he did think he might give it up soon. However, he has changed his mind.' Her look was a little accusing and Helene felt that she was being blamed for his decision.

'I think if I were a man, I should choose to remain in the army. It must be exciting to travel to foreign lands.'

'Do you think so? I should not care for it,' Miss Marshall said. 'Oh, do look at this landscape. It is rather fine, is it not?'

Their conversation was concentrated on the pictures for some minutes after that, and when they parted company Miss Marshall seemed to have recovered her usual good humour. She kissed Helene on both cheeks and said that she looked forward to seeing her very soon.

It was as Helene and Emily were emerging from the library half an hour later that they met Lord Coleridge. He stopped and doffed his hat, smiling at them.

'I hope you are looking forward to tomorrow evening, ladies? I believe it may keep fine, though it is cooler today, is it not?'

'Yes, a little fresher,' Emily said. 'We are very much

looking forward to joining you tomorrow, Lord Coleridge—
are we not, Helene?'

'Yes…yes, we are,' Helene said. She could not meet
Lord Coleridge's eyes, her cheeks hot as she glanced down
at her shoes. He would not look at her so kindly if he knew
the way things stood between her family and the Duke of
Annesdale. 'I am sure it will be a very pleasant evening.'

'Have you visited the new art collection?' Max asked.

Helene risked a glance at him and saw that his eyes were
serious as he looked at her. He must be able to sense the
reserve in her, because she had always been so free with
him. She tried to smile, but knew it was a woeful effort.

'We have been this morning,' she said. 'There were
some fine landscapes after the style of Mr Constable—
though not quite as good in my opinion.'

'You enjoy good art?' Max asked and Helene nodded. 'I
have been collecting for a while, though most are in store
until I am ready to hang them.'

'At your home in the country?'

'Yes, I think so. I stay at my club while I am in town—
as yet I have no need for a town house, though that may
change,' Max said. 'I think you must excuse me, ladies. I
have an appointment and I am sure you have things to do.'

'We are going on to a poetry reading at Lady Jamieson's
house this afternoon,' Emily told him. 'She is sponsoring
a new poet—a gentleman by the name of Mr Tarleton.'

'Henry Tarleton,' Max nodded. 'I have read something
of his—the man is a Cit and has no soul.'

'That is unfair, sir!' Helene cried. 'To say that he has no
soul merely because he is in trade is abominable. I did not
imagine you to be such a snob!' Her cheeks were flushed
and she felt hot as his eyes dwelled on her.

'I beg your pardon if I have offended you,' Max replied.

'It was a careless remark. The man's poetry is dull and I find it without passion or soul. His being a Cit is certainly nothing to the point.'

'I should hope not,' Helene said. 'A man cannot help his birth and those born to privilege should respect others for their character and not their social standing.'

Max frowned, but said nothing in reply, his eyes reproachful as he gazed at Helene. Her cheeks were flaming, but she would not look at him.

'I believe we ought to hurry on or we shall keep everyone waiting for nuncheon,' Emily said, looking at Helene in concern.

'Then I must certainly not delay you longer,' Max said. 'I look forward to tomorrow evening.'

'As do we,' Emily answered, but Helene merely looked at the ground. Her feelings were in such disorder that she hardly knew how she felt and could not bring herself to speak.

The two ladies walked on in silence. After a moment Emily glanced at Helene. 'You have not quarrelled with Lord Coleridge?'

'No, of course not,' Helene said. She still felt hot and uncomfortable, and was realising that she had been unnecessarily sharp. 'I just felt that he was unfair.'

'When you have listened to several of Mr Tarleton's poems, you may feel that Lord Coleridge was less unfair than you imagine.'

'It was not his remark about the poetry that made me cross. However, you are right to censure me, Emily. I should not have been rude to him.'

'I do not think Lord Coleridge a snob. We are all in the habit of calling persons in trade by that name, but it is not necessarily meant to disparage,' Emily said. She looked at Helene's face. 'If something is troubling you, I would be happy to listen, Helene.'

'You have been a good friend,' Helene said. 'There is nothing to tell you, but I do thank you for the offer.'

Helene's eyes stung with tears, but she refused to let them fall. She had made so many good friends and it made her sad when she thought about the future. When they left town she would probably never see any of them again.

Lord Coleridge's remark might not have been meant to disparage, but it showed what he must think of persons in trade. What would he say if he knew that Helene was the granddaughter of a tanner?

Helene had never believed that she was at a disadvantage because of her background. Even when her mama had warned that Lord Coleridge's family might find it objectionable she had believed that Max was above such things—but now she was not as sure.

Supposing he decided that she was beneath his touch! To see him turn away in distaste would be so hurtful, she did not think that she could bear it.

When Helene woke the next morning she was aware of a heavy feeling, as if a cloud hung over her. She wished that she had not promised to visit Lady Annersley, but Mama had told her that she must keep her word and of course it would be rude to cry off at the last.

Helene dressed in a dark blue walking gown; it was severe but elegant and made her feel equal to the task. Lady Annersley's house was in a fashionable square near by. She did not need to order the carriage, and she had no intention of asking Emily to accompany her. Instead, she summoned her maid.

'I have a morning call to pay,' she told the girl. 'You

will accompany me and wait in the hall. I dare say I shall not be more than a few minutes.'

Tilly dropped a curtsy. 'Yes, Miss Henderson.'

Helene chose an elegant pelisse of deep yellow, which went well over the gown of dark blue, matching the ribbons on her bonnet. She was determined not to appear cowed. Whatever the lady had to say to her, she would remain polite and dignified and she would not lose her temper!

Lord Coleridge's opinion of Mr Tarleton's poetry had proved justified in part. Helene would not go as far as to say he had no soul, but his work was certainly without passion. She was uncomfortably aware that she had been hasty in her condemnation; her temper was sometimes volatile and she must learn to control it!

She held her head high as they reached their destination, standing back while her maid knocked at the door and then announced to the footman who answered that her mistress had come to call on Lady Annersley. Helene had had visions of being sent to the tradesman's entrance, but the imposing front door was held wide and the footman inclined his head.

'You are expected, Miss Henderson.' He looked at Tilly. 'You may sit there, girl. I shall take your mistress upstairs.'

'I shall not be long.' Helene looked apologetically at the girl, for she was a little apprehensive now that they were inside what was obviously a much grander house than Miss Royston's. 'Remember we are going shopping later. We shall buy you a new bonnet.'

'Yes, miss.' Tilly summoned a grin.

Helene followed the footman up the wide staircase. It was hung with paintings of men and women, possibly past Dukes of Annesdale and their ladies, she thought, since it was the duke's house.

At the head of the stairs the footman turned to the right. They walked to the end of the landing and he threw open a pair of magnificent mahogany doors.

'Her ladyship will be with you in a moment.'

'Thank you.' Helene walked into the room. It was furnished with heavy pieces of mahogany with richly brocaded upholstery. The walls were hung with more paintings, some of them landscapes, and there was a cabinet filled with what Helene thought must be gold objects at the far end. Everything was slightly opulent, almost decadent; it was clearly the home of a very rich and important family.

She was studying one of the landscapes when she heard footsteps behind her. She drew a deep breath and turned slowly to face the woman who stood there, dipping in a slight curtsy.

'Ma'am, I am come as you requested.'

'I am glad of it,' Lady Annersley replied. 'I wish to talk to you for a moment alone—and then I should like to make you known to my father-in-law.'

'Why?' Helene lifted her head. 'I do not know what the duke can have to say to me, ma'am. I certainly have little to say to him.'

'He has wanted to make himself known for some time,' Lady Annersley said. 'We were not informed of your birth, but it was brought to our attention some years later. Until recently it was not thought of any consequence. However, my husband died soon after the stillbirth of my last child.'

'I am very sorry to hear that, ma'am,' Helene said, her hackles rising at the woman's arrogance. 'I do not see what it can have to do with me?'

'Has that woman told you nothing?' Anger glittered in Lady Annersley's eyes. 'She ruined your father by marrying him and she has deliberately withheld the knowledge of your birth from Papa—and now she has withheld Annesdale's offer from you. I do not know what your father ever saw in her. She was the daughter of a common tanner. Passable to look at, I dare say, but he could have done much better!'

'You are wrong, ma'am. I know that I am the duke's granddaughter—but still I have nothing to say. Because of the arrogance of Papa's family, Mama has had much to bear.'

'She is the daughter of a tanner. How your father can have been so lost to his duty as to have married such a person I do not know!'

'I do not think you should say such things to me, ma'am,' Helene said, feeling angry. 'Mama has done you no harm...'

'No harm? She brought our family into disgrace—'

'You are the disgrace, ma'am,' Helene cried as her good intentions fled. 'I will have you know that I am proud of my mama and her family. I have had more kindness from them than from—'

'You are insolent. If I had my way, you would not even have been invited here—'

'Sarah, if you please...' A gentleman had walked into the room. Helene knew at once that he was the duke. She was quivering with anger, stung by the unfairness of Lady Annersley's attack. 'You may leave us now, if you will.'

'She should be made aware of her duty to you—to the family,' Lady Annersley began angrily, but he lifted his hand and she was silenced. 'Very well, have it your way...' She walked from the room, clearly angry.

Helene looked at the gentleman. His hair was white, his eyes a faded blue, his cheeks lined with age and perhaps illness. However, he stood straight, unbowed, pride in every line of his body. She made him a curtsy while keeping her head high and her expression proud. He nodded, a faint smile in his eyes.

'Forgive my daughter-in-law, she is very loyal to me and she has a temper, which I think perhaps you have, too, Miss Henderson.' He was silent for a moment, his gaze intent. 'You are something like my second wife—your father's mother...' Helene gave a little shake of her head, as if in denial. 'I called on your mother and I have written to you many times. You did not receive any of my letters?'

'No, sir. I believe my mother may have kept them from me—and I imagine you will understand her feelings in this matter. She has been treated ill by you and others.'

He frowned, but did not reply, going on as if she had not spoken. 'Your father was my youngest son, but my favourite. I suppose that was why I was so angry when he threw his life away.'

'By marrying my mother?'

He inclined his head. 'Yes, by taking a wife who was not of his class.'

Helene was silent for a moment, then, 'Is a man less for having been born poor, then? My grandfather was one of a family of six boys and five girls. He had nothing but his wits and his hands, but he built a considerable business, which he passed on to his children. My uncle was sent to a good school and is generally thought a gentleman, and my grandmother was the daughter of the younger son of a country squire. I have every reason to be proud of Mama and Grandfather. I shall not hang my head in shame because he happened to be a tanner by trade.'

'You are very proud. In that you are like me.'

'Mama's father was also proud. He did not wish her to marry into a family who would not acknowledge her.'

'You think we acted unfairly towards your mama?'

'I am certain of it.'

'You do not understand. Our family goes back to the Conqueror.'

'So?' Helene's eyes glittered.

'We could not admit your mother to the family,' he said heavily. 'It would not have been acceptable. You may think me hard, but I had no choice. I had my sons to consider, their wives and children. I did not know then that I should lose them all. It is a hard thing for a father to lose all his sons, Helene. I should have died with my grandchildren around me, secure in the knowledge that they would succeed me. I have no one—at least only Sarah. I am grateful for her company. She might have married again, but she has refused to desert me.'

'That was noble of her.'

'Ah, you speak bitterly. You are angry because I have told you the truth. I could not lie to you, Helene. If we are to trust one another, we must be honest from the start.'

'Why should I trust you?'

'You have little enough reason. I know that your situation is precarious. I could make things so much better for you. If I acknowledge you as my granddaughter, you will make a good marriage. Houses that have not yet been opened to you will receive you. You will inherit most of my disposable fortune when I die—and if your husband is willing to add my name to yours, I will make your children my heirs.'

'Why would you do this for us now?' Helene looked at him suspiciously.

'I offered your mother an income if she would give you

up to me as soon as I learned of your father's death. It was only then that I knew I had a granddaughter.'

'If she would give me up? You are saying that you want me—but not Mama?' Helene felt the disgust choking her. 'She told me of your offer, but I could hardly credit that you would dare to make me such an offer to my face.'

'I see you do not mince words. I think you get that from me. Your father was honest also. He told me that if I would not accept his wife, he would have nothing to do with me—and he kept his word.'

'What makes you imagine that I would be less honourable than my father, sir? Why should you think that I would give up my mother for your sake?'

'You have much to gain—and perhaps even more to lose.'

Helene's gaze narrowed as she saw the glint in his eyes. 'Are you threatening me, sir? Mama feared you. She has been in great distress of late and now I understand why.'

'She has tried to keep you from me. You are my only grandchild, Helene. My only hope of an heir.'

Helene felt the anger rising inside her. 'Then why did you not offer her a home? I should have come with her and you might have known me as a child. Why did you make her wait in the kitchen while my father spoke to his mama? Why did your family treat her as if she were nothing?'

'Your mother is a tanner's daughter. I am a proud man, Helene.'

'And I am a tanner's granddaughter.' Helene raised her head and looked him in the eyes. 'I am not ashamed of who I am, sir. If I am ashamed of anything, it is that I carry your blood.'

His face went white and he seemed to stagger for a moment, but he righted himself and his eyes were hard.

'Then you refuse my offer? Your mother would have her own home somewhere in the country, and you have my word that the estate would go to your heirs.'

'I am not for sale,' Helene told him proudly. 'Had you offered us both a home when Papa died, I should have honoured and loved you—but you are despicable. Excuse me, I must leave.'

'If you go, you may ruin yourself. I know that you have hopes of Lord Coleridge. His father was a proud man. You may not know it, but we are close, almost as father and son. A word from me and your hopes would be at an end. He is distantly related and I had intended that he should inherit the Annesdale estate, though my private fortune would have come to you had you not refused me. Do you imagine he would give that up for the granddaughter of a tanner?'

Helene did not turn her head to look at him. His words were like a dagger thrust into her heart, but she would not allow him to see her pain. He could do his worst—she had already made up her mind that honour must make her walk away from the man who might have brought her so much happiness.

'Do not go, Helene…' The duke's voice held a world of pain. 'My wretched pride…you are my only hope…'

Helene walked down the corridor and then the stairs. Tilly was sitting in the hall, flirting with one of the footmen.

'We are leaving,' Helene said and forced herself to remain calm. 'I think we should go shopping, for I may not be in town much longer.'

Helene paced the floor of her bedchamber. She felt so angry that she did not know how she would face her friends or her mother. She could not bring herself to tell Mama that she had quarrelled with the duke. Mrs Henderson had done all she could to avoid the confrontation, but Helene had walked straight into it and had behaved recklessly. Her anger had made her speak out and now he would ruin Helene's chances.

Helene knew that she did not wish to marry any man of her acquaintance save one. That must be at an end! So she would not marry.

Poor Mama! She had not deserved to be treated so scurvily. They would have to return to Uncle Edgar's house, and her mother would continue to be unhappy.

Helene would have to find work, somewhere they could both live. She knew that she would enjoy working with children as Ann Saunders did. Amelia had spoken of setting up a second home in the country if she could find the right people to take care of the children. Perhaps she would offer the chance to them.

Helene would do most of the work. Her mama could keep accounts and perhaps help with the cooking. It was the only way out of this mess as far as Helene could see.

But first she had to get through this evening. Helene was almost certain that Lord Coleridge had planned the evening for her benefit. It was exactly the kind of thing she loved, but tonight it would be difficult to keep a smile in place. It would be difficult to face Max Coleridge knowing that she had quarrelled with a man he thought of almost as a father. Perhaps the duke had already summoned him? It might be that he would cancel the outing that evening rather than spend time with her.

Chapter Seven

Helene dressed in a gown of emerald silk that evening. Her maid styled her hair back in a complicated twist, allowing tendrils to fall about her face. Afterwards, Tilly looked at her doubtfully.

'You are pale tonight, Miss Henderson. Would you like me to apply a touch of rouge to your cheeks?'

'Thank you, but no,' Helene said and touched her hand. 'Do not worry, Tilly. My looks do not matter. You have dressed me most elegantly and I am satisfied with my appearance.'

The ache in her heart had been steadily growing all day, and she thought that the only answer for her pain was that she was indeed in love with Max.

Clearly she could not go on seeing him. Her quarrel with the duke had put an end to any hopes she might have had in regard to Lord Coleridge. Helene was determined to speak to her mama the next day and ask if they could go home. However, she could not bear to give up her last chance to see Max. She would make the most of this evening, and then she would refuse all future invitations from him.

It had been made clear to her that she was not to be allowed her happiness. The duke had sufficient influence with Max Coleridge to put an end to her hopes. Mama had warned her that they were close, but Helene's temper had led her astray. The quarrel with Annesdale had sealed her fate. Max would not give up friendship and fortune for her sake—nor would it be right to expect it. Helene had believed that he might just accept the fact that her grandfather had been in trade, though his careless remark about Mr Tarleton had made her wonder if she knew him as well as she had thought. She had intended to tell him the truth when they next met and take her chances, but now she saw that a marriage between them would be impossible.

Max dressed with care that evening. He smiled as he used his third neckcloth in an effort to perfect a style he had been toying with for a few days, achieving his aim at last. He looked tolerably well—respectable and wealthy, in the prime of his life. He had a comfortable home in the country and the wherewithal to buy a town house if his chosen bride wished to visit often. Was it enough to tempt her?

Max had come to the conclusion that Miss Helene Henderson was the lady who would best fill the position of his wife. There were other beautiful ladies, some of them heiresses—but none of the others had captured his attention as Helene had. He enjoyed her company, missed her when he did not see her, and he found her very attractive, desirable. He had kissed her on impulse when he rescued her from the apple tree and the fierce hunger that seized him as he held her had surprised him. He was not sure whether his feelings amounted to being in love, for he had never felt more than a passing desire for any other woman.

However, he had come to the conclusion that he should ask Helene before someone else stole a march on him.

Vauxhall was an ideal place to propose, because there were many secluded areas. He could draw her aside into a pretty arbour and make his feelings known to her. If she indicated that she would be happy to accept, he would call on her mama the next day.

Smiling because he was relieved to have made a decision, Max added a magnificent diamond stickpin to his cravat and slipped his signet ring on his little finger. This evening would, he believed, settle his future.

Helene smiled apprehensively as Max greeted her. He had called to collect them in his carriage, an impressive vehicle with his family crest emblazoned on the side panels and a team of the most magnificent horses Helene had ever seen. She knew that he was a member of the prestigious Four-in-Hand club, though he was not driving his team himself that evening.

'You look beautiful,' Max told her as he handed Helene into the carriage and climbed in beside her. 'I have been looking forward to showing you Vauxhall. The gardens are lovely at this time of the year, and there are some interesting booths. We may see artists and even playwrights offering their wares for sale, as well as other merchants.'

'I am looking forward to the fireworks,' Helene replied, dropping her gaze. He was staring at her in such an intimate way that she could not doubt he meant her to know he liked her very well. If only she had not agreed to meet Lady Annersley! If she had not quarrelled so dreadfully with the duke, she might have gone on as before.

'Oh, so am I,' Emily said from the opposite seat. 'No matter how often I see them, I am charmed.'

Helene nodded and smiled. She would not allow herself to think of the future this evening! If it were to be her last in Max's company, she would make the most of every second.

Toby Sinclair joined them as they strolled past the booths, glancing at various trinkets displayed for sale. They stopped to glance at some enamelled snuff boxes and scent flasks, and Toby considered buying a fine example of Bristol blue glass, but did not part with his blunt in the end.

It was as they lingered at a booth displaying some rather exquisite miniature paintings done on porcelain, which could be made up into jewellery or set into picture frames, that a gentleman came up to them. Helene had never met him, but she saw at once that the gentlemen all knew each other well. Amelia also seemed to know the newcomer, but Helene could not tell whether she was pleased to see him or not, for her face did not reflect any emotion, though her hands curled into tight balls at her sides for just one moment. In another second she was smiling as she turned to Helene.

'Helene dearest, may I introduce the Earl of Ravenshead—my lord, this is Miss Helene Henderson. She is staying with me in town.'

'Delighted,' the earl said, nodding his head towards Helene. He looked a little puzzled as his gaze returned to Amelia. 'I have just today arrived in town. Max was good enough to invite me to join you all, for I have no engagements as yet.'

'I am giving a card party on Saturday,' Amelia said. 'Perhaps you would like to join us, sir?'

'Yes, thank you, I should,' he replied and arched one

eyebrow. 'I may call before that if you have a free moment. I have something I should like to discuss with you concerning my daughter. Max has been telling me that you are the patroness of an orphanage, Miss Royston. I should be most interested in seeing it.'

'Yes, of course. You may call tomorrow morning if you wish.'

Somehow they had separated into three couples. Amelia walked a little ahead with the Earl of Ravenshead. Toby Sinclair followed with Emily and Helene walked at Max's side.

'You are a little quiet this evening,' Max said and glanced at Helene's face. 'Is something troubling you?'

'Oh, no, certainly not. I was just thinking of our visit to your orphanage. I very much admire Miss Saunders and my thoughts return often to her and her wonderful work. I think it must be very satisfying to do such work with children—especially those who have come from poor homes.'

'You are very right. When I first took them there, some of the lads had been starved and beaten, forced to do work that even a grown man would find tiring. It is unbelievable what some masters expect of their apprentices. I think the boys find it difficult to believe that their new life isn't just a dream.'

Helene nodded. 'I dare say it must seem that way to them. With an education behind them, they will find it much easier to gain employment of a more congenial kind when they are older.'

'We shall have clerks and bankers, and tailors—perhaps even the new prime minister,' Max said, laughter in his eyes.

'I do not think it likely, though of course there is no

good reason why not,' Helene said. 'Though I believe such honours go more usually to a more privileged class.' She arched her brows at him.

'Do I detect a note of disapproval in your voice?' Max looked at her, gaze narrowed. 'I know there are rotten boroughs where the rich and influential bribe people to vote for their candidate, and of course my seat in the House of Lords is hereditary—but I think on the whole we are honest and well meaning, even if we make mistakes.'

'I did not mean to question such privilege,' Helene said. 'I dare say there is nothing wrong with it, providing someone does not abuse their position. However, I have often wondered why a lady may not vote or stand for a seat in parliament.'

'Have you indeed?' Max chuckled deep in his throat. 'I see you are a radical, Helene—but I shall not harangue you with all the reasons why it would not work. Perhaps if you invited ladies of like mind to your salon, you could bring about the changes you desire.'

Helene's cheeks flushed. 'I did not say that I wished to change things, sir—only that I have wondered why it is so. Besides, I do not think that I shall ever be in a position to have a salon of my own.'

'Do you not?' Max's gaze was soft as it dwelled on her face. 'I believe it might be arranged quite easily if your husband chose to help you—and I am sure that a liberal-minded man would not object to his wife taking an interest in politics and good works. I know that I should not.'

'Oh…' Helene's gaze flew to his face. What she saw there made her heart race. He was going to speak. She was certain he was about to propose to her. He must not! She had to stop him somehow! 'But I do not intend to marry.' The words were out before she could stop them, falling over themselves in an effort to save them both embarrassment. 'I have decided that I shall find myself a position similar to that of Miss Saunders and devote my life to looking after deprived children.'

Max's eyes narrowed; the laughter was gone from his face. Helene felt as if a knife had struck her in the heart as she saw his expression become closed, a little angry, hurt—even offended. She almost wished the words unspoken, but knew that this was how it must be. The duke hated her now. He would certainly forbid the marriage even if she agreed to it.

'Are you sure that is your wish?' Max asked in a careful, guarded tone. 'You must know that as the wife of a wealthy man who cared for you, you could help children by giving them your patronage—as well as other things that might be near to your heart.'

'Yes, I am aware of that,' Helene said, her manner strained. She looked down, because she could not bear to see the glow fade from his eyes. She could not doubt that he liked her, but marriage was out of the question. 'If it were possible for me to marry, I should have considered it and I think it might have made me happy.' Her voice was close to breaking, but she held her misery inside, pride making her lift her head though she could not meet his gaze. 'However, it is impossible. Circumstances—there are reasons why I shall never marry. It is quite impossible.'

'Would you care to tell me those reasons, Helene?'

Something in his tone compelled her to look at him. 'I am unable to do so, for they concern others, as well as myself,' she said, her composure remarkable considering the rending pain in her heart. This was the hardest thing she had ever had to do! It hurt her so very much. 'I am sorry...'

'You need not apologise to me,' Max said, and his eyes were once again intent on her face. 'I must tell you that I shall be leaving town shortly. I have to pay a visit to my estate. I may not be back for some days.' He hesitated, then, 'In the matter of a position of the kind you envisage…I may have an opportunity in the future. If you were willing to receive me when I return, I could have some news that might interest you. If you are quite determined on your future?'

'I am certain that it is for the best,' Helene said and swallowed hard. She could see the others had turned to look at them. 'I believe Amelia and the others are waiting for us. I dare say they are ready for their supper.'

'And I am remiss in my duties as the host,' Max said. 'Please do not be distressed by anything that has occurred this evening, Miss Henderson. I hope that we shall continue as friends?'

Helene murmured something appropriate. He had taken her at her word and seemed to have recovered easily from his first shock and anger. Perhaps he had not truly cared for her at all, merely thinking her a suitable wife. If that were the case, he would soon forget her and turn his attentions to another young lady.

Max watched Helene for the remainder of the evening. She hid her emotions well, but he sensed her distress, though he did not know the reasons for it. Her prompt action in preventing him from speaking had saved them both embarrassment, but he did not think that she was embarrassed. Something else was making her look sad whenever she thought herself unobserved.

She conducted herself well throughout supper and the remainder of the evening, though she declined to dance with Toby when he asked. Max thought it might be that she did not wish to dance with him and had made some excuse about having eaten too much supper. She had eaten only a few mouthfuls and was clearly ill at ease, though when the firework display began she seemed to forget for a while and her delight was genuine. Once she turned to him and smiled when a particularly fine display made her clap her hands.

'Oh, this is so much fun. Thank you for bringing me, sir.'

'It was my pleasure.'

Max wished that he had waited to speak. He had arranged the evening for her pleasure and then spoiled it for her. It might be that she was frightened because she did not know him well enough—and yet he did not believe that anything truly frightened her. What reasons could she possibly have for saying that it was impossible for her to marry?

His emotions were mixed: anger, disappointment and hurt pride warring in his mind. Yet, despite his feelings, something was telling him that Helene's distress was at least as great as his own.

He knew that ladies often said no the first time in the hope that they would be asked again, or by someone more important or richer. However, he acquitted Helene of playing games or of hanging out for a more prestigious title. She genuinely believed that she ought not to marry—but why?

He had told her that he would be out of town on impulse, wanting to give them both a breathing space before they met again, but it made sense. He had delayed his journey because he wished to continue his friendship with Helene. Now was surely the right time to make the visit to his home and to think about the future. Helene's refusal had made Max all the more certain that she was the only woman he wished to marry.

Damn it! He would not give up at the first fence. If he withdrew because his feelings were hurt, he would be a fool. If Helene had a problem, he would do what he could to discover it and see if it could perhaps be solved in some way.

Helene had no way of knowing Max's thoughts. She had managed to put on a brave face all evening, but alone in her room later that night she gave way to tears. Oh, how awful it all was! Had she been able to accept Max's proposal, she would have been the happiest of women! If she had been in any doubt of her feelings for him, she was clear now. She loved him so much that it had broken her heart to refuse him—at least, to prevent him from speaking. It would have been cruel and heartless of her to allow him to continue knowing what her answer must be. If only the Duke of Annesdale had never come to town! If she had controlled her damnable temper…

Helene cried herself to sleep at last.

Her dreams had been wild and made her toss and turn, crying out in anguish. She awoke, shaking, for she had seen Max lying on the ground with blood seeping from a wound to his chest. The dream was vivid, leaving her cold and frightened.

'No…oh, no,' she wept. It was a foolish dream—there was no reason to suppose that the rogue who had fired at him in Richmond park would do so again. Surely it had been just someone intent on robbery or some such thing? Helene forced herself to put the dream to the back of her mind, for there was nothing she could do and it was merely a dream.

She washed her face, dressing herself in one of her plainest gowns. She went downstairs and found her way into the walled gardens at the back of the house. It was very warm again and she thought it might turn out to be one of the hottest days of the year so far. She knew that she had engagements for most of the day. At some time during the day she must speak to Mama—beg her to take her home. Max had told her that he would call when he returned to town and perhaps have news of a position for her, but she did not think she could bear to work for him. It would mean she would have to see him, talk to him—and all the time she would be conscious of what she had lost. It would be best to make a clean break.

Perhaps Amelia would be willing to offer her a position? If Mama could come, too, it would be better for her than living in her brother's house—if she did not wish to, then Helene would take the position herself. If Amelia could not help her, she must either seek work as a governess or advertise for the kind of position she would most enjoy.

She hoped that she would not have to meet Max in company again, because to see that look of disapproval in his eyes would break her heart. She sighed as she went back upstairs. She must get ready for her first engagement of the day, and if her mama were awake she would tell her that she wished to go home as soon as possible.

'Go home? Why, Helene?' Mrs Henderson was sitting propped up against a pile of pillows, a tray of chocolate and soft rolls with honey beside her. 'We have at least another three weeks in town. It would seem rude if we were to break all our engagements and leave. No, we shall most certainly not go home, Helene.'

'We may be forced to...'

'What do you mean?'

'I visited Lady Annersley yesterday morning, Mama. The Duke of Annesdale is staying with her and he came into the room. He offered to make me his heir if I would live with him and abandon you. I told him that I wanted nothing to do with him—I am afraid we quarrelled dreadfully.'

'Helene!' Mrs Henderson looked at her in horror. 'You should not have done it, really you should not. You should at least have considered, dearest. You would have clothes, jewels and consequence—all the things I cannot give you. You would be foolish to give all that up.'

'Do you think those things mean anything to me? Had he offered us both a home with him I should have thought him generous and kind, but he made it plain you would not be included in our world, though he did say he'd grant you a comfortable home to stay in. You are my mama and I love you. I would not live with that man now if he were the last man alive!'

'He could have given you so much, Helene,' Mrs Henderson told her. 'Sometimes I have felt so guilty for denying you what might have been yours—but your father would have nothing to do with the family after the way they treated me, and I could not betray his memory.'

'And nor shall I,' Helene said. 'But I think we should go home, Mama. The duke was furious when I refused his offer. If he were to cut us in public, it might be uncomfortable, for some people would be sure to take his side.'

'But your only chance of a future is to marry well, Helene.'

'I have decided I shall not marry. Instead, I shall seek a position as a housekeeper in a children's home. I shall ask for Amelia's help to find a place.'

'Helene, please do not! You are behaving very foolishly. I am sure that some of our friends would remain loyal and you might still marry well. Lord Coleridge—'

'No! It is impossible. He is too close to the duke.'

'But a position as a teacher…it is not what I wanted for you.'

'Mama, I must do something. I cannot continue to live at my uncle's expense—and I would prefer not to be married at all.'

'But you like Lord Coleridge. I know you do.' Mrs Henderson looked at her in distress. 'I know I have warned you against him, but if the marriage was arranged perhaps the duke would relent.'

'Lord Coleridge was about to ask me last night, but I told him I could not marry.'

'Helene! Why did you do such a foolish thing? I do not understand you.'

'The duke said that he had planned to leave the Annesdale estate to Max, but would disinherit him if I accepted an offer of marriage. I could not cause a breach between them, Mama.'

'Oh, Helene…I am so sorry. I have ruined your life…' She reached for a kerchief and dabbed at her eyes. 'Forgive me, my love. I have always disliked that man, but I did not imagine even he would be so vindictive.'

'I made him angry, Mama.'

'I warned you to be careful.'

'I know, but he made me so angry—the things he said…' Helene's head went up, her eyes moist with tears she would not shed. 'I should not have lost my temper, but it is done and there is nothing I can do to change it. I have made up my mind, Mama. I cannot marry Lord Coleridge and I shall marry no other.'

'Helene, dearest,' Mrs Henderson said, 'there are other gentlemen…you might find one you could care for if you gave yourself time.'

'Perhaps one day, when I have forgotten all this unhappiness,' Helene said. 'I know this is hard for you, Mama, but I think it is for the best.'

'Give me a few more days,' Mrs Henderson said. 'I have longed for this visit for your sake, Helene. I have dreamed of seeing you as the wife of a good man with a home and family of your own—let me come round to your new idea gradually.'

'Very well, Mama—a few more days,' Helene agreed reluctantly. 'But please understand that I shall not marry anyone—and if you prefer to return to my uncle's house, I shall find work for myself alone.'

Helene returned from her walk with friends to discover that a posy of roses had been left for her in her absence. The note said that they were from Mr Nicholas Bradwell, and asked if he might call on her in two days' time.

Helene frowned as she took the flowers to her room. She poured some water into a silver vase and arranged them on the dressing table. She had just set them down when her mama walked in.

'The roses are lovely,' Mrs Henderson said. 'Who sent them to you, my love?'

'Mr Bradwell.' Helene frowned at her. 'He has asked if he may call the day after tomorrow.'

'I am sure he means to offer for you,' Mrs Henderson said. 'Would you not consider taking him, Helene? It would be so much better for us both. I do not wish to live with Edgar—nor do I wish to become the matron at a children's home.'

'I am sorry, Mama. I could not bear to marry Mr Bradwell, even for your sake. I really could not.'

'Perhaps you need not give up all hope of Lord Coleridge. I have written to the duke and begged him to forgive you.'

'Mama!' Helene stared at her in horror. 'How could you do such a thing to me? I would never have asked him to relent. You know that I would not.'

'Perhaps you should give him what he wants?' her mother suggested. 'I have refused him for the sake of your father's memory, but perhaps I was wrong.'

'Never say such a thing again! I shall not give him what he wants and I shall write and tell him that you did not have my permission to write as you did.'

'Then marry Mr Bradwell. It must be either one or the other. You are my daughter and I shall not give you permission to work as a governess or a housekeeper.'

Helene stared after her as she walked from the room. She sat down on the edge of the bed, feeling sick. How could Mama make such a threat—and what was she to do?

Mama did not truly mean it! She was distressed and Helene did not blame her for her little show of temper. Neither of them wished to return to live under Uncle Edgar's roof again. The only alternative was for Helene to find work. Mama might resist the idea, but she would relent in time—because Helene would never consent to marry Mr Bradwell.

'I am going down to my estate in the morning,' Max told Toby as they sat drinking a glass of wine together that afternoon. 'I asked Gerard if he would care to come, but he has other things on his mind for the moment. I do not suppose you would care to accompany me?'

'It would be my pleasure,' Toby replied. 'I can stay for a few days, and then I should go home. Mama says there is something she needs to discuss with me, but it is not urgent.' He frowned. 'You have something on your mind, I think?'

'I had a letter some while back,' Max told him. 'It has disturbed me and I think I ought to make some inquiries. And then there was the attack on me in the park...'

'You have had no more incidents?'

'None. I am not even certain that the shot was meant for me—though it certainly passed close by. My agents have discovered nothing, and I have searched my mind for a name, someone I have offended. I can think of no one who would want me dead or who could benefit from my death...'

'Except your cousin. I believe you told me that, as things stand, he would inherit everything?'

'Yes...though I have left a letter of intent should I die violently or in mysterious circumstances.'

'He does not know this?'

'No. I might make Robert aware of what I have done. It depends on how I find him—and if there is any truth in what my neighbour wrote to me.'

'Do you care to tell me what the letter contained?'

Max looked at him thoughtfully, then got up and went to the drawer. He opened it and took out the letter, handing it to Toby. The younger man read it through and whistled.

'These are serious accusations, Max. He does not lay the blame on anyone, but you can see where his thinking lies.'

'It seems that my cousin may have been behind these vicious attacks on young women,' Max said and frowned. 'I have to discover what I can. The attacks might go on—and I need to know the truth.'

'It is very odd that they should have begun just after your cousin moved into the dower house. Who else lives with him?'

'My aunt and her physician. He is a gentleman and seems everything he ought. I do not like him—his manner is too smooth—but he does not look like a man who would attack young girls. I would have thought he would not find it difficult to find a willing wench if he chose.'

'But your cousin… It is a serious charge, Coleridge.'

'One that I should not bring lightly,' Max agreed. 'The devil is in it either way, Toby! I have decided that I must discover the truth. Besides, I have some serious thinking to do about the future—and I shall do it best out of town.'

'Yes…' Toby looked thoughtful. 'I know exactly what you mean. Sometimes it is hard to make your choice when you are too close to things.'

'That sounds as if you have a decision of your own to make, Toby?'

'Yes, I have,' Toby replied and shook his head. 'It will keep for the time being. Your problems are more pressing than mine, Max. I am at your service. I may not have served under Wellington, but I am pretty handy with a pistol.'

'I pray that it will not come to that,' Max said and laughed. 'I am thinking of spending the evening at White's—do you care to come or have you another appointment?'

'I said I might look in at Lady Annersley's soirée, but I don't care if I give it a miss.'

'The duke is staying with her. I know that people think him stiff in the neck—and he did cut his youngest son off without a penny when he married a girl of whom he disapproved. However, I believe that he has suffered for it. He was great friends with Father and has always been good to me. I had a letter from him yesterday, asking me to call today, but I have not had the time. I must do so as soon as I return to town, however.'

'Unfortunate business, that—cutting his son out of his will,' Toby said. 'I should not care to be in that position, but it would not happen. My father would give me a lecture and then accept my decision.'

'Quite right, too,' Max said and smiled at him. 'Thinking of putting him to the test any time soon?'

'I am not sure,' Toby said, trying to look innocent, but failing badly. 'I have a call to make, Max. I'll see you at White's later.'

Max nodded. He frowned as his visitor left. His agents had come up with nothing in the matter of the attack on him, but before he left town he would set them another puzzle to solve.

Helene frowned as she looked through the notes on the salver in the hall and found one addressed to her. She did not recognise the hand, but when she turned it she saw that it had been sealed with the crest of Annesdale. She thrust it into her glove as she went upstairs. She had written to the duke, as she had told her mama she would—was this his reply? She had hoped that he would simply ignore both letters and she wondered if it would be best to destroy the letter without reading it.

Two days had passed since the argument with her mother. Helene had not yet spoken to Amelia about the position as a teacher, but she felt that she could not bear to go on like this for much longer. Mama was still cross with her, but she really could not bear to marry Mr Bradwell.

Perhaps the worst of all was that Mr Bradwell was calling that afternoon at three. Helene had not written to him herself, but she knew that her mama had sent him a note inviting him for tea. He was sure to take it as encouragement. It was too bad of Mama!

Alone in her room, the tears suddenly welled up and began to trickle down her cheeks. How could she marry someone she did not like when her heart belonged to Max Coleridge? Yet if she did not, she must find work and Mama was against it. Helene did not wish to be at odds with her mother, but she could not bend to her will in the matter of this marriage.

A sob broke from her as the door of her bedchamber opened and someone walked in. Helene hurriedly brushed the tears from her eyes as she saw Amelia.

'Helene, my dearest,' Amelia said, 'whatever is the matter?'

'Oh...nothing...' Helene said and reached for her kerchief, wiping her face. 'I am being foolish...please ignore me.'

'No, I do not believe you would cry for nothing,' Amelia said and sat down on the bed beside her. 'Will you not confide in me, Helene? I would help you if I could, you must know that, dearest?'

'Mama is so cross with me...'

'What have you done that is so very terrible?'

'She wants me to marry Mr Bradwell, but I cannot. I really cannot—even though it means we must return to Uncle Edgar or find work.'

'You know you are welcome to live with me.'

'I know, but we could not expect more of you, Amelia. You have been so very generous.' Helene lifted her head. 'You know that Mama's father was a tanner—and that the Duke of Annesdale is my grandfather? Oh, it is such a coil! I do not know what to do.'

'Yes, I know. Your mama told me her story long ago. I do not see why any of this should distress you, Helene.'

'The duke wanted me to live with him. He offered to leave me a lot of money—but I should not be able to see Mama, at least in public.'

'That was an outrageous offer. I imagine you refused?'

'I—quarrelled with him,' Helene said and sighed. 'I should not have done, for it has made things worse. He... he threatened me...'

'What did he say?'

'You know that he and Lord Coleridge are close?' Amelia nodded. 'Well, he says he shall leave Max his estate—but not if I refuse to live with him and give up Mama. He is so proud! He thinks Mama unfit to belong to his family because her father was a tanner.'

'Ah, I see,' Amelia said and frowned. 'Annesdale is a fool! What did you say to him?'

'I told him that...my shame was in having his blood, not Mama's.'

Amelia looked shocked. 'That was a little reckless, Helene. Annesdale is a proud man. I imagine he was angry?'

'Very angry indeed. It was after that the threat to Max was made.' Helene looked at her in distress. 'Mama is reluctant to go back to her brother's house. I wanted to find myself work, perhaps in an orphanage taking care of the children, but Mama will not permit me. She says that I should accept Mr Bradwell if he asks me—and I am sure he means to do so this afternoon. I do not wish to quarrel with Mama, but I truly cannot marry him.'

'Now I understand your tears,' Amelia said and nodded. 'Marie has been a little unfair to you. I understand how she feels. She has had a hard life and she wants you to have a better one, Helene.' Amelia's gaze was thoughtful. 'It is a pity that Coleridge did not come up to scratch before he went to the country. You might have been happy with him.'

'He…almost did, but I prevented him,' Helene said, her cheeks slightly pink. 'I could not let him speak after what the duke threatened.'

'No, you could not have done differently in the circumstances.' Amelia stood up and went over to the window, glancing out into the street. 'I must think about this, my love. My advice is to go to bed with a headache. I shall tell your mama that you cannot come down for tea this afternoon—and I will tell her something that may make her less eager for you to marry Mr Bradwell.'

'Do you not like him, Amelia?'

'I have heard rumours that he is in debt from gambling. How bad his situation is I have no idea, but it may give your mother pause for thought.'

Helene hesitated, then said, 'You once seemed as if you did not quite approve of Lord Coleridge.'

'Did I? If I gave you that impression, I am sorry, Helene. Max is a good friend. Something happened years ago, but I know he was not involved. I did think he might be interested in someone else, but then he began to pay attention to you.' She smiled. 'I should have liked to see you wed to a decent man. You have behaved in an honourable manner, my love—but I rather think something may be rescued from this mess. For the moment I believe you should plead a headache and let things rest.'

'You are so kind,' Helene told her. 'I thought you might be angry because I have wasted my chances.'

'I brought you to town because I like to have my friends about me. You owe me nothing, Helene—as for returning to a house where you are not welcome, I think there will be no need. I am sure I can find a home for you in one of my properties.'

'For Mama,' Helene said. 'If I cannot marry where I choose, I would rather work for my living in a children's home, where I might do some good for others.'

'That would be an easy solution to both your problem and mine,' Amelia said, 'but I do not give up so easily.'

'I am not sure I understand?'

'Do not bother your head, my love. Go to bed and rest—and then I am sure things will seem better.'

Helene undressed and crept into bed as Amelia left her. Her crying bout had given her an unpleasant headache so Amelia would not be telling Mama a lie.

The letter from the Duke of Annesdale lay forgotten with the gloves she had taken off when she came in.

Chapter Eight

It was late in the evening and dark when Max and Toby arrived at the Coleridge estate. Max frowned as he saw there were no lights in the windows of the house. He rapped sharply on the door, but it was a minute or two before someone came to open it. The sleepy footman stared at them in dismay, his mouth falling in dismay, his candle flame wavering in the breeze from the open door.

'Forgive me, my lord,' he apologised as he realised who it was. 'Mr Hale did not tell us that you were expected, sir.' He stood back to allow them to enter. 'The letter announcing your arrival could not have reached him.'

'I did not send one,' Max replied. 'My orders were that this house should be kept ready at all times. I did not expect to arrive and find it in darkness at this hour, even though I know it to be past ten.'

'Mr Hale took to his bed a few days ago, for he had a chill, and Mrs Hale has been busy running after him, sir.'

'Do I employ no other servants?' Max said angrily. 'You will inform Mrs Hale that I have arrived. I shall expect her to wait on me in the morning. I trust the bedchambers have been aired recently?'

'Yes, my lord—at least, that is Mrs Hale's department. I shall ask her.'

'Please do so, and light some candles. Let's have a little life in this house. We shall want something to eat and drink before we retire. If the chambers are not ready, rouse some of the maids and have them made ready immediately. We shall want to retire in an hour.'

The footman sprang to life at once, lighting a branch of candles from his own and then another. As the light began to brighten the gloom a little, Max picked up one branch of candles, leading the way into a small parlour to the left of the door.

'We shall manage here for the moment,' he said and began to light more candles. 'Damn Hale! Even if he is unwell, he should have made certain that the house was running as it ought.'

'I dare say it would have been better prepared if they had known of your imminent arrival,' Toby observed with a wry smile. 'Mama says servants will get away with doing as little as they can, unless you have a good butler and housekeeper.'

'I thought Mr and Mrs Hale were reliable,' Max said with a frown. 'Even when I came back after the war the house was as clean as a new pin. I do not understand it. Forgive me. I think this is poor hospitality and I shall want an explanation in the morning.'

'It does not bother me,' Toby said, though his mother always had the family home running like clockwork.

Mrs Hale came bustling into the parlour a few minutes later. She was all apologies for the welcome they had been given.

'I am sorry, sir. Hale has been ill and I gave the servants

permission to go to bed early. Mrs Heronsdale gave orders that candles were not to be wasted so I thought it best to close the house at nine. Of course, if we'd known you were coming…'

'Since when has Mrs Heronsdale been the mistress here?' Max glared at her. 'I gave Hale my orders. The house was always to be kept in a state of readiness for visitors.'

'Well, I'm sure I'm sorry, sir—but she seemed so sure…' The housekeeper paused and looked bothered. 'Mrs Heronsdale comes to the house most days and she gives us orders, sir. We were told not to clean the guest chambers every week, because they were not needed—and she let two of the footmen and the upper parlourmaid go, my lord.'

'Indeed?' Max was angry, a little nerve flicking at his temple. 'You will bring the staff up to its original level as soon as possible, Mrs Hale—and in future you will refer Mrs Heronsdale to me.'

'Yes, sir,' the housekeeper said, a little smile of satisfaction on her lips. 'I did tell Hale to write to you, but he didn't want to bother you, my lord.'

'If you should have a similar problem in the future, I want to know—but I dare say it will not happen, for I shall speak to my aunt. She may do as she pleases at the dower house naturally, but this house will run as I see fit. I should like some wine, and something to eat—if you have anything in the house?'

'Oh, yes, sir. There is a cold ham in the pantry, bread cooked this day and a bit of mutton, if that will do you with some relish this evening? Tomorrow I'll draw up some menus for you to approve. May I ask how long you will be staying this time, sir?'

'A few days. I must be back in London by the end of next week, but certainly three days, ma'am.'

'Hale will be pleased, sir. It always seems better when you're down, my lord.'

'Yes, well, I dare say I may bring a party of friends down later in the summer,' Max said, his anger fading. He had purposely not sent word of his visit, but he had not expected to find his orders countermanded. 'I shall let you know in good time.'

'Why did you not let them know this time?' Toby inquired as the still-anxious lady went away to see to their supper. 'I am sure they would have had everything just as you like it.'

'I had a reason for not doing so,' Max told him with an odd look. 'I am sorry we came to a closed house, but I was hoping to take my aunt by surprise. It seems she has taken the role of chatelaine on in my absence. It will be interesting to discover what else has been going on.'

Toby nodded. 'You need not apologise to me, my dear fellow,' he said. 'I shall be quite comfortable. As you say, perhaps it was for the best, otherwise you might not have known what was going on down here.'

'Precisely,' Max told him. 'After that incident at Richmond, I believe it is time that I made some changes here.'

'Coleridge.' Mrs Heronsdale came rushing into the parlour where Max was having breakfast with Toby the following morning. She was a large lady, heavy boned but thin, her face all angles and planes, her skin sallow against the black of her mourning gown. 'Why did you not let me know you were coming down? I could have made sure that everything was in order.'

'Aunt Tilda,' Max said as he and Toby both rose to their feet. 'May I introduce you to a friend of mine, Mr Sinclair—Toby, my aunt, Mrs Heronsdale.'

Toby murmured something and bowed his head. The lady looked a little surprised to see him, a flicker of what might be annoyance in her eyes.

'Forgive me for disturbing your breakfast, sir. Please carry on.'

'Will you not join us, Aunt?' Max asked. 'At least sit down so that we may also sit. May I give you some coffee?' He signalled to a footman, who set a chair for her, and another poured some of the fragrant liquid into a cup and set it before her. 'I am sorry if it disturbs you that I arrived unannounced, but I do not make it a habit to inform others of my movements. I expect my servants to obey my wishes and have my house ready at all times.'

A faint flush appeared in Mrs Heronsdale's cheeks. She glanced down at her delicate porcelain coffee can, her hands moving nervously in her lap. 'I may have spoken out of turn, Coleridge. I have been used to practising economy and I hate to see waste.'

'You may order the dower house as you please, of course, but I prefer to make my own arrangements here,' Max said smoothly. 'However, no harm was done. And we shall forget it. Did my cousin not accompany you this morning? I have come down on purpose to see him.'

'Then you have had a wasted journey,' Mrs Heronsdale told him. 'Robert has been ordered to his bed. He has been very ill, Coleridge. We truly thought we might lose him this time.'

'I am very sorry to hear that,' Max said and looked grave. 'I know you trust your own physician, but I really think you should let Dr Clarke advise you, ma'am. My cousin is a young man. He should not suffer from such frequent bouts of illness. I shall ask Dr Clarke to call later today.'

'No! You must not,' Mrs Heronsdale said and looked agitated. She jumped to her feet, obliging the gentlemen to rise, too. 'Oh, do sit down! I am going. My son is too ill to be troubled by a new physician. Excuse me, I must return to him at once. I left him only because I thought it my duty to welcome you home.'

The gentlemen remained standing until she had left the room. Toby threw Max a look of enquiry. 'Is she usually so agitated?'

'Whenever I suggest that Robert should see a different doctor she makes the same excuse. Robert is too ill to see anyone. I accepted it at first, for it might be true—but you saw the letter I had. I think I must make an effort to meet my cousin this time. I do not believe that a visit from me would endanger his life—do you?'

'I cannot think it,' Toby said and frowned. 'It seems an odd situation, Max. When shall you go?'

'Almost immediately, I think,' Max said. 'If you have finished your breakfast, Toby, perhaps you would care to walk down with me? I have tried to visit my cousin with my aunt's permission several times, but been refused. This time I thought I might use a little subterfuge and you may assist me, if you will.'

'Naturally—please explain, dear fellow.'

'Ask Mrs Heronsdale to show you the garden,' Max said as they walked through the gardens towards the dower house. 'It is the one thing she seems to have a passion for other than her son. I shall make an excuse to leave after we have been there for a few minutes—but you must keep her talking for long enough for me to slip up the back stairs to my cousin's room.'

'Do you think you ought?' Toby said and looked uncomfortable. 'It is a little deceitful. Could you not just demand to see Robert?'

'I have tried it before,' Max said. 'If this makes you uneasy, I'll find another way—but I am determined to see him for myself.'

'I'll do it, of course,' Toby said at once. 'I imagine she will be very angry when she discovers what you've done. It may be unpleasant for you.'

'I do not mind her anger,' Max said, looking concerned. 'Something is being hidden from me, Toby. I have to discover what it is and this is the only way I can do it. She defends her son like a dragon and there has to be a reason for it.'

'Yes, I do see that,' Toby agreed. 'Besides, you have to know if it was your cousin that took a pot shot at you in Richmond park.'

'That, too,' Max agreed. 'It points that way, of course, but I am not certain. I need to talk to Robert myself. So you'll keep her busy while I slip upstairs to Robert's room?'

'I will do my best,' Toby said. 'What excuse will you give for coming like this, so soon after her visit?'

'I shall apologise for my abruptness earlier, beg her to forgive me—and then you will show interest in her garden. She has been asking me if she can change some things in the main gardens, so I have no doubt that she will try to influence you if she can, because so far I have resisted her plans.'

Toby looked thoughtful, then inclined his head. 'I am

interested in gardens so it will not be too hard. If she has some unusual plants, we could be talking for hours.'

Max smiled. 'Half an hour should be sufficient. Well, here we are. Leave the talking to me for a start. I think that there are a few repairs needed to the house. I had set them in hand, but I shall enquire about the roof and a damp patch at the back of the house.'

'I was intrigued by what you are doing with the gardens here,' Toby said after they had been talking for some ten minutes or so. 'Would it be too much trouble to ask if I could see your gardens, ma'am? If I am not mistaken, I believe you have a new variety of magnolias, one I have been wanting to purchase.'

'Are you interested in gardening?' Mrs Heronsdale turned her sharp gaze on Toby. 'I have been trying to persuade Coleridge that he should have a magnolia walk.'

'Do you know, I have that very thing in mind at my own estate,' Toby said quite truthfully. 'Of course, my estate is quite small, nothing like this place, but I think it could be improved and I should like to plant a walk. I should like to talk to whoever has been planning your garden, ma'am.'

'I do it myself,' she replied, her mouth softening slightly. 'Would you care to see some of my rarer plants?'

'Yes, very much so,' Toby told her. 'May we go now?'

'I shall leave you. I must speak to someone about estate business,' Max said. 'Do not mind me, Sinclair. Spend as long as you like looking at plants. I shall see you later. Ma'am...I will speak to someone about that damp patch at the back of the house immediately.'

'I am not sure that I wish to speak to you,' Mrs Henderson said when Helene went to her bedchamber that morning. 'I had to make excuses to Mr Bradwell yester-day—and despite what Amelia said to me, I still believe he might be a good match for you, Helene.' She gave her daughter a look filled with reproach. 'Amelia was so kind as to offer me a home with her. It is quite lowering to be in my position, Helene. I accepted this visit for your sake, but I cannot take more from Amelia, though she swears I should be doing her a favour by living in a house that would otherwise be left empty.'

'Amelia is truly generous, Mama. She found me crying and would not rest until I told her why. I really could not bear to marry Mr Bradwell. I would much prefer to work for my living—as Papa and Grandfather did.'

'Well, I suppose you will have your own way. I hope that you will never have to live as I have, Helene. I do not think you have considered what your life will be if you do not marry.'

'Oh, Mama,' Helene said, 'I am so sorry for all you have suffered and I did not like to be at odds with you. I truly wish that I could make things better for you. It is because of the way that the duke has treated you—would continue to treat you!—that I do not wish to be taken up as his granddaughter. Had he acted towards you as he ought, I should have honoured him and loved him.'

'You are a good girl and I am sorry if I made you cry,' Mrs Henderson said, pulling at her delicate lace kerchief in an agitated manner. 'Run away now and make the most of the time we have left to us. You will not get a chance like this again.'

Helene left her mama's room with a heavy heart. She wished that she might have married and obliged her mother, but she simply could not marry Mr Bradwell.

For a moment Helene allowed herself to think of Max

Coleridge. How long would he be away—and would she ever be able to meet him without feeling that deep ache in her heart?

Max walked round to the back of the house and let himself in by a little-used door. He could hear voices in the kitchen, but he passed it without being discovered and used the servants' stairs to gain access to the landing, which led to the main bedchambers. He knew that he had to be quick, because if he were discovered it would be awkward and he might be forced to leave without achieving his purpose. The first two doors were slightly ajar and a quick glance inside told him that they belonged to the mistress of the house. The next door opened at his touch, but it looked unoccupied. The fourth door was locked, which made him frown—if Robert were locked in, it would seem to confirm his fears. He tried the last door and immediately the smell of sickness told him that he had found the right room.

He went through the sitting room into the bedchamber behind. The windows were tightly shut, which accounted for the slightly unpleasant odour, and the blinds were drawn. If he had his way, he would pull back the blinds and open the window, but he did not wish to impose his authority as the head of the family—unless it was strictly necessary. As yet he did not know the nature of Robert's illness.

The man in the bed was lying on his back, the sheets pulled up to his chin. As Max approached, he could see that Robert looked pale, his eyes tightly closed. He bent over him, studying his face for a few moments.

Robert's sleep seemed odd...as if he were heavily sedated. When someone was ill, the bedcovers were normally messy, as if they had been tossed back. These were too tidy. He laid a hand on Robert's forehead. The young man opened his eyes and looked at him; for a moment he just stared and then he smiled.

'Cousin Max…' he said. 'You have come to visit me. I am glad to see you…'

Max gazed down at him. 'I am sorry to disturb you, Robert. I was anxious, for you have been ill each time I visit. I wanted to make sure you were being well cared for.'

'Have I been ill?' Robert seemed confused. His eyelids flickered and closed.

'Robert…' Max touched his shoulder. 'Robert…can you talk to me?'

'Robert had a disturbed night,' a voice said from behind Max. He turned and was in time to see the physician enter the room. 'I was forced to give him something to ease him earlier this morning. It makes Robert a little tired. You must forgive him.'

'Doctor Clarke.' Max inclined his head. He was immediately aware of a prickling sensation at the nape of his neck. The man's manner seemed genuine, but there was something about him that he instinctively disliked. 'Would you be good enough to tell me the nature of my cousin's illness? He is a young man and his appearance, though sickly, is not truly that of an invalid.'

'Robert is prone to violent chills and inflammation of the lungs,' the physician said, but he avoided looking at Max as he spoke. 'You may leave him to my care. I have cared for Robert since he was this high.' He held his hand waist high. 'He is as a son to me.'

Max stared at him, eyes narrowed. He had never liked the fellow; he thought him sly and he was certain something was not as it should be, though he could not quite decide what was wrong. Both Mrs Heronsdale and this man were hiding something!

'Nevertheless, I believe it will be best if I ask my own doctor to call and see him. Robert has been ill too often. I shall call in the morning. If there is no improvement, I shall return with my doctor.'

'That is your privilege, my lord.' Doctor Clarke inclined his head, his eyes glittering with a suppressed anger he dared not show. 'You will find nothing wrong, milord. I assure you that his mother is very satisfied with my care.'

Max inclined his head. 'I shall call in the morning. I expect Robert to be able to receive me.'

He saw the physician's eyes narrow, hiding his anger. Max smiled inwardly as he walked past him and down the stairs. In the hall he saw his aunt, who had just come into the house.

'I have seen Robert, but he was under the influence of some drug and unable to speak to me,' he said. 'I have told that fellow who calls himself a physician that I shall call tomorrow, ma'am. If there is no improvement in my cousin's condition, I shall have him taken to the house so that my own physician may take care of him. I am not satisfied that he is receiving the proper care here.'

'Coleridge!' Mrs Heronsdale stared at him, seeming dismayed and nervous. 'I thought you had left…'

'I am sorry it was necessary to deceive you, ma'am, but I am convinced something is wrong here. You may trust that fellow, but I do not. Robert should not be for ever ill. He is my cousin and I intend to take an interest in his health in future. Do not try to deny me, madam—if you wish to continue living on my estate…'

Mrs Heronsdale turned pale. She put a hand to her throat. 'I do not know why you should speak to me thus, my lord. You cannot think that I would harm my own child?'

'Something is not as it should be, ma'am. As yet I do not know what it may be, but I am determined to find out. Expect me in the morning—and remember that I wish to speak to Robert.'

Max walked past her and out of the house before she could recover her powers of speech. He was thoughtful as he left the dower house. What were she and that sly fellow hiding from him?

Max decided that he would not return home just yet. He would visit the neighbour who had written to him about the attacks on village girls that had begun to happen in the past few months. He needed to get to the bottom of this affair, because if his cousin were guilty—but that did not bear thinking about!

He knew that the evidence was stacking up against Robert, but to his mind something smelled wrong. His instincts were telling him that he should look to others and that Robert might need his protection.

'Tyler apologised for troubling me,' Max said as he and Toby sat drinking a glass of wine that afternoon. 'He says a man from a village some ten miles away has been taken into custody after molesting a girl and they believe he may have been responsible for what happened here. He had been drinking and apparently has a history of violence.'

'I am glad to hear that the attacker has been apprehended,' Toby said. 'That must have relieved your mind, Max. You were concerned that those attacks might have had something to do with your cousin, were you not?'

'Perhaps and perhaps not...' Max said. He frowned. 'I am certain they are hiding something from me concerning my cousin. I told you that he had been drugged, though he did open his eyes for a moment. He knew me and smiled, but then he fell asleep once more—and Doctor Clarke arrived. For some reason he and my aunt seem not to want me to speak with Robert.'

'What reason could they have for keeping you apart?' Toby asked and looked puzzled. 'It is a mystery, Coleridge. I do not see what they could gain from it.'

'No, it is difficult to imagine a reason, but there must be something. However, I have issued an ultimatum. Either I am given access to my cousin when he is properly awake or I shall have him brought here where my own physician may care for him.'

'At least you know it could not have been your cousin who shot at you,' Toby said. 'If he is being kept a virtual prisoner in his room, it is unlikely that he took a pot shot at you.'

'Most unlikely,' Max said. 'I am relieved on that score, of which I am heartily glad. I should not have enjoyed the feeling that Robert wished to murder me so that he could step into my shoes. However, it does make me wonder who did fire at me—or could it be that someone else was the intended victim that day?'

Toby stared at him. 'Good grief! You do not mean Miss Henderson? Surely not? Why would anyone wish to kill her?'

'I have no idea,' Max replied. 'But if I was not the intended victim, it must have been Miss Henderson, though I cannot imagine why. Or who could possibly want her dead.'

Toby shook his head. 'I do not think it, Max. Miss Henderson is not an heiress. I believe she has something, but not enough to make anyone wish to shoot her so that they could inherit her fortune. I dare say you will find that the mystery lies closer to home. Are you sure Robert was drugged when you saw him?'

'You think my cousin may have been faking it this morning?' Max looked at him oddly. 'I had not considered it, but it is one possibility. Yes, you are right about the shooting. I believe I was the one meant to die at Richmond, but as yet I cannot decide who was behind the attempt or why someone wants me dead.'

Helene had been to the lending library. Tilly was with her and they were walking home when the carriage drew to a halt at the side of the road just ahead of them. A groom jumped down and spoke to someone through the window, then approached Helene.

'Miss Henderson. Lady Annersley asks if you will step inside her coach for a moment.'

'Lady Annersley...' Helene glanced at her maid. 'Stay close to me. Tilly.' She looked at the groom. 'I will speak to her through the window.' She approached and saw that the lady had the window down. She was heavily veiled so it was impossible to see her face. 'You wished to speak with me, ma'am?'

'You are an ungrateful wretch,' Lady Annersley said harshly. 'How could you refuse Annesdale's generous offer? If you had the sense you were born with, you would do as he asks.'

'Indeed?' Helene looked at her coolly. 'Had my grandfather seen fit to apologise for his behaviour to my mother I might have been more inclined to think about his offer, though I cannot approve of the way it was made.'

'And who do you think you are, miss?' The older woman was plainly furious. 'If it was left to me, I would treat you with the disdain you deserve. You and that mother of yours should be drummed out of society for pretending to be something you are not, but His Grace wishes to see you again. I was on my way to request you to call on us.'

'Then I have saved you a wasted journey,' Helene said. Her pride was hurt and she felt angry. How dare this woman speak to her so! 'If the duke cares to call on my mother to apologise, I may consider a part of his proposal—but it will be on my terms. I should certainly not agree to a settlement that did not include an invitation to my mother. I dare say we have nothing more to say to one another, so I shall not detain you.'

'Vixen! I dare say you imagine Coleridge will offer for you and that you can afford to ignore the duke—but I assure you that once he knows the truth he will withdraw.'

Helene's eyes flashed with anger. 'Indeed, then perhaps you should tell him yourself, ma'am. Good day, my lady. I have an appointment I must keep.'

Helene walked on, head in the air, face proud. She was angry that Lady Annersley had chosen to interfere in something that did not concern her and that she had lost her temper. It was very wrong of her, and something she seldom permitted herself to do, but she did not regret it. Lady Annersley's threat did not worry her—if it had not been for her own pride and sense of honesty, she would already have become engaged to Lord Coleridge.

She had wanted to leave town before he returned, but both her mama and Amelia seemed determined that she should finish her Season.

She had no idea when Max would return, but it could not matter, for he would hardly bother to call. He had behaved as a perfect gentleman that night, but he must have resented her refusal to listen. No doubt he would despise her now.

* * *

Max walked down to the dower house alone that morning. Mrs Heronsdale greeted him, her face pale and anxious. She greeted him politely, but did not smile, a look of resentment in her eyes.

'I hope that Robert is awake and ready to receive me, ma'am?'

'It seems that you know your own way, sir. I shall not come up with you.'

'As you wish, ma'am.' Max inclined his head. Clearly he would have some fences to mend with his aunt, but firm action had been necessary if he were to get to the bottom of this mystery.

He went up the stairs, walking along the hall to his cousin's bedchamber. He noticed that the smell was different. Someone had used lavender polish and, as he went into the bedroom itself, he saw that the blinds were partially drawn and the window was open a crack to let some air in. Robert was sitting propped up against a pile of pillows. His face was pale, but he looked slightly better than he had the previous day.

'Robert,' Max said. 'I trust you are a little better today?'

'I think I must be,' Robert said and looked puzzled. 'Doctor Clarke tells me I have had another bout of sickness, though if truth be known I do not remember much of it. I am sorry that I was sleeping when you called yesterday.'

'I am relieved to see you so much better,' Max said. 'I should like to have my own doctor call on you—just to make sure you are receiving the right treatment. I intend to bring some friends down to Coleridge to stay in a week or two and I had hoped that you might be well enough to join us.'

'I should like that…' Robert frowned, his eyes drawn

across to the physician who stood near the window. 'Clarke—shall I be well enough, do you think? Should I have this other quack to take a look at me?'

The physician inclined his head, his eyes lowered. 'It must be your decision, Robert. If you think I have neglected something in your treatment, you must say.'

'He's sulking,' Robert said and laughed. 'Clarke has looked after me since I first became ill. I dare say I might have died had he not nursed me devotedly. I thank you for your concern, Max. I am sorry that you should have been denied access when I was in the fever—but I dare say Mama thought you might despise me for my weakness.'

'How could I?' Max said. 'Illness strikes the best of us. I am sorry that you should have so many bouts of sickness, Robert. My offer remains if you should change your mind—and I hope you will be well enough to join my guests when we dine.'

'I think I shall be well for a while now,' Robert said. There was an odd, slightly defiant look in his eyes as he stared at his physician. 'If I am in any doubt, I shall avail myself of your physician's advice, Max.'

'I am glad to hear it,' Max said. 'Are you comfortable here? Is your allowance enough for your needs?'

'I have very few needs,' Robert said and once again there was an odd, militant expression in his eyes as he looked at the physician. 'Do I, Clarke?'

'I think perhaps you should rest now,' the physician said, looking grave. 'It will not do to exhaust yourself, Robert—or you may have a relapse.'

'I told you, he is sulking,' Robert said and laughed. 'You had better go, Max. I am sure I shall be well enough to join you when you have guests.'

'I am glad,' Max said. 'If you need anything more, you

have only to send me word.' He nodded his head to the physician. 'Good day, sir. I shall see you again in two weeks, Robert.'

He walked from the room. He was frowning as he left the house and made his way home. Everything had appeared quite normal, but Max's intuition was telling him that the situation here was far from what it ought to be. However, with the man who had been attacking girls in custody, and his cousin seeming to be well enough to talk sensibly, there did not seem to be much to keep him here beyond the morrow.

He would be glad to get back to London, for there was something he needed to do…and if things went as he hoped he would not be alone when he returned in two weeks' time. Helene had prevented him from speaking when they last met, but he had decided that he would review the situation when they met again. Of course, it was possible that she might truly prefer not to marry and that would be a shame.

Helene spent the morning walking with friends in the park. She had wondered if Lady Annersley would drop a hint of her background to her friends, but it seemed the lady had kept their secret so far. If anything, Helene seemed to have more friends each day. She mentioned the fact to Amelia, who smiled at her.

'You have a quiet manner and you do not put yourself forward, Helene. I believe that is the reason you have become popular with the ladies as much as the gentlemen.'

'People are very kind, but of course they do not know my background.' She was unsmiling. Lady Annersley's spite had made her very aware that she did not belong in exalted circles.

'I believe you would find that most people would accept you despite it,' Amelia told her. 'Your father was a gentleman—and you are related to Annesdale.' She smiled. 'Your mama had such a bad experience that she has allowed it to cloud her judgement, but I do not think it would weigh with many of your friends.'

Helene was thoughtful. Her mother's father had been an honest working man. She lifted her head proudly. She would not allow a spiteful woman to make her ashamed of her grandfather!

A part of her wished that she had opened her heart to Lord Coleridge that night at Vauxhall Gardens. The duke had told her that Max would not wish to marry her once he knew it would disoblige him, but she had not given him the chance to choose and she had never ceased to regret it.

Max glanced through the notes and cards handed to him when he returned to his rooms at his club in London. One of them was from Amelia Royston, asking him to call as soon as he returned to town. He frowned over it for the tone seemed urgent, but decided it could wait until the morning. He would send a note to tell her that he would call tomorrow, and then pay a visit to a gambling house that he sometimes frequented. In the meantime, there was a call he must make. He had ignored Annesdale's letter asking him to visit and he must certainly put that right without delay.

His valet had put up a change of clothes for him, his manner of dignified silence reminding Max that he had offended the man by dispensing with his services for the past few days.

'Do not look so stiff, Carter,' Max said and grinned. 'You will be coming with me next time—and, if things go as I plan, we shall be acquiring our own house in town. I am thinking of settling down and taking a wife.'

'If I may say so, it is not before time, my lord.'

'You are very right,' Max said and grinned. 'I am not certain the lady will have me, but I mean to make a push with her.'

'I dare say most ladies would consider it an honour, milord.'

'No? Do you?' Max said and chuckled softly. 'This one is not so easily convinced, believe me. I shall not be late back, Carter—but I shall want my best coat tomorrow. The new blue one...'

'Ah, yes, sir. That is very suitable. I shall have it ready in the morning.'

Max nodded and took his leave. He went out into the gathering gloom. It was after he had been walking for a few minutes that Max had a sense that he was being followed. He glanced over his shoulder, but could not see anything. He might have imagined it, but he was alerted to danger, his instincts telling him that someone had been following at a discreet distance. He touched his pocket, where the pistol was heavy, already primed for use. He did not intend to be taken unawares again. Then, seeing a hackney waiting for a passenger drawn up at the side of the road, he hailed the driver. It was better to be safe rather than sorry.

He was smiling as the cab set him down in front of Annesdale's house a little later. The duke was an irascible old devil, but he happened to like him.

Chapter Nine

'I am going to the lending library with Emily,' Helene said that morning as she met Amelia on her way down-stairs. 'Mama has requested a book—is there anything you require? Unless you wish to accompany us?'

'Thank you, dearest,' Amelia said and shook her head. 'I have several things to do. I must go through the list of acceptances for my costume ball, which is next week. It is amazing how time has flown. The ball seemed such a long time away and now it is almost here.'

'I am looking forward to it,' Helene said, for she had decided that she must make the most of things since she was forced to remain in town. 'I think it should be amusing to guess the identity of one's friends.'

'I am glad you are looking forward to it. Run along now, Helene. I have much to do…'

Helene felt that Amelia's manner was a little odd, for it was almost as if she wanted to be rid of her, but, no, she must be imagining things. Amelia was the kindest of friends.

Emily was waiting for her when she reached the hall. She picked up a small parcel of books she was returning.

'Are you ready, Helene? I was hoping we might have time to visit the milliner's shop after we have been to the library. I ordered a new bonnet and I think it will be ready.'

'Yes, of course,' Helene agreed. 'I am sure there will be plenty of time. We have no other engagements until this afternoon.'

They spent half an hour choosing the books they had come to find and then left, carrying two each. Another twenty minutes was spent in the milliner's shop. Helene tried on three pretty bonnets, but could not decide between them. She was uncertain if she wished to spend her pin money on a new bonnet, because if she returned home without finding a new position she would have to make what little money she had last until she could find herself work. Uncle Edgar would not be too pleased to have them back, especially if he learned that she had turned down a suitable offer.

They had left the milliner's shop and were on their way home, just crossing the square to Amelia's house when it happened. Helene saw the man coming towards her and her heart took a flying leap. She felt her throat tighten with sudden longing. Max looked even more handsome than she remembered; he was wearing a very smart blue coat that fitted him so well that it could only have been made by Weston, that most exclusive of tailors. Her heart began to beat very fast and she was feeling a little confused, which was why she did not immediately notice the odd behaviour of the man behind Max. It was only as he raised his arm that she was alerted to danger. He was holding a knife in his hand. When she saw what he meant to do she cried out, but her warning was a second too late. The man's arm was raised poised to plunge a long, thin dagger into Max's back; Max's interest was fixed on her and he seemed unaware of the danger.

Afterwards, Helene did not know if it was her cry of alarm or Max's instinct that made him turn in that instant. He grabbed for the assassin's arm, tackling him as the knife struck. Because of his action, the knife slashed through the arm of his coat; she was sure that it would otherwise have been plunged into his back. She screamed as they struggled, rushing towards them and crying out for help. The assassin became aware of her and suddenly broke free, dropping his knife as he ran off. However, the alarm had been raised and at least two men set off after him.

'Stop! Foul murder!' The cry was taken up all around them and several passers-by set up a hue and cry. Two burly costers went running after the rogue who had attacked Max. Helene rushed towards him, her embarrassment at this meeting forgotten in the shock of seeing what had happened.

'My lord—Max,' Helene cried. 'That wicked rogue! He tried to kill you… I saw the knife…' She gave a cry of distress as she saw the blood seeping through the slash in the arm of his coat. 'You are hurt…you must come back to the house and let me tend it for you.'

'Be careful, Miss Henderson,' Max warned. His face was a little white, but he seemed steady on his feet and able to think clearly. 'You will get blood on your clothes if you come too close.'

'What can that signify?' Helene asked. 'I insist that you

come with us. Your arm must be bound, for it is bleeding a great deal. It may be best if you allow us to send for the doctor.' She glanced at Emily. 'Please take my books and warn Amelia. We shall need linen and salves.'

Emily took her books and ran across the square. Helene watched Max anxiously. He refused to let her assist him, holding his right hand over the wound to his left arm. She could see the blood oozing through his fingers and knew that it must be causing him pain, but he said nothing as she hovered, ready to catch him if he should faint.

'Do not look so anxious,' Max told her. 'I have suffered worse, believe me.'

'In the war, I dare say,' Helene said. 'I fear your coat will be ruined, but we must be glad if that is all.'

'You may be glad,' Max grated with an attempt at humour. 'I will have you know that this coat was made by Weston. If he could see what I have done to it, he would never waste his time on me again.'

'Oh, you are funning as always,' Helene said, her throat tight with tears. 'But you are losing too much blood…' She grabbed him as he staggered. He righted himself in a moment, but she could see that it was costing him to stand upright. 'We should go through to the back parlour, sir. There is a wooden floor and it will wipe clean.'

'I should not want to damage the carpets,' Max said and smiled just before he swooned.

Fortunately, a footman had come out to see what was happening and helped Helene to catch him. Between them they managed to support Max into the house and set him on a wooden settle in the hallway.

Amelia had come down the stairs. 'Good lord! When did this happen? I was expecting Lord Coleridge to call before this.'

'Someone tried to kill him with a knife,' Helene said. 'They stabbed him in the arm. It is bleeding terribly and he is a little faint, but had he not fought back, the knife would have entered his back…'

'Not dead yet,' Max said. 'Sorry, my love. I have bled all over your gown.'

'It does not matter about my gown, Max,' Helene said, her throat catching with the tears she refused to shed. 'We must get that coat off, Max—and bind your arm to stop the blood.'

'The best thing will be to cut it,' Amelia said. 'The coat is ruined anyway—and it will be easier to bind his arm without it. I think we should attempt it ourselves now, and then put him to bed. The doctor may do more when he comes.'

Max made a murmur of protest, but Amelia was in charge. She summoned her footmen, had them bring what she needed and bound the wound tightly, before instructing the men to carry him upstairs. He attempted to walk, but could not have managed it without help. Amelia followed the little procession with an anxious Helene close behind.

Max had recovered his senses by the time the doctor arrived. He suffered the man's probing in silence, and waited until his arm was stitched and bound once more. However, he was provoked into speech when told that he must stay in bed for a week.

'I thank you for your attentions, sir, but I must tell you that I have no intention of staying in this bed. If Miss Royston will be good enough to call for a cab, I shall take myself off.'

'No, sir, you shall not,' Amelia said from the doorway. She came towards the bed, smiling, but looking determined. 'You were murderously attacked outside my door and you nearly passed out before they could bring you here. You are weak from loss of blood and need to rest. I insist that you stay until you are feeling better—at least tonight and perhaps tomorrow. The doctor will call in the morning, and we shall see how you go on.'

'If you will take my advice, you will stay here for at least a week,' the doctor said and went out.

Amelia lingered. 'I know you feel that you will be a trouble to us, sir—but I assure you it is not the case. Besides, I believe that you should take full advantage of what has occurred. It is not my place to say this, but Helene was very upset when you were attacked. If you wish to break down that foolish reserve she has built up against marriage, you could not do better than stay here for a day or two.'

'Miss Royston, I believe you are a devious schemer,' Max said and grinned at her. 'If you will put up with me, I believe I shall stay.'

'I have learned that sometimes one must dissemble to gain one's way,' Amelia replied. 'I am aware that you think this wound is nothing, for you have suffered worse injuries, sir. That much was obvious when we tended your arm—there were old scars…'

'We?' Max said and frowned. 'I was out of it at the start and cannot quite remember. Do you mean to tell me that you allowed Helene to help you?'

'She was there and helped as much as she could,' Amelia said. 'I am certain her feelings for you are genuine. It is her stupid pride that makes her say she will not marry. I may not tell you the whole, but if you were to ask her she might be prevailed on to speak. I know that she has been breaking her heart over something.'

'You need say no more, ma'am. I visited Annesdale last night and he was kind enough to tell me everything. Including his own infamous behaviour, for which I believe him to be truly sorry.'

'Annesdale told you—and you still intend to wed her?' Amelia looked awkward. 'Forgive me, I have gone too far, but I care for Helene's happiness.'

'No, you have not gone too far. I shall make her my wife—if she will have me,' Max said and frowned. 'Though I am not sure it is wise—it is obvious I have a dangerous enemy. I had thought the first attempt at Richmond might have been nothing more than an opportunist or even a mistake—but now I know that someone wishes me dead.'

'At Richmond? Did something happen there?' Amelia exclaimed as Max recounted what had happened. She shook her head. 'Neither Helene nor Emily breathed a word of it to me. It seems clear that someone does indeed intend to kill you if they can. You must take some precautions, sir—but I do not think you can allow this rogue to ruin your life.'

'I have no intention of letting the rogue have his way, though I shall need to take more precautions.'

'You cannot think who your enemy might be?' Amelia asked, but he shook his head and looked thoughtful.

'I recall that an attempt was made to kidnap you last summer,' Max said. 'Gerard had you watched for months afterwards—but nothing more occurred. Have you ever wondered why that should be?'

'I have tried to think of a reason, but can find none—none that satisfies me anyway,' Amelia told him. 'I have been careful not to go for long walks in woodlands, but otherwise I do not let it disturb me.'

'It is curious, none the less,' Max said and his eyes narrowed. Something had occurred to him, which he might mention to Ravenshead when he saw him, though he was not certain enough of his theory to put it to Amelia just yet. 'I am not certain who would wish me dead. The obvious person is my cousin, for as things stand he would inherit the most, but he suffers bouts of ill health. I cannot think it was he—and I have never seen the ruffian who stabbed me before in my life.'

'A hired assassin, I imagine,' Amelia said. 'Would you like me to send for your valet? He could stay here to attend you if that would make you more comfortable.'

Max arched his right eyebrow. 'I see I have no choice, but I shall not stay in bed above one day, Miss Royston.'

'I dare say that may suffice,' Amelia said and smiled. 'You helped both Susannah and I last year, Lord Coleridge. This is my chance to repay you if you will let me.'

'I think I should be a fool if I did not,' Max said and grinned. 'Now that I understand Helene's situation, nothing is going to prevent me asking her to marry me—but I shall make sure that my back is protected in future. I should not wish her to become a widow before she is a wife.'

'I think that is very wise,' Amelia said. 'Now I shall go and find Helene. You are bored in bed and threatening to get up. To do such a foolish thing might cause your wound to open. I dare say a little light reading might help. Helene has an understanding of books. She will find something suitable and bring it to you.'

'How can I thank you, Miss Royston?'

'By inviting me to your wedding,' Amelia said and went out.

Max laughed softly, then the smile faded, his own problems forgotten for the moment. It was odd that no more attempts had been made to kidnap Amelia since last summer. What had changed in her circumstances that might make someone feel that it was no longer necessary to kidnap or dispose of her?

Max could think of only one thing. He needed to talk to Gerard Ravenshead about certain things, but that could keep for the moment. Max had two rather more pressing problems on his mind. The first was to discover who had paid to have him killed, for he was certain that Amelia was right—it had been a paid assassin who had tried to stab him in the back. Two failed attempts on his life had been made so far. When would the third happen? He was certain there would be another attempt. Someone clearly wished him dead—but why?

Nothing had happened while he was at his estate. He had walked alone there without harm. It had been the perfect opportunity if someone had wished to dispose of him and yet no attempt had been made to kill him. Why? Was it because it was too close to home? Was the person behind this afraid of being discovered?

A convicted murderer could not inherit property. If Robert wanted Max dead so that he could inherit the estate, he would not want suspicion to fall on him. The explanation made sense and there was certainly some mystery surrounding his cousin. Max could not make up his mind whether Robert was the sort of person likely to entertain murder to gain what he wanted. He hardly knew his cousin—or his aunt, come to that—but he instinctively disliked the physician. No, he would not believe that Robert could be behind these cowardly attempts. There must be some other reason...

He thrust the unwelcome thoughts from his mind. When inviting him here this morning, Amelia had obviously planned to ask him his intentions towards Helene, and perhaps reveal something of her background, but Max's visit to Annesdale had made that unnecessary. He had spoken forcibly to the duke, who now understood him very well and had made his apologies. Whether it would be as easy to convince Helene was another matter. Max was vexed that she should have believed he would be swayed by the duke's threats, yet he understood her pride and her reasons for thinking she must prevent him from speaking.

He knew her to have spirit and that she could sometimes be provoked to a show of temper. Her reprimand when he had spoken disparagingly of the poet had only made him admire her the more. Helene was not afraid to stand up for what she believed. She seemed to imagine that he was the kind of snob Annesdale could be on occasion, and he wondered how he could convince her that he was no such thing.

If she cared for him, she must see that the matter of her mother's birth was not important beside the way they felt about each other. Even if it became generally known, which at the moment it was not, it should be easy enough to drop a few hints in society; the fact that one grandfather had been in trade could be balanced by the knowledge that she was also Annesdale's granddaughter. Max looked grim. Once Helene was his wife, no one would slight her. He would make certain of that!

Would the foolish girl realise that these things were of no importance? Or would he have to take drastic measures to persuade her?

Helene took her time choosing between the books she had borrowed from the library. She did not know what kind of poetry Max preferred, and she was almost sure he would not enjoy the Gothic romance she had brought for Mama. Perhaps he might care for Miss Austen's work, she thought, and smiled to herself as she took the book upstairs. She knocked at the door of his bedchamber and was invited to enter. Max was sitting propped up in bed, looking annoyed and frustrated, just as Amelia had told her. He was still wearing his breeches, though his shirt had been removed. Amelia had found him a silk dressing robe, which he wore around his shoulders. His frown was replaced by a smile as he saw her.

'I am once again grateful for your help,' Max said, a gleam in his eyes. 'Are you destined to keep saving my life, Helene?'

'I did nothing of the kind, for I was too late to warn you of the attack,' Helene said. She was very aware of the bronzed and muscled torso exposed by the opening at the front of the dressing robe. A spasm in her stomach made her uncomfortably aware of the physical reaction the sight of him caused her. Heat was flooding through her body. She swallowed hard, licking her lips with the tip of her tongue. He was so very handsome and masculine! 'I merely assisted you to Amelia's house. Her footmen carried you here.'

'And you both bound my arm to stop the blood,' Max said. 'Amelia told me and the doctor said that it had been done very well. I fear I must have ruined your dress.'

'Well, if you did, we ruined your coat by slitting the sleeve—and it was a particularly fine coat,' Helene replied. 'I care nothing for a little blood, sir. Someone has tried to kill you twice now and I find that disturbing. I should be very distressed if this rogue were to succeed next time.'

'Would you?' Max's gaze was intent on her face. 'I vow it was worth the inconvenience if it has made you aware of me as something more than a friend. You must know that my greatest happiness would be to have you as my wife. I tried to ask you before I left London, but you did not wish me to speak. Have you changed your mind? Will you allow me to make you an offer—not at this moment, but when I am on my feet again?'

'My lord...' Helene stared at him. She was so startled that she hardly knew what to say. 'I did not mean to say that—at least... You must know that I have a high regard for you. I know I told you...I mean...' She floundered and looked flustered. 'Well, perhaps I do think more of you than is proper, but it can make no difference. I could not accept an offer of marriage.'

'Because your mama was the daughter of a tanner—or because Annesdale had the effrontery to say that he would cut me out of his will?' Max asked and saw her eyes widen in shock. 'Do you really believe that I care two farthings if your grandfather was in trade? As for Annesdale's fortune, he may leave it to whomever he desires—I do not need a penny of it! I do care for the man, but not if he persists in such abominable behaviour towards the woman I adore. He is now aware of my feelings and I believe he will not make such a mistake again. Next time you meet, I think you may discover that he wishes to apologise. Foolish Helene! How could you think me so shallow?'

'Forgive me. I did not at first, but then...'

'I called that damned poet a Cit and you assumed me to be a snob?'

'Well...yes, at first, though afterwards I realised that I had been hasty. I should not have spoken to you as I did. Amelia says that it is a term often used, but not necessarily a disparagement.'

'Unfortunately, too often it is,' Max admitted ruefully.

'And I fear I am as guilty as the next man. However that does not mean that I have no friends amongst persons who find their living from trade or that I despise them—and since your father was a gentleman, your grandfather's trade is too far in the past to be a problem, Helene.'

'Do you think so? Mama has never forgotten the way she was treated and Lady Annersley said—'

'That lady is a vixen. She is not well liked, Helene. You should ignore anything she said to you.'

'Oh...' Helene's heart fluttered as she looked into his eyes and saw them flame with passion. 'Does it truly not trouble you that Mama's father was a tanner?'

'Not one jot. I love you and would love you if you were a tinker's daughter. Nor do I care for the opinions of others. As my wife, you will be accepted by my friends,' Max told her firmly. 'Anyone who snubbed my wife would no longer be my friend. I think we should have as much company as we cared for, both in the country and in town.'

'Oh, but you cannot...' She shook her head as Max swung his legs over the side of the bed. 'You must not get up. You may harm yourself.'

'Come here and sit beside me, then,' Max said. 'I want to hold your hand and kiss you. I think it is time I told you how much I love you.'

Helene moved slowly towards him, her heart beating wildly. The shock of seeing him so near to death had broken down her defences. If he did not care that her grandfather came from the lower classes, why should she? She sat next to him on the edge of the bed and he reached for her hand with his uninjured arm.

'Really, you should not. I ought not to be here. Amelia said it was perfectly proper because you were not well, but I do not think Mama would agree. I fear she would be most shocked…'

The words died in her throat as Max leaned towards her, kissing her softly on the lips. There was such sweetness and tenderness in his kiss that Helene sighed and sat perfectly still, her lips parting as his tongue probed between them. She felt a tingling sensation inside, warmth spreading through her and a joy she had never experienced before.

'Oh…' she whispered as he drew back and looked at her. 'Are you sure?'

'Perfectly sure, my foolish love.'

'Mama did not wish me to marry a title.'

'We must see what we can do to change her mind,' Max said and held her hand, caressing it with his thumb. His touch set off little butterflies of sensation inside her, making her feel very strange. She wanted to melt into his arms, to be kissed until she could think of nothing else. 'I shall ask you properly another time, my dearest girl—but you will make me happy, won't you?'

'If it is truly your wish,' Helene replied, looking at him shyly. 'I have been very unhappy since that evening at Vauxhall, but I could not let you ask me. It would not have been fair or right.'

'I understand perfectly,' Max said. 'It was honourable, but foolish, my love. I knew what was in your mind the moment Annesdale told me what he had said to you.'

'I should have told you myself. Indeed, it was in my mind that I would do so when you were well again.'

'I wish you had told me at the start. Promise me there will be no more holding back, Helene. If something upsets you—you must tell me.'

'I am afraid that the duke will not be pleased if you marry me and allow Mama to visit us—you will allow it?'

'Of course. She may live with us or have her own home, but she will always be welcome.'

'Oh, Max...' Helene's throat caught. 'The duke will be so angry—and you are fond of him.'

'You may leave the duke to me,' Max said, such a grim look in his eyes that Helene almost felt sorry for her grandfather. 'If he wishes to visit us, he must learn to respect you and your mama.'

'You are so determined—' Helene stopped as he kissed her once more, her throat tight with emotion. 'I do care for you very much, my...Max...'

'That is very much better,' he said and smiled. 'I have decided to ask some friends to stay at my country home in two weeks' time. I think we should announce our engagement in *The Times* as soon as possible and then we shall go to the country—if the idea pleases you?'

'Yes, please,' Helene said. 'We could leave after Amelia's masquerade ball. If that is suitable for you?' She glanced at him uncertainly. 'You will have to speak to Mama...'

'I shall as soon as I am on my feet again,' Max told her and winced, clearly in pain. 'My arm is still a little sore. Perhaps I should rest for a while.'

'I shall go and leave you to sleep,' Helene offered, rising to her feet.

Max lay back against the pillows, his eyes soft with laughter as he looked at her. 'I would rather you stayed and read to me from that excellent book you brought with you. If it makes you feel easier, you may sit in the chair. I assure you I am not strong enough to ravish you, my love, even if I wished to, and I would much rather you gave yourself to me when you are ready. Love is mutual and should be enjoyed equally by both parties—do you not think so? Now I have made you blush. Read to me and I shall behave—as best I can.'

'Oh…' Helene gave him a look of admonishment. 'You love to tease, Max. I was not sure if you liked Miss Austen's work?'

'I think everyone enjoys her stories. I know Prinny is very fond of them,' Max told her. 'No, I am not one of the Regent's set, though we have visited the races at the same time and sat down to cards more than once.'

'Lie back and rest,' Helene said and opened the book to begin reading. 'I have not read *Pride and Prejudice* yet, but I have been told that it is vastly amusing…'

'Is it true that you spent almost two hours with Lord Coleridge?' Mrs Henderson said when she came to Helene's room that evening. 'It is all very well to assist in a sick room when someone is injured, but it is improper for a young girl to visit a gentleman's bedchamber.'

'I knew you would think so, Mama,' Helene told her. 'I assure you that nothing improper took place.' *Well, almost nothing, anyway!* 'Besides, we have an understanding. When Lord Coleridge is better, we shall become engaged. He will announce it in *The Times* soon and he has invited us to go down to his country house and stay for a while when we leave town.'

'Coleridge came up to scratch?' Mrs Henderson looked at her with a mixture of disbelief and dismay. 'You told me that you had refused him—why did you change your mind? Did you tell him what the duke said to you?'

'I did not tell him, Mama. However, the duke must have done so, for I believe they have had words,' she

said. 'However, Max says that he does not care two farthings that Grandfather was a tanner. Nor does he care for
Annesdale's fortune. You are to have a house, if you so
choose—but you will always be welcome to stay with us,
and we shall visit you. Max says if the duke wishes to know
us and our children, he must acknowledge you in public.'

'Helene…' Tears stung the lady's eyes. 'This is more
than I could ever hope for—but are you sure, my love?
There will be some who may whisper behind your back—
you will be envied your good fortune.'

'It does not matter,' Helene said. 'Max says that anyone
who will not accept me will no longer be his friend.'

'He must truly love you, Helene. You are fortunate, my
love.'

'I know.' Helene kissed her cheek. 'Shall you like your
own home, Mama—or would you rather live with us?'

'That would not be right. I should like my own home,
though I shall visit often—at least when you are in the
country. I do not care for London so very much.'

'I dare say we shall spend much of our time in the
country. You will not insist on a long engagement, I hope?
I know Coleridge means to ask you as soon as he is better.'

'Well, we shall see,' Mrs Henderson said. 'But what
of these attacks on his life? Amelia says it has happened
twice—and you were there both times. What does he
mean to do? You can hardly marry until this unfortunate
business is cleared up, Helene. You might have been hurt
yourself. Lord Coleridge will have to convince me that he
is able to protect you before I give my consent. However,
I shall consent to take you down to the country, if I am
certain he respects you as he ought, I shall allow the marriage to go ahead—perhaps at Christmas.'

'Coleridge will discuss all the details with you, I am

sure. We have only spoken of our plans—he did not feel it appropriate to make me a formal offer in his present situation. I am sure he will do so as soon as he is able.'

'Yes, I suppose he will,' Mrs Henderson said and her frown eased a little. 'I shall be satisfied once I have heard what he has to say—but I suppose I should wish you happy, dearest.'

'Thank you, Mama,' Helene said and smiled. 'I am very happy.'

'I was a little done up yesterday,' Max said and kissed Helene's hand when he took his leave of her the next morning. 'However, I am much recovered this morning. I could not quite squeeze my arm into the coat my man brought with him, but I may find something a little more accommodating at home. I have things to do—one of them to send a notice to *The Times*. I shall ask them to announce it the morning after Amelia's costume ball. We shall let it be known to our friends that evening. By then I am determined to be wearing a decent coat—and to have my ring on your finger.' He smiled down at her anxious face. 'Is there any particular stone that you have a fondness for, my love?'

'I shall love it whatever you choose,' Helene told him. 'You are quite sure you are well enough to go home?'

'Quite sure. I may not call tomorrow—but it will be the day after for certain.'

'I shall look forward to it,' she told him. Her grey eyes were still uncertain, deeply thoughtful. 'You will take care? Two attempts have been made on your life...'

'I shall be escorted home, by my man, and my groom, also Jemmy,' Max said, gazing down at her. 'Do not worry, my love. I promise I shall be safe—and before I walk anywhere again I shall make certain arrangements to protect my back. I am not that easy to dispose of, believe me.'

'Then I suppose I must let you go,' Helene said with a reluctant sigh. 'I shall count the hours until we meet again.'

'They will seem long to me,' Max told her and kissed her fingertips. 'I would stay longer, but I need to be at my lodgings. I have people to talk to, things to arrange. I promise you, nothing will happen to me, my darling.'

'Go, then,' Helene said and stood back. 'I shall not keep you since you wish to leave.'

'I hope it will not be long before I need never leave you again.'

Helene watched as he left the house, his valet close behind him. It was not likely that the assassin would make another attempt on Max's life so soon, but she would be uneasy until they were in the country. He had been safe there. His enemy had attacked him soon after his return from the country, so it made sense that whoever the rogue was, he lived in London.

Helene frowned as she wondered who wanted Max dead and why. He had offered no explanation other than saying that it might have been robbery, but Helene did not believe it and she did not think that Max did, either. If he had his own suspicions, he was not sharing them with her.

'What made you think of it?' Gerard asked as he shared a bottle of wine with Max after dinner that evening. 'Do you really think that someone tried to kidnap Amelia last summer because they thought she might marry me?'

'It occurred to me and it seemed to fit,' Max told him. 'We were all staying with Harry at Pendleton. You had paid some attention to Amelia at Susannah's dance—and then again at Pendleton. Someone who was not of our party might have thought you intended to ask her to marry you. Indeed, I wondered myself. I believe you knew her some years ago?'

'I suppose Harry told you?' Gerard frowned. 'I was in love with Amelia when we were younger. I asked her to marry me and I approached her brother. He refused me for reasons he never explained—and when I said that I would not take no for an answer, he set his grooms on me. They bound my hands and then...he took his riding crop to me. Some of the scars remain to this day.'

'Good grief! The man is a scoundrel! Does Amelia know?'

'I did not tell her.' Gerard frowned. 'He told me that the beating was a gift from her to punish me for my impertinence. Even in my anger and humiliation I did not believe him, but I left a letter for her in our secret place. The letter was found and taken, but she did not meet me as I begged her. I thought that she must wish for our affair to be at an end. It was only later that I wondered if the letter had gone astray. I think Amelia loved me once...though that was long ago and forgotten now.'

'What had you done to upset her brother?' Max frowned. 'Royston is a bore and a bully, but I would not have believed he was capable of such behaviour if you had not told me.'

'I believed at the time that it must have been because he thought me impertinent to ask for her in marriage,' Gerard said. 'My father had near ruined us. If it had not been for a lucky inheritance, the estate might have had to be sold. Yet I would swear there was something more—something more personal to Royston.'

'You still do not know why he hates you?'

'I have no idea,' Gerard said. 'Unless...I saw something

once, but I have never been sure what happened. I shall not tell you, because I prefer not to malign someone if I do not know the whole truth. Royston could have thought I knew more than I did.'

'From what I have seen of Amelia Royston, she would never have been a party to something of that nature, Gerard. She could not have known what her brother did to you.'

'I am certain of it,' Gerard replied. 'At first I was bitter. I needed time to lick my wounds and I joined the army. I came to realise that I had been a fool to let Royston drive me away, but by then I was married and my daughter was born.' He frowned. 'I did have thoughts of asking Amelia to marry me last summer, but I am not certain that she wishes for it. Or that it would suit my plans. Besides, there were other things to settle…' Gerard frowned. 'You have given me something to think about, Max. However, I would say your own problems are more pressing.'

'They are certainly something I could do without,' Max agreed. 'You are the first to know, but I have asked Helene Henderson to be my wife. She has agreed. We are going down to Coleridge after Amelia Royston's costume ball. I intend to ask Sinclair and a few others to stay, you included, of course…make a party of it. Mrs Henderson has not yet agreed the date of the wedding, but I hope it may be sooner rather than later.'

'I begin to understand,' Gerard said. 'I see your thinking, Max…why you put two and two together in the matter of Amelia's little fright in Pendleton woods. I suppose the situation is somewhat similar in a way.'

'Amelia is quite an heiress these days…'

'Unfortunately.' Gerard grimaced. He laughed as Max

raised his brows. 'It is a part of the reason I hesitate to ask her. Pride—foolish, I dare say. In your own case, your thinking may be sound, my dear fellow. Once it is announced that you are to marry, there may be some urgency in someone's mind. Another attempt is almost certain to be made quite soon.'

'They might wish to make certain that I do not make it to the altar.'

Gerard looked thoughtful. 'Yes, I see that it might spoil someone's plans if you should marry. It could be dangerous, Max—and not just for you.'

'That is why I need your help, Gerard. Last year you arranged protection for Amelia. I rather think I may need a similar plan.'

'Yes, of course.' Gerard's mouth settled into a grim line. 'I am at your disposal, my friend. You know you may call on me. As Harry once said, we are bound together by a single thread after what happened out there in Spain. You will not ask him to assist you?'

'He is settled in the country with Susannah, and she expects her first child. I should not want to take him away from his wife at such a time.'

'No, indeed, that would be inconvenient—and we shall do very well with Sinclair, a few fellows I know, and ourselves, of course. I have a lot of time for Sinclair.'

'Yes, I think he is coming along nicely,' Max agreed with a smile. 'Well, that is settled. We shall go down at the end of next week.'

'Shall you invite Amelia Royston?'

'I was considering it. She has been a good friend to Helene—and me.'

'Then please do so,' Gerard said. 'It will be interesting to see if anything happens, if nothing else.'

* * *

Max managed to squeeze himself into a size larger coat than he normally wore the next morning and set out for his destination. He drove himself in his curricle with his groom beside him and Jemmy up on the back as usual. It was unlikely that he would be attacked again so soon, but he certainly would not be walking alone for a while.

Max had given his situation much thought; someone wished him dead and the obvious suspect must be his cousin. Yet Max could not quite believe that Robert was behind the attempts on his life. There was something more...something hidden. It was difficult to see what benefit his death would be to anyone else...unless... Yes, of course!

Max's brow cleared as he began to see the fiendishly clever thinking at the root of the plot. He must be very careful—the mind that had formed this devious plan was dangerous.

Robert would inherit if Max were dead, but if he should marry things would be different. The title might still pass to Robert unless Max had a son, but Max's estate was not entailed and he would be making a will that would make certain that his wife and children inherited everything. Therefore a further attempt must be made before it was too late.

He was taking a huge risk, which might lead to his death. Max could take certain steps to make sure that Helene would be wealthy even if he died before their wedding; it should not happen if he could help it, but some risk could not be helped. If he left things as they were, something worse than his own death might occur.

Arriving at Miss Royston's house a little over an hour later, Max asked for Mrs Henderson. He was shown into one of the best parlours and asked to wait. The lady arrived, looking anxious, some twenty minutes later.

'Forgive me for keeping you waiting, sir. I was dressing.'

'I am sorry if I called too early,' Max told her. 'Had you sent word, I could have returned later.'

'It is best to get this over with,' Mrs Henderson replied. 'You may tell me your intentions towards my daughter, sir—but I must warn you that I have reservations.'

'I have learned of some injustice towards you when you were first married,' Max replied. 'I am sorry that you were treated so harshly. It will not happen again. I have spoken to Annesdale. He knows that if he wishes to attend the wedding—or any other function that my wife may care to hold—he must treat both you and her with respect. I do not believe that that gentleman or his daughter-in-law will cut you in future. I cannot promise that they will welcome you to their homes, but they will behave properly in mine.'

Mrs Henderson looked a little disbelieving, but there was an air of authority about Lord Coleridge at that moment that was very impressive. 'I should not wish to be invited to their homes—but I shall wish to see Helene and her children sometimes.'

'Whenever you please,' Max told her. 'At the moment my aunt and her son occupy the dower house. I may find another house for them somewhere. It would then be made ready for you, if you wished to live there—or you may live in Bath if you choose and visit us when you wish.'

'I should be able to see my family most days if I lived at the dower house,' Mrs Henderson said. 'But I should not wish to take your aunt's home from her.'

'Let me see what I can arrange,' Max said. 'Something will be agreed that will suit us all. In the meantime, I shall be pleased to have you stay with us—if you care to?'

'You are generous, sir,' Mrs Henderson said and then frowned. 'But what of this other business? I have not asked how your arm goes on, sir.'

'Very well,' Max said. 'I was fortunate. It is little more than a scratch. If I had been stabbed in the back, I dare say I should be dead.'

'You will take better care in future—of yourself and Helene?'

'I assure you that Helene will be watched over,' Max said. 'I should not want anything to happen to the lady I love.'

'You do love her, I know.' Mrs Henderson studied him for a moment and then nodded. 'Very well, you have my consent. When do you wish to marry—at Christmas?'

'I think I would prefer the wedding to be in one month's time,' Max told her. 'The church at Coleridge is not large, but I dare say it could hold more than a hundred guests. If you wish for a larger wedding, we could come back to town...'

'I have only one brother and a couple of real friends,' Mrs Henderson said. 'I dare say you may have many friends, sir.'

'Only a few I truly count as friends,' Max replied. 'We shall have a family wedding and then hold a large reception in town a month or so later.'

'Yes, I believe that would suit both Helene and myself,' Mrs Henderson replied. 'It seems that things have been agreed between us. You will, of course, settle something on Helene?'

'Helene will be wealthy even if I die before we marry,' Max told her. 'There is no need to mention this to her, for she would not care to know such things—but you may set your mind at rest, ma'am.'

'Thank you. I did not want her to be left in poverty as I was when my husband died.'

'If Annesdale had been any kind of a man, he would have made you an allowance,' Max said. 'In future you will be secure, ma'am. The papers are already in hand.'

'You leave me nothing to say but to offer my sincere gratitude.'

'That is unnecessary. You are giving me your daughter—and she is more precious than any marriage settlement.'

Mrs Henderson smiled. 'In that case I shall go upstairs and send her down to you, sir.'

Chapter Ten

Helene touched her fingers to her mouth. She could still feel the tingle of Max's kisses, which had made her body throb with what she now understood was desire. The feeling was so new to her, her joy so complete that she felt she must be dreaming. Surely it was not possible to feel as happy as she did now? She glanced at the magnificent diamond-and-sapphire ring on her finger. She found it difficult to believe that she was actually engaged to be Max's wife. He had left her for a few hours, because he had some business to arrange, but he would dine with them that evening. They had no other guests, because they had decided on a quiet evening at home on the eve of Amelia's costume ball.

Helene could not help smiling as she glanced at herself in the mirror. It was really true! She would soon be Max's wife, because her mama had agreed that the wedding should be set for the following month. Only a short time ago she had resigned herself to a life of service, because she was certain nothing good could ever happen to her again, and now she was to marry the man she had come to love so very much. It was far more than she had ever expected!

Helene knew that she owed her happiness to Amelia's generosity. Not only had she made this Season in town possible, she had also made Helene's mother see that it would be unjust to deny her the happiness of being married to the man she loved. Helene owed her so much. She was filled with a desire to see Amelia and tell her how truly grateful she was for all she had done.

Having dressed for the evening, Helene went along the landing to Amelia's room. She tapped in the door, which was opened by Amelia's personal maid.

'Oh, Miss Henderson,' the woman said. 'Miss Royston has gone down to the parlour. I am sure you will find her there.'

Helene thanked her and went down the stairs, still feeling as if she were floating on a cloud. The door to the parlour was slightly open, and as Helene approached she heard a man's angry voice. Helene would have turned away immediately, for she would not have dreamed of eavesdropping, but the words were so harsh that she was frozen to the spot.

'I hear that you have been seeing that rogue again, Amelia. I told you last summer that I shall not stand for it. If you continue to defy me, you will be sorry!'

'You may be my brother, Michael—and I would not wish to show you disrespect,' Amelia replied in a much calmer tone. 'I believe I told you last year that I should not stand for this dictation. Aunt Agatha made me her heiress and because of that I am independent. If I wish to count the Earl of Ravenshead as one of my friends, I shall do so.'

'On your own head be it!' Sir Michael thundered at her.

Helene was startled as the door to the parlour was

thrown back and Amelia's brother came storming out. She had retreated to the stairs, but he did not even glance her way as the footman opened the front door for him.

Helene ran back down the stairs. She knocked at the parlour door and then entered. Amelia was standing by the fireplace, leaning her head against it, her shoulders hunched as if in some distress.

'Amelia…are you all right?'

Amelia straightened. She paused for a moment before turning to look at Helene, her face pale but determined.

'Yes, I am perfectly well, Helene. You may have over-heard something my brother said to me. Michael some-times forgets himself. He will shout and that is foolish—a quiet word is often more effective.'

'It was unkind of him to be so harsh to you,' Helene said. 'It was not my business to listen and I would not have done so had he not shouted so loudly that I could not help hearing.'

'I acquit you of eavesdropping,' Amelia said. 'My dear-est Susannah did so quite deliberately at times—she was concerned for my sake—but I know you did not mean to pry.'

'No, I did not,' Helene said. 'I am, however, concerned for your sake. I came to thank you for what you have done for me, Amelia. Had it not been for your kindness—your generosity—I would not have met Max. I know I owe my happiness to you and I wanted to thank you.' Helene took a step towards her, impulsively kissing her cheek. 'I do thank you from the bottom of my heart—and if there is ever anything I may do for you, you have only to ask.'

'Thank you, Helene,' Amelia said and smiled. 'Helping others to find their happiness brings me a great deal of pleasure, you know. However, you must not be concerned for me, because I am well able to stand up to my brother. His visits can be unpleasant, but I know that I have good friends to support me. Now tell me, when do you leave for the country?'

'It is your costume ball tomorrow. We shall leave at noon the following day for Max's home. I know he has asked you to stay with us—I hope you will do so.'

'I shall certainly come down in a couple of weeks and then stay until the wedding,' Amelia told her. 'Emily and I have decided to go down to Bath a day or so after you leave us. I have some business to set in hand there. When it is complete we shall come to you.'

'And after we are married—you will stay with us sometimes?'

'Yes, I hope so,' Amelia told her. 'I am not certain of my future plans. It is possible that we may travel for a while—but I shall certainly be at your wedding.'

Helene nodded. Amelia had made light of the incident with her brother, but she suspected that Sir Michael's visit had upset her friend more than she would admit. She wished that there was something she could do to help Amelia, but it was not her place to meddle in Amelia's affairs.

Helene considered telling Max about what she had overheard when he came to dinner that evening, but after some consideration she decided that it would be wrong of her to discuss what was a private family affair. Amelia would not have spoken of it to her had she not happened to hear Sir Michael shout at his sister. Besides, Max was full of his plans for the wedding and their honeymoon, and the incident was soon put to the back of Helene's mind.

She had already sent word to the seamstress who had

made several beautiful gowns for her, and received a message that the lady would wait on her on the morning of
Amelia's ball to discuss materials. She was prepared to
make the journey into Hampshire to do the final fitting
and finish Helene's wedding gown in time for the wedding.

'You may wish to order a few new gowns for the honeymoon,' Max told Helene. 'But I want to show you Paris,
my love—and we shall visit the best couturiers to buy your
wardrobe. You look well in rich colours and I shall enjoy
helping you choose.'

Helene's pulses raced as she gazed into his eyes and
saw the love reflected there. How fortunate she was to
have found a man like Max Coleridge.

Helene did think about the argument she had overheard
when she undressed for the evening, but plans for her wedding pushed it from her mind as she snuggled down into
her feather mattress and fell asleep.

Amelia's costume ball was a brilliant affair. Everyone
was masked and their disguises ranged from pirates to eastern sheikhs and sultans, pharaohs and even one Viking for
the men. The ladies ranged from Roman vestal virgins to
Marie Antoinette and Elizabeth I—and one daring lady
came dressed as a pageboy in satin breeches, silk shirt and
fancy waistcoat. Her face was completely masked, her hair
covered by a wig. All the gentlemen were trying to discover
her identity, but she was deliberately disguising her voice.

'I should think she will disappear before the unmasking,' Emily said to Helene. 'I doubt she will dare to reveal
her identity.'

'Oh, my dear, it is not half so shocking as what Lady
Caroline Lamb wore—or rather did not wear!—when she
masqueraded as Lord Byron's little black pageboy,' Sally

Jersey said. 'Now that was totally beyond the pale and it began her downfall, you know. Poor Caroline. I wonder that she ever dared to show her face in society again, but she continued her scandalous behaviour until she sank into a decline. Her behaviour was outrageous, but I have always felt a little sorry for her.'

Helene listened, but did not join in the conversation. It was a little shocking to appear in public wearing a man's clothing, of course, but she did not think it so very wicked.

Helene danced for most of the evening, often with Max or his particular friends, who wished to congratulate them both. It was almost supper time when she went to stand by the open window for a moment, because the room was so warm and her own costume of an early Tudor lady was a little heavy. Max was dancing with Emily and Helene was waiting for Toby to claim her. He was wearing a pirate costume, but there were several gentlemen wearing similar costumes and as yet Toby had not found her.

'Will you dance, lady?'

Helene turned and saw a man wearing a pirate costume. She smiled, thinking it must be Toby at last, though it was difficult to tell.

'Would you mind very much if we just stood and talked for a few minutes?' she asked. 'It is rather hot in here.'

'We could go on to the terrace if you prefer?'

'Yes, I think—just for a moment,' Helene said. She turned and went outside, drawing a breath of air. It was so much fresher out here! 'This is fun, isn't it? I cannot guess who some people are—can you? I knew you were wearing a pirate costume of course, because Max told me, but—'

She broke off as the man grabbed her arm, his fingers

digging into her flesh so deeply that she winced. 'Stop gabbling, you little fool!' the man's voice was harsh and it struck a chill into Helene. Something was wrong! This was not Toby! Now she thought about it, he was of a different build. 'Listen to me, girl! I shall give you one warning. If you go through with this marriage, you will be a widow before you have hardly become a wife!'

'What do you mean?' Helene tried to break away from him, but his grip was too strong. 'Let me go! Who are you? Why do you say such a wicked thing?'

His grip tightened so that she cried out in pain. 'I told you to listen. You must break off this engagement or you may be the next.'

Helene struggled, but she might not have been able to break away from him had someone not come out on to the terrace at that moment.

'Miss Henderson…is that you?' Toby's voice called.

'Remember, I shall give only this one warning,' the man hissed in her ear. Then he let go of her and made off across the lawns.

Helene sighed and swayed slightly. Toby was at her side in an instant.

'Who was that fellow? Did he threaten you?'

Helene breathed deeply. 'It was a mistake. I thought it was you and told him I needed a little air. We came out and…but he has gone and you are here. Shall we have what remains of our dance?'

'Damned fellow!' Toby growled. 'These affairs are all very well, but not when some rogue threatens a lady. Shall I go after him and give him a thrashing?'

'No, please do not cause a fuss,' Helene said. 'Let us go back inside. I should have made certain it was you before I came out. Thank you for coming in search of me, sir.'

'You are very welcome. You must know that I am always at your service should you need me.'

'Thank you, I shall not forget your kindness,' Helene said.

She tried to dismiss the incident, but it was difficult; the pirate's words had frightened her—not for herself, but for Max. She was confused and distressed, but determined not to show it. However, the threat was serious and she must speak to Max as soon as possible.

Helene wished that she had not gone to the terrace with the pirate. His threats had spoiled the evening, even though she tried not to let her unease show as she went to join Max.

'Is something wrong?' Max asked as he sensed her agitation.

'I have something I must tell you...' She glanced over her shoulder. 'This is not the right place or the time, but it is important.'

'Something has happened?' She nodded. 'Tell me now, Helene.'

'I have been warned not to marry you.'

'Damnation! Who said such a thing to you?'

'I do not know who he was, for he wore a mask, but he said that if I did not break off my engagement I should be a widow before I was a wife.' Helene caught his arm, her eyes dark with emotion. 'I am sure he meant his threat, Max, though I do not know why he threatened me.'

'You have told no one else?'

'No, of course not. It was a little frightening, but Toby came and the man ran off.'

'You did not know him?'

'He was wearing the costume of a pirate. I thought he

was Toby, but then he grabbed my arm and said…horrible things. Who could it be—and why does he wish to stop our marriage?'

'I have a good idea…' He shook his head. 'It is best if you do not know for the moment. Tell me, Helene—do you wish to break off the engagement in the circumstances?'

'No. If he wants you dead, he will try to kill you whether or not we are married—unless you…?'

'No, of course not. We shall not give him the satisfaction, Helene. I suspected something like this might happen and I am prepared for it, but I did not expect it to happen so quickly.' Max frowned, hesitated, then, 'I do not think you are in danger for the moment, Helene—and I think we have no choice but to carry on as if nothing had happened.'

'You will take care, Max?'

'Of you and myself,' he replied and smiled. 'Will you trust me, my love?'

'Yes, of course,' she said. 'But Mama must not know anything of this or she will say we must abandon the wedding.'

'Mrs Henderson must certainly not be told—the fewer who know anything at all the better.'

Helene found it impossible to sleep as she tossed and turned on her pillow later that night. The pirate had told her she must break off her engagement to Max or he would die—but two attempts had already been made on his life. She was relieved to have told Max and he had taken the news in his stride. Indeed, he seemed to have been expecting something of the sort.

Who was his enemy and why did he want Max dead? Helene wished that Max had told her more, but she knew he was playing his cards close to his chest. All she could do was wait and pray that he would be safe.

Helene slept at last and it was past eleven in the morning when her maid woke her. She ate a light breakfast and then dressed, ready for the journey to Max's estate. They could not accomplish the whole journey by nightfall and were to stay at a good posting hotel for one night. In the rush of making sure that everything had been packed into her trunks, Helene had no time to think about the previous evening.

She took a lingering farewell of Amelia, hugging her and wishing her well. 'Thank you so very much for everything,' she said, tears stinging her throat. 'You have been the best friend anyone could ever have.'

'You have been a delight,' Amelia told her. 'I look forward to your wedding, my dear.'

Emily came forward to kiss Helene on the cheek. 'I shall miss our walks and the conversations we had,' she said. 'I, too, look forward to your wedding.'

'You must come and stay with us sometimes,' Helene said and hugged her tightly. 'You have been a real friend, Emily. Please write to me when you have time.'

'Of course I shall, but you must go. I am sure that I heard the carriage pull up a moment ago.' She smiled as the doorknocker sounded. 'Lord Coleridge has arrived.'

Helene went to greet Max as he was admitted, giving him a searching look, but he only smiled and kissed her cheek.

'You look beautiful, my love.'

'Max…we must talk. I have been anxious.'

'Believe me, there is no need. Everything is in hand.'

Mrs Henderson came up then, looking expectant. The

last goodbyes were said with thanks expressed to the servants, and then they were outside on the pavement. Max handed both ladies inside his travelling carriage, and then climbed in himself, tapping the roof with his stick to let the coachman know that they were ready to leave.

'Well, this is very comfortable, Coleridge. You looked a little concerned just now, Helene—is anything the matter?'

'Nothing at all, Mama,' Helene said. 'I was merely apologising for having so many trunks and bags.'

'And I was assuring Helene that my grooms will bring everything on the baggage coach,' Max said smoothly. 'As for having too many trunks, my love, I am sure your mama will agree that a lady can never have too many pretty clothes. I dare say we shall have twice as many when we return from Paris.'

'You will spoil her, Coleridge!' Mrs Henderson said and looked satisfied. 'Well, I dare say I may leave everything to you now. It is amazingly pleasant to have a gentleman to take care of one.'

'And I intend to take good care of both you and Helene,' Max told her with a smile. 'I think we should send out invitations to the wedding almost at once, do you not agree? A month is not so very long after all.'

Mrs Henderson's attention was immediately turned to all the preparations, and she passed the first of several miles happily discussing the various dinners, receptions and the dance that was to be held just before the wedding at Coleridge House.

Helene allowed her mama to talk, smiling at Max as he answered all Mrs Henderson's questions patiently, and occasionally glancing out of the window.

It was just after they left London that a curricle moving at speed came up behind them and then overtook them, passing so close to their carriage that the wheels almost touched. Helene caught a glimpse of the man driving, but it was impossible to see much of his face, for he wore a black hat pulled low over his face and a muffler that covered his mouth and nose.

'Damned idiot!' Max remarked and looked out of the window at the back of the curricle as it disappeared into the distance. 'Why must people be in such a hurry?'

'Some people have no manners,' Mrs Henderson said. 'He could easily have caused an accident.'

'My coachman had the sense to pull over to the side of the road and let him pass,' Max said with a slight frown. 'Besides, the coach is heavier and more substantial than that light rig. He must have come off the worst, and I dare say he knew it.'

Helene studied Max's face. A little pulse was flicking at his temple. She had a feeling that he was more concerned about the incident than he would allow. They had been in no danger, because the curricle had been too light to inflict substantial damage on their coach. However, something had made Max thoughtful, for he was silent for several minutes, clearly deep in thought. Had they been alone, Helene would have asked what was concerning him, but she did not wish to alarm her mama. Mrs Henderson had taken it as the thoughtlessness of a careless driver, but Helene could not help wondering if the driver of the curricle had hoped to cause an accident.

They stopped for the night at a prestigious posting inn. Helene and her mama were immediately shown to their rooms and Mrs Henderson declared that she would rest for a while before supper.

'I shall come down to the private parlour in half an

hour,' she said. 'You should not go down too soon, Helene. It will not do for you to be alone with Max in a public place. I know you are engaged, but you must still observe the niceties of polite behaviour, dearest.'

'Yes, Mama. Do not worry, I shall do nothing to arouse censure,' Helene promised. However, she took no more than ten minutes to tidy herself before going down to the parlour. As she had expected, Max was already there.

'I wished for a moment alone before Mama came down,' she said. 'I hope you do not think it improper in me?'

'You could never do anything improper in my eyes,' he told her with a warm smile. 'You are worried about the incident in the carriage?'

'Do you think it might be him—the man who threatened me?'

'It is possible—even probable. He may have wished to cause an accident or perhaps just frighten us.'

'Who can it be?'

'I am not yet certain, though I believe I know what is going on. Forgive me, dearest. Believe me when I say it may be best for you not to know.' He took her hands, gazing down at her intently. 'You must not let this overset you. I promise that all will be well.'

'He shall not prevail,' Helene said and raised her head proudly. 'I am not afraid for myself, Max—but you must know that any threat against you distresses me.'

'Yes, it must,' he said, his expression grave. 'If a threat were made against you, I should be anxious. He did not threaten you?'

'No, at least only vaguely,' Helene replied, not meeting his eyes.

'Damn him!' Max was angry. 'Something about that rig made me feel I should know the driver, though he had made sure to hide his face. I have a feeling that that curricle belongs to someone I know.' His gaze narrowed. 'If I thought you were in danger, I would call the wedding off until the rogue has been caught and punished.'

Helene moved towards him, her expression urgent. 'I am not afraid of him, Max. I was startled when he threatened me, but I shall be alert from now on. I believe that our wedding angers him. The thought of your marriage might be enough to bring him out of the shadows. It may be that you can turn the tables, use it against him in some way.'

'That would mean a certain amount of risk on your part, but if the rogue is who I think he is, he will be watched constantly. If you have any doubts, please tell me now, for I do not wish to distress you, my love.'

'If this person believes he has his way he will take his time and perhaps strike when you have relaxed your guard—but if he feels that time is short he may grow careless in his urgency. Besides, why should we sacrifice our happiness?'

'You are very brave,' Max said, reaching out to touch her cheek with his fingertips. I am sorry that you should have been exposed to two attempts on my life.'

'I am glad I was there for the first time, you might not have noticed the man with the pistol,' Helene told him. 'However, I must ask you to keep even the merest hint of danger from Mama. She would insist on postponing the wedding if she thought I might be in danger.'

'She would be anxious for you and rightly so,' Max said. 'It will be much better if she knows nothing—I think she might unconsciously betray us if she were aware of what may happen.' He tipped her chin to look at her. 'You realise that this rogue may try anything to ruin our plans?'

'Yes, Max,' she said and raised her eyes to his. 'I know that he will try to thwart us if he can.'

'But we shall not let him?'

'Certainly not!'

Max laughed softly, and then bent his head to kiss her on the lips. For a moment he held her close, the kiss becoming hungry, demanding. Helene felt as if she were melting into his body, becoming one with him. It was a blissful sensation and she pressed herself closer. They were both breathing hard when he released her.

'Forgive me,' Max said. 'I should not have done that here, for someone might have walked in on us, but I could not resist. You are one of the bravest ladies I know and I adore you.'

'So I should hope,' Helene said and laughed up at him. 'It is quite expected of new husbands, you know—though in some instances it does not last too long.'

Max arched his brows. 'I hope that does not mean you will tire of me too soon?'

'No, sir—it means that I accept that some gentlemen tire of marriage. I hope that you will not be one of them, and I shall do my best to make sure that you prefer your wife's bed to that of a mistress.'

'Helene?' Max's eyes danced with mischief. 'Do you think that quite a proper statement for a young lady of quality?'

'I dare say it is most improper,' Helene replied demurely. 'However, it is the truth—I think that marriage is more than the exchange of contracts and duty. I hope for a lifelong love match.'

'That is exactly my own wish,' Max said. 'I think I need to k—'

His words were lost as the door opened and Mrs

Henderson entered. 'Ah, there you are, Helene,' she said. 'I went to your room, but as you were not there thought I should find you here.'

'You are just in time, ma'am,' Max replied. 'I believe our supper should be here at any moment.'

Helene met his eyes, a tingle of pleasure running through her as she saw the reflection of his desire. She knew that he wanted to kiss her again and she felt his frustration. It was difficult for a young lady to be alone with her fiancé in society, but perhaps when they reached Coleridge it might be possible sometimes.

They reached Max's estate in the early afternoon the next day. Grooms came running to help with the horses and open the door when the carriage pulled to a halt. By the time Max had helped Helene and her mama to alight, the front door was opened and a welcoming party of servants came out to greet them.

A lady dressed all in black apart from a neat white collar came forward and dipped a curtsy. 'I am Mrs Hale, the housekeeper at Coleridge House,' she said. 'We are delighted to have you here, Miss Henderson—Mrs Henderson.'

'Thank you,' Helene said and smiled at her. 'We are very pleased to be here.'

'May I introduce you to the servants, Miss Henderson? This is Hale, our butler and my husband, your own personal maid, Vera, the parlourmaids, Jenny, Susan, Jane and Millie. The upper footman Jenkins, his under footmen, Rawlings, Phillips...'

Helene was taken along a line of smiling men and women who all inclined their heads and murmured something about being pleased to see her. Obviously, they had

been told she was their master's fiancée and were eager
to welcome her. She tried hard to memorise their names
but knew she might forget one or two until she became
accustomed to their faces. However, she would not forget
Vera, who was to be her own maid.

'Shall I take the ladies up now, sir?' Mrs Hale asked
Max as he stood watching benevolently. 'Or would you
wish for refreshment to be served immediately?'

'I would think the ladies would prefer to see their rooms
first,' Max said. 'Shall we say half an hour?'

'That will be much better,' Mrs Henderson said. 'Come
along, Helene. I am anxious to change this gown for a fresh
one after so much travelling.'

'Yes, Mama.'

Helene followed her mama, listening as the housekeeper
talked about the house and how good it was to see it come
to life again now that the master was home from the wars.

'We thought at one time that he might settle elsewhere,'
she said. 'It will be good to have a party of guests again…
and to see his lordship happily settled at last.' Mrs Hale
looked at Helene with approval. 'I do my best here, but the
house needs a mistress.'

'A house like this needs a great deal of order,' Mrs
Henderson said. 'However, I must say that it looks just as
it ought.'

'His lordship put the repairs needed in order some
months ago. He has spoken of further improvements, but I
dare say he was waiting for the right time. Colour schemes
are sometimes the better for a lady's eye—would you not
say so, ma'am?'

Helene did not join in the conversation. She was too
busy looking about her at what was to be her new home.
Coleridge House was a fine building of pale yellowish

brick, with long-paned windows and three storeys. From what she had seen so far, the décor was both stylish and comfortable, which was not always easy to achieve. However, the entrance hall and staircase were not enough to judge the whole. She was curious to see the room she had been given, and when she was shown into a suite of three rooms, all of which were decorated in shades of green, white and gold, she thought them luxurious.

'These are the best guest apartments,' Mrs Hale told them. 'I thought that you would like to be together, Miss Henderson.'

'Yes, thank you,' Helene said, lingering in the sitting room. 'They are lovely. I am sure we shall be very comfortable here.'

'His lordship's apartments are in the west wing, Miss Henderson. We always used to house guests in this wing. His lordship had this part of the house refurbished first. I believe he means to have his own apartments done next.'

'I see,' Helene said. 'Thank you for telling me, ma'am.'

'I shall leave you to refresh yourselves,' Mrs Hale said. 'If you need anything please ring. I think you will find warm water in your rooms, and Vera will be here to assist you in a moment.'

Helene thanked her and she went away, leaving them to make themselves at home. Mrs Henderson walked round the sitting room, nodding her approval before going through to the bedrooms.

'Which would you prefer, Helene?' she asked. 'They are both very comfortable—but this one has a better view. You can see a water feature beyond the lawns.'

'You have this one,' Helene said. 'I have a view of the woods.'

'You should have the best view,' her mama said, but

since she was standing by the window, clearly entranced by the view, Helene chose the slightly smaller room, which was over a small courtyard that backed on to what looked as if it must be a park.

She took off her pelisse and deposited it on the bed. She was just attempting to unfasten the back of her gown when someone knocked at the door and Vera came in, carrying a yellow silk teagown.

'May I do that for you, miss?' she asked. 'Some of your things were sent on ahead and arrived earlier. I took the liberty of unpacking the small trunk and I pressed this for you. I hope it will do, Miss Henderson?'

'Thank you,' Helene replied. 'That was kind of you, Vera. It will do very well. In the largest trunk you will find a dark green evening dress. I would like to wear that later—if you can manage to press it for me?'

'Of course I can,' Vera replied. 'I am so happy to have been chosen as your maid, miss—and I hope you will be pleased with me.'

'I am sure I shall,' Helene said. She wriggled free of her gown as the girl finished unfastening her. 'Thank you. I want to go down as soon as I have changed, because I should like to take a look at the gardens, though I am not sure if there will be time before we have tea.'

Helene did not wait for her mama. She had caught sight of some beautiful gardens and was eager to explore. A footman was standing by the door when she returned to the hallway.

'I should like to explore the pretty rose garden I glimpsed as we arrived,' she told him with a shy smile. 'Could you please direct me?'

'Of course, Miss Henderson. Follow me, I shall show you the best way to access the rose garden.'

He preceded her to the back of the hall and then opened the door into a very pretty parlour, which had all the sun in the afternoons and was very warm, despite the open French windows.

'The garden is just out there, miss,' he said, 'and refreshments will be served in the front parlour on the first floor.'

'Thank you...Rawlings...' She smiled, pleased that she had remembered his name. 'You have been very helpful.'

'It is our pleasure to serve you, miss.'

Helene nodded and walked across the parlour to the open window. She went out into the garden, thinking how peaceful and pleasant it was. She could smell the heavy perfume of musk roses and hear the sound of birds twittering in some graceful trees at the far end of a smooth lawn. She was so lucky that this was to be her home.

She walked towards the rose arbour, inhaling the lovely scents and bending to sniff one particularly beautiful red rose.

'Hello...' a voice said behind her. 'I think you must be Miss Henderson—Max's fiancée?'

Helene turned and saw a man of perhaps two and twenty years. Of medium stature, he had a pale complexion and his hair was black, his eyes grey. She thought that perhaps he might have been ill at some time recently, for his pallor was not quite healthy.

'Hello,' Helene said and smiled; he was not unattractive and seemed friendly. 'I am sorry, but I do not know who you are.'

'No, I suppose Max did not think to mention me. I am Robert Heronsdale—his cousin.'

'Oh, yes, I remember something. I believe Max told us that you and your mama live at the dower house?'

'Max was good enough to give us a home after my father lost all his money and then suffered a fall from his horse,' Robert told her with a strange smile. 'He was ill for some months before he died and then we discovered that he had gambled away almost everything he owned. We were forced to leave our home. When Max heard of our misfortune, he generously asked us to come here.'

'Yes, that is so like him,' Helene said. 'I hope you will visit us sometimes? I have not met Mrs Heronsdale as yet, but I look forward to it.'

'Mama will call on you later,' Robert told her. 'I am sure she would have come this afternoon, but she is a little unwell. I hope you did not mind that I came at once? I must admit to being curious about the lady Max is to marry. I must congratulate him on his choice. You are very pretty, Miss Henderson.'

'Oh...' Helene was not quite sure how to answer. His eyes were bright as he gave her an intent look. 'Thank you.' She did not know what she would have found to say next, but she was saved by the arrival of Max. He came striding towards them, a smile on his lips.

'Helene, my love. Rawlings said I would find you here.' His gaze moved to Robert and his expression became thoughtful. 'Robert. It is good to see you up and about at last, my dear fellow. I trust that you are quite well now?'

'Yes, thank you, cousin,' Robert said. 'I should like to speak to you in private when you have time—but I am happy to report that my health has improved since *your visit*.' He seemed to give significance to the last two words. 'You understand me, sir?'

'Yes, I believe I do,' Max said and smiled at him. 'I am

happy to hear that things have improved. I see that you have met Helene.'

'I envy you your good fortune,' Robert said and offered his hand. 'You have found yourself a lovely bride and I wish you both all the happiness in the world.'

'Thank you, Robert,' Max said and took his hand in a firm clasp. 'We are about to have some refreshment. I do hope you will join us?'

'I should get back, for Mama is unwell. I dare say she will be better in the morning. Her little turns only last a few hours. Perhaps you will invite us to dine one day?'

'Of course. You may call whenever you wish,' Max said. 'Send my good wishes to Mrs Heronsdale.'

'I shall do so, of course,' Robert said and inclined his head. 'Until we meet again, cousin—perhaps tomorrow morning.'

Max stood watching as he walked into the rose arbour and disappeared from sight through a tunnel of white, climbing roses.

'Is something the matter?' Helene asked, as he remained silent.

'I am not sure,' Max told her, his expression serious, and looked at her. 'Do not be alarmed, Helene. I believe you may trust my servants implicitly—but take care when speaking with anyone from the dower house.'

'You cannot think...' Helene was shocked. 'Surely not?'

'I do not think it,' Max replied. 'But Robert is the only one who would benefit from my death until we marry—at least, that is what he or others may believe.'

'Yes, of course I shall be careful of him—and of anyone else I do not know well,' Helene said. She was thoughtful as they walked back to the house together. She had not disliked Robert Heronsdale on sight; he had seemed pleasant enough, but Max's warning was clear. He must be in a position to know more than she, of course.

It was very worrying—until the person or persons who had attacked Max were discovered and caught, his life would continue to be in danger. She had come to love him so much and she could not bear it if anything happened to him. Max seemed in command of the situation, but it could not hurt if Helene kept a watchful eye. She would listen and observe, as she always did, and perhaps she might discover something of interest.

Max smiled at her, taking her hand to kiss the palm. The touch of his lips made the heat flood through her, making her aware of all the reasons she wanted to be his wife. 'You must not worry too much, my dearest one. I warned you only so that you should not be fooled by a false message, but I promise you that I have everything under control.'

'I know that you will have taken every precaution, as much for my sake as your own,' Helene told him, her eyes warm with love. 'But you must take care, too—and perhaps the obvious is not always as it seems.'

'What do you mean by that, my wise little love?'

'I just think that sometimes we are misled by the things others say,' Helene replied thoughtfully. 'I have nothing in particular in mind.'

'No, how could you?' Max said, an odd look in his eyes. 'However, I think you may be right.'

Helene had no chance to ask him what he meant, for they saw Toby Sinclair walking across the lawns towards them. They greeted each other with pleasure and then went on up to the house.

Chapter Eleven

The Earl of Ravenshead was the next guest to arrive. He joined them in the drawing room for sherry before dinner that evening. Helene knew now that the three men were close friends and were meeting for a purpose. She caught snatches of their conversation, hearing the words Harry, and Northaven, a couple of times.

The earl seemed to be of the opinion that Northaven was up to his tricks again, whatever that might mean, but Max was clearly doubtful. However, they soon changed the conversation when the butler came to announce that dinner was served.

Max took Helene in to dinner; the earl offered his arm to her mama, who seemed pleased with the attention. The company consisted of three gentlemen and two ladies that evening—most of the guests were not expected until the next day.

'I have requested the pleasure of my aunt and cousin's company tomorrow,' Max told Helene. 'I dare say Dr Clarke may accompany them; he is a physician—or so I am led to believe—and I can hardly exclude him altogether.

We shall have several guests by then, I hope, so you will hardly notice him.'

'If he is a pleasant gentleman, I shall be happy to meet him,' Helene said. 'Remember, I am a tanner's granddaughter.' Her eyes twinkled with amusement. 'I am hardly in a position to snub a physician.'

'Perhaps I deserved that,' Max retorted. 'However, it was not meant in that way—merely that I think we should reserve judgement for the time being. Besides, you are also the granddaughter of a duke.'

'Do not remind me,' Helene said, her smile fading.

'Annesdale has written to me,' Max said. 'He asks if I will add his name to mine in return for his fortune for our sons.'

'What did you answer?' Helene looked at him hard.

'I have not done so as yet,' Max told her. 'I know you are very angry with him, Helene. I thought you should have time to consider our reply.'

'You are consulting my wishes?'

'Of course. Would you expect me to do otherwise?'

'I know that matters of property are generally dealt with by gentlemen and their wives are seldom consulted.'

'I would never bother you with mundane details of business. However, this concerns you closely, Helene. You must certainly decide in this matter. I would not dream of accepting something that might distress you.'

'Thank you,' she said and sent him a look of gratitude. 'May I have some time to think about this, please?'

'Naturally you will wish to consider your answer. I should be sad if you were to reply without giving this thought. Annesdale is a proud man, but he is also an old man and perhaps he regrets things he has done in the past—as many of us do.'

'Yes, perhaps,' Helene replied.

The subject was dropped, as the conversation became general. They were dining in the small parlour that evening because there were only five of them. Toby entertained them all with the latest gossip from town. Helene laughed at his audacious description of something the Regent was reported as saying, thinking that it boded well for the future. They had good friends and it would be a happy life here at Coleridge.

The gentlemen did not linger over their port and soon joined the ladies in the drawing room. Helene played the pianoforte for a while to entertain them, but at ten o'clock her mama said she was tired and they left the gentlemen to their own amusements.

'The Earl of Ravenshead is a pleasant gentleman,' Mrs Henderson remarked as they went upstairs. 'He was telling me that he has joined his friend Lord Pendleton in a venture to import French wines into this country. Apparently Lord Pendleton suggested it to him as a way of repairing his family fortunes and it has been successful.'

'I believe Amelia likes the earl very well,' Helene said. 'Do you think she may marry him, Mama?'

'I should not think so for a moment,' Mrs Henderson said. 'She seemed very wrapped up with her plans to travel. I believe she means to take Emily and travel to Italy this winter.'

'Oh…' Helene did not continue the conversation—after all, it was not their affair—but she could not help wondering if Amelia's plans had come about because she was unhappy.

However, she did not dwell on the thought long for she had other things to consider. She was certain that even now the three gentlemen downstairs were plotting something.

She had noticed significant glances between them at dinner and she imagined they were thinking of a way to draw out the rogue who had twice tried to murder Max.

Several ladies were amongst the guests that arrived the next day. Helene helped Max to receive them, feeling a tingle of excitement as the house began to fill up. She knew most of them, for they had been Max's friends in town, but one or two neighbours also came to call during the morning. Helene paid particular attention to learning their names for they would be her friends when she lived here. Max received an urgent message just after nuncheon and made his excuses.

'I must attend to some urgent business. You will excuse me, Helene. I shall not be away long. Perhaps you will make my excuses and see that our guests are received. You know everyone and most of those still to come are your own particular friends.'

'Of course,' Helene said. 'I shall be pleased to welcome them in your absence, and to explain.'

Amongst the flurry of arrivals, she almost missed the brief visit from Mrs Heronsdale. However, when Helene returned from greeting Captain Paul Marshall and his sister, she discovered Max's aunt sitting with her mama.

'Miss Henderson. I am Coleridge's aunt,' the lady said, rising as Helene entered. 'I believe you may have met my son yesterday? He told you I was indisposed. I had a slight headache. I was sorry not to have been here when you arrived. Please forgive me.'

'Robert made your apologies, ma'am,' Helene replied and offered her hand. She was drawn into an embrace, inhaling the almost overwhelming perfume of rose water and lavender. 'I am very pleased to meet Max's aunt.'

'Coleridge sent word that he wished to see me,' she said. 'However, he was out when I arrived, I believe on estate matters.'

'He will be sorry to have missed you,' Helene told her. 'However, I know that he invited you all to dine this evening. I am sure you will be able to speak privately then if you wish.'

'Yes, I dare say.' Mrs Heronsdale looked at her intently for a moment. 'My son was very taken with you, Helene—I may call you that, I hope?' She looked pleased as Helene inclined her head. 'I have seldom known him take to anyone so quickly. Robert is inclined to keep his own company, but he told me he was keen to know you better.'

'Oh…' Helene recalled the rather intense look in the young man's eyes and her cheeks felt warm. 'That is kind of him.'

Well, I must go,' Mrs Heronsdale said and stood up again. 'Will you walk with me to the door, Helene?'

'Yes, of course—but will you not stay for tea? Some of my friends have just arrived. I am sure they would like to meet you.'

'This evening,' Mrs Heronsdalc said. She was silent until they left the parlour, then she placed a hand on Helene's arm. 'I had to speak to you alone. Please, Helene, take this as a friendly warning—do not trust Robert too much. I say this for your own sake. If he asks you to walk with him anywhere…be careful…'

Helene felt an icy trickle down her spine. Mrs Heronsdale's grip on her arm was almost painful and the look in her eyes was frightening.

'I am not sure I understand you, ma'am?'

'Robert is…excitable at times. Oh, he means no harm,

and he truly likes you—but be careful of being alone with him.'

'I should not walk alone with any gentleman but Max,' Helene assured her. 'But surely you cannot think…?'

Mrs Heronsdale looked as if she might burst into tears. 'I do not wish you to think the less of him. It distresses me to say these things…but Doctor Clarke says that Robert becomes a little odd at times. It is the reason he has to—' She gasped and looked anxious. 'Please, say nothing of this to my nephew. If he knew, he might…' She shook her head. 'I have said too much…excuse me, I must go.' She walked quickly to the door and then glanced back. 'Do not forget my warning.'

Helene puzzled over her words. She wished that she could speak to Max concerning his aunt's warning. Mrs Heronsdale had begged her not to tell Max, but Helene knew that she must talk to him, and as soon as possible.

However, they now had ten extra guests. Max had invited three ladies he knew to be Helene's particular friends. They were all delighted with the news of her wedding and she found herself caught up in the chatter and excitement. Even when Max joined them for tea a little later she had no chance to speak with him alone.

It was the same for most of the evening. She saw Max talking earnestly to his aunt at one point, though neither the physician or Robert were present, which was rather strange. When she tried to catch Max's eye, he just smiled at her.

Helene did not have a chance to speak to Max alone until much later that evening. The hour was late and most of the ladies had decided to go up. Helene went to say goodnight to the gentlemen and Max drew her aside for a moment.

'I am sorry we have had no time to ourselves today,' he said. 'Perhaps I may take you for a little drive in the morning?'

'Yes, please,' she told him. 'I have something I wish to say to you.'

'Is it urgent, Helene?'

'Yes, it is—or it may be.'

'Then you must tell me now.' His gaze narrowed. 'I can see that you are distressed.'

'I hardly know how to say this, but it concerns something your aunt told me about Robert.'

Max frowned. 'Yes, this is important. Tell me exactly what she said to you, Helene.'

Helene repeated the warning almost word for word and Max was silent for a moment. 'It seemed strange for I cannot think that the young man I met yesterday would do anything to harm me.'

'No, he would not,' Max replied. 'But there may be more to this than we yet know.'

'Surely she would not lie about her own son and yet...' Helene shook her head. 'It is puzzling.'

'I believe I may begin to see what is happening here,' Max told her. 'However, it may be as well to heed her warning, my love.'

'Max, you do not think...?' Helene was shocked. 'He would not...'

'I warned you that there might be danger. Would you wish to leave?'

'Certainly not! I shall do whatever you tell me, Max—but I shall not leave you.'

'You are quite certain?'

'Yes, quite certain.'

'Very well.' His eyes seemed to burn into her. 'I cannot wait for the morning. I want you to myself so that I can kiss you, my darling—but it would have been rude to leave our guests on the very day they arrived. By the morning they will have found their own amusements, and many will not rise before noon. If we leave at nine thirty, we shall be back before anyone knows we have gone.'

'Yes, we shall,' Helene said. 'I shall look forward to it.' She took a reluctant leave of him.

Helene was thoughtful, a little restless as she undressed, for the mystery had deepened. Why should Robert's mother warn her to be careful of her son? Was she trying to point the finger of blame? Oh, it was all so disturbing and strange! It was difficult to know who could be trusted.

After she had dismissed her maid, she blew out her candle, drew back the curtains and sat by the window looking out. At first there was little she could see, for the moon was shadowed, but as the clouds moved away she saw its silvery light touch bushes, trees and statutes. She was gazing at what she thought might be the statue of a man when it moved. Helene was at first startled, then her interest was caught as the man came towards the house. Now she could see that he was wearing breeches, but no shirt, which was why he had appeared to be a statue in the moonlight. She leaned forward and her movement seemed to attract his attention. He peered up at her window, clearly straining to see her.

'Helene…' he called softly. 'Miss Henderson…come down, please. I must warn you.'

Helene shivered, for she was certain that the pale torso she could see must belong to Robert Heronsdale. His face had seemed very pale when they met in the gardens and instinct told her that it was he. She did not answer him, for his mother's warning was echoing in her mind. Besides, it was most improper of him to be wandering about the countryside without his shirt—especially outside the bed-room window of his cousin's fiancée!

'It is a matter of life and death,' Robert called. 'I am trying to help you…'

Helene stood up, still hesitating. As she wondered whether to open the window wider and call down to him, another man came from the shadows suddenly and grabbed Robert from behind. There was a short tussle and then Robert seemed to collapse into his arms. The newcomer hoisted Robert over his shoulder and retreated into the bushes.

Helene shivered. If she had not witnessed the whole with her own eyes, she would not have believed it. How could anyone overpower a young man so easily? And why would they do such a thing?

She frowned as she retreated to her bed and sat down. Her thoughts were confused as she tried to work out what she had just seen. She was uncertain of what she ought to do, because she could not be sure what had happened. It was such a shocking thing to happen! Either Robert had been kidnapped or…he had been controlled by the physician.

Helene's mind was beginning to work out a theory based on the warning that Mrs Heronsdale had given her earlier that day. She had told her that Robert had taken a liking to her and that she was to be careful because Robert sometimes became excitable. What was that supposed to mean…unless…but that was too horrid!

Helene's mind veered away from what she had just

pieced together. It would fit in with what Max had told her about his cousin being ill at times…and his absence that evening. If perhaps he were not quite as he ought to be…and that when one of his…mad fits was upon him, he attacked young ladies.

No, it was too awful! Helene did not wish to believe such a thing. She admitted that the young man had been a little intense when they met in the gardens, but insane… No! She could not think it. His manner when he called to her outside her window had certainly been urgent, but she would not have said he was in a mad fit. Yet his mother's words had been intended to make her wary of him.

Oh, how horrible it all was! She would not have taken so much notice had not Robert cried out that it was a matter of life and death. Someone had tried to kill Max twice, and his cousin was his heir. The finger of blame pointed in Robert's direction, so why did Helene feel that something terrible had just happened?

She could not simply retire to bed and let this thing go unnoticed. She must speak to Max immediately.

Putting on a thick wrapping gown and a pair of slippers, Helene took her candle and went downstairs in search of Max. She did not know if he would have retired yet. If he had done so, she would have to ask the hall porter to fetch him, because he ought to know what was going on.

'Mrs Heronsdale informed me this evening that Robert has gone missing,' Max told his friends as they sat together in the library drinking a last nightcap. 'She says that it has happened half a dozen times in the last six months. He is—she says—of a nervous disposition. When he returns from these mysterious disappearances he is sometimes very ill and takes to his bed for weeks at a time.'

'Do you believe her?' Toby asked. 'You spoke to him yesterday. How was he then?'

'He seemed fine, if a little nervous,' Max replied. 'I told you that fellow Clarke had been keeping him drugged... If what my aunt says is true, it would appear that they do it for his own good.'

'What of these village girls who have been attacked? You said that they had arrested some yokel,' Gerard said and frowned.

'Yes, they did, but it seems that he is foolish, but harmless. At the time the attacks in our village took place, he was with his mother—or so she swears. The magistrate sent him to a place for idiots. My neighbour visited him and is of the opinion that he did not attack the girls in our village.'

'You are thinking that it was your cousin?' Gerard asked.

'I am not certain—' Max broke off as someone knocked at the door and then Helene walked in, wearing a heavy silk robe over her nightgown. 'Helene—is something wrong? You are not ill?'

'Forgive me for disturbing you,' she said, a faint colour in her cheeks. 'I know I am dressed improperly, gentlemen—but I have seen something disturbing and I believe you should know about it, Max. It concerns your cousin.'

'Good grief!' Gerard said. 'It was very sensible of you to come, Miss Henderson—please tell us.'

'I was restless because of something Mrs Heronsdale said to me earlier,' Helene told them. 'I blew out my candle and sat by the open window, looking out. At first I thought him a statue because he was so pale...he wore only his breeches—no shirt, coat or shoes on his feet, I think...' She saw that she had their attention. 'He called to me.

He said that it was urgent that he speak to me because it was a matter of life and death…and then someone came up behind him. He struggled, but he was overpowered very quickly and went limp, as if he had suddenly been drugged.'

'Good grief! Was it Robert?' Max asked her.

'I believe so.'

'Thank God you did not go down to him!'

'I believe I have too much good sense,' Helene said. 'And yet I think he may truly have been trying to warn me of something.'

'Why is that?' Max asked, his gaze narrowed. 'I have been told that he disappears sometimes for days and when he returns he is ill. Apparently, he remembers nothing.'

'Did Mrs Heronsdale tell you that this evening?' Helene asked. 'You did not tell me.'

'She returned to the house and spoke to me privately after you retired, Helene. Besides…I am not certain I believe her,' Max said. 'She said she thought it her duty to warn me, but there is something not right. I cannot put my finger on it just yet.'

'Do you think that…?' Helene shook her head. 'No, I am being foolish.'

'You suspect her of something? What?' Gerard asked, giving her an intent look. 'Why would she concoct such a story about her own son?'

'There have been two attempts on your life,' Helene replied. 'I suppose she could not inherit if her son were dead—or convicted of murder?'

'Actually, she might,' Max said. 'My estate is not entailed to a male heir. It would go to Robert first if I died before we marry, Helene—but after that it would go to her, for she is my father's sister. At least it would have done had I not made certain changes.'

'Have you made Mrs Heronsdale and Robert aware of those changes?' Gerard asked, his eyes narrowed and thoughtful.

'No, I have not.' Max frowned. 'I could do so, of course, but then I might never discover what has been going on.'

'You are taking a huge risk,' Gerard said.

'Yes, I know. That is why I asked you to take certain precautions.'

Max threw a look of apology at Helene. 'Forgive me for bringing you to a situation like this, my love. It is more involved and dangerous than I imagined.'

'The situation is not of your making,' Helene replied. 'Besides, I want to be here. If you are planning anything— and I am certain you are—I should like to help.'

'You have already helped us,' Max told her with a smile. 'We do have a plan, but there is nothing you can do, dearest. Just be careful.'

'What of Robert? Will you send men to search for him?'

'I think we shall wait until tomorrow. I shall call on my aunt first thing in the morning and hear what she has to say.'

'You do not think he is in danger?'

'No…' Max shook his head. 'If what I think is going on is right, Robert is perfectly safe until I am dead.'

'Oh…' Helene wrinkled her brow in thought. 'Yes, I see…of course.'

'Forgive me if I tell you nothing more,' Max said. 'Go to bed and try to sleep, my love. I promise you I shall take great care. Gerard and Toby will help me—and once it is all over I shall explain everything.'

Helene hesitated. She would have liked to be included in

their plans, but she knew it was unlikely Max would allow it. Whatever they had in mind carried a certain amount of danger and he would not wish her to be involved.

'I shall go up,' she told him. 'I felt that I should tell you what I had witnessed, Max.'

'I am grateful you did—you have confirmed something I was not sure of,' Max told her. 'I may have to postpone our drive until tomorrow afternoon, Helene.'

Helene nodded. She wished the other gentlemen good night and left them alone to talk. She did not think she would find it easy to sleep, because Max and his friends were clearly involved in some plot to make the murderer show his hand. The thought that he was in danger was disturbing, but she knew that she must do everything he asked of her and be as patient as she could.

Helene was up early in the hope that Max might still have time to take her for the drive he had promised, but when she went downstairs Mrs Hale told her that his lord-ship had gone out riding with two of his friends. Helene knew who the friends were and sighed inwardly. She would have liked to know exactly what was going on. The fear that Max might be in imminent danger made her restless.

She decided that she would take a little walk in the gardens, though she would not go out of sight of the house. The sun was shining and it was such a lovely morning that she had no desire to sit alone in the house, and most of the guests would not rise before noon.

Helene found a sunny spot on the lawns and sat down on a wooden bench. The warmth on her face and head was so pleasant that she was lulled into a sense of peace and well being.

'Miss Henderson?'

Helene looked up. She had never to her knowledge seen the man addressing her before. He was a thin faced, dark-haired man, his eyes deep set and his nose a little crooked.

'Excuse me?' she said, standing up a little warily. 'I do not think we are acquainted?'

'You are Miss Helene Henderson?'

'Yes, I am Miss Henderson,' Helene replied. 'And you are, sir…?'

'I am Dr Clarke. You may have heard that I look after Robert? I need your help because Lord Coleridge is in grave danger.'

'Max is in danger?' Helene was immediately alert, her nerves jangling. 'Tell me at once. What is going on?'

'Robert has lost his mind,' Dr Clarke said. 'It pains me to say this, for I have looked after him for years. I love Robert as my own son, but he is not always as he should be. He has an illness that manifests itself at certain times.'

'You are saying that he has bouts of insanity?' Helene felt cold shivers down her spine. Looking at him closely, she was suddenly certain, 'You are the one who grabbed him last night as he called to me. I saw someone take him.'

'You were in danger,' the physician told her. 'Robert has been getting much worse of late, more cunning. He came to himself before I could administer sufficient quantities of the drug we use to control him during his mad periods. He knocked me on the head and then ran away. He will kill both you and his lordship if he can.'

'You should be telling Lord Coleridge this,' Helene said, feeling uneasy. 'I do not see what I can do to help you.'

'Robert has Lord Coleridge tied up. I searched for him all night and finally found him, but it was too late. Lord Coleridge is his prisoner. If you come with me now, we may still save him. Robert likes pretty girls and he wishes to speak with you. He will not speak to anyone else—if you bring another person, he may lose control completely. I beg you, Miss Henderson, if you care for Lord Coleridge, you must come with me now.'

Helene's unease was growing. She was not sure what to do—ought she to return to the house and fetch help? Supposing Dr Clarke was telling her the truth? Any delay and it might be too late.

'Yes, I will come,' she said, making up her mind. 'Where are they? Please lead on, sir.'

'You must hurry,' the physician urged. 'When Robert is like this, he might do anything.'

Helene frowned, because something was making her more and more uneasy. Her instincts were warning her she ought not to trust this man, but what choice did she have? If Robert were really mad and would only speak to her, she must do what she could to save Max's life.

She set off in his wake through the shrubbery. Her mind worked quickly. She did not trust this man! She was almost certain he was lying and it was possible he was leading her into a trap. Glancing at a delicate lace kerchief in her hands, she noticed that she had torn the lace in her anxiety. She would use it to leave a trail for others to follow! She pulled a piece off and dropped it onto a bush, her fingers working at the fine material until she had another little shred that she could drop.

If someone came to look for her, she could only hope that they would understand what she had done.

'Robert is missing,' Mrs Heronsdale said when Max inquired after his cousin that morning. 'His bed has not been slept in. He claimed to be ill when he came back yesterday, but when Dr Clarke went to look for him he had gone. He has not returned and we do not know where he is.' She twisted her hands in distress. 'Forgive me, Coleridge. I should have told you long ago about his disappearances, but I was afraid that you would send us away. I have nowhere else to go and without Dr Clarke…my poor Robert would end in Bedlam, chained up for the rest of his life.'

'I am certain we can do better than that for him,' Max told her. 'He must obviously be confined for his own safety and that of others.'

'My poor, poor boy…' A tear ran from the corner of her eye and she dabbed it away with a lace kerchief. 'I do not know what I would have done without Dr Clarke.'

'You trust him?' Max's gaze narrowed.

'Completely! I know he has to drug Robert at times, but it is for his own good. When you forced us to leave it off… I cannot answer for what he might have done.'

'You will allow me to look in his room?'

'Of course—but he is not there. Doctor Clarke is out looking for him now. Do you wish to search the house? We have already done so, but I shall not deny you if you wish to do so yourself. Indeed, I should be happy for you to set your mind at rest.'

'Very well, I believe you,' Max told her. 'I think I shall not need to search his room after all. You should have told me from the beginning, but we shall discuss that at another time. I must organise a search for Robert.'

'I pray you find him before he does more harm,' Mrs Heronsdale said and gave a little sob of despair. 'My poor boy…'

Max inclined his head and went out. She was afraid of something and he suspected that she was lying to him! He was not sure why she would lie, but he was fairly certain he knew exactly what had been going on here. It was imperative that he should find Robert before Dr Clarke did, because his cousin's life was in danger!

Helene looked uncertainly at what was clearly a summerhouse. There was an unused air about it, as if no one ever came here. She felt very nervous, her stomach beginning to tie itself in knots. She was certain now that the physician had lied to her. This was a trap! Even as she hesitated, the physician stopped, turned back and looked at her. His gloating manner frightened her. She turned, prepared to flee back the way they had come, but he was on her at once. His powerful hands grasped her arm, his fingers digging into the flesh as he held on to her.

'Has the penny dropped at last, Miss Henderson?' he asked, and suddenly she knew him. She had heard that voice on the night of Amelia's costume ball. He was the man who had threatened her with dire happenings if she would not give up her engagement to Max. 'I thought you might know me, even though I disguised my voice that night at the ball. But of course all you thought of was your precious Lord Coleridge. How foolish a woman in love can be!'

'Let go of my arm,' Helene said. 'You are an impostor, aren't you? You never were a doctor at all.'

'Oh, yes, I do have a certificate and I have worked in Italy as a physician. I was forced to earn my living after my father cut me off without a penny for disgracing his name. It was not my fault that the stupid girl struggled so hard I broke her neck...' His lip curled in a sneer. 'Women are all fools. They will believe anything you say, providing that they believe you love them.'

'You made Mrs Heronsdale believe her son was mad.'

'Actually, it is Mrs Clarke. It suited our purposes to keep the marriage a secret.'

'Does she know that you have tried to kill Lord Coleridge twice?'

'You ask too many questions,' he said and his fingers tightened their hold, making Helene wince.

'You are hurting my arm,' she said as he took a key from his pocket with his free hand and unlocked the door of the summerhouse. He thrust her inside and followed, closing the door with a bang. Helene kicked out at his shins in a desperate attempt to free herself, and in subduing her once more he neglected to lock the door behind them.

'Behave and perhaps I shall let you live,' he said. 'You really should have listened to me, Miss Henderson. You are a stubborn wench. I should enjoy taming you—as I might have done had you done as your grandfather asked you. Why would you not give up Coleridge and live under Annesdale's roof? I could have disposed of those who stood in my way of a fortune—and then I might have come courting. I think I should have enjoyed that.'

'What are you talking about? If you imagine that I would ever have married you...' Helene began, but a look from him silenced her.

'You might have had no choice,' he said. 'When the grandson of his long-lost cousin turned up, Annesdale would have been glad to give you to me.'

'You are related to Annesdale...' Helene stared at him in disbelief. 'How could you know of his offer to me? I do not believe you are his cousin. Were you planning to dupe a lonely old man by impersonating a member of his family?'

'Do you imagine I would tell you?' He smiled. 'But I

shall tell you that a certain lady is my friend. She told me all about you, because she hates you.'

'If you are going to kill me, what difference does it make?' she asked, and then, hearing a strangled sound behind her, she turned and saw the figure of a man struggling against the bonds that bound his ankles and wrists. He was lying on the floor, with his back towards them, but she knew at once that it must be Robert. She ran to him, kneeling by his side and pulling the gag from his mouth. 'Has that devil hurt you?'

'I wanted to warn you,' Robert gasped. 'I didn't know what he planned for a long time, but of late he had grown careless and talked to me when he believed I was drugged. When Max insisted on bringing in his own physician, he stopped drugging me. I began to remember things…I wanted to warn you. He is going to kill Max, blame it on me and then Mama will inherit the money. Once he can persuade her to give it to him, he will marry her and then she, too, will die.'

'You are somewhat behind the times,' the physician's sneering voice told them from his position near the door. 'Your mama is my wife. You, my so-dear Robert, will be killed after Coleridge is dead—and then in a while I shall dispose of my sweet lady when we are abroad. I shall return, wealthy, the prodigal son as it were, to be welcomed with open arms…' He smiled oddly as they stared at him in horrified silence. 'I killed your father, Robert—did you know? He was ill and it was easy to poison his medicine so that he faded slowly. I was Harriet's lover. After your father's death, we married in secret, because she did not want you to know—she feared your disapproval. When we discovered that your father had been in debt and there was no money left, we came here. I realised it would be simple to kill Coleridge and later you, the plan to blame the murder on you came afterwards, when he began to take an interest in marriage.'

'You devil!' Robert said and struggled furiously with his bonds. 'Your plan will backfire—no one will believe that I killed my cousin.'

'Poor Robert. You have been suffering from bouts of madness for a long time. Your dear mama believes me. She will swear to it, because she does what I tell her. When Max finds his beloved fiancée dead, he will blame you. I shall kill you both and put the pistol in your hand. You raped and killed the delightful Helene and then you killed Max in a fit of madness. Realising what you had done, you killed yourself in remorse.'

'Damn you!' Robert said and renewed his struggles. 'You are a cold devil! I will kill you for what you've done.'

'Unfortunately for you, you will never have a chance,' the physician sneered. His gaze moved to Helene. 'It would be a pity to kill you too soon, Miss Henderson. I enjoy pretty women, especially when they fight. I believe we have time to get better acquainted before Coleridge comes looking for you…'

'Stay away from me!' Helene screamed. 'I would rather die than let you touch me.'

She looked for a weapon, but could find none. Robert was still struggling to free himself, but the knots were too tight.

'Scream louder,' the physician said. 'I love it when you scream.'

He advanced towards her, but even as he did so the door crashed open and Gerard Ravenshead entered, closely followed by Toby Sinclair. Both of them were carrying pistols, which they had firmly trained on the physician.

'Lay one finger on Miss Henderson and you die instantly,' Gerard told him. 'Max thought if we gave you enough rope you would hang yourself.' He looked at Helene. 'I am sorry it took us a while to follow you inside, Helene, but we needed to hear his confession. It was the only way we could prove that he made those attempts on Max. We couldn't be sure it would work, but Max said he was an arrogant fool and would fall for it.'

'Damn you!' the physician said and lunged at Helene. He grabbed her and held her in front of him. He took a knife from somewhere about him and held it to her throat. 'Stand aside or I shall kill her.'

Even as Gerard hesitated, Robert threw off the bonds that secured his hands and, though his ankles were still bound, lunged at the physician, clinging to his leg and biting at his ankle. The sharp pain made the man grunt and for a second he released his hold on Helene. She brought her arm back sharply in his face and then ran towards the door. Toby pushed her outside. She heard a sharp scream of pain from inside and then a shot. Shocked and distraught, she hesitated, and then, seeing Max striding towards her, she ran to him.

'Max,' she cried, flinging herself at him. The words came out in a passionate torrent, 'He tricked me into coming here—and he was going to kill both Robert and me and you, too, when you came looking. The earl and Toby listened to his bragging confession and then came inside. He grabbed me and held a knife to my throat, but then Robert bit his ankle and he let go of me.'

'Helene, my love.' Max put his arms about her, holding her as she trembled. 'I am so sorry. I followed your trail. I was afraid something might happen and Gerard would be too late.' How pale her cheeks were! 'Forgive me, Helene.

You were the bait. After what happened at the ball, I suspected that it must be Clarke. When his attempt to frighten you into crying off failed, he became desperate. I thought he might try to use you to trap Robert and me. He had to get us both together—somewhere he could be private. We knew it was a terrible risk, but Gerard and Toby promised they would not let me down. Can you forgive me? Had they not followed you closely, he might have harmed you and then I should not have forgiven myself.'

'I would have gladly taken the risk for your sake had you told me,' Helene said. 'He was the pirate at the ball, as you guessed. He claims to be Annesdale's distant cousin but I am not sure if he lies.'

'I care not who he is, providing you are unharmed—and will forgive me. I have been shockingly careless of your safety, my love.'

'I do not think it,' Helene told him with a smile. 'I was watched over the whole time. I was told that you had gone out with your friends, but I see now what you were planning last night.'

'We wanted people to think we had gone riding, but then we split up. We knew that if I was right, both Robert and I were safe until he could get us together. Gerard and Toby watched for you while I went to my aunt. I was sure that she was hiding something. I am not certain that she knew what Clarke was up to, but I believe she suspected something. I came to look for you immediately. I found the shreds of lace you had cleverly left for me and followed the trail.'

'I think someone has been shot…' Helene began and then stopped as the door to the summerhouse opened and three men came out. Robert was limping. He had blood dripping from a wound to his hand, but otherwise seemed unhurt. Gerard and Toby had put away their pistols.

'The rogue is dead,' Gerard said. 'He would have killed Robert so I had no choice but to shoot him. It is best for everyone that he is out of the way, because he was a dangerous man. Had he succeeded in his plans, there is no telling what he would have done next.'

'We heard his confession,' Toby said. 'Robert can tell you more.'

Max looked at his cousin. 'What did your mama know of his plans?'

'I think she had begun to suspect him of something, for I heard them quarrelling,' Robert told him. 'She asked him where he had been one night when she found blood on his shirt. He told her that he had cut himself on a nail, but she did not believe him. After you insisted that I should not be drugged, Mama forced him to stop. He told her that I could be dangerous, but she wept over my bed when he was away for a few days. I believe she may have been afraid of him, because perhaps she had begun to realise that he was the one to be wary of, not me—and yet she did not challenge him. Indeed, she gave me the medicine he prescribed.'

'I dare say he may have exerted a great deal of influence over her. She married him and felt herself trapped,' Max agreed. 'I knew she was hiding something from me, but I was not sure how much she knew of the attempts on my life.'

Robert looked angry. 'He had bragged to me of his plans as I lay drugged, but I knew nothing of his attempts against your life until he brought me here. You must believe me, cousin!'

'I have acquitted you of any involvement since I found you lying in a drugged state. Before that I admit that you seemed the most likely person to want me dead. Although I disliked and distrusted Clarke from the first—if, indeed, that is his name, which I doubt—I could not see what he hoped to gain from my death. Had I known he was your stepfather, I should have understood much sooner.'

'Mama kept it from me,' Robert said. 'It seems he killed my father—but she is not blameless, for she was his lover while my father lived. She must have told him about her wealthy nephew, for it was his idea that we should come here—and it was only after we moved into the dower house that he began his evil work.'

'I do not understand why your mama allowed him to drug you,' Helene said. 'I had met you but once and you did not seem mad to me.'

'Thank you,' Robert said and smiled. 'You must understand that I was always prone to chills and ill health. Clarke came to look after me and at first he was considerate, even kind, but after my father died and he realised there was no money he changed. I did not realise that he had married Mama. He began to give me drugs, which made me sick and ill. I had black holes in my memory. He told me that when I was ill I did bad things, and, because I could not remember, I believed him. After a while I accepted whatever he told me.'

Max nodded. 'I distrusted the man from the start. I shall contact the magistrate and tell him that his mystery has been cleared up. I think we can be sure that our Dr Clarke was the rogue who attacked the village women.'

'What village women?' Helene asked in disbelief. 'You did not tell me your suspicions!'

'I wasn't sure,' Max said, looking at her white face. 'I assure you, you were always watched. You have been for a while, even in London—not by my friends, but by others.'

'Excuse me...' Helene said, feeling distressed. 'I think

I should go home before Mama realises I have gone out and starts to worry.'

She started walking very fast. Max's revelation about the village women had come as an unpleasant shock to her. She was prepared to face danger, but that he should know what kind of a rogue the physician was and not tell her had upset her.

'Helene!' Max's voice called to her. Angry and upset, she started to run. Max ran after her, catching her at last. He took hold of her arm and swung her round to face him. 'Forgive me. I was not sure of anything until my aunt told me that her son was dangerous when he had one of his fits. It was then that I began to understand what was going on—and I realised that it must be Clarke or whatever his name may be. I am not sure whether he was trying to blacken my cousin's character in order to establish the myth of Robert's madness—or drew pleasure from the attacks.'

'He would have abused me had Robert not managed to free himself. Your friends could do nothing—he had a knife to my throat and he would have taken me with him.' Helene suddenly burst into tears. Max took her into his arms holding her close. 'He was horrible...'

'Yes, my darling, he was,' Max said and stroked her hair as he held her close. 'Evil is the right word in his case, I believe. He treated Robert abominably and my aunt allowed him to do it, for like you I believe she must have known her son was not mad. However, I acquit her of complicity in the attempts on my life.' Max's arms tightened about Helene as she looked up at him. 'I had to catch him out. Believe me, neither of us was safe while he continued to stay in the shadows. Can you ever forgive me?'

Helene glanced up at him. Her heart slammed against

her ribs, her breath catching in her throat. She inclined her head slightly and he lowered his head to kiss her. The kiss was long and sweet, making her feel as if she were melting into him, becoming a part of him, never to be parted. She knew that she wanted to be his completely, wanted to know him in every way, and whatever happened to them she would always be his. He was the man she loved and would love until she died.

'I have to forgive you,' she whispered, her lips parting on a sigh, 'because I should only be half-alive without you.'

'I love you more than my life,' Max said. 'You are all that I have ever wanted in my life. I knew our plan was a risk, and at first I resisted—but I trusted Gerard and Toby. If we had simply waited for that devil to make his move, he would have had the advantage. I was afraid that you would be his next target and the only way to keep you safe was to give him his opportunity. Besides, you are so brave that I was certain you would know just what to do—and you did.'

'Brave or reckless?'

'That, too,' he agreed, a faint smile on his lips.

'I wish you had told me,' Helene said. 'I almost didn't go with him. Supposing I had refused? Supposing I hadn't gone outside alone?'

'Then we should have had to think of something else,' Max told her. 'But Toby said he was sure that if Clarke approached you, you would take a risk—and, knowing how impetuous you can be, I thought he was right. I knew that you would be restless and I was sure the garden would tempt you outside on such a lovely day. It was a perfect opportunity and Clarke could not resist the bait.'

'You know me too well,' Helene said ruefully. 'I understood it must be a risk when I went with him, for he told me that I must speak to Robert if I wished to save your life. I suspected he was lying, for I saw him capture your cousin last night. How did he do that so easily? Robert is a strong man.'

'I believe he must have learned how to control a violent patient by placing his finger on a pressure point,' Max replied. 'These things are known to certain medical practitioners; the Chinese have long known the secret and I dare say others, too. Clarke, as he called himself, may well have studied medicine. He certainly had access to powerful drugs—some of them unknown in our culture, I imagine.'

'How evil he must have been!' Helene looked at him. 'Your aunt—she was not a party to the scheme to kill you, but she did allow him to mistreat Robert. What will happen to her?'

'I shall consult with Robert. I do not know if he can forgive her. I am convinced she knew her husband was lying about Robert's madness, yet she tried to convince me of it. Perhaps she was afraid of what her husband would do if she defied him. Robert must decide her fate himself.'

'And your cousin?'

'If Robert will let me, I shall set him up with a residence, either in the country or in town. My fortune is sufficient to give him a decent allowance. I believe he deserves a chance to prove himself, Helene. He has had a wretched life and I should like to see him happy.'

'Yes, he does deserve his chance,' Helene agreed and looked thoughtful. 'You are generous and forgiving, Max. I think that makes me love you even more.'

'Then you have truly forgiven me?'

'Yes,' Helene replied and reached up to kiss him softly

on the mouth. 'Providing you do not tell Mama what has been happening here.'

Max laughed huskily. 'You are so brave, my darling— and yet you fear your mama's displeasure?'

'I do not fear it,' Helene told him. 'It is just that she would make such a fuss and probably want to cancel the wedding.'

'Then you may be sure that I shall make every effort to make certain that she does not discover what happened this morning.'

'You may think me a fool, Helene, but I am not,' Mrs Henderson said and frowned at her daughter. 'I know something has been going on these past few days. You have tried to keep it a secret from me, but I have seen the glances between you all. Why has Mrs Heronsdale gone off so suddenly—and why has Lord Coleridge's cousin come to live in this house?'

'Mrs Heronsdale has been called to the bedside of a sick relative.' Helene could not look at her mama as she told the lie. Robert had banished his mother to stay with friends abroad until he could bring himself to forgive her, which might not be for some time. She was to have a small pension while she remained there. Helene did not know exactly what had taken place when the two met in Max's presence, but she understood that Mrs Heronsdale was much chastened and had confessed that her husband had threatened her when she began to question him about the precise nature of her son's illness. At first she had loved him blindly, but at the last she had begun to fear him.

'I still do not see why Robert should come to live here.'

'It is only until after the wedding,' Helene replied. 'Robert is to have a house in Bath. Max has an interest in a wine-importing business, as I told you before, and Robert will be in charge of outlets both in Bath and in London. He has no need to work, for Max has made him a generous allowance, but he wishes to do something in return. It is just so that Max can have the house made ready for you, dearest.'

'Well, I must say I like Robert well enough, but I still do not know what is going on,' Mrs Henderson grumbled. She looked at her daughter awkwardly, then, 'I have had a letter of apology from Annesdale. He says that he will provide me with a residence in Bath and an allowance. I am not sure how to answer him…'

'Max wrote to him and invited him to the wedding,' Helene replied. 'I have decided to forgive and to accept him in my life. Perhaps you should do the same, Mama?'

'He has written me a very decent letter, apologising for what happened years ago. It is not easy for me to forgive him, Helene. However, I quite see that it would be awkward to be on bad terms with him once you are married, for we may meet in company, therefore I must try to come to terms with him. Coleridge is having the dower house refurbished for me, and he has also made me an allowance—but I do not see why I should not take what is rightfully mine, for I can divide my time between Coleridge House and Bath. I am not sure what your father would have thought.'

'If Papa knew that his father had apologised, I believe he would tell you to accept, Mama,' Helene said. 'You may be easy in your mind on that score. I am sure he would say we should not continue to hold a grudge, but let the past go and enjoy the future.'

'Very well, since you are so well settled and happy, I dare say I may accept Annesdale's offer.' She smiled at her daughter. 'So it is your wedding day tomorrow, my love—and you are truly happy?'

'Happier than I ever expected,' Helene told her. 'I cannot wait to be Max's wife.'

'You look beautiful,' Amelia said and kissed Helene's cheek. 'I am so happy for you, my dearest. I know you will be loved and spoiled by your husband—and I am glad that you have mended fences with Annesdale.'

'Max showed me by example that it was best to be generous and to forgive others,' Helene told her. 'I could not do less, Amelia. I want Max to be proud of me.'

'I am certain he already is,' Amelia replied. 'You are a beautiful bride, my love, but you are also brave and wise. Max told me what happened here and it seems that you behaved very creditably. I am sure that you will make him an excellent wife.'

'I shall try,' Helene said. She glanced at the diamond-and-sapphire bracelet on her arm. 'You have spoiled me once more, Amelia. After all you had already done, this bracelet is almost too much.'

'I wanted you to have it. Aunt Agatha had it as a girl and I know she would have been happy to see you wearing it at your wedding.'

'Thank you so much,' Helene said and kissed her cheek. 'Annesdale sent me a magnificent sapphire-and-diamond necklace and tiara set. He has also settled ten thousand pounds on me—and the remainder of his fortune will go to our sons.' Helene blushed. 'I hope we shall have at least three sons and two daughters. I was an only child and I would like a large family.'

'Does Max feel the same?'

'Yes, he does. He had a brother once, but Tom died

when he was seven. Max says that he would like a house filled with children. You haven't seen him with his orphan boys, of course—they adore him! We are going to set up another home in one of the houses he owns locally so that I may take an interest in the children. And we are to set up a campaign to make it unlawful to force boys up chimneys, besides other projects I have brought to Max's attention.'

'Well, it seems that you will share your interests and that must bode well for the future,' Amelia said and a little sigh escaped her. She turned as the door opened behind her. 'Here is your mama, which means that you must go down if you are ready, Helene.'

'Yes, I must not keep Max waiting,' Helene said and smiled. 'I am perfectly ready, Mama...'

Helene turned her head as the vicar pronounced them man and wife, her heart beating fast as Max lifted her wedding veil to kiss her softly on the mouth. She seemed to be walking in a dream of happiness as they signed the register in the vestry and then went out into the sunshine to be met by the sound of church bells and a little storm of rose petals.

Max's eyes were warm with love as he turned to her. 'You are so lovely, my darling,' he said in a husky voice. 'I cannot wait to have you to myself. I am tempted to sweep you up now and run off with you.'

Helene laughed, because she too was impatient for the moment when she became truly his, but she knew that he was teasing her. Max was a gentleman. He would never desert his guests or behave in a manner that would cause hurt or offence to others—and perhaps that was why she loved him so very much.

'Be patient, my love,' she whispered back. 'We have the rest of our lives.'

'I like the sound of that,' he replied. 'If you will not run away with me, I dare say we should go back to the house and entertain our guests.'

'Well, Lady Annesdale-Coleridge, I must congratulate you on your choice of a husband,' the Duke of Annesdale told Helene a little later that day. 'Coleridge is a fine man. He has told me about his home for orphan boys. I hear that you intend to open one for girls? Coleridge asked me if I would associate myself with the project. I shall be happy to do so, for I like children—perhaps there is yet time for me to see my great-grandchildren before I die?'

'I hope that we shall oblige you, sir,' Helene said, a faint blush in her cheeks. 'I think I ought to apologise for the way I spoke to you before.'

'No! I deserved it,' the duke told her and there was a twinkle in his eye. 'You were the first person to stand up to me since your father. I have been fawned over too much, Helene. I was proud and cold and I have been much at fault. It was time someone refused me. Your comments shocked and hurt me, but they also made me realise that my unhappiness was my own fault. I am grateful that you forgave me and allowed me hope for the future.'

'Max is so generous and forgiving,' Helene said and her mouth curved into a tender smile. 'As his wife I could do no less. I am pleased to have a grandfather and I sincerely hope that you will have many more years left to you.' She leaned up and kissed his cheek. He patted her arm awkwardly, clearly unused to such displays of affection.

'Your husband has come to claim you, girl. I dare say he wants to be off.'

Helene turned as Max came up to her. 'Is it time for me to change, Max?'

'Yes, I think so,' he told her. 'Your mama was looking for you a moment ago.'

Helene knew that her mama would not approach her while she was with Annesdale. They had acknowledged each other at the wedding, but it would be a long time before they truly forgave each other.

'I shall go up,' Helene said, gazing up into her husband's eyes.

'At last,' Max said and drew her closer, his eyes burning her with the heat of his passion. She felt desire pool low in her abdomen as she lifted her face for his kiss. 'Have I told you how much I love you?'

'Only six times since we got here.' Helene laughed.

They were in the bedroom of a house loaned to them by one of Max's many friends. Their intention was to stop here one night and a day and then travel on to the coast where they would take ship for France.

'Not nearly enough,' Max said hoarsely. He swept her up in his arms and carried her to the bed, depositing her gently amongst scented sheets. Max lifted her nightgown, pulling it over her head so that he could feast his eyes on her lovely body. 'You are so lovely. I want you so very much, my darling.'

Helene shivered with pleasure as he removed his robe and then gathered her close, the touch of his flesh searing her with the heat of desire. His kisses thrilled her, making her body arch with pleasure as he explored her with lips and tongue, his hands stroking the satin smoothness of her skin.

'I love you…' she whispered, feeling as if she were being carried away on a wave of love and need.

Helene responded to his seeking heat, as the hard urgency of his manhood penetrated her, giving one little cry of pain as he broke through her maidenhead. Then, as the pain was forgotten in surging joy, she clung to him, her body moving with his in the sweet dance of love. She whimpered and moaned as the pleasure mounted unbearably and then cascaded through her in wavelets of pleasure that made her writhe and call out his name.

'I adore you, my sweet Helene,' Max murmured against her ear. 'You are all that I want and more.'

'I was so fortunate that you came to my rescue that day when we stopped that awful man beating poor Jezra,' Helene said and smiled as he looked down at her. 'If you had not seen me, we might never have met or fallen in love.'

'I think we were destined to meet,' Max told her as he kissed her softly once more. 'You are my soulmate, Helene. We were meant to be together for always.'

'Yes,' she said. 'I think we are.'

* * * * *

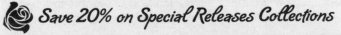

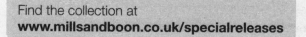

The World of Mills & Boon®

There's a Mills & Boon® series that's perfect for you. We publish ten series and, with new titles every month, you never have to wait long for your favourite to come along.

Blaze.

Scorching hot, sexy reads
4 new stories every month

By Request

Relive the romance with the best of the best
9 new stories every month

Cherish™

Romance to melt the heart every time
12 new stories every month

Desire™

Passionate and dramatic love stories
8 new stories every month

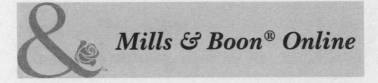